A TASTE FOR GREEN
TANGERINES

Barbara Bisco

A TASTE FOR GREEN TANGERINES

ISBN: 978-0-9560276-0-3

Printed and bound in Great Britain by
The Good News Press Ltd
Ongar, Essex, UK, CM5 9RX

Published by
BLACK LOTUS PUBLISHING LTD
25 Belsize Crescent
London, UK, NW3 5QY
Registered under the Companies House Act
Number 5,928,807
website: www.blacklotuspublishing.com

Black Lotus has been registered as a Trade Mark with the
UK Patent Office

A CIP record for this book is available from the British Library

Papers used by The Good News Press Ltd are natural, recyclable products made from PEFC wood free paper. The Manufacturing processes conform to the environmental regulations of the country of origin.

FOR MY HUSBAND AND DAUGHTER

CHAPTER ONE

A wave of excitement, tinged with a flicker of apprehension, swept over Bethany Parker as she peered out the window of the tiny Twin Otter plane that was taking her deep into the interior of Borneo. Below her the rainforest stretched out in a vast jumble of dark green, emerald green, lime green, every kind of green and she wondered, as she had for the thousandth time since she had left London, just how suited she was for a career as an anthropologist.

She supposed she should have thought of that sooner, at least, that's what her boy friend Nigel Compton had said after she had told him about Kanyalang.

'What's that?' he had asked, without much interest.

'An eco-tourism project in Indonesia.'

'Good God, what do you want to go there for?'

'It sounds like an exciting idea, a research centre, some sort of conservation effort too, that will be financed by the profits from a luxury hotel.'

Nigel showed no sign of finding this exciting at all.

'Of course, I'm just a last minute substitute,' Bethany continued, 'because Professor Brown, you remember the American I was doing research for last term, had to let them down. But I suppose it can't be that easy to find someone who can just drop everything and take off for Borneo at a moment's notice.'

'Quite,' Nigel had said.

'But luckily for me, I can.'

'Lucky?' Nigel had sounded astonished.

'Everyone in the anthropology department thinks it is,' she had insisted. 'They would all kill for a chance like this.'

'Everyone at the bank would kill to avoid it,' Nigel had replied, acidly.

This had prompted a heated exchange about lifestyle choices but they were so used to bickering these days that it hadn't deterred Nigel from turfing Pumpkin the cat off the bed, tumbling Bethany down onto it and kissing her where he imagined she liked it most.

She had nearly pushed him off so they could talk about how a year and a half apart would affect their relationship but it hadn't seemed like the right time. After a few brief minutes of foreplay she had felt him plunging down inside her and as usual had faked the enthusiasm he seemed to think his performance merited.

Oddly enough, the right time for that conversation about their future together had never quite arrived. Instead, they had settled for a sort of unspoken agreement to put things on hold while she was away. They would keep in touch, of course, Nigel would take care of Pumpkin, and they would see how they felt when she got back.

Almost before she knew it, he had been seeing her off at Heathrow and she had been on her way to her first job as a full-fledged anthropologist.

Yet now, as the plane was crossing and re-crossing the path of a meandering mud-brown river, Bethany was a little less sure about some of the lifestyle choices she had made. For instance, how was somebody who hated snakes as much as she did going to get along in the rainforest? And could she live without a corner shop that sold Mars bars? And how would she manage when her supply of anti-frizz shampoo ran out? Was she making a terrible mistake?

No, of course not, she told herself firmly, she was just totally exhausted. After all, it had barely been three weeks since she had heard about the job and the time had passed in such a frenzy of activity that she had hardly slept at all. She lay back in the seat, closed her eyes and for a moment almost wished she was back in the safety and security of her tiny flat in Islington with Pumpkin purring softly on one side of her and Nigel made hissing sounds through his teeth on the other.

Gradually, as the plane droned on, the throbbing of the engines began to take on the rhythm of Pumpkin's purring and she drifted into a light doze.

She had no idea how long she slept but when she opened her eyes again she was shocked to see that the luxuriant green of the forest canopy had been replaced by the barren grey of a moonscape. For a moment, nothing made sense to her. Then she remembered about all the logging that was going on and the damage it was doing to the equatorial rainforest. She had read about it, of course, but the scene below her had an emotional impact that the printed word hadn't delivered. Nothing could possibly be left alive down there, she thought, turning away from the window with a shudder, nothing except rats, anyway.

It was a while before she could bring herself to look out again but when she did, she was relieved to see that they were once again flying over the myriad greens of a living rainforest. And when she sensed the plane beginning to lose altitude for the approach to the airstrip at Putussibau, her enthusiasm for the adventure ahead of her came flooding back.

She was drawing in her first breath of the hot, humid air of Borneo, redolent of garlic and spices and animal dung, when a tall man with a slightly Asian cast to his features called out her name.

'Bethany?' he asked, coming toward her and holding out his hand.

She nodded.

'I'm Bima Van Wick,' he said, in a deep voice tinged with a Dutch accent, 'from Kanyalang. I'm the lucky one who got to come and meet you.' And nodding in the direction of a small helicopter a few hundred yards away, he added, 'The pilot's waiting for us. It will just be a short ride from here so we should be there in time for lunch.'

Bethany had never been in a helicopter before, and the rapidity of the vertical ascent gave her an alarming sensation of having left her stomach somewhere on the ground. Fortunately, it didn't take long to reach cruising altitude, and her insides managed to catch up with the rest of her.

Bima launched into a running commentary on the landscape as they went along but Bethany had some trouble following it over the noise of the rotor blades.

'We're leaving the lowlands now,' he was saying. 'See, the rivers are much narrower here and some of them, like the one that runs in front of Kanyalang, are barely navigable a good part of the year. That's mostly because of the rocks, but the rapids are a problem, too. Unfortunately though, we aren't really high enough to escape the heat.'

'I won't mind that,' Bethany yelled back. 'Non-stop summer will be heaven after London.'

'You might change your mind when steam starts coming out of your ears,' Bima laughed. Then a moment later his tone became serious as he said, 'Look down there and you'll see what the loggers have done.'

She did, and saw an expanse of stripped and denuded terrain much like the one she had flown over earlier.

'That's not going to go on anywhere near us, is it?' she asked, in alarm.

'I hope not,' he said. 'Fortunately we're right on the edge of a huge conservation area so we should be alright.'

'That's a relief,' she said, but she wasn't certain he heard her. She suspected that his deeper voice carried more effectively over engine noise than hers did so she contented herself with the role of a listener.

'We've all been looking forward to your arrival,' he said. 'At the moment, the research team has only got a botanist, that's Marguarita Barnet, and a zoologist, Catherine Everton, so we've been very much in need of an anthropologist. If the people who actually live in the rainforest are ignored it could make the whole project look bad.'

'Where do you come in?'

'More on the tourism side of things,' he said, 'the part that's supposed to bring in the money to support the research centre. I'm an architect and I designed the hotel. I usually just pop in now and then to check on things once the construction actually gets started but Kanyalang is my all-time pet project and it's so isolated that I'm staying around to keep an eye on things.'

He had barely finished explaining this when he drew her attention to a cluster of simple thatched-roofed structures nestled in the bend of a river.

'There it is,' he announced, 'that's Kanyalang. As you can see, we've kept everything entirely in the style of the local Maloh Dayak people, on the outside at least. We'll try to do that as much as possible on the inside too, but we'll have to make a few concessions to meet the demands of the affluent twenty-first century tourist.'

'Such as?' she asked.

'Well, decent showers and things like air conditioning in the bedrooms and —'

'Won't that sort of spoil the effect?' interrupted Bethany.

'Not if we do it right, using solar panels and things like that.'

'But on a thatched roof —' protested Bethany.

'Good God, no, we'll put them in a separate clearing fifty meters or so from the hotel and channel the power to the rest of the compound from there. In the meantime we're making do with a couple of generators and —' He broke off, aware that Bethany was no longer listening.

The helicopter had begun its descent and her attention was riveted on the scene below.

Bethany wasted no time clambering out onto the landing pad and surveying the clearing around her. From the tops of the tallest trees, some of them so high they stole the lion's share of sunlight for themselves, to the vines and lianas that twined their way snake-like up the bark of their unwilling hosts, to the moss and fallen leaves that carpeted the forest floor, she saw a world of green.

'It's more beautiful than I ever thought possible,' she exclaimed, as her eyes drank in the countless species of palm trees, ferns and shrubs that surrounded her.

'But you haven't seen anything yet,' Bima protested. 'Come on, I'll show you where we all live. Don't worry about your cases. Someone can bring them up for you later.'

'Great,' she said and felt that she was in heaven as they started down a wide path where the vegetation that pressed in from either side was so thick that it almost gave the effect of a tunnel.

They hadn't gone far when the illusion of heaven came under attack. A disgusting stench, one so revolting that she thought for a minute she was going to be sick, assaulted her nostrils.

'What's that?' she asked.

'Just this,' laughed Bima, indicating a plant with an unabashedly phallic-shaped flower, 'something called Maiden's Veil. The thing to do is just hurry past it as fast as you can.'

She followed his advice and quickened her pace even though the heat and the humidity were so intense that she soon felt like she had been dipped in a kettle of steaming water but she forgot about the temperature when they reached a clearing beside a shallow river.

There, looming up in front of her, stood a wooden house, one that was so long it seemed to go on forever, balanced serenely on a series of ironwood pilings.

Bethany immediately recognised the style of a traditional Dayak longhouse in its high thatch roof designed for maximum coolness, its wide veranda where the life of an entire community could take place, and its tall pillars that kept the main part of the structure some twenty feet above the ground.

'This is where we all live,' Bima said, proudly, 'but I have to admit, we've cheated a bit on the access. Everybody rebelled at the idea of climbing up and down a notched log like the locals do whenever they wanted to go in or out so I put in wooden steps with a handrail instead.'

Bethany regarded Bima's innovation doubtfully, wishing that it looked a little sturdier but she didn't want to seem like a wimp so she kept her reservations to herself.

'Everybody's probably on the veranda by now,' he said, glancing at his watch, 'relaxing and having something cold to drink before lunch. At least, that's what we like to do if we have time. Anyway, so let's go up and see. With any luck you can meet the whole crowd at once.'

He was right about the veranda and the drinks, but no one was relaxing. Tension hung like a tangible presence in the air.

Bima sensed that something was very wrong, but was about to go ahead and introduce Bethany anyway when Elliot Martin, the project leader, strode out and cut him off in mid-sentence.

'Tarique's dead,' Elliot announced, gruffly.

A chill that defied the heat of the Borneo noon swept over the little group on the veranda as they absorbed the news. Tarique Radjeb had been very much alive at breakfast that morning.

Catherine was the first to react. 'It can't be true,' she cried, leaping up and rushing off to the dead man's room.

She found him there, stretched out in perfect stillness on the bed.

'You fucking bastard,' she hissed, to the inert form, 'you can't do this to me.' And as a wave of morning sickness washed over her, she reached out and slapped the unresponsive face. 'Get up, damn you. Get up.'

Tarique, enveloped in the indifference of death, did not stir.

Outside on the veranda, a state of collective shock prevailed and Bethany's arrival was barely acknowledged.

'How did it happen?' Bima rasped when he had recovered the power of speech.

'Snake bite,' Elliot replied, grimly.

'But we've got a first aid kit, for God's sake,' Bima protested. 'It must have an antidote for something like that.'

'The snake was a banded krait,' Elliot explained, 'and Tarique was nearly an hour's walk away from the longhouse when it happened. There wasn't time.'

'Jesus,' was all Bima could say.

'Better try Allah,' a bearded Australian named Mike Roberts muttered in a heavy Queensland accent. 'Tarique was Muslim.'

'Yeah, well, it looks to me like Allah wasn't on his side this morning,' said John Wolfenson, an American with sharp eyes and a beaky nose known as Wolf.

'Either that or he changed his mind about protecting the bastard, decided he wasn't worth making an effort for,' suggested Mike.

'Smuggling a shit like that into heaven would be no easy task, that's for sure,' added Wolf.

'Hey, watch it,' said Bima. His mother had been a Javanese Muslim.

'Sorry,' Wolf mumbled hastily, 'I wasn't thinking.'

Elliot, his mind on the troublesome obligations that were certain to fall on him as a result of the morning's events, barely noticed the altercation between the two men. 'Damn Tarique,' he was saying to himself, 'and damn the snake and damn Borneo.'

The first thing he'd better do, he decided, was go down to the office and ring Tarique's wife. He dreaded being the one to give her the news. It would really be hell if she broke down during the conversation. He would have to contact the French consulate, too, and let them know what had happened because, although Tarique had been born in Tunisia, he had been naturalised as a child. And considering the fact that the Rainforest Research Fund was financing the start-up costs of the project, he supposed they would have to be told as well. It was, he admitted, grudgingly, the sort of situation that justified having the outrageously expensive iridium phone.

Marguarita, also wrapped up in her own reflections, was silently reliving the moment she had seen the snake uncoiling itself and getting ready to strike, the moment she could have called out a warning to Tarique but hadn't. Had that been something close to murder? Some people might think it was. But then was it her fault that a banded krait's venom took effect so quickly or that it was nearly always fatal? No, of course it wasn't. She hadn't killed Tarique, the snake had done it. She had just happened to be there at the time. It was fate, a well-deserved fate, and if a word from her might have saved him, well she could live with that.

Bima would not have agreed that Tarique's fate had been deserved although, looking back on it now, he wondered how he could have been crazy enough ever to have lent him any money. He started to add up the total in his mind and then broke off in disgust. How could he think about things like that when the guy was lying dead a few doors down the veranda?

Bethany, in the meantime, had been left to get on with things as best she could.

She was actually beginning to wish that she had listened to Nigel and stayed in London when Mike strolled over to her and said, 'It must be tough walking in on all this. After all, you didn't even know the guy.'

'It is a bit difficult,' she replied, acknowledging to herself that even in circumstances like this, there was something disconcerting about being invisible.

'Come on, I'll show you your room,' he continued, 'so you can wash up before lunch, if you want to. You'll want something to eat, even if none of the rest of us are very hungry. But hold on a second, I'll just get your gear.'

Bethany saw that her two cases had mysteriously arrived at the top of the stairs and she watched gratefully as Mike went loping over to pick them up. His gait made her think of a friendly gorilla and his build and demeanour added to the effect. But when he came back, a case in each hand, she noticed that the brown eyes peering out above his bushy beard seemed surprisingly kind for someone who, just a few minutes before, had talked so callously about his dead colleague.

'Here you are,' he said, opening one of the many doors that led off the wide veranda and showing her into a hot stuffy room not much bigger than a closet. Furnished with Spartan simplicity, its only possible concession to comfort was a window air conditioner that blocked the light, obscured the view and currently wasn't running.

'I hope this will do,' Mike said, in the uncertain tone of someone who wished he could offer something better.

'It'll be fine,' she assured him. 'I didn't expect anything more.'

'You know,' he began, rather awkwardly, as he set her cases down, 'we're basically not as bad as you might think from everything you heard out there. It's just that, well you see, some of us think Tarique wasn't the greatest guy in the world.'

'I could see that,' she replied.

He wondered unhappily what else he could say to make this appealing girl with the nicely rounded figure think well of him.

'I guess you've met everyone now, except Pashetta,' he said, hoping a new subject would do the trick.

'Who's he?'

'She,' Mike corrected. 'She's supposed to be the team leader's PA but she actually does things for all of us. You'll like her. She might still be down in the office trying to get through to the doctor in Putussibau. I don't know if anyone's told her it's too late. You'll probably meet her at lunch. That is, unless you've been so put off by everything that's happened here that you're on your way back to London by then.'

'It hasn't been a very good start,' she admitted.

'It's not a very good project, either,' he said.

'What's the matter with it?' she asked, surprised. 'From what I've heard about it, it seems like a great idea.'

'Yeah, that's what I thought when I first came here.'

'But you don't anymore?'

He shook his head. 'It's absolute madness, building a luxury hotel in the back of beyond like this and expecting it to make enough money to support a research centre, even a small one.'

'Oh,' said Bethany, disappointed. She had thought it sounded like a brilliant plan and she told him so.

'On paper, maybe,' Mike replied, 'but if the numbers don't work out, well research is an expensive proposition, isn't it?'

'I suppose so but why do you stay here if you think things aren't going to work out?'

'I like my job. It's great. That part couldn't be better.'

'But you just said –'

'The project is crazy but I've no complaints at all about what I do. In fact, I love it. Forestry is my thing, especially the tropical rainforest, so if some organisation is willing to pay me to be out in it and lead a conservation corps, doing whatever I can do to keep it from being wrecked by loggers and gold miners and guys who want to plant oil palms, then I'm their man. I just don't think the hotel we're building is ever going to make enough money to support a research centre, that's all. I'll be surprised if it even supports itself. In my opinion it's not going to be long before the project, the ecotourism part of it anyway, runs out of money and comes to a screeching halt.'

'What will you do then?'

Mike shrugged. 'Get another job.'

'Don't you mind?'

'No, nobody stays in jungle jobs very long. You haven't signed up for the next twenty years, have you?'

'No, just the next eighteen months.'

'There you are then. But you shouldn't worry. The money will probably hold out that long.'

'I hope you're right.'

'Well, I'd better get out of here so you can wash up,' he said, and nodding in the direction of a table that had a metal pitcher and a plastic bowl on it, he added, 'Sometimes there's running water and sometimes there's not so you'd better keep that thing full whenever you can.'

'I'll try.'

'There's a loo and an Indonesian style bath, just a big vat of water really, down at the far end of the veranda,' he continued. 'But you see when the project's up and running this place is just going to be housing for the staff so it doesn't get all the luxuries the hotel's going to have.'

'It seems to have air conditioning anyway,' she observed, pointing to the small window unit.

'Part of the time,' he said. 'Kolop, he's the cook-houseboy, usually gets the generator going around six in the evening so you can turn it on then. The office is the only place that's got electricity during the day.' He paused with his hand on the door. 'Do you think you'll be okay here?' he asked, doubtfully.

'Absolutely,' she assured him.

Yet when he had gone she admitted to herself that she wasn't so sure. She didn't mind a bit about the simple accommodation. The truth was that she rather liked it. It gave everything the air of being an adventure. What made her a bit uneasy was a feeling that the people she was going to be working with, some of them anyway, were going to be a little hard to like.

When Bethany went back out to join the others, she found them drifting toward the far end of the veranda where a table had been laid for lunch.

This time her new colleagues seemed to recognise that she existed but once everyone was seated around the table they all focused their attention on what Elliot had to say about his conversation with Tarique's wife.

Madame Radjeb, he reported, had shown no sign of distress when he had told her the news. It had only been when he had mentioned shipping the body back to France that she had shown signs of being upset. Then, in unexpectedly clear and emphatic

15

English, she had insisted that this was out of the question. Tarique had been Muslim, she had reminded him, and must be buried in accordance with Islamic law. That meant before sundown on the day of his death.

Bethany only half listened to this recital. Instead she watched in amazement as her companions, their appetites apparently undiminished by the sudden arrival of death in their midst, devoured heaping plates of rice and spicy chicken. Only Catherine, who looked terrible, merely toyed with her food and ate next to nothing.

Part way through the meal a young woman, whom Bethany gathered must be the as yet unknown Pashetta, slipped quietly into an empty place on the other side of the table. She tried to catch Wolf's eye, looked disappointed when she didn't succeed, and then smiled a greeting at Bethany before ladling an enormous helping of rice onto her plate.

How can she eat like that and stay so slim, Bethany wondered, as she returned Pashetta's smile. She was just deciding that she was going to like this girl when an outraged exclamation from Wolf drew her attention.

'Christ, doesn't Tarique's wife realise that we know fuck all about Muslim funerals?' he said.

Other voices joined in the indignation and Bethany, who didn't realise that Muslim funerals were considered men's business, wondered why, as the only Indonesian there, Pashetta wasn't consulted.

The solution to the problem arrived in the form of a rotund and jovial Madurese doctor from Putussibau and, as there was little for him to do except sign the death certificate, he was invited to join them all at lunch.

Elliot and Marguarita vied with each other to give him the most complete account of what had happened and Wolf laid their present predicament before him.

The Madurese doctor proved to be as kind as he looked and he relieved everyone's worries by offering to turn the funeral arrangements over to the imam at the mosque in Putussibau. 'That is,' he said, 'if a helicopter can bring him to Kanyalang.'

Elliot said that could be arranged.

'Now,' the doctor said, pushing his chair back from the table, 'please, I must go.'

'But you've scarcely eaten anything,' protested Marguarita.

'I eat at my house,' he declared, glad to escape the Kanyalang food. It was Dayak fare and he didn't like it – no one from the island of Madura would. He was certain of that.

'Pashetta will take you down to the landing pad and see about having the pilot bring the imam here this afternoon,' Elliot said.

Bethany, noticing that Pashetta had barely had time to make inroads on her chicken and rice, decided that a boss who didn't give her time to eat might be one of the reasons for her great figure.

With the problem of the funeral thus transferred to more capable hands, the conversation turned to Tarique himself and soon became quite heated. The debate centred around whether or not he could have been involved in any underhand dealings with the logging companies and opinions on this subject differed as sharply as did the accents, British, American, Australian, and Dutch, in which they were expressed.

Catherine was fierce in her insistence that everything Tarique had done had been above reproach. Bima echoed this view but with less conviction, while Marguarita maintained that he had been guilty as hell. Wolf and Mike shared this opinion but, as Elliot pointed out, without any real evidence to support it.

Bethany only half-listened to what was being said. She was finding everything so strange that it was a relief just to sit back and let the discussion flow over her. Not even something as basic as breathing seemed to come easily here. The air was so humid that she could almost feel herself growing gills and the spicy food that had tasted so good at the beginning of the meal was now starting to burn her throat. It made her desperate for a glass of cold water but everything on the table, the food, the water, the tea, was tepid.

Toward the end of the meal Kolop raised Bethany's hopes for something refreshing by bringing out a bowl of fruit.

'Here, have an orange,' Wolf said, handing one to Bethany.

'It's actually a tangerine,' corrected Marguarita.

'But it's green,' Bethany protested.

'All the tangerines here are green,' Marguarita explained. 'It's just a different species, that's all.'

'Go on, try it,' said Wolf, peeling one for himself. 'They're not too bad.'

Bethany tried hers and thought it was awful, dry and fibrous and sour, but she struggled through it anyway.

She had just managed to swallow the last bite when Wolf pushed his chair away from the table and announced, 'I gotta get going. There's a lot to do before this funeral.'

Everyone seemed to take this as a cue to get up and leave and for a moment Bethany thought she was going to be forgotten again.

Then Wolf surprised her by turning back and saying, 'Hey, do you want to come along to the office with me? That way you can see where you'll be working, when you're not hanging out with the Dayaks, that is. I'd better warn you though, it's pretty basic.'

'I don't mind "basic",' she replied.

'Good,' he said, giving her a vigorous nod of approval. It sent a shock of floppy dark hair down over his forehead, almost grazing his remarkable nose.

Looking up at him, she wondered briefly if he had ever been Cyrano in a school play but then hastily put this ungenerous thought aside and took him up on his offer.

CHAPTER TWO

Out in the sunlit clearing between the longhouse and the river, Bethany decided that the temperature must be somewhere between roast and bake and wondered if she would ever be able to get used to it. Wolf, she noticed enviously, appeared to be quite undaunted by it.

'This is such an exciting project,' he was saying in a voice filled with enthusiasm. 'I mean totally ground-breaking. And if it's a success – which it's bound to be – it's going to catch on like a house afire.'

She looked at him in surprise. This certainly wasn't the way Mike had talked about it.

'It's going to have a tremendous effect on research into the eco-system around here,' Wolf continued, his American accent somehow giving added emphasis to his words, 'and I'll bet you anything that before you know it sister projects are going to spring up all over the place.'

'Aren't you being a little overly-optimistic?' she asked. 'It's not as if eco-tourism is a new idea, you know. You can read about it in any travel magazine.'

'You've totally missed the point,' he exclaimed. 'We're going to have a completely new kind of eco-tourism here, one that's going to make the world sit up and take notice.'

'In what way?'

'All the profits from the tourism section, basically the hotel, are going to be ploughed back into the research and conservation sections. You see, there's no way that any of the organisations interested in the environment are going to come up with enough money these days to finance more than a tiny fraction of the research that's needed. And the funds available for conservation are peanuts, too.'

'But foreign aid donors are interested in this sort of thing, aren't they? And they have money.'

'Forget it. That well dried up when the Cold War ended. Not that anything more than a pittance ever found its way into research anyway, even when the going was good.'

'How about the Indonesian government then?'

To her intense mortification, this idea drew a loud guffaw from Wolf. 'You gotta be kidding,' he exclaimed.

'Actually, I wasn't,' she replied, coldly. 'I know this is a poor country but –'

Wolf, cutting her off and in a tone so patronising that it infuriated her, said, 'What you must know is that this government, Suharto and all his relatives and cronies, can't be relied on for anything. They're hand-in-glove with the loggers who are cutting down every tree in sight.'

'Are you quite certain about that?'

'I'm certain that's what they'll do if they can. Listen, money's king around here. Those fat-cats in Jakarta don't give a rat's arse about the eco-system or the ozone layer or the habitat of a few hairy orang-utans. Money, the more of it, the better, is all they care about. And they want it to go directly into their own pockets and not be wasted on the general public.'

Bethany was taken aback by the bitterness in his voice.

'But if our project is successful – and like I said, it's absolutely bound to be –' Wolf went on, 'it's going to launch a revolution in the financing of small-scale research centres and conservation projects. Of course, there'll be a lot of scrounging to do around the foundations and the development banks to get hold of the initial seed money but that'll be a one-off. Once these centres are up and running, they should be able to cover their operating expenses with the profits from an income-earning venture.'

'And you really think it might work?' she asked, still sceptical but wanting to believe it.

'It will, if it's done right. I mean, look at what's going on here already. We've got the start-up money from a major hotel chain and from the RRF –'

'The what?' she began, unused to the acronym, and then she twigged. 'Oh, you mean the Rainforest Research Fund.'

'Right, and when we open our centre and our super deluxe hotel, we'll be able to give the tourists a jungle experience they can dine out on for years without having to give up on the pleasures of a comfortable night's sleep or an ice-cold drink or a delicious dinner. Something like that's got to be a winner.'

'Hardly a very authentic winner,' Bethany observed, scornfully.

'Don't worry about that,' he laughed. 'We'll give them all the hard-hitting stuff they can take, maybe more. We'll lay on tours through the primeval forest that will include as many authentic leeches and scorpions and fire ants as you could want but it'll be worth it because on lucky days there'll be a chance of seeing some thoroughly genuine indigenous fauna like bearded pigs or flying foxes or maybe even a bearcat or two. We'll give them a botanical and zoological treat that'll blow their minds, I promise you. But at the same time anyone who tosses out any non-biodegradable litter will get strung up by the thumbs. You just wait and see.'

'Are you just making that up, about those improbable sounding animals, I mean?'

'No, but we'll show them some very probable species that are worth looking at too, gorgeous butterflies, huge colourful birds and mile-long crocodiles. God knows how many kinds of fauna run, crawl or slither around here. And that's only the beginning.'

'You mean there's more?' she asked, allowing a hint of mockery to creep into her voice.

'Damn right there is. Our tourists will be taken into the rainforest by the actual scientists and conservationists who've been working there and who can clue them in on what they're actually seeing – stuff that's specific to the area and that's come straight out of our centre.'

'I hate to say this but what makes you think your scientists and conservationists are going to be willing to play tour guide?'

'It's obvious. They'll jump at the chance. Just think about it, a couple of hours a week talking about their work to people who are sufficiently interested to go tramping through the jungle to hear about it. That has to be a small price to pay for a fully funded research opportunity like this place is going to offer. In any case, it can't be any worse than teaching an undergraduate course. Now you've gotta admit, that's a pretty impressive proposition.'

Bethany wasn't prepared to admit anything of the sort but she set her doubts aside because they had arrived in front of another longhouse, one that was set on shorter stilts than the one they all lived in, had a narrower veranda and served as an office.

Here we are,' he announced, with a flourish. 'This is our soon-to-be-famous research centre.'

'I can't think of a lovelier place to work,' Bethany exclaimed, starting up the veranda stairs ahead of him.

It'll be good having a little more feminine fauna around the place, Wolf reflected, standing back and watching her, even though he didn't consider this particular specimen to be exactly a sex symbol. Still, he liked the way her hair bounced over her shoulders as she walked. The colour, sort of like pale honey that had had some carrot juice splashed on it, was intriguing and her eyes were an unusual shade, too. He had noticed them at lunch, sort of a yellowy-brown with greenish flecks in them, and had wondered where he had seen ones like that before. It dawned on him now that it had been in the lion enclosure at the zoo. The big cats had eyes that colour, although he couldn't remember seeing any greenish flecks in them. Still the resemblance was there all the same. He was on the point of telling her about it when he thought the better of it. She might not like being compared to a wild animal. He wouldn't mind it himself but women could be funny about things like that.

Her bum, distinctly on the generous side, was another one of her attractions, he decided. In any case, something about her was giving him a hard-on and that was probably it. But then, he reminded himself, just about anything new and female and homo sapiens would probably have that effect in a place like this.

'I'm afraid this dismal, little cell,' he announced, flinging open the door to an almost empty room, 'is all the RRF provides for your comfort and convenience. Still, if it's any consolation, none of us except Elliot have anything better. The old man gets VIP treatment on account of being team leader.'

Bethany gazed delightedly around the tiny office. Although it had the same stark simplicity as her bedroom in the other longhouse, there was an important difference. The air conditioner in this one, set in the wall below the window, didn't block the view. Instead, it allowed a dense thicket of bamboo on the other side of the pane to act as a softly tinted curtain.

'I know it's pretty bad,' Wolf said, sympathetically, 'but do you think you can make do?'

'Make do? I love it. It's like a wonderful little tree house.'

'Don't tell me you're a closet romantic,' he said, disapprovingly.

'Is that such a bad thing to be?'

'Damn right, it is. That sort of thinking can get you in a lot of trouble in a place like this. The jungle —'

'Jungle,' she repeated, disdainfully, 'isn't that a rather old fashioned word for a forward looking environmentalist to use? I mean, you are the environmentalist on the project, aren't you?'

He nodded.

'I thought that word went out with Rudyard Kipling,' she said.

'Well, it shouldn't have,' he declared. 'All these politically correct words like rainforest make it sound too benign. I promise you that it is very much a jungle around here and it's brimming over with insects and reptiles that don't share your rose-coloured view of the world. You're the enemy in their book, you and your fellow human beings, and they want nothing more than to give that Madurese doctor another death certificate to sign, possibly yours. So while you're revelling in a load of romantic garbage about this "rainforest" as you will probably insist on calling it, they're sizing you up as the easiest prey since —'

'You're not making me sound romantic, just stupid,' she said, angrily, 'and I don't like it.'

'Temper, temper,' Wolf scolded, with a mocking smile, 'but seriously, I didn't mean to hurt your feelings. I'm quite sure you're not stupid. I just wanted to give you a timely warning, that's all.'

'Thank you,' she answered, coldly, 'but I'd rather learn for myself.'

'That appears to be what Tarique did,' he remarked, cheerfully. 'Of course, in his case it might have been a good thing. At least, it got him out of the way.'

'Doesn't it bother you to say such frightful things about him when he hasn't even been buried yet?'

'No,' he said firmly. 'When do you think it's okay to start telling the truth about someone? Five minutes after the funeral, will that do?'

23

'Of course not, not when it's that kind of truth.'

'How long do we have to wait then, ten years, a hundred years, a thousand? Do we dare say nasty things about Attila the Hun, or Caligula, or any of the countless ogres who've been a scourge on the planet since the beginning of time?'

'Now you're being absurd.'

'No, I'm being perfectly rational. Tarique was an A-number one shit when he was alive and I doubt if being dead has improved him any. Actually, on second thought, maybe it has. At least, it has stopped him feathering his nest at the expense of the jungle while the rest of us are working our butts off trying to save it.'

'That may be your opinion, but I noticed not everyone at lunch agreed with you.'

'That's because they're blind.'

'Oh,' she scoffed, 'and I suppose you're the only one who's smart enough to have figured things out.'

'No, not the only one.'

'Generous of you to share the credit.'

'I'm glad you're finally beginning to appreciate me,' he returned with a chuckle.

'I appreciate the fact that you have a highly inflated opinion of yourself.'

'How do you know it's inflated? You haven't been around me long enough to find out.'

'I think I have.'

'Really? Then maybe I'm not the only one around who's overflowing with confidence in his, or in this case, in her, own opinions,' he teased. Then glancing down at his watch, he added, 'Jesus, I'd better get a move on. That burial's got to happen before sundown.'

An instant later, he was gone and Bethany was alone in her tree house office.

She stared after him for a moment and then wandered over to the window and looked out. And as she did so, she wondered whether she would ever come to see this place as Wolf saw it, a jungle, filled with the menace of savage predators and strangling vegetation or whether she would always see it as a rainforest, a life-giving font of oxygen and food and well-being for the world.

Unable to resolve the question, Bethany turned away from the window and went back to her room to unpack.

It didn't take her long to empty her two cases, and she had almost finished arranging their contents in the available drawers when there was a tap on the door and Marguarita waltzed in.

'I just stopped by to see how you're getting on,' she said.

'Fine,' Bethany replied.

'I don't see how you can be fine,' Marguarita remarked as she moved one of the cases aside and sat down. 'I mean it must be a real shag, coming all this way and finding everything at sixes and sevens just because some fool has let himself be bitten by a snake.'

'I don't suppose he could help it, could he?' Bethany replied, icily.

'Help being bitten or help being a fool?'

Bitch, Bethany thought, and didn't deign to reply.

'But I'd like to put all that out of my mind for a while and hear about you, instead,' Marguarita continued.

Bethany regarded her frostily. 'There really isn't anything to tell.'

'Nonsense, everyone has something to tell. For starters, whatever made you sign up for a lengthy sentence in an isolated place like this? I mean, it isn't exactly a holiday resort, not yet anyway and definitely not for us. I hope it won't totally drive you round the twist.'

Bethany laughed. 'I don't think it will. I'm an anthropologist, remember. We all have to do field work, want to do it, I should say.'

'Yes, but why do you lot become anthropologists in the first place?' Marguarita demanded. 'What are you trying to escape?'

'Don't you think that's a rather personal question?'

'Absolutely, that's what makes it interesting.'

'I'm glad it amuses you.'

'It doesn't very much but we're all desperate for diversions in this place. You'll find that out soon enough so you might as well forget what you were taught about not asking personal questions and go for it.'

'Alright then, I'll start with you. What are you doing here?'

'Oh, this is my natural habitat,' Marguarita replied, airily. 'I was born in the jungle.'

'That's a little hard to believe,' Bethany said, thinking that her new colleague, tall and slim, managed to look more like she had been born in a Versace showroom than in a tropical rainforest, even though she was just wearing jeans and a tee shirt.

'I promise you it's true though,' Marguarita declared. 'I was born in the Yucatan when my parents – they're both archaeologists – were excavating a Mayan site there. Mummy was too obsessed with her work to think about doctors and mid-wives until it was too late so I was literally born in the jungle. Daddy had to help deliver me.'

'That sounds rather romantic, actually,' Bethany said, and then glanced hastily around to make certain that Wolf wasn't anywhere within earshot.

'I don't think Daddy quite saw it that way,' Marguarita returned with a laugh, 'just the reverse, I'm afraid. He must have been seriously disgusted by it all because he decamped shortly afterwards and went off to work on an Inca site in Peru.' Her countenance clouded over for a moment before she gave a dismissive shrug and observed, 'But then, families are crap, aren't they?'

Bethany's memories of her own childhood kept her from springing to the defence of family life so she contented herself with asking, 'Did you grow up there, in the jungle, I mean?'

'No, Mummy dumped me on my Mexican grandparents until I was eleven and after that Daddy managed to pawn me off on the English ones.' With a glint of amusement in her eyes she added, 'I must not have been a very appealing child.'

Bethany could well imagine that she had been an absolute horror – a true descendant of some ancient Aztec or Mayan ancestor who had carved out human hearts as a sacrifice to his gods. Certainly her shiny black hair and widely sculpted cheekbones would give added credence to this possibility, Bethany thought, before she put a firm check on her imagination.

'Do you still go back to Mexico?' she asked, interested now in spite of herself.

'Not much anymore but I used to spend the summer holidays there when I was at school, university, too. Of course, Mummy was always frightfully busy rooting around with brush and trowel but that left me with masses of time to spend wandering around looking at plants, especially orchids. They've always been a grand passion of mine, still are, although now I've got other pet interests, as well.'

'Such as?'

'Mainly plants with potential for medicinal uses. They're going to be the key to saving the rainforest, I'm certain of that.'

'What makes you so sure?'

'The inherent greed and selfishness of the human race. The only thing that will make people reach into their pockets and dredge up some money for conservation is the prospect of getting something out of it for themselves. And it has to be something they really want like miracle drugs to cure their aches and pains and possibly even prolong their pathetic little lives.'

'You're a bit cynical,' observed Bethany.

'More than a bit,' Marguarita admitted, readily, 'but when you think of all the deforestation that's going on, only a complete fathead could be anything else.'

'I'm not so sure about that,' Bethany protested. 'I know lots of people who care about virgin forests and animal habitats and the way of life of indigenous peoples and aren't thinking about getting anything particular out of it for themselves. They just don't want to see all the natural beauty of our planet destroyed, that's all.'

'I know people like that, too,' Marguarita said, dismissively. 'They'll go on incessantly about organic food and recycling and greenhouse gases and that sort of thing but heaven forbid you suggest cutting back on their plane tickets or buying smaller cars or not eating strawberries in December. And don't even get me started on the subject of all the cosmetics that are made using oil palm when irreplaceable tropical hardwoods are being chopped down to plant it.'

'And what are you doing about it that's so much more impressive?' Bethany demanded, scornfully.

Somewhat to her surprise Marguarita didn't take offence at this. Instead she seemed to regard it as something of a joke.

'What a breath of fresh air you are,' she cried. 'Everybody else around here tries to get me to shut up about what I'm doing because they're so sick of hearing me go on about it. Of course, you will be too before long, you'll see.' And she immediately set about proving this point by launching into an exhaustive account of her various projects.

Bethany did see.

'But all this is frightfully unfair,' Marguarita said, when she eventually wound down. 'Here I am rattling on about myself but I haven't found out a thing about you. And it should be the other way around because you haven't been here long enough to get thoroughly bored yet. I'm the one who's frantic for some entertainment.'

The idea that anyone could find her life story entertaining was preposterous to Bethany and she was about to say so when Mike poked his bushy head around the door.

'Here you are,' he said, reproachfully, to Marguarita. 'It's nearly time for the funeral. Everybody's waiting for you.'

'But it's just a burial actually,' objected Marguarita. 'I didn't think women went to them in Muslim countries.'

'Well, you're in luck,' he said, cheerfully. 'They're going to this one.'

'Why?' Marguarita asked, clearly appalled at the prospect.

'For one thing, it doesn't look good in front of the locals if hardly any expats come. And this Imam from Putussibau seems to be a reasonable old codger. I think he realises that when the dead guy is the only Muslim around the whole thing's got to be a little unorthodox. Anyway, he's agreed that women are okay. I think they're supposed to sort of stand in the back though.' Then turning to Bethany, he added, 'You don't have to come if you don't want to.'

'Lucky you,' said Marguarita as, with undisguised reluctance, she followed Mike out of the room.

CHAPTER THREE

Marguarita left the door slightly open behind her and Bethany could hear the hum of voices drifting down along the veranda. They sounded more like they came from people gathering for a picnic than for a funeral, and for a moment she was almost tempted to go out and join them. Then her better judgement prevailed. Even thinking of such a thing, going to the funeral of a complete stranger just to avoid being alone in this big empty longhouse, would be ridiculous.

She closed the door resolutely on the voices and sank down on the bed, thinking about some of the things Marguarita had said. Little as she liked her, Bethany had to admit that a few of her comments were spot on, the one about families in particular. And it was certainly welcome after the nauseating platitudes that floated around about families, platitudes that flew so directly in the face of Bethany's own experience.

Her thoughts drifted back to the beginning of the end of her own illusions about families and stirred memories of her mother's wedding day. No one except her new stepbrother, Jeremy, had even noticed that she had completely missed the ceremony. He had found her afterwards and had brought her a piece of wedding cake along with a glass of champagne even though she was only eight. It had made her a little dizzy but it had lifted her spirits and loosened her tongue. Before long she had found herself pouring out her woes to Jeremy, telling him how much she hated the man her mother had just married. Then she had clamped her hand over her mouth in embarrassment as it had dawned on her that the man she was talking about was this kind boy's father.

But Jeremy, wonderful Jeremy, had made her feel better by declaring that he really couldn't stick the old tosser either. He had said that his strategy had been to make such a nuisance of himself that he would be sent away to boarding school. It had worked for him and if she tried the same plan, it would probably work for her, too.

It did.

The only problem had been the holidays. When Jeremy was at home too they had been heaven. She could have had Dracula himself for a stepfather and she wouldn't have minded. But Jeremy hadn't come home very often or stayed very long when he did. He had an outgoing nature, was always ready for a good laugh, and had been an ace rugby player. As a result, he was very popular at school and had no shortage of holiday invitations.

The same had not been true for her. She had been shy, studious, and a disaster on the lacrosse pitch, with the result that when holidays came around she rarely had any place to go except home.

It had been near the end of the Easter holiday just after her fourteenth birthday that everything had gone so terribly wrong. Her mother hadn't been feeling well and had gone upstairs to take a nap after Sunday lunch. Jeremy, home for a few days before the start of his last term at Oxford, had mumbled something about meeting a couple of friends at the pub and had gone out. That was when her stepfather had surprised her by talking to her with unprecedented geniality, urging her to regard him as a friend instead of an adversary, and had insisted on sealing what he declared was their bargain with a kiss.

The next thing she knew he had forced her down on the sofa and pinioned her there by pressing all his flabby weight down on top of her. With one hand glued over her mouth so she couldn't alert her mother, he had used the other to pull her skirt up and her knickers down. Then with thrust after brutal thrust, he had sent a searing pain, one so terrible she had felt she was being torn in two, deep inside her.

Deliverance from the torture had finally come when Jeremy, back from the pub sooner than his father had expected, had seen what was going on. In a thunderous fury he had wrenched her stepfather's great weight off of her and then had proceeded to hit him so hard on the jaw that it had sent him sprawling, bloody-mouthed and semi-conscious, onto the floor.

Her mother had filed for divorce and Jeremy, after a titanic quarrel with his father, had stormed off to his cousin's place in Cornwall and fallen madly in love with the beautiful, sophisticated

Caroline. After that there had been no more room in his life for his gawky teenage stepsister.

Bethany resolutely pushed the recollection from her mind and looked around the room for something to distract her. The possibilities were limited but she did, at least, have her laptop. She would e-mail Nigel, she decided, and let him know she had arrived safely. After all, it wasn't as if they had totally broken up or hated each other or anything and it would give her a chance to ask if Pumpkin was showing any signs of missing her.

Then she remembered that e-mails weren't an option at Kanyalang because it was too far from any server. And she couldn't even write a letter on her laptop and send it snail mail because she had run down the batteries and wouldn't be able to charge them up again until the electricity came on. It was hard to believe this was really 1996.

Oh well, she sighed, fuck Nigel.

The phrase made her smile. Actually, fucking Nigel was what she had been doing for over a year now and, considering everything, it hadn't been too bad. After all, being with someone was better than being alone all the time and it seemed that if you wanted to share your life with someone then sex had to be part of the mix. She supposed it was worth it although sometimes she wasn't quite sure. But at least, it didn't bring her stepfather's face and hands and ... well, everything to mind as often as it used to.

What she couldn't understand was why so many women claimed to like it so much. They must have all had a 'first time' once, and while it was unlikely that it had been as bad as hers – she had even heard some friends go on about how great it had been – she couldn't imagine that it had been brilliant.

At least, Nigel hadn't been as sex-mad as the other men she had gone out with. That was one of the good things about him. There were other things, too, lots of them, really. In fact, he seemed more attractive to her now than he ever had in London. Perhaps she would write that letter, after all, she decided. There were still such things as pen and paper, weren't there?

She tore a page out of a notebook she had brought along for field work, rummaged in her handbag for a pen and set about describing her arrival in Borneo, determined to convince him that she had done the right thing in coming out. She found that it didn't take much – a little tweaking here, a few omissions there – to make it all sound rather exciting and certainly very exotic. By the time she got to the end of her letter, put in a bit about missing him – almost true – and signed it with love – not altogether false – her spirits had lifted and her outlook had become positively cheerful.

A very different mood prevailed amongst the small gathering that watched as Tarique's body, laid out on a hastily cobbled-together stretcher and covered with a white cloth, was lowered into the earth. And when the final cadence of the Arabic prayers had drifted over the newly-made grave and the only tears had been Catherine's, it was a very silent and thoughtful group that made its way back to the longhouse.

Back on the familiar veranda, everyone set about trying to put the dreadful scene of the last hour behind them.

Foraging in the ice-chest for a cold drink was the first step toward accomplishing this and Wolf had polished off nearly half a bottle of Bintang beer before he looked around and noticed that their newest arrival was missing.

'Hey, what happened to Bethany?' Wolf asked, after he had assuaged his thirst. 'Did somebody put her in deep storage or something?'

'She's probably still in her room,' Marguarita said. 'That's where I left her a while ago, anyway. I'll go and tell her everything's over, shall I? Perhaps she can cheer us up.'

This time everyone greeted Bethany with all the warmth and interest she could want. Mike leapt up and poured her a beer, Elliot quizzed her about her flight out, and Wolf set about regaling her with teasing portraits of them all.

'Now Elliot, here,' he declared, waving his glass in the team leader's direction, 'is a cagey bastard, the quiet type, kind of gives you the impression he's a deep thinker but you can't be sure what's really going on behind that owlish façade of his. He sits in his office interpreting the aerial photographs and mapping everything out so that the uninitiated can understand what's going on. They're beautiful maps, by the way, and if you're nice to him and swear not to sue him for sexual harassment, he'll probably invite you into his lair to have a look at them.'

Elliot smiled with tolerant amusement at this picture of himself but he was finding it difficult to enter into the light-hearted atmosphere that Wolf was making such an effort to generate. As far as he was concerned, it was just too soon after everything that had happened.

He hadn't actually liked Tarique very much. Nobody had — well, none of the men anyway. The women were a different matter. Catherine was the only one who had been thoroughly infatuated with him but he had a feeling Marguarita had been rather taken with him, too. Only Pashetta had seen the man's dubious charm for what it was. She, at least, had shown a little sense.

Elliot frowned as a burst of laughter provided a discordant background for his thoughts. Then he reminded himself that the others must have felt much the same way he had when they were all at the graveside. Now they were just trying to drive the chill of death away with their laughter. He wished that sort of thing worked for him but it didn't. He needed a whisky, a double one, or perhaps a triple.

Catherine could use one, too, he thought. He hated to see the despair in her lovely grey eyes. Her face was so drawn and pale, so fragile-looking, it tore at his heart. And her hair looked like it hadn't been brushed for a week. He wished — damn it, he mustn't wish anything where Catherine was concerned. He should remember he was old enough to be her father, well, not quite. It just seemed that way because she didn't look much older than his daughter. Actually she must be nearly thirty and he had only recently turned fifty but what did that matter? It was going to take her a long time to get over Tarique, he was certain of that. It was hell to see her suffer though.

Elliot, deciding that he couldn't wait any longer for that whisky, went into his room and brought out a bottle. Everyone apart from Pashetta, for whom a single glass of beer was an exceptional amount of alcohol, eagerly held out their glasses.

33

Catherine drank hers straight and requested a second before anyone except Wolf had finished their first one. What the fuck was she going to do, she asked herself for the hundredth time that day? Of course, she couldn't have married Tarique even if he had lived. He already had a wife. And she had the sort of career that wasn't at all conducive to marriage and children. But she could always change that. She didn't absolutely have to do field work all the time. She could teach zoology or entomology somewhere. And he could have worked anywhere. Everybody needed accountants. It was the most transferable skill in the world. If she could just have persuaded him to go back to Australia with her when this project was over, they could have settled down and made a life together. And they would have been happy. She knew they would.

It took only an instant for reality to intervene and begin eating away at this fantasy. How could she ever have been happy with a man who cared nothing for her feelings, someone who actually seemed to enjoy hurting her? And how could she have endured it when he started playing around with other women as he would certainly have done? Wasn't he already beginning to fancy Marguarita?

Catherine could feel her blood congealing at the thought. Why did he have to turn her on so much that she could hardly bear it? Why couldn't she have just stayed away from him? Why couldn't she have had the self-respect to refuse to accept the way he treated her? And why did her life seem so bleak and miserable now that she knew she would never make love to him again?'

She'd have to get an abortion and get one fast. She was already a bit more than two months along. She couldn't postpone it much longer.

How could she have even thought of actually having the baby, she wondered? After all, it might turn out to be a boy, a younger edition of Tarique who would be a part of her life for the next twenty years or more. She could get rid of a man who pissed her off and she could probably forget him but she'd be stuck with a child even if it turned out to be a monster.

She couldn't let that happen. She couldn't give Tarique the chance to look down at her from wherever he was, or look up from hell, that was more likely, and laugh at the idea of leaving her with a carbon copy of himself to torment her for years and years to come.

The very idea made her want to have the abortion immediately but she had no idea how she was going to pay for it. And she'd have to go somewhere but where – Singapore, Jakarta, back to Australia? Those places meant plane tickets and hotels as well as everything else, and she just didn't have the money.

She felt sick at the thought of how idiotic she had been to turn so much of her salary over to Tarique to 'invest in their future'. But he had become obsessed with the news about the mining companies, some of them large international ones, that were putting money into the gold deposits that turned up along some of Borneo's rivers. He had gone on about the wonderful future a small investment could bring them, a future they would share, of course, and his dreams had been contagious.

Now those dreams didn't bear thinking about. She even wondered how she could have thought she wanted a future with him. One thing was clear, though, without that money she wasn't going to be able to have an abortion anywhere but here. That would mean having it Dayak style, whatever that was, and she was at a loss to know how to go about arranging it. Of all the major fauna in the area, the species she knew least about was her own.

It was a pity Bethany hadn't come sooner, she thought looking over at her. An anthropologist might know about Dayak abortions, who did them, how they did them, all that sort of thing.

Bethany felt Catherine's appraising glance on her and was interpreting it as a tentative overture of friendship when the arrival of Bima, looking like a thundercloud, diverted her attention.

'What's up?' Wolf asked. 'If it weren't such bad taste I'd say you look like you'd just been to a funeral.' And pushing Elliot's whisky toward him, he added, 'Here, have some of this. It'll do you good.'

Bima didn't hesitate. He downed the whisky as quickly as Catherine had, although under more ordinary circumstances neither of them were serious drinkers. 'It's those damn loggers,' he fumed, banging his glass down on the table.

Wolf was immediately alert. 'What loggers?'

35

'I'm not sure. But I've just been talking to Liu —'

'Who's that?' asked Marguarita.

'The new guy Tarique brought in to oversee the builders. I'm surprised you didn't notice him at the funeral. He told me that rumours about a new road have been floating around Putussibau. Apparently it's going to be built just a few kilometres from here, right through the heart of the conservation area.'

A concerted gasp of dismay went up from the group.

'A logging road?' demanded Marguarita.

Bima nodded. 'To get the logs down to where the river is navigable.'

'We all know what that means,' said Mike.

'Yes,' Marguarita said, bitterly, 'the rape of the rainforest.'

'But they can't violate a conservation area, can they?' exclaimed Bethany.

'You bet your arse they can. Just watch them,' replied Wolf. 'Tropical hardwoods mean money, plenty of it and that's all these dickheads care about.'

'Can't anything be done to stop them? I mean, what's the point of having a conservation area if people can just go in and chop it down?' protested Bethany.

'Good on you,' said Mike, but a ripple of laughter from Wolf and Marguarita made her feel she had said something extremely stupid.

'The point,' Wolf explained, 'is that a conservation area looks good on maps and gives a few uninitiated fools the idea that the government is doing something useful. And, of course, it's money in the bank for the bandits in the Ministry of Forestry.'

'How do they get anything out of it?' Bethany asked.

'You don't expect those guys are going to turn a blind eye for peanuts, do you? They've got the logging companies by the short and curlies and they know it so they hold out for big bucks. And they get it, worse luck.'

'But if you know all that, other people must, too,' Bethany persisted, 'so why don't they —'

'Jesus, you really haven't done your homework, have you,' Wolf interrupted. 'The corruption in this country goes all the way up to the top. Suharto and his relatives and cronies are raking in billions from plundering the forests. Everybody knows that. I would have thought that even newly-arrived anthropologists knew it.'

'Then you would have been wrong, wouldn't you?' Elliot observed.

'Never mind about that,' Marguarita said, her eyes lighting up with a wicked twinkle. 'I know what we should do about it.'

'What?' demanded Wolf, looking at her in astonishment.

'The same thing that chap, Harrison, did when he was parachuted behind Japanese lines during World War II,' Marguarita suggested, gleefully.

'I don't get it,' said Mike, trying to remember exactly what it was he had heard about Harrison.

'Think about it,' Marguarita laughed. 'The Dayaks are head-hunters, aren't they?'

'Were head-hunters,' corrected Elliot, placing special emphasis on the past tense.

Marguarita ignored this. 'He let it be known that he would pay the Dayaks a shilling or something like that for every Japanese head they brought him.'

'I believe it was 'a bob for a nob',' put in Elliot, who remembered the story well.

'All right then, taking inflation into account,' Marguarita went on, 'suppose we offer ten pounds for the head of each person they catch brandishing a chain saw.'

'Hell, let's give them fifty,' put in Mike, seeing eye to eye with Marguarita for once.

'Make it a hundred,' urged Wolf. 'It would still be the most cost effective conservation programme around.'

'I'm afraid you're a little late,' Elliot said, noticing that Bethany wasn't looking entirely happy. 'You seem to have forgotten that the Dayaks' head-hunting days are over.'

'Don't be too sure of that,' replied Wolf. 'How about those headless bodies that turned up not far from the Sarawak border a couple of years ago?'

'They were Madurese,' said Pashetta, as if that explained everything.

Bethany thought of the kind Madurese doctor and shuddered.

'There was a big pool of blood where their heads should have been. My brother saw it,' Pashetta added with relish.

'It's lucky they didn't get his head, too,' Bethany said, in a misplaced effort at friendliness.

To her surprise, Pashetta was outraged. 'They wouldn't,' she exclaimed. 'My family is not Madurese. We are Orang Melayu.'

'I'm not sure we want to go on about this right now,' Elliot said, reprovingly. 'It might put Bethany off working with the Dayaks.'

'Don't worry,' she assured him, eager to prove to Wolf that she had actually done her homework, 'I know about the head-hunting and about that treaty they signed back in the 1890s agreeing to stop it.'

She shot Wolf a look of triumph but it didn't elicit the result she had intended.

'There's a small detail that seems to have escaped you,' he pointed out. 'They agreed not to hunt each other's heads anymore. There wasn't anything in it about not taking a few non-Dayak heads here and there.'

Mike was becoming impatient with a conversation that, in his opinion, was straying into the realm of the absurd. 'This business with the logging road just goes to show what I've been saying all along,' he declared.

'Oh, did you say something?' Marguarita scoffed. 'I must have missed it.'

He glared at her and then went on. 'If this project ever manages to rake in any profits they should go toward protecting whatever is left of the rainforest, not to doing more research on it. I mean what's the point if it's not going to be around in ten or twenty years?'

Marguarita gave him a scathing look. 'If it's going to disappear,' she retorted, 'that just increases the importance of finding out as much as we can before that happens. Surely even you can see that. Or are you just trying to get more project money allocated to your forest rangers?'

Elliot could see an all-too-familiar argument between Mike and Marguarita developing and, deciding that the day had already been bad enough without that, resolutely changed the subject and began questioning Bethany about her trip out from London.

More drinks were splashed into glasses and a curtain was determinedly brought down on the events of the day.

Yet the day wasn't quite over and later that evening Marguarita decided to finish writing up her recent findings on the medicinal potential of various species of wild ginger, particularly the costus speciosus.

She was the one person who liked to bring her laptop out on the veranda after dinner and work there. Everyone else claimed that it was too dark so she was certain to be undisturbed. Tonight was no exception but for once she had trouble concentrating.

Tarique's face as she had last seen it, so uncharacteristically passive in death, kept looming up in front of her. It was hard to believe that only that morning she had watched him wading out of the river after a Dayak-style bath, his hair damp, his sarong clinging to his hips and legs.

God, he had looked attractive, she thought. There was no denying that, nor could she deny that he had been spectacularly good in bed. How many times had it been? Not many, actually, and always in the middle of the night. She supposed she should have been furious and sent him away but she hadn't been able to do it. She didn't think she had even protested. The sensation of waking up to the touch of his hands and his mouth and his cock had been too tantalising to resist.

Had it been a mistake to have let things go that far, she wondered? When he was with her like that she just hadn't let herself think of the appalling way he treated Catherine, constantly putting her down with mocking and belittling comments. He would always claim that he was just teasing but it was a vicious sort of humour, untempered by the hurt in Catherine's eyes. And there had been times when it had been clear that the abuse had been more than just verbal. Once Catherine had gone around with a black eye for several days, claiming that she had bumped her head on the branch of a tree. Everyone except Wolf had taken care not to ask too many questions but Wolf, being Wolf, hadn't minced words. He and Tarique hadn't spoken for weeks after that.

Well, no man is ever going to drive me to fabricating silly stories about tree branches, Marguarita thought fiercely, no matter how great the sex is.

She tried to turn her attention back to the costus speciosus, but other disturbing thoughts about Tarique kept whirling around in her mind. They were, she acknowledged, really just suspicions based on unsubstantiated feelings and highly debatable interpretations of events. Still, she couldn't help thinking that something underhand had been going on, something that would not have been in the best interest of the rainforest.

Well, whatever it was she had put an end to it now, she reflected, or rather the banded krait had. She hadn't done anything. And Tarique had brought it on himself, actually. He should have been in his office working on the accounts, that was what he was paid to do, not out in the jungle following her about. If he hadn't cheated on Catherine, she reasoned, if he'd kept his dick where it belonged, he'd be alive now.

Satisfied that a primitive form of justice had prevailed, Marguarita turned her attention back to the wild ginger family.

CHAPTER FOUR

Wolf, lying in bed waiting for Pashetta's arrival, was also thinking about Tarique. He couldn't quite shake off a gut feeling that the guy had known something about this new logging project. But if so, why hadn't he said anything, he wondered? Could someone have been paying him to see that the thing was kept under wraps until it was too late to stop it? But what would have been the point of that? There was virtually nothing anyone at Kanyalang could do about it even if they did know. Or could Tarique have been involved with the loggers somehow, maybe fed the company some useful information about where the best tropical hardwoods could be found? But how would he have known that sort of thing when his work rarely took him out of the office?

Elliot, not Tarique, was the one who would know exactly where the best pickings were. After all, he was the high chief in charge of mapping as well as being team leader. Surely he should have been the one to spot what was going on inside the conservation area and if he didn't, or didn't mention it, could he have been the one who was hand-in-glove with the loggers?

No, impossible, Wolf told himself. Elliot was such an upright guy, he couldn't do anything like that although, a thought struck him, weren't straight arrow guys exactly the kind who could get away with murder? If they were faced with money problems or something, mightn't they stoop to some pretty low manoeuvres and get away with them because everyone thought they were above reproach? Whereas an obvious shit like Tarique would have had a much harder time because people would instinctively mistrust him and be on the alert for any hanky-panky. In this case someone, probably Marguarita, would eventually have gotten the goods on him. She had the sharpest eye and would have had the fewest scruples about how she got hold of information. Sex, he suspected, could be a powerful weapon.

Thinking about sex made him wonder where Pashetta was and then a horrible idea crept into his mind. She went into all the offices and did anything on the computer that anyone shoved at her. She knew everything that was going on in and around the place. And he'd be surprised if her commitment to the jungle went much beyond lip service. Could she have given Tarique the information he wanted?

A little extra money would go a long way for her, he realised. Pashetta's parents had found out that she had been screwing her English teacher and had thrown her out. So she could use a little cushion to fall back on. Poor kid, he thought, it must be pretty awful to come from a background where a little fooling around was that much of a social no-no, for girls, anyway. He guessed the English teacher had pretty much cabbaged any future marriage prospects for her. Still, she had spunk. There was no doubt about that. Not many girls from strict Muslim families would have had the courage to break out on their own the way she had. And she was smart, too. Look at the way she had learned English and got to be a whiz on the computer. She wasn't someone who would let opportunities slip through her fingers.

But this project wasn't going to go on forever and no one, not even Pashetta, would want to stay here too long even if it did. At some point she might find herself in a pretty precarious situation for an Indonesian woman. Tarique might not have had to fork over very much in the way of money to buy her help.

Shit, how had he let himself get so involved in his work that he hadn't taken the time to find out exactly what Tarique was doing and who might be doing it with him?

Before he could come to terms with these disturbing questions his thoughts were interrupted by the squeaking sound his door inevitably made as it was pushed open. A moment later Pashetta, smelling of the gardenia scented powder she always used after a bath, came quietly across the room, let her sarong slide onto the floor, deftly parted the mosquito netting that encircled the bed and slipped in beside him.

Wolf lay back to let her hands, soft and caressing, perform their magic and drive his daytime demons away, but tonight they didn't have their usual effect. His mind kept turning back to darker subjects so after a while he propped himself up on one elbow, scrutinised her face and opted for conversation.

'What's wrong?' she asked, surprised at this unexpected response to her overtures.

'Listen Pashetta, tell me, did you ...' He felt like a real shit lying in bed with her and asking her point blank if she had been supplying Tarique with useful information for the logging companies. And what was the point, anyway? She was no fool. If his worst suspicion was true, she would certainly deny it and if it wasn't, well, her answer would be the same, wouldn't it?

Maybe the best bet would be to approach the whole thing sideways, he decided, although he knew he wasn't very good at doing that. Still, it was worth a try. 'What did you really think of Tarique?' he asked, attempting to sound casual.

After a moment's thought, she replied cautiously, 'Catherine loves him very much.'

'That's not what I asked. What did you think?'

'He is good looking but not as good looking as you.'

'Crap,' Wolf exclaimed, in exasperation, 'I'm not looking for a lot of phoney compliments. I want your real opinion.'

'What is "phoney"?'

'Not true.'

'You accuse me of telling lies?' she demanded, indignantly. 'I am not telling lies. Why are you so horrid tonight?'

'Okay, okay,' he said, 'forget it.' And in an attempt to make her do so, he lay back down, pulled her over him and began kissing her neck and breasts. But his inclination for lovemaking, usually so swiftly and effectively aroused when Pashetta was in bed with him, seemed to have evaporated.

It was with some difficulty that he reassured her that he still found her attractive, that he wasn't tired of her and that he didn't want their relationship to end, although he secretly harboured a few doubts on this point. And if by any chance she had cooperated with Tarique – but it was too soon to hang that one on her.

It was only after he fabricated the superstition that Americans thought it was bad luck to make love after a funeral that she felt better and curled up and fell sleep beside him.

Oblivion was longer in coming to him. He lay on his back with his hands behind his head listening to the familiar sounds of the jungle night. The croaking of the frogs, the squawking of the gekko lizards and the distant howls of the jackals, all had a soothing effect on him and eventually he was lulled into a state of quasi-consciousness between sleeping and waking.

As his eyelids grew heavier, the silent predators of the night gradually gained prominence. Clouded leopards crept on velvet paws through his dreams, ready to pounce on their intended kill. Cold-eyed reptiles slithered through the undergrowth to inject their venom into unwary victims. Scorpions scurried on many sets of legs to spray a deadly acid on their prey before appeasing their appetites with the still-living morsel. Yet these fearsome images held no horrors for him. They were all a part of the irreplaceable ecosystem he was trying so hard to save from destruction by the fiercest menace of them all – man.

With that thought, he reached an arm protectively over Pashetta and knew nothing more until the morning song of the siamang apes drifted across the forest canopy and drove the visions of the night away.

When Bethany finally woke up she was horrified to see that it was after nine. She had been told that everyone was usually at work by eight so they could accomplish as much as possible before the onslaught of the mid-day heat.

How embarrassing to be late for work on her first day, she thought, hoping that neither Elliot, who seemed a little intimidating, nor that obnoxious Wolf would notice.

'Fuck,' she muttered to no one in particular when, nearly half an hour later, she took another look at her watch. Why had it taken her so long to bathe and dress? She supposed it was because of the challenge of trying to get clean by dipping cold water out of a large vat and pouring it over herself. And why hadn't anyone warned her that there were fish, real, live fish, actually swimming around in it? She hadn't noticed them until she had accidentally poured one over her and felt the scaly, squirmy thing slithering down her back. The experience left her rather shaken and very much in need of coffee. Well, she was so late anyway, she reasoned, another few minutes wouldn't matter.

To her surprise, she found Catherine still at the breakfast table with half a cup of tea in front of her.

'Sleep well?' Catherine asked, looking up with a smile that Bethany thought seemed a bit forced.

'Too well, I'm afraid. It's dreadful to be so late on my first day. But what's going on with that bath, anyway? There were fish in it.'

'I know,' Catherine laughed, 'there always are.'

'Why doesn't someone do something about them?'

'No one wants to. They keep the mosquitoes away.'

'They do?'

'Yes, a vat of standing water like that is a perfect breeding ground for them. Without the fish to eat the eggs, we'd all be bitten within an inch of our lives every time we took off our clothes in there. Don't worry, you'll get used to it,' Catherine assured her. 'Do you want some tea? There's coffee, too.'

'Coffee, please.'

Catherine pushed a tin thermos in her direction and Bethany wondered whether she should return the question about sleeping well. It was so obvious from the drawn look on her companion's face that she hadn't.

'I had a hell of a night,' Catherine said, rescuing Bethany from her indecision. 'A lizard, a huge one by the sound of it, was croaking right outside my window from midnight on. And then it was joined by a whole throng of its friends and relatives, God only knows how many. It sounded like hundreds. Do you know, the ridiculous thing is that some of my friends in Melbourne thought it was going to be lovely and quiet in the jungle. Quiet! Can you imagine? It's incredible how idiotic some people can be.'

Bethany shifted uncomfortably, thinking that she would certainly have been one of the idiotic ones. 'I suppose you can't really understand what the rainforest is like until you've experienced it,' she ventured.

'Probably not,' agreed Catherine. Then, in a voice tinged with both regret and bitterness, she mused, 'I think the rainforest does things to you, changes you, warps your judgement and distorts your vision.'

This observation left Bethany without a reply so she turned her attention to the possibilities for a quick breakfast. A few slices of papaya had been left on a platter beside a pyramid of green tangerines and a bunch of miniature bananas. There was also a plate of sliced bread, an open tin of butter, and a dish of yellowish jam.

'The bread's not bad,' Catherine said, passing the plate to her. 'Kolop bakes it every day. He makes the jam, too, pineapple, but I warn you, it's gruesome. He'll fry you an egg though, if you want one.'

Bethany accepted the bread but declined the egg and Catherine retreated into her own thoughts. But, after a few minutes, she broke the silence, saying tentatively, 'You must know all about how the Dayaks do things, how they live and all that.'

Bethany demurred. 'I should know and I've been doing my best to learn as much as I can as fast as I can but there hasn't been much time. This job only came my way less than a month ago. Before that, I was finishing up my thesis and working part time as a research assistant for a visiting American professor who was doing a series of articles on the Dayaks. He was spending a couple of terms at SOAS –'

Catherine looked blank.

'The School of Asian and African Studies in London,' Bethany explained. 'I was getting my degree there and Henry Brown, the American, was the anthropologist who was supposed to be coming here. When he had to turn the job down he sent along my name as a possible replacement.'

Catherine nodded. 'Yes, I gather he went to Papua New Guinea or somewhere after that and picked up some dreadful parasites he can't get rid of. That's why he had to leave us in the lurch the way he did.'

'I knew you lot had to be rather desperate,' Bethany said, with a slightly nervous laugh, 'or an opportunity like this would never have come my way. It's my first real job.'

'Well, Henry recommended you very highly, described you as terribly bright,' Catherine said.

'Oh, that's not true,' cried Bethany, embarrassed, and quickly changed the subject. 'How long have the rest of you been here?'

'I've been here a bit over a year. For some of the others like Elliot and Wolf, it's been more like two.'

'Shouldn't there have been an anthropologist here long before this?' Bethany asked.

'Absolutely.'

'Then why wasn't there?'

'I don't know,' she said, with a shrug, 'money issues, I expect. Anyway, everyone agrees that we really need one, especially me.'

'Why especially you?'

'No reason,' Catherine replied, silently ticking herself off for having said too much.

'You must have some reason,' Bethany persisted, hoping to hear how necessary anthropologists were to any project.

She was disappointed.

Catherine, after giving her an appraising look, decided to do a little testing of the waters. 'If I asked you a question, would you promise, I mean, seriously promise, not to tell anyone?'

'Yes, if you want me to.'

'You're sure?'

'Of course.'

'Well, then,' Catherine paused for a moment and then continued, 'do you know anything about how Dayaks do abortions?'

Bethany, suppressing her astonishment, ran her mind back over the books and articles she had read about life amongst the peoples of Kalimantan. Most of them had been written by men.

'I'm afraid I don't,' she admitted, 'but if you like, I'll try to find out. I'm interested in traditional medicines anyway and especially in things that affect the lives of women.'

'You should get on well with Marguarita, then. She has a whole pharmacopoeia of local cures and potions in the botany lab.'

'Why don't you ask her then? She probably knows more about things like that than I do,' Bethany suggested.

'I did ask her and she knows a few plants that might be used but the trouble is, they're all poisons and —'

'Poisons?'

'Yes, the idea is you take just enough to kill the foetus but not enough to kill yourself. The catch is how much is "just enough"? Frankly, the idea scares the hell out of me.'

Bethany was stunned. 'You're not thinking of trying any of them yourself, are you?' she cried.

Catherine grimaced. 'I don't much like the idea either. That's why I'm hoping the Dayaks know some other way of doing it. Or at least, if they do use a poison, that they really know what they're doing.'

'Then you're ...'

Catherine nodded. 'A little parting gift from Tarique.'

'But you can go to Singapore, can't you, or Jakarta, or even back to Australia? Why are you even thinking of having something like that done here?'

'Short of cash.'

'Surely someone here can lend you the money. I wish I could but this is the first job I've had that's paid anything more than a pittance. I've been scraping along on university grants for the past few years but couldn't you ask —'

'I'd rather not.'

'For something this important, it's scarcely a question of what you'd rather do. It's what you have to do. I mean, women die in unsafe abortions, for God's sake.'

'I'm tough. I'll be alright.'

'You don't look tough, just the opposite, actually.'

'Appearances are deceiving,' Catherine said with a laugh. 'Anyway, you don't understand how they all felt about Tarique.'

'What difference does that make?'

'If they find out about the mess he's left me in, they'll all be saying, or at least thinking, that they could have told me so. And I couldn't bear that.'

'Well, fuck them. It's not worth risking your life just because of what other people might think, is it?'

Catherine didn't answer.

'Look, I know I have no right to interfere,' Bethany persisted, 'but I just have to tell you what I think.'

'Don't bother. I already know what you're going to say.'

'Of course you do, and that's because there's only one sensible thing to do and that is to bite the bullet and ask someone to lend you the money. Then you could go someplace where abortions are safe. Of course, you won't like doing it. Who would? But it is the lesser of two evils, isn't it?'

Catherine shook her head. 'I can't do it,' she said, firmly.

'But, why?' Bethany cried, scarcely able to believe her ears.

'Because I'd have to explain why I don't have the money myself.'

'Isn't that your own business?'

'Nothing at Kanyalang is your own business,' Catherine declared, in a voice that seethed with resentment. 'Everyone here knows everything about everybody.'

'That's dreadful.'

'I know but that's the way it is,' Catherine agreed, but her tone was calmer as she went on, 'You see, we all make decent salaries and have almost nothing to spend them on except the occasional holiday. So I couldn't possibly let on that I need money without everyone asking why.'

'That's not a question you have to answer, is it?'

'If I didn't, it would just hang in the air like some kind of rotten horrible thing. And everybody would be speculating and wondering about it.' She paused and then added, 'Just the way you are now.'

''I'm not.'

'Yes you are. I can see it in your face.'

'Well, I'm human, aren't I? I mean, after what you just said about salaries and all that, I can't help being slightly curious, can I?'

'I suppose not.'

'But I'm not asking,' Bethany added, hastily.

'At this point, you might as well,' sighed Catherine. 'The problem is that Tarique fucked me over in more ways than one.'

'What does that mean?'

'Well, he did it in the obvious way, of course. Everybody knows about that. What they don't know is that I was fool enough to hand over virtually every cent I had to him. And I just can't bear to think of everyone finding out. They'd be delving into my finances and asking a million questions and it would be too humiliating. It doesn't bear thinking about.'

'Aren't you worrying too much about what other people think? It's not really that important, you know.'

'In a place like this, it is. You can't get away from it. It presses in on you every minute of the day. So you see, I'd a thousand times rather take my chances on a Dayak abortion than have the others realise what an imbecile I've been.' She gave Bethany a searching look and added, 'Can you understand?'

'I'm trying but, to be honest, it isn't easy,' replied Bethany, thinking that Catherine must surely have a better reason than that.

The appearance of Kolop to clear away the breakfast things alerted Catherine to the time.

'Good God,' she exclaimed, 'I'm being awful, inflicting my sordid problems on you, when you want to be starting your new job. You must think I'm the most selfish person in the world, apart from being the weakest and the most generally fuckwitted.'

'I don't think your problems are sordid,' Bethany replied, although she did think that Catherine seemed awfully ditsy for a scientist, she was the project zoologist, wasn't she? It was curious, she thought, but then nothing at Kanyalang was turning out the way she had expected.

CHAPTER FIVE

The first thing Bethany and Catherine heard when they got to the office was the sound of desk drawers being roughly opened and closed in a room near the veranda steps.

'Who's going through Tarique's things?' Catherine asked, although she didn't expect Bethany to know the answer. 'I swear if it's Wolf, I'll —'

Catherine had flown off to investigate before Bethany could catch the end of the sentence. So, drawn by curiosity, Bethany followed her to the open doorway of Tarique's room and peered in.

'Just what do you think you're doing?' Catherine was demanding, indignantly.

'Isn't it obvious?' Wolf replied, indicating a disordered pile of papers and computer disks that had apparently been taken out of the drawers.

'You've no right to go snooping around in here,' she cried. 'Elliot's the only one who has any business going through Tarique's files.'

'The problem is that he doesn't appear to be doing it,' Wolf replied.

'Then let it wait,' she said.

'I don't think that's a very good idea,' he returned, 'nor do I think this room is the best place for you right now.' And taking her by the arm he ushered her firmly out the door.

Elliot, roused from his maps by the fracas, came out to see what was going on.

'What are you doing?' he asked when he peered in and saw Wolf sitting at the dead man's desk.

'Taking a look at all this,' Wolf said, indicating the jumble of papers and disks. 'We'll never find out what he was up to if we just bury this stuff along with him.'

'What does it matter now?' Elliot asked. 'If he was up to anything he shouldn't have been, well,' he shrugged, 'it's over now, isn't it? Best put it all behind us.'

'I don't know what you think you can find out, anyway,' said Marguarita who had heard the argument and paused to put a word in. 'Tarique wasn't stupid. He would scarcely have left a trail of incriminating evidence around, would he? It's just wishful thinking on your part to believe you can find anything.'

'You're probably right,' Wolf acknowledged, 'but anybody can get a little careless. There just might be something interesting on his computer or in his desk if anyone bothered to sniff it out.'

This last remark was directed at Elliot, who caught the intent behind it and didn't like it. He was getting thoroughly tired of having Wolf nipping at his heels, trying to encroach on his role as team leader.

'It's my responsibility to go through Tarique's papers, not anyone else's,' Elliot declared, looking pointedly at Wolf.

'Okay, you're the boss,' Wolf replied, trying, with minimal success, to hide his irritation at the rebuke. He scooped up the discarded papers, shoved them into the nearest drawer and sauntered out of the room with what he hoped was an air of cool indifference.

Back in his own office, Wolf decided to keep the door open for a while. He enjoyed the early morning coolness, such as it was, and didn't care to entomb himself in air conditioning until the temperature approached the boiling point.

He sat down at his desk and flicked on his computer but he had trouble concentrating on his work. His mind kept drifting back to Catherine. She looked so pale, like she hadn't slept. Poor kid, she must be really torn up about Tarique's death. Otherwise why would she have made such a fuss about his going through the guy's desk? Somebody had to do it and it could be months before Elliot would get around to it.

It was rather odd, he thought, for her to be so pale still, not getting tanned like everybody else. Of course, no one got very brown when they were actually in the jungle. The sun didn't penetrate that thick arboreal cover, at least not much. But everyone else at Kanyalang had tanned faces, arms, and hands just from walking around the compound or taking a bath, Dayak style, in the river.

But enough of that, Wolf told himself. It was time he got some work done. And with that in mind he got up and shut the door, walling out the distracting voices that were beginning to waft in from the veranda.

'I know a girl who'd be interested in a job as your assistant,' Mike was telling Bethany.

'Assistant?' she repeated, with surprise. 'I hadn't thought of having one.'

'You should, you know. There's a line item for it in the budget. Elliot mentioned it to me the other day because he thought I might be able to help you find one.'

'Well, I'm not quite —' she began, doubtfully.

'You'll need someone who can get you into a longhouse, introduce you to the headman, that sort of thing. You can't just walk in cold.'

'To tell you the truth, that's something I've been a bit worried about. It seems like such an intrusion.'

'The people who live there would probably agree and not give you a very friendly reception. You might even find that nobody would talk to you and that wouldn't be very good for an anthropologist, would it? I mean, isn't talking the main thing you people do?'

Bethany laughed. 'It's listening that's important, actually,' she said, 'but a village where nobody would speak to me would be a disaster.'

'How about the language? Can you manage?'

'I don't know any Dayak yet but I studied a bit of Indonesian at university and since that's the national language I'm hoping it will get me started.'

'It should be okay for talking to the men and the older kids, the ones who've been to school. And for the younger women, too, but not for the grannies. You'll need an interpreter who speaks Maloh Dayak, if you want to talk to them.'

'They're the ones I most want to talk to.'

'Why?' he asked, thinking this was a rather odd preference.

'Because they're the ones who'll know the most about their traditions and culture,' she explained. 'What's this girl like, anyway, the one you have in mind?'

'She lives at Nanga Palin, that's the closest longhouse. All the guys who work with me in the conservation corps are from there,' he continued, 'and one of them has got a sister named Sarika. She's been through SMP, that's a sort of pre-high school, nine years of schooling, I think. You won't find many girls around here with more than that. Anyway, I know she'd be interested, if you are.'

'When can I meet her?'

'Soon. I'll be seeing her brother later today and I'll set it up.'

Mike was as good as his word. A meeting was arranged and the following morning he showed Bethany the way up the notched log that served as a staircase to the longhouse at Nanga Palin.

Built to house nearly eighty families, one to each room, it amounted to an entire village and was considerably longer than its counterpart at Kanyalang. It was also noticably less sturdy-looking and to Bethany's distress, the veranda floor, made only of parallel stalks of bamboo laid out next to each other, had a disconcerting way of rolling under her feet when she walked across it. Another difference was that there was virtually no furniture at Nanga Palin.

Yet, as at Kanyalang, the front veranda was the centre of longhouse life, serving not only as communal sitting room and dining room but as village hall, high street, park, café, and playground, as well. The cooking was done on the narrower back veranda and the individual rooms, dark and largely empty in the daytime, were used primarily for sleeping and storage, with items of special value kept on a bamboo platform suspended high in the eaves.

Sarika proved to be a God-send. She was a tiny girl who claimed to be eighteen, although Bethany suspected she was younger. Nevertheless, she demonstrated a quick intelligence and an easy humour, and she showed no impatience with Bethany's halting Indonesian, translating it when necessary into Dayak. In addition, she was generous with her own kinship ties, introducing Bethany in the longhouse as 'my older sister' and thus giving her a place in the social order. And as Sarika was a granddaughter of the headman, this was an excellent place indeed.

The role was, of course, an honorary one and no one was in danger of forgetting that Bethany was an outsider. But the consensus of opinion was that she wasn't a bad outsider. She was respectful to the old people. She took a great interest in the ways of the longhouse. And to everyone's surprise, she was even making an effort to learn their language. They expected strangers to speak Indonesian but only one of them had ever tried to learn to talk to them in their own language. That was Mike, the initially fearsome man who was in charge of the conservation corps.

Mike had first come to Nanga Palin to check on the progress of one of his rangers, a boy named Raran, who had fallen into an animal trap and broken his leg. Mike had astounded them all by calling in a helicopter and taking Raran all the way to Putussibau where a doctor there had made pictures of the inside of his leg and bound it up in a hard white plaster. After that, Mike had come every few days to check on how Raran was getting on. His visits were usually in the evening, and he generally brought beer and cigarettes with him and sometimes even packets of coffee and sugar for Piang Thumbi, the headman's wife, as well.

In a community where privacy was unheard of and where, if it had been thought of at all, it would have been equated with loneliness and regarded as a bad thing, the arrival of a guest was an event to be shared and enjoyed by the entire longhouse. Thus whenever Mike came, everyone would crowd onto the veranda, the men sitting in a semicircle in front, the women and children clustering behind them, to look and listen and be entertained.

At first it had been a mixture of gratitude for his help and fascination with his appearance that had drawn them to him. He seemed so big and so hairy, had such clumsy manners, and in the beginning knew so few intelligible words that it was rather like observing an animal. But animals couldn't speak, not even badly. At least, no one at Nanga Palin had ever heard one speak although there were rumours that orang-utans could talk when they wanted to. They just avoided letting human beings know about it for fear of being made to work. The schoolteacher said this wasn't true but not everyone was convinced.

Gradually Mike began to pick up more and more Dayak words from the men he worked with, and, as few outsiders ever learned their language, they found his efforts to speak it uproariously funny. Even so they usually managed to get the gist of what he was trying to say and took gleeful delight in adding bawdy words to his vocabulary whenever they had an opportunity.

By the time Bethany put in her first appearance at Nanga Palin, Raran's leg had healed and Mike didn't come so often. But he hadn't given up his visits entirely and Bethany couldn't help being a little envious of the affection with which everyone seemed to regard him. It surprised her that the man she would have pegged as the least culturally sensitive person at Kanyalang was actually the one expat who made a real effort to get to know the local people. She didn't really count herself because it was her job.

Bethany soon found herself spending every morning at Nanga Palin making a constant effort to absorb everything she saw and heard. And it was more of an effort than she had expected.

She had to figure out who everyone was and what his or her relationship was to everybody else. At the same time she had to work on adding to her small but growing vocabulary in Dayak. By noon she was always mentally exhausted and wildly hungry so whenever possible she retreated to Kanyalang for lunch and didn't go back to Nanga Palin in the afternoon. More often than not, she spent the rest of her day in her office, writing up her notes, memorising Dayak vocabulary lists, and planning her strategy for the next morning.

Catherine asked her almost every day, 'Have you found out anything yet?'

'I will as soon as I can,' Bethany told her repeatedly, 'but abortions just aren't the sort of thing I can spring on people right away.'

'But you will soon, won't you?' Catherine constantly urged.

'Yes, I promise,' Bethany always replied, guiltily aware of the pressing nature of Catherine's plight, yet wary of broaching a subject that might prove to be sensitive.

She compromised by embarking on a tactful, she hoped, circle around the edges of the abortion question. There was nothing secret or forbidden about having babies and she soon discovered who it was that acted as midwife for the longhouse and, by extension, as consultant on women's problems. This was a gnarled old crone called Piang Kati.

Although Bethany had learned that 'piang' simply meant grandmother and was a term of respect for any older woman, she couldn't help thinking that it was particularly ill-suited to the midwife. There was nothing warm or motherly about her piercing eyes, skeletal features, or cackling laugh, all of which made Bethany see her as more of a wicked witch than a comfortable granny. To make matters worse, her mouth was besmirched with blood-red stains, the result of years of chewing betel nut, that made her look like she had just been devouring the insides of a wild animal.

It didn't take Bethany long to discover that everyone regarded Kati with great awe and deference but it was some time before she learned the full range of the old woman's powers.

Kati was highly skilled in the interpretation of auguries and could look at the flight patterns of birds or the entrails of sacrificial animals or other configurations of natural phenomena and understand the messages that were being sent from the shadowy denizens of the spirit world. She was, therefore, the female belian, the shaman, of the longhouse and she possessed mystical powers that greatly enhanced the potency and effectiveness of her cures. Her status at Nanga Palin was surpassed only by that of the headman.

Unlike most of the people in the longhouse, Kati evinced little interest in the odd-looking foreigner in their midst, possibly regarding her as too big — Bethany towered above the Dayak women — and too ugly ever to be in need of obstetrical services.

Bethany, for her part, found it extremely difficult to approach Kati with the sort of questions that would be of interest to Catherine. And Sarika proved worse than useless in this regard. As ill-luck would have it, she was a far more serious Catholic than was typical at Nanga Palin, where the imported religion formed little more than a veneer over the traditional animistic beliefs known as Kaharingan. The one subject on which Sarika was determinedly unhelpful was abortions.

57

'No one ever has them,' she declared, firmly.

Initially Bethany was tempted to believe her. After all, one of the first things she had noticed about the people at Nanga Palin was how much they loved and valued children. They passed babies around from one woman to another so casually that she often had difficulty figuring out who the actual mother was. There had even been a couple of times when, after seeing a baby suckling at a woman's breast, she learned a little later that the enterprising infant had merely been enjoying a snack and a cuddle from some other baby's mother. Toddlers were played with and watched over by affectionate fathers, uncles, and grandparents, as well as aunties, siblings, and cousins. It was easy to see that this was not a place where terminations would be much in demand. Perhaps Catherine's hopes of finding a solution to her problem here would have to be dashed and that, Bethany told herself, might not be a bad thing.

She was on the brink of a decision to tell Catherine that it was no-go when she fell victim to one of her worst ever attacks of period pains.

The temperature on the front veranda at Nanga Palin that afternoon soared to levels generally associated with the fires of hell. In a desperate search for a touch of shade, Bethany wandered onto the back veranda where the cooking was done, and her timing could hardly have been worse. Sarika's cousin, Lika, was lowering a dead snake into a cooking pot and Bethany was treated to an unobstructed view of the repulsive thing, buoyed by the motion of the bubbling water, swirling around as if it were alive. Convinced she was going to be sick, she grabbed the veranda rail and leaned over it.

'What's the matter?' Sarika cried, in alarm.

'Nothing,' Bethany gasped, not wanting to admit that the contents of the cooking pot were causing the problem, 'just monthly cramps but they're awfully bad today.'

'I'll go find Kati,' Sarika said.

'No, don't,' protested Bethany, whose one interest at that moment was in distancing herself from the snake stew. 'I'm okay.'

Sarika wasn't convinced so she went in search of the medicine woman anyway while Bethany fled to the more congenial atmosphere, the heat notwithstanding, of the front veranda.

Sarika, accompanied not only by the fearsome midwife but by a coven of grannies intent on observing the proceedings, found her there a few minutes later.

Bethany was ordered to sit down on a mat on the veranda floor while Kati touched her skin, checked the clarity of her eyes, inspected her tongue and felt her pulse, breasts, and abdomen. Then, nodding to herself as though satisfied, she disappeared into the sleeping room she shared with her youngest daughter, son-in-law, and four grandchildren.

'Is she going away, just like that?' Bethany asked, greatly relieved.

'She's going to make a special tea to help the pain,' Sarika explained.

Bethany, not entirely happy with this plan, became positively alarmed when the old woman reappeared and presented her with a murky-brown drink.

'What is it?' Bethany asked, suspiciously.

'Medicine,' Kati replied in a curt tone, making it clear she would welcome no more questions.

Bethany persisted none-the-less. 'What kind of medicine?'

A murmur of consternation rippled through the onlookers and they cast surreptitious glances at Kati to see how she would react to this impertinence.

At first she didn't appear to take it well. Her face darkened and became even more menacing than usual but then to everyone's surprise, she actually answered the question.

'Gerangau merah,' she said.

Bethany, who had no idea what that was, realised with a sigh that she might as well not have asked.

'Drink,' Kati ordered.

'It will be good for you,' Sarika added, encouragingly.

'I don't think I need it, after all,' Bethany declared, waving it aside. 'I'm feeling better already, really I am.'

Sarika received this news with ill-concealed horror. 'But Kati made it for you,' she cried. 'It would be very rude not drink it. You don't want to be rude to Kati, do you?'

Bethany assured her that she didn't.

'Then drink it, all of it. Do it now,' the usually docile Sarika insisted.

Reminding herself that it was vital to keep on the right side of this important woman, Bethany steeled herself to give the evil looking liquid a try. She raised the glass to her lips, sniffed the surprisingly sweet aroma that wafted up from it and ventured a cautious sip. The actual taste, by contrast, proved to be as bitter and horrid as she had initially suspected.

I don't care what Sarika says, I simply can't drink this, she thought, and was about to put it down and declare her rebellion when something in the faces of the old biddies watching her told her this was a critical moment. Accepting Kati's medicine would be viewed as an endorsement of their traditional ways. Refusing it would be an insult to their ways of doing things and would not be readily forgiven. The effect on her work could prove disastrous. She couldn't risk it.

Well, if this kills me, at least I'll be dying for science, she told herself, gloomily, as she drank it down.

Her relief at finding herself still alive when she had finished was nothing compared to her amazement a couple of hours later when she realised that the pain had completely disappeared.

'I'd never tasted anything so totally foul in all my life,' she told Catherine and Marguarita that evening, 'but the effect was absolutely amazing.'

'Was it mixed with boiled water, at least?' Catherine wanted to know.

'It would have had to be, wouldn't it?' Marguarita pointed out. 'The medicine woman, or whatever she is, couldn't have made an infusion otherwise. What was in it, anyway?'

'I've absolutely no idea,' Bethany admitted.

Marguarita gave her a scathing look. 'Didn't you ask?'

'Of course I did and she told me some name or other but I didn't have a clue what it was.'

Marguarita thought for a moment and then suggested, 'It couldn't have been Boesenbergia, could it?'

'It didn't sound much like that,' Bethany replied.

'But, of course, she would have told you the Dayak name for it, wouldn't she?' said Marguarita, thinking out loud.

Bethany nodded. 'But what makes you think it might have been – what you just said?'

'The sweet smell, along with the bitter taste, and of course the effect. Boesenbergia is an analgesic and a mild stimulant and I think it may have antispasmodic properties as well.'

'Is it dangerous?' asked Catherine.

'Is what dangerous?' demanded Wolf, sauntering over to join them.

They told him and he furrowed his brows in disapproval.

'Do you think it was smart to mess around with that stuff?' he asked, his tone of voice making his own view very clear.

'I drink their ordinary tea every day,' Bethany said, immediately on the defensive, 'so why shouldn't I drink a medicinal tea?'

'Because you know what's in an ordinary tea but you have no idea what was in that concoction.'

'Well, whatever it was, it was brilliant. It made me feel so much better, I can't even begin to tell you. I'm really glad I drank it.'

'Well, don't do anything that dumb again,' he ordered, as if he had a right to tell her what to do. 'Fucking around with jungle potions can get you into big trouble. If an aspirin won't do the job, go and see a real doctor.'

'But the drug companies must think there's something to be said for local medicines,' Catherine interjected, 'or they wouldn't spend so much time and money testing them, would they?'

'The drug companies know what they're doing. Bethany doesn't,' Wolf replied.

Bethany glared at him but realised there was little she could say. She was well aware that jungle cures were a dodgy business at best and she had been a tad worried at the time. Still, she thought it was horrid of Wolf to make her feel such an idiot about it. And actually, she hadn't been so stupid after all. It had worked, hadn't it? She felt like a new woman. Taking it had been absolutely the right thing to do.

She was so firmly convinced of this that she decided she would go ahead and ask Kati about Catherine the next morning.

Finding the old healer alone wasn't an easy proposition in the communal life of Nanga Palin, but eventually Bethany caught her coming out the door of her sleeping room and hurried over to her.

A disapproving Sarika followed her reluctantly.

Skimming over the polite preliminaries as quickly as Dayak etiquette allowed, Bethany soon came to the point.

'My friend is pregnant,' she explained, modulating her voice in the hope that she wouldn't be overheard, 'but she doesn't want to have the baby. Can you help her?'

No interpreter was needed to convey the look of disdainful refusal in Kati's sharp eyes.

Fuck, Bethany thought, had she picked a bad time, after all, or was it still just too soon? Perhaps she should have waited. But Catherine couldn't wait much longer.

Yet Bethany's timing proved to be far better than she could possibly have predicted because just at that moment a loud whooshing sound, made by the flapping of giant wings, drew everyone's attention as a flock of rhinoceros hornbills flew overhead.

The midwife's gaze was riveted on the majestic birds as they made their way across the sky, and Bethany watched her expression change from interest to astonishment to awe as they vanished into the distant clouds.

When Kati finally turned back to Bethany her attitude toward Catherine's problem appeared to have undergone a significant change.

'Your friend, how many months?' she demanded, in her cackling voice.

'A little over three, I think,' Bethany ventured, silently wondering if it could be four by this time.

'Bring her and I will see,' Kati replied.

Bethany, instead of feeling that she had won a victory, was left with a vague sense of misgiving. Something had happened and she didn't understand what it was.

CHAPTER SIX

The oldest woman in the longhouse, Laban, stared at Kati in disbelief when she heard what the mid-wife had in mind. Was she really thinking of giving an outsider the benefit of her medical skills, she wondered? It had never been done before, at least, not as far as she knew. And she could remember back to the time when the heads her father and grandfather had taken in battle had still been hanging in the rafters above their sleeping room.

Surely even someone who was as respected as Kati couldn't make a decision like that on her own. After all, it might go wrong and then – well, who knew what difficulties it might bring on the entire longhouse?

The headman's permission would be needed, she reflected, so Baki Lunsa would have to be consulted. And Baki Sangalang, too. After all he was the male belian and even though this particular situation didn't have much to do with his usual concerns – war or hunting or growing rice – he would still have to agree. And of course nothing so important could be done without the approval of the elders and they were always very cautious. She knew they would want to discuss all the aspects of the situation before they took any decision.

With commendable self-control, the betel-chewing grannies refrained from giving voice to these thoughts as long as Kati was within earshot but as soon as the medicine woman was drawn away by a misdeed of her naughtiest grandson, they besieged each other with questions. What would Lunsa, say? And how about Sangalang? How would the other elders, the men, react? Surely they would never sanction such a plan.

'Kati gave medicine to Mbak Bethany,' one of old ladies pointed out, coming as close as she could to pronouncing Bethany's name and preceding it with the honorary title, 'Older Sister'.

'That wasn't very strong medicine,' her friend replied.

'Not dangerous,' someone else murmured.

Everyone nodded sagaciously.

Abortions, they all knew, were a different matter – they could go very wrong. Sometimes women even died. And Kati's medicine, intertwined as it was with the intercession of the spirits, would be considered black magic by the Indonesian government if they found out about it, and there were laws against such practices. If it became known that a death had resulted, there could be trouble. Of course, if one of their own died, from whatever cause, the authorities were unlikely to know about it – and even less likely to care – but the death of a foreigner in their longhouse would be noticed, and who knew what the result might be? Surely Baki Lunsa would never countenance such a risk.

By the time the headman assembled the elders on the veranda that evening they all knew what the subject of the discussion would be. And they all knew a great deal more about Kati than Bethany did.

They knew that she derived her cures not only from the plant and animal products she obtained in the surrounding jungle, but, more importantly, from her ability to communicate with the world of the ancestors. She had the power to placate the evil spirits that caused disease and misfortune, and when necessary, could even journey into their shadowy world herself to bring back a human soul that had been abducted. She knew how to draw the evil forces out of the body of a sick person and send them away.

All of these talents combined to make Kati the best healer in living memory but her value to the longhouse didn't end there. She was unsurpassed as an interpreter of dreams and a reader of auguries. And it had been her command of the last of these vitally important skills that had made her consider the extraordinary possibility of allowing an outsider to receive the benefit of her medical knowledge.

Kati explained to the gathering of elders that she had been on the point of refusing Bethany's request when a flock of rhinoceros hornbills had flown overhead. Here she paused to give maximum effect to her next words, 'flying from north-west to south-east.'

A collective gasp went up from her audience. Everyone knew that at this time of year the giant birds flew from south-east to north-west.

It was this astonishing sight, she told them, that had made her reconsider the answer she had been about to give Bethany.

Kati was as skilled in the arts of persuasion and manipulation as she was in the techniques of forecasting and healing so she didn't fail to emphasise the point that this was too important a decision to make without obtaining the agreement of the oldest and wisest people in the longhouse. But the rhinoceros hornbill was the messenger from the gods, she reminded them – although they knew this as well as they knew their own names – so a change in the behaviour of this sacred creature could only mean that a change was required in the behaviour of the people at Nanga Palin. And failing to respond to the expressed will of the gods could bring disaster upon them.

Everyone nodded. Kati was far too old and too wise for her words to be taken lightly.

One of the few people who had enough status to challenge her, was Lunsa. 'If the girl dies, that might bring trouble, too,' he said, speaking so quietly that everybody was forced to listen with extra attentiveness to what he said.

No one could deny this possibility but the society at Nanga Palin was not one that welcomed debate. Unanimous decisions were the only ones with which people felt comfortable, so a prize cock was slit open and its entrails were examined for further advice from the spirit world. The results left no doubt in the minds of either of the two belians about what action should be taken.

It was Sangalang who explained the full implication of the auguries to the others.

'We are living in difficult times,' he told the assembled group, 'yet we make only paltry offerings to the ancestors and the gods. Many years have passed since we have brought them human heads or given them human slaves. The Dutch rajas didn't understand these things and now the new Javanese rulers are no better.'

There were murmurs of agreement.

'The young men these days are not strong of heart like their grandfathers were. This is what happens when they go to school. But the old ways are dying so they need school now. And the ancestors are unhappy because they are placated with nothing more than animal sacrifices.'

Disapproval of the worthless young was clearly registered on many of the wrinkled faces.

'And what has been the result?' Baki Sangalang demanded.

A spellbound silence prevailed as they waited for his answer, even though each person could have given it himself.

'The Madurese devils have come and stolen our land. The logging companies have cut down our forests. And the Javanese in the government have tried to stop us from making offerings to quell evil spirits, and from paying homage to our ancestors and our gods.'

As always when subjects like these came up, expressions of outrage flew from person to person.

'If we continue to neglect our gods and our ancestors,' Sangalang continued, 'they will neglect us in return. They treated us well in the days when we offered them human heads and human slaves. It is clear that the animal sacrifices we offer them now are not enough. They want human blood.'

This was something their grandfathers had known, and everyone suddenly felt ashamed to have forgotten it. They listened intently as their male spiritual leader went on, 'But we no longer have any slaves to sacrifice and our sons are made weak by school and by the lust for money. They care more for bringing home radios and foreign music than for bringing back heads and this makes the gods angry. If we do not soothe them with the offerings they want – human blood – they will come down and take it from us.'

A shiver of unease reverberated through the crowd as everyone looked to their two belians for ways in which such a manifestation of celestial anger could be avoided.

Kati's response was truly shocking. 'This is not the first time the gods have been angry with Laban,' she said.

The elders could scarcely believe they had heard her correctly. Laban was very much respected.

'The gods sent her only one child, a daughter who died giving birth to Nyuta,' the medicine woman continued. 'But now Nyuta herself is not so young anymore and, in spite of many pregnancies, she has not yet given birth to a healthy child.'

Of course everybody knew this, but they all listened patiently as they realised the medicine woman must have her reasons for reminding them of it.

'Now once again Nyuta's time has almost come,' Kati continued, 'and if anything goes wrong it will mean that Laban's blood line, one so ancient she can trace her ancestors back for ten generations, may disappear forever.'

Everyone nodded. They all remembered that Nyuta's first two pregnancies had bled away sometime during the early months. Then she had given birth to a perfectly formed baby boy, one that had stayed inside her for the full nine months but had been blue when it had come into the world. The cord had been wrapped tightly around its neck and it had never drawn breath. The result of her next pregnancy had been even worse, a monster, born with four legs like an animal, two normal arms like a human and two additional hands sticking directly out of its chest. No one except Kati and the two other women who had been helping with the delivery had seen it, and one of them had had to rush out of the room and throw up over the veranda rail. Only Kati knew what the creature's eventual fate had been.

Nyuta had seemed to give up on having a child of her own after that but her bad experiences hadn't diminished her eagerness to hold and care for the other infants in the longhouse, to romp and play with the toddlers, and to tell the older ones wonderful stories in the evenings.

Then one month her bleeding didn't come. She was getting on a bit by then so no one except Kati thought to keep an eye on the size of her breasts or the roundness of her stomach. And when it became apparent to all but the youngest members of the longhouse that a baby was on its way, the usual delight in such news was noticeably absent. What would go wrong this time, they all wondered?

So far, nothing had and Nyuta seemed healthy and happy. The baby's kick was strong, and now, as the time for its birth approached, Kati's experienced hands could detect nothing that should cause alarm.

Yet she was anxious nonetheless – at least she was until the request from Bethany, coming almost simultaneously with the unexpected direction of the hornbills' flight, had shown her a way to ensure the continuation of Laban's ancient line.

'Sangalang is right,' she said, 'we have angered the gods with all our new ways. The hornbills were sent to tell us that offerings of animal blood are not enough. Our ancestors gave them human blood – the blood of our strongest and fiercest enemies. That is what they want. It has been a very long time since our gifts have been worthy of them but now we have the opportunity to give them something that will make them look on us with favour again. We can offer them the blood of this unborn white child. It will be foreign blood, powerful blood, the blood of people who tried to rule us during Dutch times, and who may try to take our land again. That is the blood that will strengthen the spirits of our ancestors and persuade them to bring us wealth and happiness again.'

Her argument was convincing. And, now that they understood what the gods wanted and what must be done, agreement was unanimous. Kati would perform the abortion and the blood of the foetus would be offered to the spirits in return for prosperity and good fortune.

The younger people, many of whom would have taken issue with this plan, did not have sufficient status to have been consulted.

Two days later, a terrified but determined Catherine followed Bethany up the notched log to the veranda at Nanga Palin.

She wished Bethany had been able to find out exactly how Kati was going to do it. It would be so much easier to face it if she had a better idea what to expect, but apparently the midwife had been totally uncommunicative. She would also have liked to think she was putting herself in the hands of a motherly sort of person who would be reassuring and supportive, but Bethany's picture of the fierce, old medicine woman had quenched any hope of that.

After a perfunctory greeting and an examination similar to the one performed on Bethany, Kati disappeared into the back of the longhouse, leaving Catherine completely unenlightened about what would follow.

Desperate to know what was going to happen, Catherine got up and tried to follow her, but Bethany caught her arm and stopped her.

'But I want to see what Kati's doing,' Catherine protested.

'She won't like it,' Bethany warned.

'Why not?'

'Sarika says she likes to keep her magic to herself,' Bethany explained.

'Magic?' Catherine exclaimed, not knowing whether to laugh or cry. 'I thought she had real medicine.'

'She does. She just mixes in a little magic for good measure.' And in an effort to be light-hearted, Bethany added, 'Free of charge.'

Catherine was in no mood for levity. 'Can't we tell her to leave out the magic this time?'

'I don't think we can tell her anything but it doesn't matter. The important thing is that it works, isn't it?'

'God, yes,' breathed Catherine, fervently, and tried to resign herself to the ordeal of waiting. But it wasn't long before she grew restive again and urged, 'Let's ask Sarika what the old witch is doing? She must know.'

Sarika was found and duly questioned but declared in a disapproving tone that she had no idea.

'It's still not too late to change your mind, you know,' Bethany said, turning back to Catherine. 'Just because we're here, doesn't mean you have to go through with it.'

But Catherine stubbornly shook her head. 'No, I've come this far. I'll stay,' she declared, firmly.

The minutes ticked by with agonising slowness.

'I do wish the old harpy would hurry,' Catherine fretted, after more time had dragged by.

'Be reasonable,' Bethany said, soothingly. 'She can't just take a tablet out of a medicine cupboard, you know. She's probably stoking up the fire. That takes ages. And she'll have to grind up whatever roots or spices or herbs she's going to use and then wait until the water boils so she can make an infusion. And then the whole thing will have to cool down before you can drink it. At least, that's what happened with the medicine she gave me. She can't do all that in five minutes so you've just got to be patient. '

'Then you don't think she's going to poke me with a rusty coat hanger or a dirty stick or anything?' Catherine asked.

Bethany, who wasn't altogether sure, said, 'My guess is, it will be some kind of potion.'

'Some kind of poison, you mean,' Catherine said, glumly.

Bethany tried to sound reassuring. 'Well, as long as she gives you the right amount, which I'm absolutely certain she will –'

'I don't know how you can be so sure,' returned Catherine, irritated by Bethany's sudden attempt to look on the bright side of things. Although she was desperate for reassurance, comforting lies were no help.

'Kati's smart. She knows what she's doing,' Bethany insisted, with more conviction than she really felt. 'And this way, you won't get any nasty infections or bleed to death like you might with the dirty stick method.'

'The truth is, I'm beginning to feel sick just thinking about it,' Catherine groaned.

Bethany, for lack of a better idea, reached for the flask of cool water she always brought with her from Kanyalang and handed it to Catherine. 'Here, have some of this,' she urged. 'It'll make you feel better.'

Catherine accepted it gratefully and, after swallowing a few mouthfuls, said, 'You know, I think I'm beginning to change my mind after all.'

'Thank God for that,' exclaimed Bethany, who had been feeling increasingly uneasy all morning, and was now having a massive attack of second thoughts. It had all seemed so right in the aftermath of her own experience with Kati's medicine, but now, sitting on the floor of a longhouse in the middle of the rainforest, things looked rather different. And, of course, it probably hadn't taken anything very strong or very dangerous to sort out period pains, but terminating a pregnancy was another matter. Something really powerful, measured out in just the right quantity, would be needed.

Oh, God, she thought, what if Catherine dies? And, leaping up, she said, 'Come on, I'll take you home. Sarika can explain things to Kati later.'

But the Dayak girl widened her eyes in horror when this plan was explained to her. 'No,' she cried, 'you can't go now. Kati is brewing the medicine. Catherine must drink it.'

'But if you explain —' began Bethany.

'I will not explain,' Sarika cried, switching from Indonesian into Dayak in her agitation. 'I will tell Kati I made a mistake in ever working for you. I will tell her I am very, very sorry and ask her to forgive me. I will promise her that I will never have anything to do with you again.'

Bethany was astounded at the ferocity of this response from her usually helpful assistant. 'But, Sarika, you were so against the abortion,' she reminded her, 'I'd have thought you'd be delighted to have it called off.'

'Called off before it started, yes, but not now. Not when Kati is already preparing the medicine. She will be so angry.'

'Alright, then,' Bethany said, slightly amused that the prospect of antagonising the terrifying midwife was so much worse than violating the strictures of the Catholic Church. 'I'll stay here and do the explaining. You take Catherine back to Kanyalang.'

'No, I won't do that either.'

'Shit,' Bethany muttered, under her breath. But out loud, she merely said, 'Alright, I'll take Catherine home first and then I'll come back and explain.'

The expression on Sarika's usually pleasant face was mutinous. 'Then you are no longer my older sister.'

'But Sarika —'

'Things may get very bad for you here if you make Kati angry. You may find that no one will talk to you. They may not even want you here at all anymore.'

Bethany knew Sarika was right — the consequences of going against someone as respected as Kati could be dire. The encouraging start she had made here at Nanga Palin and the promising relationships she was developing could all go up in smoke and she would have to start all over again somewhere else — but where? None of the other longhouses in the area were within the same easy distance of Kanyalang. Working in one of them would mean long treks through the rainforest or boat rides on the rock-strewn river that was only navigable part of the year. On top of that, there was the disturbing question of what kind of reception would await her in a longhouse in which she didn't have the initial contacts through Mike and Sarika. And what if Elliot reported it all back to the RRF in London? What would they think of an anthropologist who fucked up in her first job?

Oh, God, she groaned, inwardly, it was all too obvious what they would think.She might even be sacked. But there was absolutely no way she could try to persuade Catherine to stay here and drink some potentially lethal concoction just for the sake of her own stupid career. And stupid was certainly the operative word when it came to describing the way she had handled things so far. How could she ever have been so idiotic, so utterly insane, as to let herself get involved in all this?

'Well, if no one wants me here anymore,' she told Sarika, using her limited Dayak to keep Catherine from understanding what she was saying, 'I'll just have to find another longhouse, won't I?'

She glanced anxiously at Catherine, who had become very quiet. Had she guessed what they were talking about, Bethany wondered and then decided that she probably hadn't. She appeared to be wrapped up in her own thoughts and not even listening.

Bethany's surmise was correct.

Although Catherine seemed to be gazing in the direction of an old man who was working on a fish trap some fifteen or twenty feet away, the image that filled her mind's eye was very different. In it she was looking down on Tarique's body as she had seen it that last time, so remote in its absolute stillness, so devoid of the passions that had animated it in life, so indifferent to the harm it had taken malicious pleasure in inflicting on her. She was staring at it now, just as she had that day, trying to reconcile that inert form with the memory of the man she had loved and hated.

But had love played any part in their relationship at all, Catherine asked herself, or had it only been desire, intense, agonising, overwhelming desire, that had been mixed with a growing hate?

Now that death had stolen his magnetic sexuality, she could see that all that was left was the hate.

Catherine tried to push his image from her mind but the more she struggled with it the more vivid the likeness seemed to grow.

72

Then a horrible thing began to happen. She saw the black-lashed eyelids flick open and the dead arms reach up toward her. Paralysed with fear, she could only watch as the familiar lips begin to part, curling at the edges in a serpentine smile, and then opening wide in a burst of unrestrained hilarity.

'Keep this child that is going to be a younger edition of me,' she could hear the laughing corpse saying, 'and you will keep me with you forever. You will never be free of me – never. I will haunt you all your life, go with you everywhere you go, be with you every minute until you die.'

'No,' Catherine screamed, so loudly that everyone up and down the entire length of the veranda turned to stare in astonishment and Kati, who was just emerging from the dark interior of the longhouse, spilled some of the drink she was carrying. But after righting the glass in time to save most of it, she brought it over and thrust it toward her patient.

Catherine, still in the grip of her macabre hallucination, and too desperate to think of anything but ridding herself of Tarique's child, seized the glass with both hands and drained it in one go.

CHAPTER SEVEN

The revolting taste of the medicine, acrid, pungent and very, very bitter, helped Catherine drive Tarique's lingering image from her mind and bring her back to reality.

If I have to kill myself to get him out of my head, it's worth it, she thought, as she handed the empty glass to Kati, took a deep breath and looked around her. Everything appeared clear and normal. She would have given a good deal for a Polo mint to take the evil taste out of her mouth but other than that she felt alright. She settled for some more of Bethany's cool water instead.

'How long is it going to be until something happens?' she asked.

Bethany translated the question but Kati's answer was too vague to leave them any the wiser so they had no choice but to resign themselves to waiting.

There was no shortage of activity on the veranda and they tried to let the morning occupations of their hosts distract them. Groups of young women pounded rice while small children, naughty and noisy, frolicked around them. Some of the old ladies plaited mats and baskets from carefully prepared strips of rattan while two others, who had newly acquired the status of granny, devoted their attention to making elaborately beaded baby-carriers for their offspring. One of the old men carved a wooden paddle for his boat, and another whittled a long spear, while others of their sex and generation merely sat about smoking.

Were they remembering the days when they had gone with the other men to clear and burn the fields for planting, Bethany wondered as she watched them? How many of them had gone to school? Now of course all the boys, and even the girls, had at least an elementary education. And when the young men came back from their work in the rice fields and played foreign music on their radios and cassette players, what did these old men think of it all? Now, as they sat and smoked and let the morning sun pour its strength into their wrinkled bodies, did they ponder the changes they had seen during their long lives? And were they doubtful about how many of those changes were good?

Catherine had more practical considerations on her mind. She was not pleased to discover that this longhouse differed from the one at Kanyalang, not only in the absence of any chairs to sit on, but also in the non-existence of a loo. At Nanga Palin the river served the multiple functions of kitchen sink, laundry, bathtub and toilet but fortunately Sarika, kind and thoughtful as ever, provided her with a plastic pail to take care of the bouts of nausea that plagued her with increasing frequency through the long morning. And it was so hot on the veranda that Catherine didn't feel much need to pee. One trip down to the closet-sized wooden enclosure built out over the river was sufficient.

As midday approached some of the women gravitated to the cooking veranda. They returned a while later with tin plates that had something foul-smelling and unrecognisable piled on top of a generous mound of rice.

'You're very lucky. Yesterday the men caught a big lizard,' Sarika said. And spreading her arms out to their full breadth, she added, 'Sooo big. I had some last night. Very delicious.'

The smell alone was making Catherine's stomach turn and the information about what it was didn't help. 'It sounds like it was a monitor lizard,' she said, pushing it away in disgust.

Bethany felt she didn't really have that option. Painfully aware of the demands of being a participant observer in the local culture, she gingerly picked up some of the slightly sticky rice, along with a chunk of the lizard meat, and forced herself to take a bite.

As everyone at Nanga Palin knew everything that went on, Catherine had been given a plate of food out of politeness rather than out of any expectation that she would actually eat it. Bethany, however, did not get off so lightly, and one woman after another came over to encourage her to eat more. Bethany tried valiantly to make inroads on the white-fleshed meat, but eventually had to hand it back half-finished. She suspected this lack of appreciation for a highly valued delicacy would do nothing to increase her standing in the longhouse but there were some things she just couldn't worry about right now.

When the last of the meal had been cleared away, mats were brought out for them to lie on and most of the villagers settled down to sleep away the hottest hours of the day.

Unfortunately, any such peaceful oblivion eluded the visitors. Catherine's woes were increasing with the onset of what felt like severe period pains and Bethany's stomach was reacting badly to the combination of lizard meat and stress.

After a while Catherine asked, 'Are you asleep?'

'No.'

'Neither am I. But I wish we didn't have to wait around like this for the medicine to work,' Catherine complained. 'And of course it must be even worse for you. You must be bored out of your mind.'

'No, I'm used to sitting around like this. I do it every day.'

'I don't know how you stand it. Don't you ever wish you had taken up something other than anthropology?'

'Actually I used to think I wanted to be an archaeologist.'

'God, that would be worse,' Catherine said with a shudder, 'digging up graves and scraping off skeletons all the time. It's positively ghoulish.'

'You dissect animals and insects,' Bethany pointed out. 'I'd hate that.'

'You get used to it. And, besides, it's really interesting.'

'So is archaeology. And the great advantage,' Bethany reflected, 'is that the people you study are all dead so you don't ever have to worry about what they're going to think. And best of all, you know they can never hurt you.'

Catherine gazed at her friend in astonishment. 'That's a shocking way of looking at things,' she exclaimed. 'Something really dreadful must have happened to you to make you think like that.'

Bethany shrugged. 'Bad things happen in everybody's life, don't they? The world's full of bastards, so everyone gets hurt – especially women.'

'It sounds like some man gave you a really hard time.'

'You could say that,' Bethany replied.

'An even harder time than Tarique's giving me right now,' Catherine reflected, 'although it's hard to imagine what could be worse than this.'

'I can think of a few things,' Bethany said.

'Like what?'

'Like rape, for instance.'

'Good God, that never happened to you, did it?'

Bethany nodded. 'Actually —'

'Was it some sort of date rape,' Catherine demanded, 'or were you attacked by a ghastly, horrible stranger?'

'Neither,' replied Bethany, tersely.

Reluctant as she was to be drawn back into events she had tried so hard to forget, remembered images from that fateful Easter holiday flooded into her mind but they all seemed to be cast in a slightly altered hue. It was, she thought, almost as if the heat of the jungle afternoon had steamed away the sharpness of the pain that had been clouding her vision, allowing her to see things in a different light. She began to wonder whether Jeremy's defection, the fact that he had never again been there for her after his hasty trip to Cornwall, had actually had a more far reaching effect on her life than her stepfather's violent assault. After all, she had gone on to have sex again but she had never loved or trusted a man again and she was sure she never would.

Still, that might not be a bad thing, she told herself. As she sifted through her memories, she found herself, for the first time since it had all happened, pouring out the whole story. And she became so caught up in the emotional release of opening her heart to a sympathetic listener that she failed to notice the increasing pallor on Catherine's face.

The old women of Nanga Palin were more observant. When they woke up from their naps and began mixing lime and areca nuts on betel leaves for their afternoon's refreshment, the ghostly-white of Catherine's complexion did not escape their notice and they whispered about it amongst themselves.

'I think those old bats are talking about us,' Catherine said, as the neighbouring voices grew louder. 'Can you understand what they're saying?'

Bethany cocked her head to one side, listened a moment and then laughed. 'The one with the long ear lobes said that you look like some kind of ghost and now the toothless one is saying that we both look like lizards.'

'Lizards?' repeated Catherine, puzzled.

'Yes, because of the colour of our skin.'

'But we're not all green and orange and black,' objected Catherine.

'Not that kind of lizard. They mean the pale translucent ones that climb around on the longhouse walls. They think our skin is like that.'

'Ugh.'

'That's their reaction, too,' Bethany said. Then regarding her friend with concern, she added, 'And come to think of it, you've gone awfully pale.'

'I'm alright,' Catherine murmured, as a voice, somewhat louder than the others, drew Bethany's attention back to the conversation about ghosts and lizards.

She didn't like what she heard. It almost sounded as though, in spite of Kati's respected position, Sarika's view of abortions might have a wider currency than she had realised. Was all this going to rebound to her discredit she wondered, perhaps even get her black-listed by the granny contingent, after all?

'Crap,' she muttered under her breath.

She hadn't intended for Catherine to hear her, but she did.

'What's the matter?' she asked.

'Those women,' she nodded in the direction of the group 'are wondering why you don't want to have your baby.'

Their opinions didn't interest Catherine. 'It's none of their business, is it?'

'Weren't you the one who told me that at Kanyalang everything was everybody else's business?'

Catherine nodded.

'Well, it's exactly the same here.'

'Yes, but we don't live here, so what does it matter?'

'I work here,' Bethany reminded her, rather sharply. 'It could matter a lot to me.'

'Oh, Beth, I am sorry,' Catherine cried, instantly contrite. 'I'm being a selfish pig. Will it help if you tell them how awful Tarique was? Would that make things any better?'

'Perhaps,' Bethany replied without conviction.

'Or that I don't have the kind of career where —'

'You can definitely forget that one.'

'Or could you say I'd die if I actually had the baby? Would that do any good?'

Bethany didn't answer because she hadn't really been listening to Catherine's feeble suggestions. Her mind was racing at top speed, looking for a way to extricate herself from this new predicament. She'd have to think of something and it would have to be really good.

Desperation produced results.

'As long as we don't have to be absolutely glued to the truth —' she began.

'Good heavens. Why should we?'

'Then I have an idea.' And leaping up, Bethany hurried over to the mat where the betel-and-gossip session was taking place. It was hard to force herself to follow the Dayak custom of not coming directly to the point when she had something she was eager to say but she knew it was important to try. So she endured several minutes of idle chatter before beginning, 'My friend is in a very bad situation.'

The old women regarded her with curiosity.

'You see,' she continued, 'my friend doesn't have a husband. The man who made her pregnant was the one on our project who died a few weeks ago. You heard about that.'

They nodded.

'There are some places in world,' Bethany went on to tell them, trying to keep as close to the truth as possible, 'where parents get very angry if their daughter makes a baby before she is married. If she does not marry the father of the baby — and my friend cannot do this now because the man is dead — the parents turn her out of the family. They tell her that she is not their daughter anymore. Then she has to go through life with no father, no mother, no sisters or brothers. Her baby will have no family and no ancestors. Her friends will go away from her too and she will left all alone in the world.'

Bethany paused for a moment. She didn't like to lie to these kind people but it seemed like the only option, so she added, 'My friend's country is like that.'

Forgive me, Australia, she murmured, silently, as she watched a sympathetic shudder sweep over her audience, accompanied by expressions of incredulity on the wrinkled faces.

Without your family, without your ancestors, who were you, the old women of Nanga Palin were asking themselves? What were you? Didn't your very humanity come from those who had given you life? And who would intercede with the spirit world on your behalf, if not your ancestors? You would be doomed not only to go through this world alone, but, even worse, to wander alone and lost through the shadowy after-life if you had no ancestors to guide you.

How could such a terrible punishment be inflicted on a daughter just because a boy had visited her in the night and they had made a baby together, the old women were wondering? It was only what all the young people in the longhouse did – what they themselves had done when they were young. Much as this foreign girl must want her baby, what could she do? How lucky she was to be here where Kati could help her instead of back amongst her own cruel people.

Bethany listened with an overwhelming sense of relief as the women gave voice to these thoughts. But when she returned to share the triumph of her story with Catherine, even though it was a little embarrassing to tell an Australian what she had said, she found that it evoked no interest at all on the part of her listener.

Catherine's face had turned the colour of old ivory, her lips had taken on a bluish cast, and sweat had broken out on her face.

CHAPTER EIGHT

Bethany immediately went in search of Kati who ordered several of the younger women to half-lead, half-carry Catherine into an empty sleeping room and help her down onto a wooden bed.

Bethany sat on the floor beside her, feeling rather sick herself, as she contemplated her responsibility in this potentially catastrophic affair.

Oh God, don't let her die, she prayed, although she was far from certain that an interventionist deity was there to hear her.

As the hours crawled by, Catherine became too racked with pain to care whether she was dying or not. She was only vaguely aware of the women who drifted in and out, caring for her under Kati's supervision, and was completely indifferent to the supplications made to the spirits on her behalf.

Eventually the nightmare afternoon drew into evening, but Bethany was much too preoccupied with their immediate situation to give any thought to whether they were being missed at Kanyalang.

Their absence at lunch had caused no concern. Bethany sometimes spent the entire day at Nanga Palin and Catherine was often too busy trudging through the rainforest in search of 'new species of anything that moved' as Wolf once put it, to come back for the midday meal.

It was only after it had been dark for several hours and there was still no sign of either of the two women that the others grew alarmed.

Elliot was in Jakarta for talks with the Ministry of Forestry so Wolf elected himself in charge.

'We've got to go and look for them,' he declared.

'At night?' exclaimed Pashetta, horrified.

'Damn right. We can't just sit here on our butts, for God's sake. If one of them got hurt out there they might be having a devil of a time getting back.'

'There is a very bad pack of wild pigs down river from here,' Pashetta reported, ominously. 'Tjilik told me about them. He saw them yesterday when he was in the jungle with Catherine.'

'He wasn't with her today,' Bima said. 'He was sterilising sample cases in the lab this afternoon. I saw him there.'

'If Tjilik isn't with them, who is?' Wolf demanded. 'They're not alone out there, are they?'

'Don't be silly. They know better than that,' Marguarita said.

'Maybe Catherine went to Nanga Palin with Bethany,' suggested Mike, 'and they're still there.'

'For a whole day and half the night — I doubt it,' returned Marguarita.

'Maybe Catherine just felt like taking a day off,' Mike shrugged. 'You know how hard she works. And where else could she go except Nanga Palin?'

Marguarita looked at him doubtfully. It wasn't easy to imagine Catherine skiving off. But on the other hand if she wasn't with Bethany, why would they both go missing at the same time? It couldn't just be a coincidence.

'The only thing to do is to get up a search party,' Wolf declared and immediately set about organising all the men, including the builders, into groups of three and four.

'Hello,' Marguarita said, tartly, 'I'm here too.'

'This is men's work,' replied Wolf, testily.

Pashetta shot him a grateful look.

'Excuse me,' retorted Marguarita, 'but I know the jungle better than anyone here.'

'News to me,' Wolf replied.

'Well, better than anyone except Mike,' she amended, 'or Batok or Tjilik,' she added, hastening to do justice to the two Dayak research assistants.

'Your modesty overwhelms me,' said Wolf, 'but if you're so hot to go, you can take some of the builders with you and sniff around that area east of Nanga Palin. You know the place I mean — the one where Catherine found that new species of creepy-crawly she's been going on about.'

'Builders,' Marguarita replied scornfully, not at all pleased about her assigned companions, 'what do they know about the jungle?'

'Possibly not much,' Wolf admitted, 'but since you're such an authority they won't need to know a lot, will they?'

Marguarita conceded the point.

'Anyway, you know what Catherine's like when she's all excited about something,' Wolf continued. 'She might've gone back to the place she found her new creepy-crawly to see if it had any interesting relatives and somehow got more than she bargained for.'

'And Bethany?' enquired Mike.

'She's probably with Catherine,' Wolf replied.

'I think I would not be very useful in the jungle,' Pashetta put in, just in case anyone should suggest that she, like Marguarita, should venture out into that tangled darkness.

Nobody did.

Wolf's attention turned instead to Bima. 'You don't get out and around this primeval Eden very much,' he said, 'so you'd better team up with someone who does. Tjilik would probably be best. He'll know the places where Catherine's likely to have gone. And you'll want one of the builders with you, too, just to have an extra man along in case of an accident or anything.'

'Okay,' agreed Bima.

'Mike, you and Kolop are obviously the ones to check out Nanga Palin,' he continued, 'because if they're not there, you can mobilise your ranger guys and search out that neck of the woods. But if they are there, just messing around getting pissed on jungle juice and screwing the local talent, strangle them. I could be doing something else with my evening besides traipsing through the greenery looking for a couple of drunken chicks who forgot to come home.'

'Right, General,' Mike said, with a mock salute that drew derisive laughter from Marguarita and Bima but bounced unheeded off Wolf's resilient skin.

From the moment Mike arrived at Nanga Palin, accompanied by Kolop and one of the builders, he noticed that things didn't seem quite right. An unfamiliar reserve hung in the air and everyone, even the rangers he thought he knew so well, seemed curiously reluctant to talk to him.

The only person to greet him with anything like the usual enthusiasm was Sarika's little cousin, the chubby, five-year-old

Untan, who rushed forward to be picked up, tossed into the air and then caught again in the hairy visitor's strong arms. This exquisite and terrifying treat, obtainable only from Mike, was not to be missed. Tonight it proved to be even better than usual as it included the delicious bonus of being swung round and round by the ankles before being turned right-side-up and set down on his sturdy little feet.

'Again, again,' he cried.

'Next time,' Mike promised him, 'now I'm busy trying to find Bethany and her friend.'

'Sleeping,' the little fellow said, promptly.

Mike noticed a look of consternation cross the faces of the surrounding adults.

'Come, I show you,' said Untan, tugging his hero's hand and feeling very important.

Christ, Mike thought, what were they doing in bed at ten o'clock at night at Nanga Palin? Could Wolf possibly have been right about them having sex with a couple of the guys here? Somehow he just couldn't see it. But why else – he looked questioningly at Sarika who chose not to meet his glance. Then he turned to Thumbi who was saying something in rapid Dayak to Untan. He couldn't quite catch her words but it sounded like she was telling the child off – something he had never heard her do before.

Fortunately, Lunsa came up to greet him so he put the question to him.

'Is Bethany here,' he asked, 'and her friend Catherine?'

Lunsa narrowed his eyes and thought for a moment before answering. He didn't want Mike to find out what was going on but Untan had sort of given the game away and he wanted even less to risk the loss of face that would ensue if he were caught in an outright lie. A careful path between truth and falsehood was required. Looking at Thumbi as he spoke, he said, 'Yes, they are here.'

'Where?'

'Not good to disturb them,' advised Thumbi, who had been quick to perceive her husband's strategy. 'Bethany's friend ate something bad in the jungle – vomiting.' And she proceeded to illustrate the procedure with gestures that left no doubts about her meaning.

'I'd better go and see her,' Mike said.

'No, she is very tired,' said Thumbi. 'Better let her sleep.'

'I'll just pop in for a minute and see if she needs anything,' he insisted, looking hopefully at Untan who appeared to have withdrawn his offer of acting as guide.

'Thumbi will take you,' Lunsa said.

Mike followed her along the veranda but when they reached Catherine's room, the old woman planted herself solidly in the doorway, effectively blocking his way inside. As a result, he could only peer over her head into the shadowy interior.

'Are you okay in there?' he called, as he made out two forms in the dim light, one sitting and one lying on a bed.

'Fine, go away,' Catherine cried.

Mike, puzzled, thought she sounded slightly hysterical.

'But what's the matter?' he asked, pressing gently on Thumbi's shoulder to indicate he'd like her to move out of the way.

She didn't seem to get the hint.

'We're pissed, that's all,' Catherine replied impatiently, not sounding a bit grateful that he had come all the way over here at night to make sure she was alright. 'Just leave us alone, will you. We want to get some sleep.'

It astonished Mike to hear that Wolf had been right after all, at least about the boozing, if not about the sex. But then he knew how strong tuak could be, even though it was only a kind of palm wine. It could catch you out if you weren't careful. He tried to explain to Thumbi that he would actually like to go into the room but his command of the language seemed to be failing him tonight because he wasn't getting through to her. She just kept standing there smiling and he couldn't think of any way to get past her without actually knocking her down.

'What about you, Bethany? Are you pissed, too?' he called out.

'Legless,' she lied, wondering if she really should be going along with this fiction.

'Do you need anything before I go?' he asked.

'No,' shrieked Catherine, 'just fuck off, will you.'

Mike was deeply hurt. This was a side of Catherine he had never seen before — hadn't even suspected existed. And Bethany wasn't being much better. Well, he decided glumly, there clearly wasn't any point in hanging around if they were going to be like that.

Bethany listened with a sinking feeling to the sound of his retreating footsteps along the veranda floor and very quickly began to regret having lied to him.

'Listen,' she exclaimed, starting up from the bed. 'You've got to let me tell him what's really happening.'

'No, you can't. You mustn't,' Catherine pleaded, grabbing Bethany's wrist with a surprising show of strength and holding her back. 'It's my secret. You can't tell. You promised.'

Had she promised, Bethany wondered, too exhausted now to remember very clearly whether she had or not. She supposed she had but weren't there times when a promise really should be broken? And if so, wasn't this one of them?

Then she reminded herself that in all likelihood Catherine was just suffering something akin to labour pains. They had been induced a number of months too early, that was all. So if the pain was only to be expected, and if Catherine didn't want her secret divulged, it would be wrong to betray her trust, wouldn't it?

Bethany had just managed to convince herself of this when, to her horror, she saw a red stain spreading slowly across the bed and the full extent of Catherine's diminished rationality was driven home to her.

Oh my God, why did I listen to her, she asked herself? Why didn't I tell Mike the truth? Her thoughts flew to the iridium phone in Elliot's office and she realised that Mike could have used it to ring up that kind Madurese doctor in Putussibau.

Perhaps it's not too late, she thought, with a surge of hope. Perhaps Mike's still here, drinking and talking on the veranda. Rushing from the room, she ran out in search of him, only to have her hopes dashed by Thumbi.

'He's not here,' the old woman said. 'He went home.'

Bethany was devastated. 'Could we send someone over to Kanyalang with a message?' she asked.

To Bethany's surprise, Thumbi received this request with an unexpected lack of helpfulness, apparently viewing it as a poor return for all their hospitality.

'Maybe we send in morning,' she replied, in a voice so dismissive that Bethany feared any argument would be useless.

'But I'm frightfully worried about –' she began, with little hope.

'Don't worry, Kati will take care of her.'

'But the pain is so bad and the blood –'

'If the baby comes out early there is always pain, always blood. It's normal,' Thumbi explained, her manner a little more kindly this time. 'I will go and see. Come along.'

Bethany found it hard to believe that what Catherine was experiencing could possibly be considered normal but then, she wouldn't know, would she? Perhaps Thumbi was right.

Catherine was writhing and moaning in a pool of blood when they reached her side but the sight, so terrifying to Bethany, apparently left the headman's wife unperturbed.

She felt Catherine's forehead and stomach with an experienced hand, nodded and declared, calmly, 'I'll call Kati.' Leaving Bethany hovering by the bed, she went in search of the medicine woman who soon appeared, followed by two of the younger women.

After an initial appraisal of the situation, Kati embarked on a ritual invocation of the spirits, chanting and dancing around Catherine's prostrate form.

Oh God, is that all she's going to do for her, Bethany thought with a sinking heart. Much as she had tried to immerse herself in the culture of Nanga Palin, she simply couldn't share the Dayak confidence in the healing powers emanating from the supernatural world.

Suddenly Catherine gave a shriek of agony, curled her entire body up like a snail and, in what seemed like a gesture of final desperation, crushed Bethany's hand in a grip so strong that it seemed certain to break every bone in it. Then, spent and exhausted, she fell back and stretched herself out on the bed, indifferent to the two women who came forward with cloths to mop up the blood.

The nightmare was over.

Helpful Nanga Palin women bathed Catherine, dressed her in a fresh sarong and held a glass of cloudy liquid to her lips. 'To make good blood,' one of them explained.

Catherine took a hesitant sip, made a grimace of distaste, and tried to push it away, but she was too weak to resist Kati's stern admonitions so, dutifully, she drained it to the end.

Bethany, by contrast, needed no urging to down the strong tea, heavily laced with sugar, that was brought to her. She drank it gratefully.

Catherine soon fell into an exhausted sleep but Bethany, feeling a need for fresh air, strolled out onto the veranda and tried to calm her frayed nerves by surveying the peaceful night sky. She was just beginning to feel herself relax a little when a slight smell of fish caught her attention and, looking around, she saw with dismay that Sarika had brought her a large bowl of fish head soup.

After thinking that she couldn't possibly touch it, Bethany decided she would try just a little so as not to wound Sarika's feelings, and to her surprise, it tasted delicious. She ended up polishing off the entire thing, along with two cakes of manioc fried in pig fat and half-a-dozen rice balls. When Bethany had finished, Sarika unrolled a mat for her and spread it out on the floor beside Catherine's bed. Dizzy with relief that everything was over, she collapsed onto it and fell into deep sleep.

Mike was experiencing no such sensation of relief as he trudged back to Kanyalang with Kolop. The whole episode at Nanga Palin had left him confused and depressed. What could have got into Catherine, he wondered, or into Bethany, for that matter?

Whatever it was, he decided, after coming up with no satisfactory answers, the first thing he had to do now was to let the others know that they could call off the search. And finding them, he was certain, wouldn't be easy.

The night was half over before everyone finally made it back to Kanyalang and Marguarita didn't have a chance to quiz Mike about it all until breakfast time.

'They were tanked to the gills,' Mike told her, in response to her questions, 'and not in any condition to make it back here.'

'That doesn't sound like Catherine,' Marguarita said with a frown, 'and it hardly seems very professional of Bethany. I mean, there are places where you get pissed and places you don't. And for an anthropologist –' she broke off and regarded him suspiciously. 'Are you sure that was all that was wrong with them?' she demanded.

'I guess so. That's all they told me, anyway.'

'No fevers or anything?'

'Why should they have fevers?'

'Because that tuak could have been mixed with water that had God-knows-what kind of bacteria and parasites in it.'

'They didn't mention anything except being pissed.'

'I can't believe you went all the way over there and didn't bother to find out a little more,' exclaimed Marguarita.

'They might have had a couple of guys in there and been having a shag, you know, like Wolf said,' Mike pointed out. 'After all, he was right about them being pissed. He might have been right about the sex part too. And if he was, then the last thing I wanted to do was barge in on them.'

Marguarita's eyes lit up with wicked amusement as she contemplated this scenario. 'Well, I suppose we can't accuse Bethany of being unprofessional on that one, can we?' she laughed.

'What do you mean?' Mike returned, fearing that, as so often happened, one her painful darts disguised as humour was heading his way.

'Anthropologists are supposed to be participant observers in the cultures they study, aren't they?' she said, delightedly. 'Perhaps our little Bethany's just taking that part of her research a bit more seriously than the job description requires.'

If Bethany could have overheard this conversation she might have credited Marguarita with being clairvoyant. How else would she have known that the issue of being a participant observer was about to become so central to her role at Nanga Palin?

But when she first woke up there was only one question that held any importance for her. Had Catherine lived through the night? Bethany scarcely dared to open her eyes for fear of what she would see. Fortunately one glance was enough to put paid to her worst fears. Not only was Catherine still breathing, but her colour was noticeably better. Miraculously, at least, it seemed like a miracle to Bethany, Catherine looked like she was going to be alright.

Relief made Bethany hungry so after a quick bath in the river — starting the day without one would have been unthinkable for the inhabitants of Nanga Palin — she went round to the back veranda in search of something to eat.

It took no more than an instant for her to sense that there was something different in the way the women around the cooking fires were greeting her. It was hard to say exactly what it was and she couldn't help wondering if she was imagining it. But gradually, as the morning wore on, she noticed other subtle changes, not in actual words or actions but in people's body language when they were with her. They didn't pay any particular attention to her or treat her with any of the politeness they reserved for Mike and other occasional visitors. If anything, they almost ignored her, but somehow it wasn't in a bad way. It was almost as if — and she hardly dared let herself think it — her presence in their midst had become so thoroughly accepted, so normal, that she was just regarded as another member of the longhouse.

She mulled this over in her mind while she fashioned a rough and misshapen version of the rattan baskets that the Nanga Palin women made so beautifully. How and why had this change in people's attitudes occurred, she wondered?

Could it be that that bringing Catherine to Kati had served as some sort of initiation rite into the deepest and most sacred aspects of Dayak culture, she asked herself? Had it been seen as an affirmation of her confidence in their traditional ways? Or had it just made her seem less of an outsider now than she had before?

The various possibilities that went through her mind were not entirely off the mark but important things had happened during the night, some of which she would never know about.

Bethany had no idea that while she had slept, the sacred ancestor figures had been taken from the rafters above the sleeping rooms where they were stored. Nor did she suspect that they had been carefully and reverently rubbed with cloths that were still wet with the life blood of a human foetus. And the rituals of the night had not ended there. Sangalang and Kati had recited the appropriate incantations over the reddened images before they had been returned to their resting places in the eaves of the longhouse, high above the daily activities of the living residents of Nanga Palin.

The glorious reward for this blood offering came within hours of the event. To the joy of the entire longhouse, the gods sent Laban her longed-for great grandchild, a healthy baby boy. The infant was born early that morning just as dawn was breaking over the forest canopy, a clear sign that the gods were pleased to have tasted human blood again. The traditional ways of the ancestors had not been forgotten. Nanga Palin would enjoy the blessings of the gods once more.

By the time Bethany found her way onto the cooking veranda that morning, everyone in the longhouse knew about the arrival of the new baby. Even the young people, the ones whose minds had been warped by school and whose memories had been stunted by reading and writing, were pleased to know that the spirits were looking favourably on them again, and that good fortune was coming their way.

Everyone, except Bethany herself, knew that in bringing her friend to their healer, she had precipitated this welcome turn of events

CHAPTER NINE

Bethany's star was not shining so brightly at Kanyalang where tempers were frayed from lack of sleep, and grumblings about Mike's performance at Nanga Palin – lacklustre, to say the least – were heard around the breakfast table.

The explanation that Bethany and Catherine had simply been too pissed to come home was generally accepted, although Marguarita wasn't so sure. But the suggestion that they were having it off with a couple of the Nanga Palin men was viewed with more scepticism, particularly by Bima and Pashetta.

'It just doesn't sound like something they would do,' Bima objected, thinking mainly of Catherine.

'Why ever not?' teased Marguarita. 'Do you think you have a monopoly on sex appeal around here?'

'Don't be absurd,' he returned, flushing with embarrassment. 'I just meant –'

'He just meant they wouldn't do that sort of thing with a Dayak,' asserted Pashetta, projecting her own low opinion of the forest people onto Bethany and Catherine.

'No, I didn't,'retorted Bima, hotly. 'I was thinking that one night stands with whoever happens to be around doesn't seem like –'

'It sounds to me like it depends on who's around,' grinned Wolf. 'A longhouse fuck can be a real turn on, you know.'

'I don't know, actually,' Bima returned, wishing he wasn't sounding quite so wet. 'And I don't know what makes you think you can speak for Catherine.'

'Okay, okay,' Wolf agreed, putting up his hands in a gesture of mock surrender. 'No aspersions on the purity of Saint Catherine, I assure you, but I think I'll just amble over there and check things out anyway.'

'It's none of your bloody business,' grumbled Bima.

'Like hell it isn't,' retorted Wolf. 'Who spent half the night tramping through the jungle looking for those two idiots, tell me that? I'm going over there and, if they don't have hangovers that are positively life-threatening, I'm going to tear them both limb from limb.'

'Hold on a second,' Marguarita said as Wolf stood up to leave. 'I'll go with you.'

'Good thinking,' he said. 'I might need you keep me from killing them.'

'That's not exactly the reason I had in mind,' Marguarita said.

'What, then?' asked Wolf.

'I'm curious about what, if anything, is really keeping them there,' she replied. 'Mike's useless little trip over there told us practically nothing.'

'Sure it did,' argued Wolf. 'It screamed an overdose of booze and sex.'

'Very likely,' Marguarita agreed, 'but just in case it's something more serious I'm going to make up some oral rehydration fluid and take it along.'

'That's the best thing for a tuak hangover too,' Mike said recalling how he had felt after several Nanga Palin celebrations.

'Okay, but hurry up,' Wolf scowled, not entirely pleased with the prospect of her company, 'I haven't got all day.'

When they arrived at Nanga Palin, the sight of Bethany, who seemed in remarkably high spirits and quite hangover-free did nothing to improve his temper.

'What the fuck do you think you're doing?' he demanded, striding over to her.

'Making a basket,' she replied, coolly.

'It's hideous.'

'I know. Did you come all the way over here to tell me that?'

'I came here, you idiot, to see if you're alright.'

'I'm fine.'

'I can see that. Do you realise I spent half the night combing the goddamn jungle looking for you?'

'We all did,' added Marguarita, not caring to have her own efforts go unappreciated.

'Whatever did you do that for?' Bethany asked, with irritating innocence.

'Because, you ungrateful wretch, we were afraid that you or

Catherine or both of you had had some kind of accident. That's why,' Wolf retorted.

'Didn't Mike tell you –'

'He couldn't exactly tell us anything until he found us,' snapped Marguarita, 'and it took him hours of searching to do that.'

'So the next time you get the urge for a booze-up and an anthropologically correct fuck –' Wolf began.

'We weren't having a fuck, anthropologically correct or otherwise,' Bethany declared, emphatically.

'Yeah, tell me another one,' he said.

'I have no intention of telling you anything,' she retorted.

'Well, whatever you were doing, the next time you feel like doing it, you damn well better let somebody know about it ahead of time,' Wolf declared.

'I'm not sure exactly how you came by the curious idea that I'm in any way accountable to you,' she retorted, 'and if you had had the good sense to mind your own business, you could have had a comfortable night tucked away in bed.'

'I was minding Kanyalang's business,' he told her, angrily, 'and that unfortunately includes scooping up the dismembered body parts of any project staff who've been careless enough to let themselves be gored by a wild pig or treed by a monitor lizard. We thought something like that might have happened to you or Catherine. Where is she, by the way?'

'Still sleeping it off.'

'Let's wake her up, then. You'd better show me where you've stashed her.'

This was not something Bethany really wanted to do but she decided it would be pointless, and might arouse his suspicions, if she tried to stop him so she led the way.

They found Catherine awake but pale and listless and not in any condition to respond quickly when Wolf said, 'I hear you went on quite a binge last night.'

'A binge?' she echoed, blankly.

'Don't you remember anything?' Bethany exclaimed, with what she hoped was a teasing laugh. 'You must have been even more pissed than I was.'

'Oh, yes, possibly,' agreed Catherine, catching on. 'I suppose, I was.'

'Have some of this then. It should make you feel better,' Marguarita said, taking a flask from the satchel she was carrying.

'What is it?' asked Catherine, who felt she had had enough revolting medicine in the last twenty-four hours to last her a lifetime.

'Just oral rehydration fluid, the best thing for a hangover, you know,' Marguarita said.

'But I don't –' Catherine began.

Marguarita looked at her sharply.

'Come on, drink up,' Wolf said impatiently, 'and then we'll get you back to Kanyalang.'

Catherine panicked. 'No, not yet,' she protested. 'I don't want to go anywhere yet.'

'Why, is something else wrong, other than a hangover I mean?' asked Marguarita, feeling Catherine's forehead to see if it was hot.

'No, I'll be alright. I just want to stay here and sleep, that's all.'

'You don't have to go anywhere you don't want to,' Bethany promised her. Then, noticing the suspicious expression on Marguarita's face, she added, 'There's no reason why Catherine can't stay here until she feels better, is there? Just leave the oral rehydration fluid and I'll give it to her later.'

'Well, the sooner the better,' Marguarita advised, reluctantly setting the flask on the floor beside Catherine's bed. 'What was it you were drinking, anyway? Was it tuak?'

Catherine looked confused. 'Tuak,' she repeated, 'I don't know, perhaps.'

'Yes, of course, it was tuak,' Bethany cried, wishing Catherine would be a little quicker on the up-take.

'Anything else? Did you eat something dodgy?'

'I don't think so,' Catherine said vaguely. 'I can't remember.'

'You know what it's like here at Nanga Palin,' put in Bethany, 'or perhaps you don't. Anyway, people are always bringing you things to eat. I'm used to the food but Catherine isn't. And of course tuak's not exactly made with pure Himalayan spring water either.'

'I'm fine, really I am,' insisted Catherine. 'I just want to sleep, that's all.'

Marguarita, somewhat against her better judgment, decided to accept this at face value but, as she thought about it on the way back to Kanyalang, she wondered if she had done the right thing.

'They were lying, you know,' she said to Wolf.

'Well, something obviously knocked Catherine for a loop,' Wolf agreed, 'but if it wasn't the tuak, what was it?'

Instead of answering him directly, Marguarita reflected, 'Catherine's been sick a lot lately, hasn't she?'

'I guess so,' he said, 'but what's new about the jungle trots in this neck of the woods?'

'Not much,' Marguarita agreed, 'but when you think how dragged out she's been looking recently —'

'Yeah, I guess Tarique's death hit her pretty hard.'

'Did it? I wonder.'

'Of course, it did. Where the hell have you been, on Mars?'

'Not exactly,' Marguarita replied slowly, her mind racing ahead of her words. 'In fact, a couple of days ago I was on the veranda when Catherine came out of the bath. She was wearing a sarong and it clung to her because it was a bit damp and —'

'Aren't you damp when you come out of a bath,' he interrupted, 'or do you get yourself dry-cleaned?'

Marguarita ignored this. 'I noticed that her stomach was rather rounded and I remember thinking at the time that it was a bit odd, considering that she eats almost nothing.'

'What are you getting at?' he asked. Then looking at her sharply, he added, 'You're not saying what I think you're saying, are you?'

'Very likely. I'm wondering if she had an abortion at Nanga Palin and doesn't want to tell the world about it.'

'Are you crazy? No one in their right mind would have an abortion in a place like that. I mean, not in a fucking longhouse, for God's sake. They just wouldn't.' But as he said this, he suddenly remembered how staunchly Catherine had defended the use of Dayak medicine when Bethany had been babbling on about some voodoo cure.

99

Could she possibly — no the idea was ludicrous. No one smart enough to have become a first rate scientist would fall for crap like that.

'I don't believe she would have done anything that dumb,' he insisted, as much to reassure himself as to convince Marguarita. 'I think she just got herself stinking drunk on tuak mixed with river water. Now you've got to admit that would be a pretty lethal combination, and Catherine's paying the price today.'

Marguarita, agreeing that Catherine was paying the price for something, merely nodded and kept any further thoughts on the subject to herself.

No one could doubt that drinking tuak mixed with river water was a very dicey proposition.

Elliot, when he returned and heard about it, immediately put the episode down to Bethany's pernicious influence. Catherine, on her own, would surely have known better, he was convinced of that. If Bethany wanted to take foolish chances that was up to her but anyone could see that Catherine wasn't strong enough to be taking risks like that. He was determined that the minute he saw Bethany again he'd let her know exactly what he thought of her judgement.

In the meantime, looking at his watch and seeing that dinner time was approaching, he nipped into his room and fortified himself with an extra-large whisky, accompanied by an extra-small splash of water, before joining the beer drinkers on the veranda.

'You're looking like death warmed over,' Wolf observed as Elliot sat down in the chair that was tacitly reserved for his use. Although a bit rickety, it was the most comfortable of the lot.

'Anything wrong?' Bima asked.

'Quite a few things,' he replied, tersely. 'For starters, the rumours we've been hearing about a logging company coming into the area are quite true. But that's only part of the story. A whole rash of new licences has been given —'

'Given?' hooted Wolf.

'Alright then, sold, paid for under the table, put it any way you like,' Elliot returned, irritably. 'The fact is, permits have been issued to several logging companies to cut a wide area of forest, beginning just a few kilometres from Nanga Palin and going right up to the border of the conservation area.'

'Where did you hear that?' asked Marguarita.

'A chap in the Ministry of Forestry told me.'

'And did he say how long it's going to be before the loggers are crossing into the conservation area?' she asked, sharply.

'I'd give them about five minutes,' declared Wolf. 'Christ, I bet you anything some greedy shit at the Ministry is already putting in his order for a new Mercedes.'

'Yeah,' said Mike, 'and once those bastards get inside the conservation area, how much more money's going to go into Ministry pockets then?'

'They'll have them by the short and curlies,' agreed Elliot. 'With a substantial investment to protect, persuading the powers-that-be to turn a blind eye won't come cheap.'

'Which is more expensive, I wonder,' mused Marguarita, 'logging with a permit or without one.'

'I'd say, without one,' returned Wolf. 'Then it's like blackmail, the guys who turn the screws can make the victims pay and pay and pay. Serves the mother-fuckers right, though.'

Pashetta flushed as she listened to this exchange. It infuriated her that foreigners criticised the Indonesians for cutting down their forests when they, the Europeans and the Americans, had made themselves rich by cutting down their own. Yet when Indonesians wanted to do the same thing, wanted to be rich instead of poor, they were called greedy bastards.

The hypocrisy of it all made her absolutely livid but she knew better than to air this opinion in front of her companions. Wolf wouldn't want anything more to do with her if he knew what she really thought, that was certain, and she didn't want to lose him, or risk her job either. So, difficult as it was to keep silent, she managed to hold her tongue.

'We're not going to let anything the loggers are doing affect us, are we?' asked Bima, whose thoughts had flown to the hotel, and who couldn't imagine anything more devastating than having to abandon his star project when it was only half-finished. 'We are going to carry on here, aren't we?'

'There will still be lots of jungle around Kanyalang,' Pashetta pointed out.

'Sure,' Wolf agreed, sarcastically, 'and rich tourists are going to come thronging here in droves to listen to the music of the chain saws. We might even get a hit single out of it, call it 'The Chainsaw Serenade'. We could offer excursions through the blighted area and show people what it's like when there's not a tree or a living creature in sight, except possibly a rat or two, of course. They'll love it. The guide books will declare it The Vacation Spot of the Year.'

'There's really no need to inflict the darker side of your imagination on us,' protested Elliot.

'Isn't there?' Wolf replied, grimly. 'I hate to tell you, but that darker side, as you put it, is usually a damn good predictor of what's about to happen.'

No one disputed this claim. Instead, everyone except Pashetta drank more than usual. Mike and Marguarita vented their feelings by resorting to their usual bickering. Bima sank ever deeper into a cloud of gloom at the thought of abandoning his beloved hotel.

Wolf was arguing with Elliot about strategies for coping with the loggers when the sound of footsteps and unfamiliar voices coming from the direction of the veranda steps made everyone turn their heads and gasp.

A tall man, with rust red hair, followed by two companions, was climbing the veranda stairs.

CHAPTER TEN

Everyone was stunned. Kanyalang never had surprise visitors.

Elliot was the first to recover from the shock and stepped forward to greet them.

'I'm Jim Nathan,' the red-headed man said when Elliot had introduced himself. 'My bearded friend here is Don Miller and this is our guide, Jabu. We're with Fairbanks Mining and Exploration.'

Enthusiasm for the visitors immediately evaporated but Elliot, feeling that jungle etiquette required him to play the polite host in spite of their affiliation, offered them a beer. 'Our American colleague insists we keep them on ice,' he explained, with a smile of paternal indulgence. 'And in this heat, you know…'

Elliot shrugged his shoulders in a gesture suggesting that, under extreme climatic conditions, a few trans-Atlantic influences could be tolerated.

'That sure would hit the spot,' Don said, gratefully, 'especially for Jim here. He's from Alaska. I'm from Louisiana myself but even so I can't help wondering what I'm doing in a cauldron like this.'

'Exactly what are you doing?' Marguarita asked, acidly.

'Looking for gold,' Jim replied. 'I'm a geologist, you see, and Don here handles the business end of things. But at the moment we're just taking a few days off and checking out the local scenery.'

'Gold,' murmured Pashetta, her hand going instinctively to the chain she always wore around her neck.

'Well, gold's mostly what we're into,' Don explained, 'but sometimes we mess around with a little copper and zinc, too, depends where we are.'

'You've got a guy named Tarique Radjeb here, haven't you?' Jim asked after an awkward silence during which the visitors quenched their thirst, and their reluctant hosts silently debated whether to offer them further hospitality or to chuck them over the veranda rail.

'You've probably heard a lot about us from Radjeb,' Jim continued setting down his glass. 'He's the one Don really wants to see. In fact that's one of the reasons we've come through here on this little jaunt.'

'I'm afraid you won't find him,' Elliot said. 'He was bitten by a snake several weeks ago and, well, we weren't able to get him to treatment soon enough.'

'You don't mean he died?' exclaimed Jim.

Elliot nodded. 'I'm afraid that's exactly what I do mean.'

'Fuck,' muttered Don under his breath and then hastily amended it to, 'I mean that's too bad.'

'A damn shame,' Jim murmured.

'Did you know him very well?' asked Bima.

'No, never met the guy,' Don replied, 'just corresponded with him.'

'Oh?' said Elliot.

Marguarita didn't share his reticence. 'What about, if you didn't actually know him?'

'Just a few business matters.'

'Funny, I thought his business was with us, not with any mining companies,' Wolf observed.

'Careful,' Marguarita hissed under her breath.

She needn't have worried. Don merely said, 'A guy can have a few outside interests, can't he, a few investments for the future?'

'Not ones that conflict with the basic purpose of this project,' retorted Wolf.

Don shrugged this off and continued, 'You see, Radjeb's one of our stockholders, at least he was. So Jim and me thought that since we were in this neck of the woods we'd drop around and chew the fat for a while.'

Elliot eyed him suspiciously. What was the fellow on about? Businesses didn't send envoys around to drop in on small shareholders, especially not ones that happened to be in the middle of the rainforest. It was too absurd.

Don could see that his explanation wasn't going down well. 'The thing is,' he said, in an effort to make it sound more convincing, 'Jim's one of these weirdos who's never happier than when he's hacking his way through the jungle. I'm just humouring him and since we had this business connection with Radjeb we were kinda hoping we could cadge a few beers off him.'

Jim corroborated this. 'Yeah, I've got a few days' leave and I'd thought about going to Pontianak, or even Singapore, but hanging around those places doesn't interest me much. I'm basically an outdoor guy.'

'You look like one,' affirmed Marguarita, viewing their visitor's lean muscular form and coppery mane with undisguised appreciation. She had never thought she liked red hair but it suited this man. She liked his eyes, too. They were a deep brown, warm and somehow very sexy. What incredibly bad luck, she thought, that the first attractive man she had met in months had to be working for a mining company.

'Hey, since you guys were friends of Radjeb's,' she heard Don saying, as she thrust these potentially treacherous thoughts aside, 'I could let you in on a very interesting investment opportunity.'

'Oh, what sort of investment?' Marguarita asked, wanting to find out what had really brought them here.

'Nothing less than – but this is top secret, you understand. The fact is, we're on to something really big, something that could make a mint for anyone smart enough to be in on it from the beginning. Any of you guys interested?'

No one was.

'Don't worry,' Jim put in, trying to assuage the bad feelings he could read in his hosts' faces, 'there wouldn't be any action anywhere near you, nothing that would hurt your business. You see, word's out that the locals around here do some panning for gold when the water level's low and we've got reason to believe there's a major deposit – I'm talking commercial quantities – up there in the hills near the Sarawak border. That news is going to bring other mining companies here in droves, ones that don't care about the environment and don't take the time and trouble to do things right like we do. That's why it's so important that we get in there first. So I'm thinking that if we just follow this river in front of your place here up toward –'

'That's the conservation area,' Elliot warned. 'I'm afraid it's strictly off-limits for all but the most carefully controlled incursions. And it's completely taboo for any logging or mining.'

Don dismissed this objection with a shrug. 'A few friends in the right places,' he declared, confidently, 'and a little money changing hands can take care of all that.'

'Do you mean to say you can sit there calmly and tell us you'd be prepared to do something like that?' Wolf thundered. 'I don't believe I'm hearing this.'

'Hey, keep your shirt on,' Don replied. 'It's no big deal. It happens all the time.'

'Right, and do you know what else happens every fucking time?' Wolf continued. 'The mercury you bastards use to process that gold leaks out and poisons everything for miles around. That's what happens every fucking time.'

'Look, you can't stop progress,' Don replied patiently as if he were explaining something to an obtuse child. 'If there's gold in them hills somebody's going to go in and get it out. And they're not going to be stopped by the environmentalists or, I might add, by the powers-that-be in Jakarta. So why shouldn't we be the ones to get the gravy? And why not you, that is if you want to take advantage of a once-in-a-lifetime investment opportunity when it's practically being dropped in your lap?'

'You've sure as hell come to the wrong place,' Wolf retorted, 'because all I can say is you won't get a dime out of any of us. We're working our butts off to save this rainforest from mother-fucking schmucks like you.'

'Hey, wait a minute,' snarled Don jumping up from his chair and clenching his fists, 'if you want to get personal —'

'Don't mind Wolf,' Marguarita interrupted, catching hold of Don's arm. 'He's rude to everyone. '

Wolf was stunned. Had Marguarita, up to now the world's most impassioned defender of the rainforest, lost her mind? Or did she think the red-headed guy might be good for a quickie? One thing was for sure. He wasn't going to hang around to find out.

'I'm not listening to any more of this crap,' Wolf announced. 'I'm off in search of better company.'

'Where?' asked Pashetta, genuinely curious. As far as she was concerned, good company was in short supply in the jungle.

'Where do you think?' he returned. 'There's only one possible place.'

'Nanga Palin?'

'Got it in one.'

'But you were there this morning,' she reminded him.

'So?' he said. 'I'm going again.' And turning to Mike, he added, 'Want to come?'

'Yeah, why not?' Mike replied, although a glance in the direction of a blue plastic bucket filled with melting ice and several bottles of Bintang beer nearly made him change his mind.

'We just might take a few of those with us,' Wolf said, reading his friend's face.

'You're on,' Mike agreed, and after gathering up several bottles, they clambered down the veranda stairs.

When they arrived at Nanga Palin they found Catherine and Bethany dipping balls of rice into a fatty-looking pig meat stew and, apart from the fact that Catherine looked a little paler than usual, they both seemed fine.

'Back again?' Bethany remarked, smiling at Mike but demonstrating no enthusiasm for Wolf's return.

'Oh, lovely, you brought some beer,' cried Catherine, before a quick kick from Bethany made her realise that she hadn't said the wisest thing.

'What's the matter, didn't you guys get enough to drink last night?' teased Wolf.

'Actually I did,' Catherine replied hastily.

'Well, it doesn't seem to have put you off your food,' Wolf remarked, eyeing the chunks of pig fat that had floated to the top of the stew and thinking that they looked like the indigestion special, not something a woman recovering from a hatchet-style abortion would be eating. Marguarita, he decided, must have got it wrong.

'I'm feeling better,' Catherine said cautiously, trying to avoid any more ill-considered comments.

'Then what kept you here?' Wolf demanded. 'It couldn't have been the cuisine.'

'I'm the one who wanted to stay on,' Bethany improvised. 'I really need to be here for several days running and Catherine's keeping me company. Anyway, it's fun.' And, looking at Mike, she added, 'You should understand that. You spend enough time here yourself.'

'And I hadn't spent any time here at all, not until now,' Catherine said. 'It's really shocking that I've been in Kalimantan this long and know so little about the local people.'

'Well, you chose a good time to do it,' Wolf said. 'Kanyalang's swarming with vermin at the moment.'

'Vermin?' exclaimed Bethany, with distaste.

'The two-legged kind,' Wolf explained and launched into a description of the visitors while Mike opened the beer they had brought and filled the glasses of anyone in the vicinity who looked thirsty.

CHAPTER ELEVEN

The next morning Catherine told Bethany that she was feeling well enough to go back to Kanyalang.

'Are you sure you're up to it, the walk and everything?'

'Yes, I had a good night's sleep and it will do me good to get back to work, take my mind off things. And it should be interesting to see if Wolf's "vermin" are really as bad as he says.'

To her disappointment, they didn't have a chance to find out. The visitors had gone by the time they got there.

They hadn't left a moment too soon for Wolf. He wasted no time before storming into the lab and giving Marguarita the third degree. 'What the hell did you think you were you doing turning traitor on me last night?'

She put down the plant press she was holding and gaped at him. 'What on earth are you talking about?'

'Making nice with those pricks who were out to flood the place with poisonous chemicals. I would have thought you cared too much about the jungle to do something like that.'

'I wanted a chance to find out what they were up to,' she replied coolly, 'and I didn't think flinging insults at them and stalking off in a childish fit of temper was the way to do it.'

'And what did you manage to ferret out — anything interesting?'

'Not much,' she admitted, 'nothing very definite anyway.'

'Don't tell me you actually fell for that crap about dropping in on one of their so-called stockholders.'

'Don't be an idiot.'

'Well, what then?'

'I don't see why I should tell you when you're being so nasty?'

'Okay, I'll find out from someone else then.'

'Do that.'

'Don't worry, I will,' he declared, and set off in the direction of the half-finished hotel in search of Bima.

Wolf found him perched on a precarious bit of bamboo scaffolding directing the placement of a finial on the roof.

'Are you planning to spend the day up there,' Wolf called, 'or can you come down for a minute?'

'Hold on,' Bima replied. 'I just want to make sure this is right.'

'Looks like you're the one who'd better hold on,' Wolf called back, cheerfully. 'We don't need another funeral around here.'

After a few parting instructions to the workmen, Bima left them to it and adroitly made his way down to the ground. 'What's up?' he asked.

'Sorry to bring you down off your trapeze there,' Wolf replied, 'but I wanted to pick your brains about our visitors last night. Do you have any idea what the fuck they were up to?'

'Does it matter?' Bima shrugged. Then to Wolf's annoyance he went on to reflect, 'You know, there's just something about gold, it affects people like a drug. They see a few grains of it in the ground or in a river and become obsessed by the desire for more.'

'That may be,' agreed Wolf impatiently, 'but what I want to know is, why those guys came poking their snouts around here?'

'Marguarita thinks they were looking for information.'

'Information?' echoed Wolf, surprised, 'what about?'

'Possibly about Elliot's maps.'

'But how could guys like that have even known the things existed?' Wolf exclaimed.

'I've no idea.'

'Well, there's only one person who could have clued them in,' Wolf said, getting angrier the more he thought about it, 'and it's pretty fucking obvious who that was.'

'I don't know about that,' Bima warned. 'It's easy to build up a case against someone who's dead and can't defend himself. Marguarita might be wrong, you know. They may have come here for some other reason.'

'She does get crazy ideas sometimes,' he agreed, remembering her theory about the abortion, 'but they sure as hell didn't come to consult a two bit shareholder.'

'Perhaps they thought they could squeeze more money out of

Tarique,' Bima suggested, 'or more likely out of some of his more credulous friends. After all, they did try to do that.'

'Yeah, but that was peanuts. Not even pricks from a cheap-shit outfit like that would go to so much trouble for that kind of money,' declared Wolf. 'Did Marguarita worm anything else out of them?'

Bima hesitated, looking rather embarrassed.

'You were there, weren't you?' persisted Wolf. 'You must have heard what they said.'

'I wasn't, actually – at least, not all the time. You see, she put on a rather good show of being interested in investing and ...' He paused, not exactly sure how to go on.

'And what?'

'Well, if you ask me,' Bima continued, 'her real interest was in the redheaded chap. At least, that was my impression and I think it was his, too.'

'And did she follow through – have it off with him?'

'I've no idea. I didn't hang around to find out.'

A sudden crashing sound sent Bima flying to the spot where the finial had just toppled to the ground and Wolf resigned himself to not learning any more from him.

Later that afternoon as Wolf was passing the lab, he was seized with an impulse to have a chat with Catherine. He found her absorbed in dissecting an unsightly specimen with God-only-knew how many legs but he interrupted her.

'Hey, you knew Tarique better than anyone else,' he began, crossing over to where she was working. 'Did he ever tell you anything about investing in a mining company?'

His voice startled her and the creature had one less leg as a result.

'No,' she replied, 'I don't think so.'

'Are you surprised to hear that's what he was doing?'

'Nothing about him would surprise me,' she returned.

The bitterness in Catherine's tone shocked him. He had never heard her talk that way before and he thought he detected something new in her manner, almost as if her pastel prettiness had been re-enforced with steel.

What could have changed her like that, he wondered? Sure, she had had a monster hangover, but that had been yesterday. She couldn't still have it today.

Wolf watched her as she turned her attention back to the centipede, or millipede, or whatever-it-was. Could Marguarita's theory about the abortion possibly have been right, he wondered? He had heard that women generally went into a kind of emotional melt-down after something like that, had depressions and crying fits and that sort of thing, but Catherine actually she looked like she was in better spirits than she had been for weeks. She just seemed to have gone a bit prickly, that was all. Marguarita must surely have been wrong.

The problem was that the hangover story just didn't ring true. Maybe the thing to do was just to go ahead and ask her.

'Tell me something,' Wolf began, 'you weren't pregnant, were you?'

'What a question,' she replied, with a dismissive laugh that only succeeded in furthering his suspicions.

'That's not an answer,' he said.

'Perhaps not but do you really think it's any of your business?'

'Okay, I admit it isn't so if you tell me to shut up I'll understand. But if I'm right then, for the life of me, I can't figure out what the hell you were doing having an abortion in a fucking longhouse instead of someplace where you'd get decent medical care.'

'Nanga Palin was the closest place,' she sighed, giving up on the hangover story.

'What kind of a reason is that? Haven't you heard of airplanes, for God's sake?'

'It was also the cheapest,' she said, hoping this would, at least, put an end to the current grilling.

'Holy shit, you can't mean you risked your life just to save a few bucks.'

'I don't have masses of money to throw around for nothing, you know.'

'Nothing – you call your life nothing! That's the dumbest thing I've ever heard.'

Her mouth turned down at the corners, rather like a child's who was about to cry but, to Wolf's considerable relief, she didn't.

'What have you been doing with your salary, for God's sake?' he continued. 'And don't tell me you were sending it all back to an invalid mother or anything like that.'

'I don't have a mother. She died.'

'Or did Tarique persuade you to sink it all into that phoney gold mine? Was that it?'

'No,' she cried, her eyes flashing in a way he had only seen once – the time she had found him going through Tarique's desk.

Scattered bits of information tumbled through his mind like the random patterns in a kaleidoscope and then fell into a clearly discernible order. 'Could it have been your money that Tarique used to buy up shares in that gold mine?' he asked.

'Don't be absurd.'

'Is that what I'm being? I don't think so.'

'Yes you are, you're talking absolute rubbish,' she replied, but she wasn't a good liar and the expression on her face told him everything he needed to know.

'That's what happened, isn't it?' Wolf said. 'Tarique helped himself to the contents of your bank account, with your fond acquiescence, of course and left you flat broke.'

'I don't know why we're having this conversation,' she retorted. 'Why should you care what he did?'

'Because it would be very interesting to know how Tarique got the money to put into that gold mine, like how much of it might have been taken from project funds.'

'Are you hoping to dig him up and send him to gaol?' asked Marguarita, breezing into the lab with two sample cases in her hands, the results of her afternoon's foray into the rainforest.

'Believe me, I would if I could,' Wolf said, with a grimace. 'For the first time in my life I wish I were a religious man.'

'Whatever makes you say that?' Catherine asked. 'It doesn't seem like you at all.'

'Because then I could be absolutely sure that the bastard was roasting in hell right now.'

'Very satisfying,' agreed Marguarita, 'but unfortunately it wouldn't change anything, would it?'

'No, but it would be nice to think that there was some kind of justice somewhere.'

'Is that so important to you?' Marguarita asked and, without waiting for an answer, she deposited her samples in a cupboard, and went to her office to write up the afternoon's finds.

'You know what's the matter with you?' Wolf began, turning back to Catherine and waving an arm in the direction of some cages at the far end of the lab. 'You spend too much time with all these beetles and weird and not-so-wonderful fauna. It warps your understanding of your own species. You should broaden your scope of work to include people now and then.'

'They're not in my job description.'

'Fuck the job description then.'

Catherine saw that his expression was turning serious again, and had an uncomfortable feeling that he was about to revert to their former topic.

He did.

'There's one more thing I'd like to know,' he began, 'but it makes me so God damn mad to think about it, I can hardly bring myself to ask.'

'Then don't,' she suggested.

He ignored this. 'Why the hell didn't you come to me when you needed cash for a decent abortion somewhere? I'd have given it to you.'

'You would?' she gasped.

He would have been the last person she would have asked.

'Of course I would have, you idiot. Don't look so surprised. Any of us would have seen you through, one way or another. You should know that.'

To her utter mortification, the kindness in these words after all she had been through during the past two days made tears well up in her eyes.

'Hey, cheer up,' he said, as eager to avoid a flood as she was, 'things aren't so bad. You were brave, even if you were completely nuts, and you came through it alright, didn't you?'

She sniffed, nodded, and almost smiled before a dreaded possibility came into her mind. 'Are you going to tell the others?' she asked, tremulously.

'Not if you don't want me to.'

'Promise?'

'Promise,' he replied with a grin and, by the force of his will, compelled her to smile in return.

It was a very new and different Catherine who breezed out onto the veranda for drinks that evening. The intoxicating sense of liberation she felt at being free of Tarique's child, and thus free forever of Tarique himself, was causing her hair to shine brighter, her eyes to look bluer, and everything about her to seem more clearly defined, more focused.

Bima, noticing this transformation, thought it seemed almost as if someone had adjusted the aperture on a camera lens. He sensed that it might have something to do with Tarique although he didn't know quite how. Perhaps she could be beginning to put that episode in her life behind her though. That might go at least a little way toward explaining the way she looked tonight. If so, he couldn't help wondering if there was any chance that she would ever be interested in anyone like him?

Flickering images from his past wafted through his mind as he considered this possibility and, as often happened when he was in a reflective mood, his thoughts drifted back to his grandparents' rambling house in Jakarta. It had always been full to bursting with an assortment of aunts, uncles, cousins, dogs, cats, birds, and generally a monkey or two. Looking back on it now, it seemed like a paradise. He and his mother had lived there for five years after his father had left them and gone back to Holland. But then when he was twelve years old, he had been abruptly and irrevocably torn away from it all, to be sent alone to a strange country to live with a father he barely remembered and a Dutch stepmother he had never met.

He would never forget the utter desolation he had felt as he had peered out the window of that enormous plane for a last look at the family that had been the rock of stability and the font of happiness in his life. He had tried his best to imprint their faces on his mind as, in spite of all their assurances that he would come back, he had been convinced that he would never see them again.

In an important way, he had been right. When he did come back many years later, he had changed so much that his Indonesian relatives regarded him as a foreigner. He, in turn, had seen them as a European would see them, exotic, charming and kind but as people whose lives he could never again really understand or share.

He had been lucky, though. His stepmother hadn't been one of the wicked ones and he had soon grown quite fond of her. She had helped him to relearn the long-forgotten Dutch of his infancy, encouraged him to use his Dutch name, Pieter, instead of his Indonesian one, and had done everything she could to ease his way into his new surroundings.

As he had progressed through his teens, he had discovered that girls seemed to like him. He had inherited the build of his northern European father and the colouring of his Southeast Asian mother, except for his eyes. They were the blue of a summer sky and the effect was startling in his dusky brown face. By the time he was fifteen, three different girls had demonstrated their enthusiasm for his good looks in a manner he had found most exhilarating. It had taken some stern discipline on the part of his father to keep him at his books, but paternal authority had prevailed. He had kept his romantic escapades to a minimum, done well on his exams, and gone on for a degree in architecture.

It had been during his university years that he had spent a summer rediscovering the land of his birth. In an effort to feel that he belonged there again, he had revived the use of his Indonesian name. Then, in the course of a trip to Sumatra, he had become fascinated with the idea of adapting traditional Indonesian houses to the demands of modern living. This would be an expensive proposition, he knew, but the economy was soaring. Major cities, especially Jakarta, were overflowing with people who had money to spend on their homes. The challenge would lie in persuading them to want traditional style houses instead of ones that looked like they had been transplanted from southern California.

When he had finished his degree, he had joined a firm of architects in Amsterdam that had a branch office in Jakarta and had begun several years of commuting between his two countries.

With the help of relatives who had contacts in the right places, he had expanded the firm's Indonesian client base and his work had become increasingly in demand, largely amongst people who were building in order to let to foreigners. Within a few years he had been offered his biggest and most challenging project of all, building a five-star hotel in the middle of the jungle, one that would look like a Dayak longhouse on the outside but would contain as many modern amenities as an affluent tourist might crave on the inside.

Saskia, his girlfriend of nearly four years, had been understanding about his long absences as he had spent more and more time in Indonesia. But when the hotel contract came through – it committed him to a minimum of two years in Borneo, with intermittent inputs for another three – she had declared that she had had enough. He had almost asked her to marry him and come out to Kanyalang with him but then had thought better of it. She was too smart, too career-oriented, too much her own person to sit around a jungle longhouse all day while he supervised the construction of the hotel. He would be working on something he loved but no such option would be available to her.

Yet often as he lay awake at night, especially when he heard Pashetta slipping into Wolf's room next door, he could almost feel Saskia in his arms again. But, he admitted to himself, recently it hadn't been Saskia but Catherine, kitten-soft and sunlight-blond, who had crept into his dreams.

118

CHAPTER TWELVE

In the following weeks, Catherine found that the happiness she felt at being free of Tarique continued. She didn't even miss the sex. When she went to bed at night, the absence of passion seemed more like a pleasant release than a deprivation, allowing her to drift lazily into refreshing dreams, populated only by her butterflies, beetles, and the colourful fauna of the rainforest.

Wolf sometimes stopped by the lab to see what Catherine was doing but he never wandered into her dreams. Once or twice, it had occurred to her that his interest in her might be a bit more than strictly professional, especially in the light of what he had said about the money for the abortion, but she soon dismissed the idea. He was probably just being nosey. In any case, Wolf's offer of money for the abortion had certainly changed her opinion about him. Until then, she had thought she hadn't much liked him, but now she was convinced that he was nothing short of wonderful.

Bethany during this time, was so preoccupied with her new status at Nanga Palin — sometimes she almost felt that she really was Sarika's older sister — that she didn't pay much attention to her relationship with Wolf or with anyone else at Kanyalang.

The only exception to this was Elliot. She knew she should make an effort to get on with him better but she didn't know quite how to do it. It wasn't that she had anything tangible to complain about, that would actually have made things easier. It was just that he seemed increasingly cold and distant. She had a vague feeling that he held her responsible for Catherine supposedly getting pissed that night at Nanga Palin and she resented being the one blamed for it. She didn't see what she could do about it though. The truth about it all would probably just make him dislike her more.

These reflections were in the forefront of her thoughts after a lunchtime discussion in which Elliot had gone on at great length about the fact that she so rarely spent an entire day at Nanga Palin.

'Aren't you even slightly curious about what goes on there in the afternoons and evenings?' he had asked.

Bethany was well aware that she shouldn't be coming back to Kanyalang in time for lunch so often but she rationalised it on the grounds that not much happened at Nanga Palin during the hottest part of the day. Everyone who wasn't out in the rice fields usually slept through the heat of the early afternoon. By the time the longhouse came to life again, she was usually too hot and too tired to cope with the difficulties of carrying on conversations in Dayak or adding much to her store of information. She was convinced, more or less, that her afternoons were better spent analysing her data, writing up her findings, and memorising lists of vocabulary words in the invigorating coolness of her air-conditioned office.

Bethany had pointed all this out to Elliot and had emphasised that it wasn't necessary to be there all day every day to know what was going on there but he had struck her at her weak point and they both knew it.

When lunch was over Bethany had managed to put the matter out of her mind but it came back to haunt her when she went to bed that night. All the brilliant things she might have said to him, but hadn't thought of until it was too late, percolated through her imagination and kept her tossing and turning until well after midnight.

Eventually, when sleep had eluded her for over an hour, she decided that some fresh air might help. She tied on a sarong, crossed the veranda and gazed out over the rail into the jungle night. She still hadn't quite come to terms with her feelings about this mysterious world of dense greenery and improbable animals. It both fascinated her and intimidated her. She was intensely aware of its beauty and there were moments when she exulted at the thought of being in the very heart of it, but tonight wasn't one of those times. Tonight she felt repelled, even frightened, by the twisting mass of vegetation that lay beyond the security of the longhouse and she visualised it only as the domain of blood sucking leeches, poisonous snakes, and stinging insects.

With an involuntary shudder, she turned away from the railing and discovered that she was not alone. Someone else was gazing out over the veranda rail a dozen or so metres away. The size and shape of the form indicated that it might be Wolf, but the posture, defeated and dejected, wasn't like the Wolf she knew at all.

He was crumpling a much-read letter in his pocket and muttering things like 'fuck' and 'damn it' and 'why the hell' over and over to himself.

It was a good thing that Pashetta hadn't come tonight, he thought. He certainly wasn't in the mood for that kind of fun and frolics. He supposed she had her period. She always stayed away on those nights. He hoped this would be one of her long ones. She was a great kid and he liked her a lot but he was getting an uncomfortable feeling that she just might have a marriage certificate on her mind. If he could manage to let their relationship taper off gradually, that would be a lot better than bringing it to an abrupt, and possibly painful, end. But he really couldn't think about that tonight.

Bethany's first impulse on realising who she was sharing the veranda with had been to slip back to her room before he saw her but she sabotaged her retreat by stepping on an unlit mosquito coil, and the resulting clatter of the metal dish on the wooden floorboards drew his attention toward the sound.

'What are you doing wandering around at this time of night?' Wolf asked, on seeing who it was. Then, deciding that a little company might not be a bad thing, he waved his hand toward the half-empty whisky bottle he had with him and asked, 'Want a drink?'

It was evident that he had already had quite a few himself.

'No, thanks, I just came out for a breath of air.'

'Suit yourself.'

'Is something the matter?' she asked, despite the fact that it was blatantly obvious that there was.

'You could say that.'

Torn between a reluctance to pry and the desire not to appear callous, she settled on, 'Can I ask what it is?'

'It's not a secret,' he replied, with a shrug. 'My grandmother died. I just got the news today. My aunt, great-aunt, really, wrote me about it.'

The fortnightly helicopter delivering supplies and post from Putussibau had arrived that morning and she had noticed that Wolf had been a veritable snapping turtle all day.

'You must have been very fond of her,' Bethany said sympathetically.

'Hard not to be, she was a great old girl. Fierce as all hell but God only knows where I'd have been without her, or where I'd be right now for that matter.' He took several large gulps of his drink and added, 'That's something I don't like to think about.'

'Are you going back?'

'Back?' he repeated, gazing at her questioningly through his slightly drunken haze.

'To America for the funeral.'

'No point. Everything's over now. It all happened nearly a month ago. Aunt Agnes said she just died in her sleep. No warning. She'd been fine, even gone out shopping that day. It was typical of her not to make a fuss about dying. Just do it and get it over with. My aunt said she was letting me know by letter instead of anything faster so I wouldn't feel I had to come. She says Gran wouldn't have wanted me to and she's probably right. But...' Bethany could see that his mouth was twisting into a bizarre grimace. 'I'll sure as hell miss the old tigress.'

Alarmed that the moisture he felt welling up in his eyes might actually escape and stream down his face, Wolf quickly tried to change the subject. 'You never answered my question,' he reminded her.

'I forgot what it was.'

'Why you're out here at this hour.'

'I don't know. I just couldn't sleep for some reason.'

'Guilty conscience?' he teased, trying to drive his darker thoughts away.

'Not really,' she said, lightly, 'just a few doubts about things, that's all.'

'Like what?'

'Like what I'm doing here.'

'Why should you have doubts about that? You're an anthropologist, aren't you? This place should be right up your alley. And you're doing great. Mike tells me you're Little Miss Popularity at Nanga Palin these days.'

Bethany sighed. 'I wish he'd tell that to Elliot. He thinks I'm a total failure. You heard what he was saying at lunch.'

'Elliot's an idiot.'

'I'd like to believe that but it's obvious he's had it in for me ever since that time Catherine and I got so pissed at Nanga Palin.'

'You don't have to lie to me,' he said. 'Catherine told me about the abortion.'

'She did?' Bethany cried, indignantly. 'After all the trouble I went to because she wanted me to keep it a secret.'

He laughed. 'Well, you did what you could for her, didn't you?'

'I don't like to think about it, actually. I mean, I tried to help but, looking back on it, my God, she might have died and it would have been my fault.'

'Bullshit, it was her idea to go to that witch doctor, wasn't it, not yours?'

'Yes.'

'So there you are, free and clear. You just sorted out a few practical details for her, that's all,' he said, splashing more whisky into his glass.

Bethany bit her lip. 'I wish I could look at it that way.'

'Try. Believe me I know what I'm talking about.'

'You can't possibly.'

'Why can't I?'

'Because you haven't been responsible for any dangerous abortions.'

'Not for a particularly dangerous one, that's true. But I got my girlfriend pregnant senior year in high school and abortions are expensive in the States. I stole a car to get the money to pay for it.'

Bethany gaped at him through the darkness. 'Were you caught?'

'Yeah.'

'What happened?'

'My grandfather bought off the guy I'd stolen it from and gave him a shiny new Buick in exchange for dropping the charges.'

'You have a very nice grandfather.'

123

'I know that now but I didn't exactly figure it out at the time. Christ, he was so mad he had steam coming out of his ears. If it hadn't been for my mother —'

'Was she sympathetic?' Bethany asked, not entirely concealing her surprise. She had heard about permissive American parents but this was going a bit far.

'She didn't have any options. She was dead,' he said, curtly.

'But you just said —' Bethany protested, thoroughly confused.

'Sorry, I'll explain. The thing was my grandparents had disowned her, thrown her out on her ear when she got pregnant with me. You see that was back in 1965 and Gran and Granddad were already as old as the hills by then. Their attitudes about sex dated more or less from the time of the Spanish Inquisition. Free sex and flower children and single moms were an anathema to them.'

Bethany couldn't help thinking of the women at Nanga Palin and what their reaction to this sort of thing would be. 'Wasn't throwing her out a bit harsh?' she asked, deciding her theories about permissive American parents must not apply to grandparents as well.

'There was more to it than just being pregnant,' he said, grimly.

'Didn't they like your father?'

'I don't think they ever knew who my father was.'

Wolf drained the remaining whisky in his glass and then refilled it. 'Sure you won't have any?' he asked. 'It's okay to change your mind, you know.'

'Well, maybe a little,' she agreed.

He looked around for another glass but didn't see one. 'Looks like you'll have to share mine but I don't think I have any disgusting diseases.'

With an unsteady hand he splashed a generous portion of whisky into his glass and held it out to her.

She took a sip and handed it back.

'What was I saying?' he demanded, two frown lines appearing on his forehead as he tried to recall what it had been.

'About your father,' she prompted.

'Oh, yeah, whoever he was.'

'You mean you don't know?'

'Nope. You see, my mother and a couple of her friends – they were at Vassar College at the time – decided that the allowances their daddies were giving them didn't quite cover their charge accounts at Saks Fifth Avenue. So they joined one of those high-class call girl rings in New York on weekends. That was the thing my grandparents really couldn't stomach when it came to light. Being pregnant was secondary. They might have been able to deal with that but the prostitution thing was too much for them and they went ballistic. They're an old Boston family, you see, very conservative, three-piece suits, the Episcopal church, Ivy League colleges, the works. Granddad was with an investment banking firm and Gran presided over dozens of charity committees. My mother was just too wild for them.'

'What happened to her?'

'She moved to Chicago, had me, and continued in the same line of work. She was very beautiful and very successful. We had a gorgeous apartment on Lake Shore Drive and lived pretty high on the hog until I was ten. Then one of her clients slashed her up one night and she died in the hospital a few hours later.'

'God, how awful,' Bethany exclaimed, but the outrage in her voice was due more to a growing suspicion that he was putting her on than to the facts themselves. It was all beginning to sound a bit too fantastic to be true and she didn't appreciate being lied to.

'What did you do?' she asked, wondering if she would catch him out in an embarrassing contradiction.

'I ran.'

'Ran?'

'Yeah, fast! Two gruesome social workers from the Child Welfare Department came to get me. I took one look at them and that was enough to know I didn't want any part of anything they had in mind so I ran. It took them two years to catch up with me.'

'How did you live?'

'Stole food and slept rough for a while. That wasn't too bad in the summer but it gets colder than a witch's tit in Chicago in the winter. I was getting pretty damn desperate, I can tell you. But then I bumped into one of my mother's ex-clients on the street

125

and he fixed me up as a sort of errand boy and pimp for a brothel he patronised.'

Bethany found this hard to believe. 'Children who drop out of school to work in brothels at the age of ten don't usually end up with university doctorates,' she said, thinking aloud.

To her surprise, he only laughed. 'True but they don't usually have my grandparents, either.'

'Where do they come into it?' she asked.

'It was after the police raided the brothel. That time they nailed me. I was turned over to Child Welfare and dragged off to an orphanage. In the meantime, the police had been trying, in their half-arsed way, to track down my mother's killer. They never did get the bastard but in the process they had checked out her background so they had my grandparents' name and address. The Welfare people contacted them and they came and got me.'

'Lucky for you!'

'You can say that again. But life with them was a real shock at first, almost worse than the fucking orphanage. They set straight to work trying to make a human being of me, and it couldn't have been easy, I'll tell you that. They cleaned me up and sent me to school and got me a tutor to make up for the two years I'd missed. Then, when I'd caught up with my class, and learned never, ever, on pain of death, to mention the brothel or my mother's occupation to anyone, they shipped me off to Granddad's old boarding school.'

'That must have been another shock,' she said, dryly. But she was beginning to wonder if, at least, some of what he was telling her might be true.

'Yeah, but it was okay. I was good at sports so I got on alright. And I even managed to make my grandparents happy by pulling decent grades and generally keeping my nose clean, that is, until Linda got pregnant and I stole the car. That practically gave Granddad a heart attack. But in retrospect I can see that he was a prince about the whole thing.'

'Wasn't that a bit odd, I mean, considering their reaction to what your mother had done?' she asked.

'Not really. You see, they never stopped agonising over the thought that if they'd handled things differently – not thrown her out like that – they might have set her straight and she'd still be alive. And I guess as far as I was concerned they realised that even the best schools couldn't completely hammer out the bad influences of the Chicago years. Or maybe they just decided I'd inherited some bad genes from my unknown father, I don't really know. Anyway, they took a very different tack with me. Of course, they gave me holy hell about Linda and about my brief career as a car thief. They even cancelled my graduation present, a zippy, little sports car with five forward gears. Let me tell you, a knife through the heart could hardly have been worse than making me give that up. They inflicted a few other parental-type tortures on me too but that one surpassed them by a mile. Still, I've got to say, they stood by me. I suspect that Gran, under that fierce exterior of hers, was a secret romantic. As much as she disapproved of my having had sex with Linda, she thought that engaging in a few criminal activities to get her an abortion was better than any of the alternatives.'

'Alternatives, what were they?'

'Sabotaging my own future by marrying her, I guess, or leaving her to cope with the joys of being a single mom on her own.'

'And your grandfather, was he a romantic, too?'

'God, no, he was a hard-arsed old codger, if ever there was one, but you couldn't help respecting him. I couldn't, anyway. But he died during my third year at Harvard. And now Gran…'

Even through the darkness, Bethany could see his face twist into an ugly contortion that for a moment made her think he was going to cry.

She had never actually seen a man cry before and the thought that macho, arrogant Wolf, of all people, might do such a thing sent her into a panic. She desperately tried to think of some comforting thing to say but her mind went blank. Unable to think of any words, she resorted to talking with her hands. Impulsively she placed one of them on each side of his face with her fingers covering his eyes, almost as if she were making a wall to hold back his tears. She held them there until she sensed that he was regaining control. Then she deftly moved her fingers across his cheekbones and brushed his tousled hair back from his forehead.

'Thanks,' he muttered hoarsely, feeling as though some of his pain had actually been smoothed away.

'For what?'

'I don't know, exactly — for listening, I guess, and for this impromptu little massage but mostly for just being here for me when I was feeling like shit.'

'It was an accident really,' she told him truthfully. 'I only happened to be here because I couldn't sleep.'

'To hell with the reason, you were here and that's what counts. It'll be easier for me to sleep now,' he said firmly and, gulping down the last of the whisky, he went quickly back to his room.

CHAPTER THIRTEEN

The next morning Bethany smiled tremulously at Wolf across the breakfast table. She had lain awake for a long time after their midnight conversation, mulling over the things he had told her about himself. Things she hadn't understood about him before – like why, in spite of his intelligence and his education, he was still a bit rough around the edges – seemed clear to her now. She was even starting to see why he had chosen the career he had. None of the massive contradictions in his life would seem very important in the rainforest. She wondered if he would ever really belong anywhere, except possibly in a place like Kanyalang, and decided that most likely he wouldn't.

Eventually she had dropped off to sleep and, although she didn't actually remember dreaming about Wolf, she sort of suspected she had. Therefore she was disappointed and thoroughly annoyed when he just went on drinking his coffee and eating his papaya without giving her any indication that he even remembered their conversation the night before, much less that it had meant anything to him.

On the contrary, he seemed to be making a distinct effort to avoid her. This became blatantly obvious when, after going down the veranda steps shortly after her, he muttered something about being in a rush and hurried off toward the hotel before she had a chance to say a word.

Well, she thought, trying to shrug off the rebuff, if last night's confidences hadn't meant anything to him, she wouldn't let them mean anything to her either. And on that note she turned her steps firmly toward the path to Nanga Palin.

It was quite true that Bethany was the last person Wolf wanted to see. The memory of all he had told her utterly mortified him in the morning light. Plus there was the fact that until last night he had followed his grandmother's instructions to the letter and never talked about his past to anyone, not that that had been any hardship. Advertising it was the last thing he wanted to do. Still, he couldn't help feeling a little guilty that as soon as he had heard about her death he had thrown her instructions to the winds. Well, that was just one of the reasons he hoped Bethany would forget everything he had said.

Bethany didn't forget but when she arrived at Nanga Palin she found that she didn't have much time to think about it. Being an effective participant observer in Dayak life, navigating her way through the intricacies of it all, still required her close attention if she didn't want to mess up or do something awful.

Today she found herself the recipient of so much kindness it was actually hard to handle. Sarika greeted her with a glass of hot sweet tea and shortly after that Thumbi insisted that she try a bowl of the fish head soup she had just made. She had barely finished it when Motut, a boy of about twelve who frequently played truant from school but was quick at picking up bits of English from Bethany, presented her with a fresh coconut, saying he had picked it especially for her and standing shyly by to watch her drink it. She hadn't had the heart to disappoint him.

The result of all this liquid was predictable. She had to pee and this was something she didn't much like doing at Nanga Palin. After delaying the inevitable as long as possible, she reluctantly made her way down to the small bamboo structure, about the size of a telephone box, that had been built out over the river. She closed its flimsy door behind her and squatted down over a strategically positioned hole in the floor.

The sound of clattering metal plates along with laughing chatter nearby indicated that dishes were being washed a little too close, in Bethany's opinion, to the loo. This was an aspect of Dayak life she still found rather off-putting, and, whenever possible, she elected to eat off a banana leaf instead of a plate that had been washed in the river.

The grannies were delighted with her preference for their traditional way of serving food. They didn't see the point of using plates when banana leaves cost nothing and could be thrown away after the meal was over. But, as they reminded each other with grave resignation, young people wanted to do things the modern way, no matter how much trouble it was.

When Bethany emerged from the bamboo enclosure, she guessed from all the giggling that the dishwashers were regaling each other with tales of the previous night's adventures. As often happened, a group of boys from a neighbouring longhouse had come over to flirt with, and hopefully have sex with, the Nanga Palin girls.

Bethany understood that this custom was something of a social necessity as young people who had toddled around on the same veranda together since infancy were generally too much like brothers and sisters to fancy each other as marriage partners. It was just one of the many things about Dayak life that made her realise how clever these people were. Without the benefit of test tubes or scientific equipment they had figured out that the mixing of bloodlines was genetically desirable.

Drawn by the fun of listening to the teasing and the gossip that inevitably followed these nocturnal visits, she sauntered over and joined the cluster of dishwashers. The trouble was that when they talked rapidly to each other, rather than speaking directly to her, it wasn't always easy to follow what they were saying. Today she was certain she must have got it wrong. It sounded like Giri, Sarika's very pretty cousin, was saying something like, 'he had three sticks through his cock.' What's more she was saying it gleefully, not at all as if the man in question had been the victim of a dreadful accident.

'Three,' Bethany could have sworn she heard one of Giri's companions exclaim, 'I haven't ever had sex with anyone who had more than two.'

Bethany shook her head in despair over her dismal progress in learning the language. She hadn't realised she had done that badly.

Then she thought she heard a slightly older girl say something like, 'That's pathetic, wait 'til you have sex with a man who has four sticks, that's when it's really good.'

'Did you see my little brother yesterday?' Giri asked, laughing.

'You mean Banyam?' asked her friend.

Giri nodded. 'Remember how he strutted around boasting about all the sticks he was going to have? Well, even though he sat in the river all morning so his willy would be cold enough to numb the pain, he ran away screaming before even one stick was all the way through.'

Everyone fell about laughing.

'What happened then?' demanded one of the girls.

'It dropped off.'

'The stick or his willy?' someone asked.

Unrestrained hilarity ensued.

'The stick,' Giri gasped, when she was able to speak again. 'Now no girl will ever want to have sex with him.'

Joining in the conversation but still scarcely able to believe that she hadn't misunderstood, Bethany said, 'But poor Banyam, wouldn't something like that hurt terribly?'

'He certainly thought so,' replied Giri, bursting out in a fresh gale of laughter.

'No, no,' Bethany corrected her, 'I mean, wouldn't it be agony for any girl to have sex with him?'

Everyone regarded her with amazement.

'No, when the skin grows back over the end of the stick, it makes it more exciting,' declared Giri. 'Don't the men in your country do it?'

'Definitely not.'

'Bad luck for you then,' Giri said, sympathetically. 'Men in your country must not be very good at sex.'

'They aren't,' Bethany agreed glumly, but refrained from adding that she didn't think putting sticks through their willies would improve them any.

When the dishes were as clean as they were ever going to be and Bethany had come to terms, more or less, with this new bit of information about life and love amongst the Dayaks, she went back up to the longhouse for a lesson in mat-weaving from Thumbi.

It looked so easy, she had watched the other women doing it, she was confident she could master it in no time. But when she actually tried to plait the strips of pandanus leaves into a creditable mat herself, the result had so many bumps and gaps in it that Thumbi insisted she unravel the entire thing and start again.

This activity kept her fingers busy but left her thoughts free to wander where they would and, before long, they drifted back to Wolf.

She wondered if he'd told Pashetta any of the things he had told her the night before. She doubted it, partly because she didn't believe that talking was the main thing they did together and partly because she wasn't convinced that there was that much of an emotional bond between them.

It seemed to Bethany that Catherine was the only person, other than Mike, who showed any sign of liking Wolf these days. Of course, Catherine was probably one of those women who always had to be in love with someone and now, without Tarique around anymore, Wolf had become the most likely one to take his place. He clearly liked her but then everybody did.

I'd give a good deal to know how in the world she manages it, Bethany thought a bit enviously. It had to be more than just her looks that drew everyone to her, although she certainly had that going for her too. She had an inner quality that just shone out and made people love her – something that Marguarita, who was far more beautiful, didn't have.

Marguarita could command a certain kind of admiration, Bethany decided, but nobody would say they really loved her.

This was not entirely true.

Jim Nathan, lying on a cot in a gold mining camp along the upper reaches of the Kahayan River, was thinking about Marguarita, if not exactly with love, with the kind of intense desire that is often taken for love.

He was recovering from a virulent bout of haemorrhagic fever and it had left him weak, fretful and utterly disinterested in anything related to work. During the long days when his temperature had soared into the danger zone and blood had oozed through the pores of his skin, Jim hadn't thought of anything except cool fresh water. But now, the worst was over and as the long days of convalescence dragged by he found himself more and more frequently falling prey to memories of the night he had almost spent with Marguarita.

Who the hell would have thought there could be such an attractive woman hidden away in the middle of the jungle, he had asked himself over and over again? And what had happened that night? Everything had seemed to be going his way until suddenly, for no reason he could see, she had frozen him out. Yet she didn't seem at all like the cock teasing kind of female, nor he did get the feeling that she had been having it off with any of the guys around Kanyalang.

Maybe it hadn't been her fault that things hadn't worked out that night. He might have botched things up somehow. It was a disconcerting idea and not one he was used to having because he was generally pretty successful with women. Still, he had to admit that it probably served him right to come up against a little resistance now and then. But why did it have to happen just when he was about to score with the sexiest woman he had met in years?

He'd just have to see her again and give himself another chance to make things go right, he told himself. That was the thing to do but it wouldn't be easy. A gold miner who had his eye on their precious conservation area would be about as welcome as a case of bubonic plague in that den of super-green types, not that he was apt to be looking for gold much longer. It was pretty obvious that Fairbanks Mining & Exploration was going exactly nowhere fast. And with the world gold price down in the cellar, finding another job was going to be tough. Most of the higher cost operations would be closing down because only a strike of enormous proportions could possibly bring in enough profits to make it worthwhile.

He was glad that grease ball Don had taken his accounts and his laptop and his dubious stock certificates and oiled his way back to the head office. He was just the kind of guy you'd expect to find around a cheap-shit operation like Fairbanks. The whole idea of working for such a shady company had been pretty hard to take but he hadn't had much choice. With only the big established companies doing any exploration at all these days, those places were deluged with job applications from out-of-work geologists like himself, guys who had been made redundant when the price of gold had tanked.

Yet gradually as his health improved, so did his spirits. The more he thought about Marguarita, the more determined he became to go back to Kanyalang and run the gauntlet of her hostile colleagues, including the obnoxious one with the animal name, and see her again. And if they gave him the shove he'd just tie his sleeping hammock to a couple of trees the way the Dayaks did and climb into it. And with any luck, he thought with an expectant chuckle, it wouldn't be long until he'd have Marguarita in it with him.

Springing out of bed with a new-found energy, and then cursing his legs for wobbling unsteadily under him, Jim went in search of his boss to arrange for some of his overdue vacation time.

As it happened, he needn't have bothered.

'I gotta tell you, you're going to get time off whether you want it or not,' Greg Mills, the operations manager, told him, 'and it starts today. I just got the news. The company's gone bust.'

'No shit,' Jim exclaimed. And then went on to add, philosophically, 'I had a hunch something like this might happen.'

'And I'm sorry to say,' Mills continued, 'you've seen your last pay cheque. We all have. Those fuckers back in Fairbanks are being hauled into court for bankruptcy and fraud.'

'Fraud?' Jim echoed, wanting to sound thoroughly surprised but doubting if he was really managing it. He had learned a lot about what the company was doing when he took Don around on that jungle tour and he didn't want to be tagged as an accomplice.

'Yeah, and maybe a grand larceny charge on top of that,' Mills went on bitterly, 'although there seems to be some doubt about whether or not that one's gonna stick. Anyway it looks like you and me are free men as of right now.'

'Okay, if that's the way it is,' Jim said, his anger partially mitigated by a returning wave of weakness. He reached for the back of a chair to steady himself.

'Hey, you don't look too good,' Mills observed. 'You better sit down.'

Jim followed his advice.

'I tell you what you gotta do,' Mills continued, 'if you want to stay around these parts, that is. You gotta get yourself to Balikpapan.

135

That place is jumping with jobs and it's got plenty of cold beer and hot chicks – better than a doctor's prescription, if you ask me. That should set you up in no time.'

'Is that what you're going to do, head for Balikpapan?'

'Me? Hell no. I'm fed up with steaming hell holes like this. I'm getting my arse Stateside quick as I can.'

Jim wasn't quite sure what he wanted to do with himself. He didn't think he needed doctors, just a few more days of rest should do the trick. The problem was that didn't seem to be an option right now so maybe Balikpapan wasn't such a bad idea. He doubted that he was quite up for the hot chicks yet but the cold beer didn't sound all bad.

'Those jobs, they're mostly oil company jobs, aren't they?' Jim asked.

'Yeah, oil and logging – although of course it's the oil companies that need guys like you to sniff around with Geiger counters.'

'I just wish that was true but those companies have probably got swarms of guys banging at their doors begging for jobs.'

'Well, try the logging companies then. Balikpapan's crawling with them.'

'Logging's a shitty business,' Jim growled, almost surprising himself at his vehemence.

'Hey, you haven't gone all green on me, have you?' Mills exclaimed, wondering if he could have heard him right.

'Just a joke,' Jim replied, suddenly wondering if lying around having fantasies about screwing Marguarita had somehow messed up his brain, 'but the thing is, logging companies don't need geologists to tell them where the fucking trees are.'

'No, you've got it all wrong,' Mills declared. 'You got to look at what they do need, not what they don't. And they need guys that know their way around the jungle. That could include you.'

Jim looked doubtful.

'And on top of that,' Mills continued, 'you got yourself a college degree, haven't you? They might snap you up for something on the admin side.'

'Yeah, maybe – I'll think about it,' Jim said, knowing that he wouldn't. Christ, if he ever showed up at Kanyalang announcing that he was working for a logging company, he'd be lucky if his head was the first thing they cut off.

Still the fact remained that he'd have to do something with the rest of his life. The question was, what? He liked the freedom and the adventure of the jungle and he didn't want to give that up. But the hell of it was that the companies, mostly logging, oil, or gold, that might take him on for a jungle assignment would basically be paying him to destroy it.

Why the hell hadn't he ever thought of that before, he wondered? How could he have been such a fucking idiot?

He supposed it was just that the jungle had always seemed so vast and so unconquerable that a few incursions into it here and there wouldn't make any difference. But now he was getting a feeling that Marguarita and that green bunch at Kanyalang actually knew what they were talking about. Maybe up to now he'd just seen what he wanted to see. Or was it only that at this particular moment he was thinking with his dick, as he did all too often. Still, the fact was that his dick and his wallet were the two most important things in his life and if he didn't look out for their interests, who would?

Jim was still feeling a little shaky the next day when he climbed into a long-tailed boat to begin the journey to Balikpapan but the prospect of a cold beer fortified his spirits and he promised himself that it wouldn't be long before he'd be ready for the hot chicks. They'd sort him out and set him straight on the subject of all that green stuff, he predicted.

To his surprise, it didn't exactly work out that way.

CHAPTER FOURTEEN

While Jim was drifting down the Kahayan River wondering what to do with his life, and Bethany was trying to learn the art of mat-making from Thumbi, Mike and the men on his patrol were caught in an unexpected downpour.

Mike didn't really mind the rain. After growing up on an arid sheep station in Queensland, he rather liked it but his companions didn't share his attitude. They glumly sought whatever shelter they could find, generally beneath large, leafy branches, and patiently waited for the downpour to end.

What the hell, Mike thought, peering at his watch, why keep the poor bastards out any longer? After all, it was getting late and they weren't going to get much more done today. And noting that they weren't very far from Nanga Palin, he decided to drop in there and get a cup of tea off Thumbi before trekking back to Kanyalang.

'Okay guys,' Mike announced, 'that's enough for today.'

Everyone except Raran greeted this news with enthusiasm.

Raran was standing still as a statue, his eyes fixed on a point some ten feet above the ground and twenty or thirty feet away.

'Hey, what's up?' Mike asked, instinct telling him to keep his voice unusually low.

'Clouded leopard,' Raran said, raising his blowpipe to a defensive position.

'Are you sure?' Mike demanded.

Ordinarily he wouldn't have questioned Raran's powers of observation but clouded leopards were nocturnal creatures, solitary and secretive. They were seldom seen by human beings at all, and never in the daytime.

'Wounded,' Raran explained, in an undertone, 'see the way it moves – not right.'

'Better go for it then,' Mike said, standing back while his men crept silently toward the dangerous cat. He hated putting all the risk on them while he kept safely out of the way but he knew that when it came to the stealthy pursuit of an animal through the rainforest, he was no match for these Dayak guys. They could slip through the dense vegetation without making the slightest sound, whereas he, clod that he was, would be sure to snap a twig or rustle a branch with just about every step he took.

They were gone longer than he expected and Mike was beginning to wonder what had happened when four embarrassed faces came into view and reported that their efforts had been unsuccessful.

The rain had nearly blinded them, they explained, emphasising that they hadn't been able to see more than a few feet in front of them.

Mike knew that the clouded leopard would have been hard to see even in more favourable circumstances. With its black spots and grey coat, the creature would have been too well camouflaged to stand out in the perpetual twilight of the deep forest.

He would just have to bring these guys back and try again when the rain stopped, Mike decided, and for a moment, he thought this solution was good enough. Then he remembered that Bethany hadn't come back to Kanyalang for lunch so presumably she was still at Nanga Palin. Although it was generally understood that project staff didn't venture into the jungle alone, there was some doubt about whether or not the well-travelled path to Nanga Palin counted as no-go territory for a solitary walker.

Mike knew that Bethany sometimes went back and forth by herself.

'It's my only time to be alone and just think about things,' she had protested, when he had warned her that she really should have somebody with her.

He knew what she meant. He had the same need himself, so he had convinced himself that she probably wasn't in any danger. But now, with a clouded leopard in the vicinity, a wounded one at that, the situation was suddenly quite different. He realised that he'd better warn her about it and bring her home himself.

Bethany was still struggling with her mat when Mike got to Nanga Palin and told her about the leopard.

Much as she hated to relinquish her freedom to come and go on her own, she didn't relish the prospect of being leapt on by a hungry leopard.

'It'll just be for a little while,' he assured her when he saw her mouth turn down at the corners, 'until we can take care of it, one way or another.'

'What does that mean?'

'Put it out of its misery if we have to but preferably just make sure it's not a danger to humans in the area.'

Bethany felt a momentary wave of sympathy for the leopard but her sentiments changed when, on their way back to Kanyalang, Mike pointed to a scarred tree branch and said, 'This is where we saw it, just in there.'

'I don't see anything,' she said, peering cautiously into the tangled undergrowth.

'Neither do I right now,' said Mike, 'but that doesn't mean we can let down our guard. Remember, if it's hungry — and it might get very hungry if it can't hunt well in its current condition — it could leap down on you from any of these branches before you had a chance to realise what was happening.'

'Actually, would you mind not scaring the shit out of me,' she said. 'I've got to come back along here tomorrow and the next day and the next and you're making me absolutely terrified.'

'That's exactly what I'm trying to do,' he explained, patiently, 'for your own safety, you know.'

'Yes, but you don't need to —'

'Yes, I do. I want to make sure you take the whole thing really seriously.'

'Don't worry, I'll be careful,' she promised. Her nerves were getting more fraught by the moment and by the time they reached the clearing around Kanyalang she was straining her peripheral vision to make sure that nothing was lurking in the foliage waiting to pounce.

Then suddenly something did pounce — at least, it swooped out of a tree, sailed through the air only inches from her right ear, and sent her into such a panic that she shrieked and threw herself onto Mike for protection.

'Silly,' he said, his voice particularly growly as he gave her a reassuring hug. 'That was just a flying fox, a kind of bat, you know. It won't hurt you unless you go after it first.'

'I'm not about to do that,' she declared, lingering longer than strictly necessary in his comforting embrace.

Pashetta was looking out over the veranda rail to see if there was any sign of Wolf when, to her astonishment, she caught sight of Bethany flinging herself into Mike's arms.

'Bethany likes Mike very much,' she told Wolf later that evening when the others had all drifted off to bed and they were alone together on the veranda.

'What makes you say that?'

'I saw them hugging and kissing each other for ages and ages, over there near the path to Nanga Palin,' she said, a mischievous sparkle lighting up her eyes.

'Are you sure?' he demanded, drawing his brows together in a frown that made his beaky nose seem longer than ever.

'Of course, I am sure,' she said, disappointed at his reaction. 'I saw them there all wrapped around each other. What were they doing if they were not kissing?'

Wolf had to admit that he couldn't think of anything.

'Are you angry with me?' Pashetta asked, amazed that he still showed no sign of enjoying her bit of news. 'I can't help it if Mike and Bethany were kissing like that.'

'Of course, not,' he agreed, trying to muster up a patience he didn't feel. He knew that Pashetta wasn't a liar. It didn't occur to him that she might be the victim of an over-active imagination.

'And do you know what Bethany –' she began.

'Let's just drop it, shall we,' he snapped, no longer trying to hide his annoyance.

Eager to get away, he seized on the first escape route that came to mind. 'I've got some work to do,' he told her, untruthfully, 'so I'd better get down to it.'

'At this hour?'

'Yes, unfortunately.'

'But you never work this late,' she pouted.

'I'm turning over a new leaf,' Wolf said, not noticing that this way of putting things was too idiomatic for her. Instead, it flashed through his mind that while he was turning over one new leaf, he might just as well turn over two, at least for now. He had been toying with the idea of breaking it off with Pashetta for some time and maybe this was the moment to do it. He'd miss the sex, of course, but he was becoming more and more convinced that she had some kind of agenda in mind and that it involved more of a commitment than he had any intention of making. If that was true, then the sooner he opted out, the better. And right now, for some reason, he was in the mood to do exactly that.

'You know,' he began, groping for a way to be completely clear, yet moderately tactful at the same time, 'I think we'd better cool it for a while, not see so much of each other.'

'But why?' Pashetta exclaimed, stunned by this sudden rejection.

'Let's put it this way,' he said, seeing the puzzled expression on her face and fervently wishing himself elsewhere. 'Why don't we try just being friends for a while?'

Shit, he thought, I can't believe I'm resorting to that worn out old line.

It didn't seem worn out to Pashetta but it didn't seem comprehensible either. 'We are friends,' she reminded him, shaking her head in confusion.

'I mean just friends, only friends, nothing more,' he said, in a lame attempt at explaining what he meant.

'Oh,' she replied, grasping his meaning, 'you mean, no sex.'

Putting the matter this bluntly made him feel like a real shit and he found himself backtracking a little. 'Yeah, just for a little while, now that I've got so much work to do.'

Pashetta looked unconvinced.

He cursed himself for not coming up with a better excuse but, since he hadn't, he decided to make this one sound a little more creditable. 'The thing is,' he began, in the most persuasive tone he could muster, 'I've got most of Tarique's work to do and I generally end up doing at least half of Elliot's job on top of that because he doesn't get around to doing it himself. I'm really going crazy with it all. But maybe when things ease up a bit, we can see how…' He noticed that she wasn't listening and trailed off.

An idea had dawned on her and she was glaring at him suspiciously. 'Is something wrong with you?' she asked.

It was his turn to look puzzled.

'Did you catch something from bad Dayak girls?' she demanded, in a voice quite unlike the caressing one she generally used with him.

'Good God, no,' he exclaimed, taken aback by the question, 'that's not it at all.'

'Then what is it? Why do you not like me anymore?'

'I do like you but —'

'But you like Catherine better?'

'No I don't.'

'I think you are telling me lies. You do like her,' Pashetta persisted.

'Of course, I like her but that's not the point.'

Pashetta didn't ask what the point was because it seemed all too clear. He was simply tired of her and unless she could think of some way to change that, all hope of going to live in America would be gone completely.

She made a brave attempt to keep the bitter disappointment from showing in her face as Wolf mumbled something about getting down to work and left her alone by the veranda rail.

For the second time that day, Pashetta turned and gazed out at the menacing green of the jungle that always seemed to be pressing relentlessly in on Kanyalang.

Foreigners were so lucky, she thought, with an envy born of desperation. What did it matter if they were big and ugly? She'd gladly be big and ugly too, even have a red face and round eyes and a nose that looked like an aubergine the way they did if she could be as rich as they were. She'd even eat disgusting things like cheese and not care about it making her smell like a goat if she could go anywhere in the world, live wherever she wanted, and do whatever she felt like in a place where no one cared whether girls were virgins or not. Even Dayaks were better off when it came to that kind of freedom than her own Orang Melayu people were.

She recalled her aunties' opinions on the behaviour of foreign women. 'They carry on like animals,' one of them had reported after a visit to the cinema. 'They wallow in their feelings without a thought for the dishonour they bring down on their families.'

'They don't have any sense of honour,' another auntie had said while the others nodded in agreement.

The memory of that conversation made Pashetta want to cry. Why couldn't she have been born into a family unburdened by a strict Islamic code of honour? What had that code ever done for her except cause her to be cast out by her parents, shunned by her neighbours and cut off from any kind of future in the life she had been born to.

Well, she couldn't change her past, she reflected, but she could and would do something about her future. And she was going to do it by marrying someone who would take her far away from everyone who had reviled and rejected her, someone who would take her to a glorious life in one of those magical foreign countries she was always hearing about.

Was it really too late to get Wolf back, she wondered, maybe not. Perhaps he was telling the truth when he claimed he just liked Catherine a little. But if that was true and if he didn't have one of those nasty diseases then why didn't he want to have sex with her anymore?

Maybe he's just having stress, she decided, and that's what's keeping him from being able to do any sex. After all he does have a lot of work to do. If that's all it is, then it's only a small problem. The Chinese have good medicines for that, ones that can make a man get it up and keep it up for a long, long time. She smiled to herself, remembering the time when Charles, just for a lark, had bought some from the Chinese apothecary near the school and they had tried it. They had been completely exhausted afterwards but it had been fun while it lasted – and it had lasted and lasted and lasted.

Yes, she must get some for Wolf. Perhaps she could buy it in one of the Chinese shops in Putussibau and somehow slip it to him without his knowing what it was but she'd better make sure what was really going on first. She didn't want to go to the trouble and expense of getting it just to have him use it with Catherine.

Pashetta decided to watch and wait.

CHAPTER FIFTEEN

The dinner table was a good place to watch people, Pashetta decided, after she had spent a few days and nights being 'just friends' with Wolf. If you were sitting across the table from someone, you really couldn't do anything but look at them. And if they were eating fish, as they were all doing tonight and trying to avoid the bones, they didn't notice if you were staring at them.

This left her free to watch Wolf and Catherine and observe any exchanges that might go on between them.

At first, the conversation was general. Exclamations of delight rose from almost everyone when Kolop triumphantly set an enormous fish, charcoal-grilled and flavoured with turmeric and ginger, down on the table. He was justifiably proud of his prowess both as a fisherman and as a cook, and tonight his skills met with all the appreciation he could hope for. There was general agreement that this particular specimen was nothing less than a sea-monster and everyone except Catherine dug into it with great enthusiasm.

'Damn,' she exclaimed, seeing that she had managed to help herself to a good part of the skeleton along with the flesh. 'Why am I always so hopeless when it comes to fish bones?'

'You just do it like this,' Wolf said, reaching over, taking her plate and, with surgical precision, removing the bones.

Pashetta eyed this procedure narrowly, suspecting that Catherine's clumsiness had been deliberate and wishing she had pretended to be equally incompetent herself.

Catherine, whose difficulties had actually been quite real, marvelled at how kind Wolf was being and wondered if he could have been like that all along but she had just been too obsessed with Tarique to notice.

Bima couldn't help wishing that he had been sitting next to Catherine so that he could have been the one to solve the fish bone problem for her. Still, he would have thought that she would have learned to do it herself by now. Certainly Kolop cooked it often enough. But then there were a lot of puzzling things about Catherine, he decided, things that were far more important than fish bones, like how quickly she had got over Tarique's death. He'd have thought her feelings went deeper than that.

If you loved me, would a few weeks be enough for you to forget me, Bima asked silently across the table.

This thought upset him so much that he failed to pay attention to the bones in his own fish, swallowed one, and succumbed to an alarming fit of choking.

Mike pounded him on the back. Elliot told him to eat a spoonful of rice, and Catherine offered him a banana. Nothing really helped until a strangle thrust, administered just under the ribcage by Wolf, dislodged the bone and came perilously close to making him disgorge the rest of the fish as well.

Later that evening Bima, still feeling a bit shaken, was having a beer on the veranda when Catherine slipped onto the rattan sofa beside him.

'You gave us all quite a fright at dinner tonight,' she said.

'I don't know why I was such an idiot,' he replied, ruefully.

'You weren't anything of the sort. I just wish Kolop didn't enjoy fishing so much, that's all. I'm getting very tired of eating the result.'

'Then we shouldn't have it,' he declared. 'You're getting awfully thin.'

'That's because of the climate. Who can feel hungry in all this heat?'

'I can,' Bima confessed.

'Even with Kolop's cooking?'

'There isn't much variety,' he acknowledged, 'but that's okay. At least it's good and spicy.'

'Too spicy for me,' said Catherine.

'My girlfriend, ex-girlfriend actually, wouldn't like it either.'

'Is that why she doesn't come out here?'

Bima laughed. 'It wouldn't have been much of a relationship, would it, if a few curries would have put her off?'

'Was it much of a relationship?' Catherine asked.

'I thought it was.'

'What happened?'

'Geography, basically, she has a job and a life back in Amsterdam.'

'She has holidays too, hasn't she?'

'Of course.'

'Then can't she come out here sometimes?'

Bima looked doubtful. 'This isn't her sort of place. She's not the kind of woman who'd like to come and sit around while I was working. She likes to lead her own life and go her own way.'

'This isn't the Middle Ages,' Catherine pointed out, helpfully. 'Most women like to do their own thing, although…' She hesitated. 'I hate to say this because it's so totally politically incorrect but –'

'Go on,' he urged. 'Why worry about being politically correct in the middle of the jungle, or anywhere else, for that matter?'

'Well, I'm not completely sure that going our own way makes us all that happy, really.'

'That's a rather extraordinary thing for someone like you to say.'

'Why me, especially?'

'Because you're a woman with a very demanding career, one that must have taken years of study, and you're obviously very committed to it.'

'Yes, but –'

'I wouldn't be surprised if you dreamed about centipedes and butterflies and bearcats and things at night,' he teased.

'Beetles, most likely,' Catherine said with a smile. 'There're more of them around than anything else.'

A moment later she was serious again. 'But we were talking about happiness, remember?'

'Well, yes,' Bima said, 'but what do you mean?'

'I think that being absorbed in a successful career is enough to make a man reasonably happy, even if his personal life is rotten, but it's not the same for women. Relationships are always the most important thing for us. They colour everything and if they aren't good, well, it's sort of like being on the edge of a yawning void, no matter what's happening on the professional side.'

'Good God,' exclaimed Bima, horrified, 'you don't feel that you're on the edge of some kind of void, do you?'

'Sometimes I do.'

'You mean since Tarique died?'

'No, actually, I felt more that way when he was alive.' And in response to the astonished expression on his face, she explained, 'You see, things weren't always that great between us. In fact, more often than not, they were awful, especially toward the end. There were times when I even hated him.'

'Then why didn't you break off with him?' Bima gasped, utterly astonished.

'I don't know, I sort of loved him and hated him at the same time, I suppose. Can you understand that?'

'To be honest, I can't, but then maybe women are just more complicated than men – either that, or I'm a complete dolt. I'm not sure which.'

'You're not a dolt. You're a darling, the nicest man I've met in ages.'

'That sounds like the kiss of death,' he protested, feeling that his hopes, never very high where Catherine was concerned, were crashing down around him.

'Don't jump to conclusions,' she smiled, reading the expression on his face. And on impulse, she reached up and kissed him on the mouth.

'There,' she murmured, drawing away, 'that wasn't death, was it?'

'No.'

'Do you dare risk it again?'

'I might, if properly persuaded, that is,' he replied with a laugh. And pulling her into his arms, he continued kissing her until the tread of someone's feet on the veranda floorboards made them jump apart.

'Don't mind me,' Wolf said, heading past them toward the kitchen. 'I'll just get myself a beer and be out of your way.'

The mood of the evening was broken. They remembered they were colleagues, not lovers, and hastily said good-night.

Jim Nathan, whose life was uncomplicated by colleagues or lovers at the moment, was sitting glumly in the Mermaid Bar in Balikpapan.

He had been there for a number of weeks now but the guys he had found to be drinking buddies alternately annoyed or bored him. And the girls he had found didn't really turn him on. Not very much anyway.

As the bartender handed him his sixth, or maybe it was his seventh, beer of the evening Jim let his mind drift back to that night at Kanyalang when he had come so close to scoring with Marguarita. But then he had screwed up somehow - not that there was really any doubt about how. No guy who turned up in that hotbed of ecological correctness would have a hope of getting laid after letting on that he was out to start up a gold mine in a conservation area.

But he was a geologist, for God's sake, and his bank balance was screaming for reinforcements. He had no choice but to work for companies that were prospecting for oil or gold. And with the world price for both those commodities down in the cellar, he was hard pressed to get the guys who did the hiring to even talk to him. They were deluged with job applications from out-of-work rock-hunters. But who else would take him on? Not anyone at a greener-than green joint like Kanyalang, that was for sure. Those guys probably wouldn't give him a job mucking out pig shit.

A friendly slap on the back distracted him from his thoughts and he swung around to face one of his frequent drinking companions, a barrel-chested fellow named Matt.

'Hey, there, what'll you have?' Matt asked. 'I'm buying.'

This was astonishing news. Jim had never known Matt to fork over a buck for anything that he had a chance of getting someone else to pay for.

'It's my lucky day,' Matt continued. 'I just got a job with the new Korean bunch that's just come into town.'

'Loggers?' Jim asked, knowing that was what most of the Koreans around were involved in.

'Yeah, I gotta admit it's a rinky-dink firm, new in the business, and I'm shit scared they're gonna go bust before they get around to paying me. But the way things're going these days, you gotta take what you can get.'

151

Jim couldn't argue with that. At least, Matt had a chance of a pay cheque. That was more than he could say for himself but it certainly wasn't the kind of pay cheque that would buy him any points with Marguarita. It would definitely be dirty money in her book. She'd probably think that mucking out pig shit was a damn sight too good for him if he had any logging money in his pocket, not that that mattered. He hadn't seen any pigs around Kanyalang anyway.

Jim's memory was correct. Kanyalang had been a pig-free zone when he had been there. In deference to Tarique's and Pashetta's religion, as well as to any Muslim visitors who might be about at mealtime, Elliot had been firm about not having pork on the table. But now that Tarique was dead and Pashetta had admitted to having tried the forbidden meat in a Chinese restaurant, the cries for a more varied diet had grown increasingly vociferous. Kolop had pressed to be allowed to cook pork, always a favourite at Nanga Palin, and the ban on the pig had been lifted.

Kolop had been over the moon and had immediately purchased several piglets in the market in Putussibau. He also began buying chunks of wild boar meat from the people at Nanga Palin whenever they brought one down with a blowgun. But meat from the domesticated piglets was far more tender than that from their wild cousins so replacement piglets frequently had to be acquired.

Elliot had raised no objections but Bima had lodged a brief protest on Pashetta's behalf.

'How would you feel if you were sitting at the table during a cannibal feast,' he had demanded, 'even if you weren't actually eating human flesh, yourself?'

Wolf, who not only liked pork but had a lot of time for pigs, considering them to be highly intelligent animals, had replied that cannibals didn't sit at tables and had given Kolop the money to buy half a dozen. He had then gone on to oversee the construction of their enclosure and, in a moment of whimsy that surprised his colleagues, hung a sign saying 'Piglets Residence' on the gate.

Wolf was less sure about the intelligence and general characteristics of clouded leopards, sightings of them in the wild were so rare, but the thought of a wounded one in the vicinity worried him so he decided to check out the spot where Mike had seen the cat.

An examination of the ground in the area yielded no clues to the animal's current whereabouts so Wolf began searching the lower branches of a strangler fig. He was just pushing aside some leaves in order to get a better view when the swoosh of an arrow made him leap aside just nano-seconds before it would have relieved him of his left ear.

The next moment Santuk, a Nanga Palin teenager who had been hired for the purpose of accompanying Bethany whenever she went beyond the outer perimeter of Kanyalang, emerged from the foliage, blowpipe in hand.

'What the fuck do you think you're doing?' exploded Wolf.

'Hunt monkey. See branch move. Think maybe you monkey,' Santuk replied, breaking into a hearty laugh.

Wolf was less amused. 'Aren't you supposed to be keeping an eye on Bethany?' he demanded, looking around. 'Where the hell is she anyway?'

'Nanga Palin.'

'Well, you'd better get back there,' Wolf ordered, sternly. 'She may be ready to pack it in for the day. And don't forget, it's your job to stay with her whenever she's out in the jungle.'

'No need,' he replied, airily. 'She tell me okay go home by herself.'

'It is not okay,' shouted Wolf. 'You get your arse back there right now.'

'Okay, Boss,' Santuk said and, with maddening insouciance, set off in exactly the opposite direction.

'Fucking hell,' Wolf fumed, as he watched the aggravating fellow's departure.

Well, it didn't matter today, he told himself. He was going to Nanga Palin anyway and could see that Bethany got home alright. But he'd definitely have a word with Baki Lunsa about it. The old man wasn't blind to the income his longhouse was raking in from Kanyalang and he could be relied on to make sure the worthless fellow stayed on the job.

After a satisfactory conversation with Lunsa, a man he regarded with increasing respect the more he got to know him, Wolf strode over to several wrinkled grannies who were clearly enjoying recounting their family histories to Bethany. They were all very good at this as they had the highly developed memories of people who had grown up with little or no exposure to the written word and it was no easy task for Bethany to take it all down in her notebook.

She made no effort to hide her irritation at being interrupted but Wolf, ignoring the death stares she was sending his way, blithely exchanged polite greetings with the old ladies.

'Come on,' he told her, when his efforts to chat up the more loquacious of the grannies reached the limits of his Dayak vocabulary, 'Get your kit and caboodle together so we can head back to Kanyalang.'

'I beg your pardon,' she said, indignantly, 'but I'm not planning to leave yet.'

'Change your plans then. I've got something I want to talk to you about and,' nodding toward the assembled grannies, he added, 'this might not be the best place to do it.'

'I'm afraid you'll have to,' she replied, icily.

'Okay, if that's the way you want it. Just tell me what you think you're doing letting Santuk go off on some monkey-hunting jaunt when he's being paid to stay with you whenever you're in the jungle.'

'Oh, is he hunting monkeys?' she asked, slightly surprised.

'That's what he told me when he almost hit me with one of his fucking arrows,' replied Wolf, impatiently.

'Oh well, maybe he wants to take one to his girlfriend,' she suggested with, he thought, an annoying indifference to any peril he might have been in. 'I told him he could go see her for a couple of days. Her longhouse is —'

'And who's going back and forth with you while Santuk's away?'

'No one. Mike's leopard can't still be around, at least, not unless it's too sick to move. In which case, it's not likely to cause me any problems.'

'You'd better let me be the judge of that.'

'Actually, I hate to remind you of this, but you're not the team leader on this project. Elliot is.'

'Right, and if you think he'll appreciate being short-staffed for months to come because some idiot anthropologist has gotten herself chewed up by a leopard then you're very much mistaken. Something this project doesn't need is another fatal accident, one was more than enough.'

'How dare you come here and talk to me like this in front of the people I work with,' she retorted, without making the slightest effort to moderate the fury in her voice. 'You know I need their respect to do my job. You have absolutely no right —'

'It wasn't my idea to have this conversation in front of an audience,' he reminded her, testily.

'Well, I didn't know that you were going to come on like the wrath of God, did I?'

'No need to worry,' he returned airily. 'You've said yourself that the grannies don't understand English.'

'They don't need to. They're not stupid. Your tone of voice makes it perfectly obvious that you're ticking me off for something and I just won't accept that in front of the people I work with. It's too fucking demeaning and I don't want to hear any more of it so will you please just sod off?'

'Like I said, I'm ready to go when you are,' he replied.

'Well, I'm not ready and I don't intend to be ready anytime soon, thank you.'

'That's a pity because I can't wait around all day.'

'Then don't.'

'I'm not going back without you. Lunsa agrees that you shouldn't be going back and forth alone. We were talking about it just now and he's promised that in the future he's going to see to it that that fool, Santuk, earns his salary. But for now we've settled it that you're coming back with me. Ask the old man yourself if you don't believe me.'

This wasn't something she was prepared to do.

'Alright, since you insist on being horrible, I guess I'll go,' she agreed with bad grace.

'Being horrible is my specialty,' he replied, not entirely displeased with this description of himself.

Bethany bade everyone goodbye in her usual fashion as they made their way along the veranda but as soon as they climbed down the notched log and reached the ground she let him know exactly what she thought of him.

'You arrogant, interfering bastard,' she began, and was in the process of embellishing this theme when she realised that Thumbi and half-a-dozen other women were leaning over the veranda rail taking an avid interest in the scene. The last thing she wanted to do was provide them with this sort of entertainment so she quickened her pace and hurried on ahead of Wolf along the path to Kanyalang.

Wolf made no attempt to catch up with her. Instead, he walked just quickly enough to keep her in sight but out of conversational range.

She was getting to have a really nice arse these days, he thought, as he availed himself of the opportunity to survey her figure but she shouldn't get any thinner, not unless she wanted to look like some kind of half-starved fashion model.

Wolf wondered how long it was going to take her to get over her little temper tantrum. He supposed he really had come on a bit strong. He didn't know what had got into him all of a sudden but he hadn't been able to resist doing the macho bit and baiting her a little. She looked sexy as all hell when she was mad. Just thinking about it was giving him a hard-on.

He'd better be careful, he told himself sternly, and not go following his dick into a relationship he might regret – not that that was likely to happen. Judging by her performance this afternoon, Bethany would as soon have it off with a moderately friendly gorilla as with him.

CHAPTER SIXTEEN

If Bethany had known what he was thinking at that moment, she would have confirmed that he was absolutely right. And by the time she reached the clearing around Kanyalang her temper had risen to a fever pitch. She was so angry that she could barely manage to conceal her feelings and be polite when, as she was passing the hotel, Bima called her to come and admire an enormous wood carving of a Dayak ancestor figure.

'We're going to put it in front of the entrance,' he said, pointing to the designated spot, 'to greet the guests when they arrive.'

Bethany wasn't sure this was such a good idea. The image was so ferocious-looking she couldn't imagine that it would be very welcoming. Still, she didn't want to tell Bima that so she managed to profess some enthusiasm for it before she made an excuse and hurried on to the office.

The first person she saw when she got there was Marguarita, just back from one of her searches for interesting plant specimens and quenching her thirst from the thermos on the veranda.

'Here, you look like you could use some, too,' Marguarita said, as Bethany mounted the stairs. 'You seem upset.'

'Upset doesn't begin to say it. I'm absolutely livid.'

'Whatever happened?'

Bethany told her about Wolf's visit to Nanga Palin and fumed, 'It's absolutely intolerable the way he puts his nose into what everybody's doing and tries to order everyone around, especially me. It's as if he thinks he's the team leader. I swear to God, he tries to usurp Elliot's position at every turn. I mean, you'd think Elliot would be absolutely furious, wouldn't you?'

'Oh, don't worry about him,' Marguarita said, 'he can take care of himself. Just don't let Wolf get the upper hand where you're concerned. If he does, he'll make your life miserable.'

'He's doing that already,' Bethany replied.

'Then you'd better put a stop to it, hadn't you?'

'Believe me, there's nothing I'd rather do. The question is, how?

God knows, I haven't been able to manage it so far. Is Wolf really Elliot's deputy anyway? I mean is it carved in stone anywhere that he's the 'Number Two Man', as he likes to put it?'

'I don't think so. It's just that he's the only one here who's a bit of a generalist. He has a degree in Environmental Studies, or something vague like that. You know what American universities are like. You can practically put a programme together with cello tape, a little bit of this, a smattering of that, and get a doctorate for it. But Elliot's background is in the interpretation of satellite maps and that's too narrow and too technical to make him the right team leader for a project like this.'

Bethany acknowledged this with a nod.

'Wolf is the only one who understands, at least to some extent, what each of us is doing,' Marguarita continued. 'He's smart as a whip. You can't under-rate him there. And he's madly interested in anything and everything about the rainforest so what he doesn't know he usually makes it his business to find out. And if you put all that together with a typical American personality, boasting and bragging and being totally full of himself, you've got Wolf. It's as simple as that. He's a bloody pain in the backside but there are times when he has his uses.'

'Still, I'm surprised Elliot stands for it,' Bethany said.

'I don't think there's much he can do about it. And the truth is that, as obnoxious as Wolf can be at times, the project would fall apart tomorrow without him. Elliot's no fool. I'm sure he sees how convenient it is to have Wolf around. In fact, in some ways, I suppose the whole situation probably suits him rather well, just the way it is.'

'I don't see how it could,' Bethany protested.

Marguarita glanced down at her watch. 'Jesus, how did it get so late? I've got some stuff I want to put under the microscope before the air conditioning goes off.' And without lingering for any further discussion, she breezed off to the lab.

Elliot, who had had the ill-luck hear all this, was incandescent.

He had been sitting at Tarique's desk trying to check some of the figures in the last quarterly report against the raw data on the dead man's computer files. He had thought it would just take a couple of minutes so, instead of turning on the air conditioner, he had merely left the door ajar for ventilation.

He hadn't expected to find a number of disturbing discrepancies in the figures and the question of whether these were indicative of nothing more than carelessness on Tarique's part, albeit to an inexcusable degree, or whether they might be the tip of an extremely sinister iceberg, had kept him there longer than he had planned.

It had never occurred to him that Marguarita and Bethany might start chattering away right outside the door – and that it would be largely about him.

All his life he had considered eavesdropping beneath contempt but gradually he found himself listening to their conversation. And infuriating as it was, he had to admit that there was some truth in what Marguarita said.

He didn't know quite what he could do about it apart from firing Wolf, an impractical solution, or remaking himself into a clone of the dreadful man, an idea as repulsive as it was impossible. He supposed he just would have to accept the perennial fate of the eavesdropper – hearing things about himself he didn't want to know.

Elliot breathed a sigh of relief when he heard the click of the generator being shut down. He had had enough for one day, he thought, more than enough. What he needed was a good stiff drink, perhaps three or four.

He was locking his office door when the sound of footsteps on the veranda stairs made his blood boil. He knew who they belonged to.

'Hey, the hotel's going great,' Wolf announced by way of greeting. 'I've just been climbing all over it with Bima. You feel like you're on top of the world when you're on that roof. And he's got a terrific woodcarver there making a big-arsed statue that's guaranteed to scare the shit out of the guests when they see it. But it'll sure as hell make them realise they've come to a weird and wonderful place.'

Elliot ignored this. 'I want to talk to you,' he said, marshalling the full force of his anger and directing it entirely at Wolf. 'Come into my office for a minute.'

159

'What's the problem?'

Elliot didn't answer until he was seated behind his desk. Wolf, who had not been invited to sit down, helped himself to a chair and straddled it with annoying ease.

'I understand you are making things absolutely impossible for Bethany at Nanga Palin,' Elliot began.

'Where did you hear that load of shit?' interrupted Wolf.

'Never mind about that. The important thing is that you've been deliberately embarrassing Bethany in front of the very people whose respect she needs to carry out her work.'

'Bullshit,' Wolf declared, but potential scenarios swirled through his head like a hurricane. Had Bethany come to Elliot complaining about him? Who else could have done it? It must have been Bethany, even though it beggared belief. He'd never have expected her to do such a low, underhand thing.

'There's another thing, as well,' Elliot was saying, 'and it's considerably more serious. I hear that you've been going around deliberately trying to give the impression that you're the one who's really in charge of this project and that I'm little more than a figurehead.'

'That's a bunch of crap, too. Whoever told you that is a goddamn liar.'

'Let's hope so. In any case, I want to make one thing abundantly clear. I am the head of this project and I am the one who will ultimately be held responsible for its success or failure. Every member of the expat staff reports directly to me and to no one else, and that includes you.'

'Okay, chief, you got it,' Wolf said, putting his right hand to his forehead in a mock military salute.

'This is not a joking matter,' Elliot reminded him, in a voice icy with anger.

'Right, any other complaints?'

'Only a suggestion.'

'And that is…?'

'If you find that confining yourself to your own work doesn't give you enough to do perhaps I can arrange with RRF to find you a place on a project that could make better use of your many talents.'

It took a mega-dose of self control on Wolf's part to keep himself from voicing the stream of epithets that were racing through his mind. But with a supreme effort he reigned in his fury and sanitised his language before saying, 'Don't put yourself to any trouble.' And with that he flung himself out of the office.

Elliot remained frozen at his desk for several minutes wondering if such a confrontational approach had been wise and thinking how ironic it was that he had ostensibly taken that step in defence of Bethany, of all people. He had thoroughly disliked her ever since she had inveigled Catherine into drinking herself senseless at Nanga Palin. But of course, Bethany wasn't really the issue. He had taken on Wolf in defence of his own position and authority and he was quite certain that was the right thing to have done.

Wolf, striding back along the path to the longhouse, was considering a different form of confrontation and control, one that centred on the pleasurable sensation of tearing Elliot limb from limb. But, once he was on the veranda, the primary thrust of his anger veered in Bethany's direction so he marched directly to her room and pounded on the door.

'You little sneak,' he exclaimed, the moment she opened it, 'What the fuck do you think you're up to?'

For an instant she was too taken aback to be angry. 'What are you talking about?' she asked, thoroughly bewildered. But her reaction quickly gave way to outrage. 'How dare you come here and talk to me like that,' she sputtered, positioning herself in the doorway in an attempt to block his entrance.

'Because I want to tell you that you're a liar and a contemptible little tale-bearer,' he declared. And ignoring the fact that she was clutching her sarong about her and that her hair, still wet from a shampoo, was dripping down her shoulders, he thrust her aside and stormed into the room.

'I beg your pardon,' she retorted, hotly, 'what makes you think you can come charging in here with your absurd accusations?'

'You know damn well why I'm here. I've just had an illuminating little chat with Elliot.'

'I fail to see what that has to do with me.'

'It has everything to do with you, and you know it. You went whining and snivelling to Elliot with some bullshit about how I was interfering with your work and –'

'Well, you are interfering with my work but I didn't –'

'Then let me say, you're pretty easily put off the rails,' he shot back.

'And let me say that I would greatly appreciate it if you would just sod off.'

'Not before I've finished. Apparently you also fed him a lot of crap about how I was angling for his job and trying to get everyone to believe that I was really the top dog around here.'

'Well, isn't that what you're trying to do?'

'No, it isn't. But even if it was, only a treacherous little rat would go and blab to the chief honcho about it.'

'I agree.'

'How extraordinary. Well in that case you must be feeling pretty disgusted with yourself.'

'I don't know why. I haven't even seen Elliot since breakfast, much less talked to him.'

'If you expect me to believe that you're a greater fool than I thought.'

'You're the one who's a fool if you don't believe me because I'm telling you the absolute truth.'

'Yeah, sure,' he flung back at her, 'and I'm the Angel Gabriel.'

With that, he stalked out of the room and slammed the door behind him.

CHAPTER SEVENTEEN

During the days and weeks that followed Bethany took care to avoid Wolf whenever possible. She saw him only at mealtimes and during the gatherings for drinks on the veranda. And she had his full cooperation in this effort because he was just as eager to stay clear of her company as she was to keep away from his.

Bethany was not the only one who was angry at Wolf. Ever since his moment of unintentional eavesdropping, Elliot had been seething with fury every time he thought about Wolf. He could just picture him strutting around trying to make everyone think that he was the real team leader. Well the bastard wasn't going to succeed, he'd see to that. He would make it very clear that he, not Wolf, was in full charge of the project.

He wouldn't do it by trying to imitate Wolf's hands-on style, he decided. He knew enough about himself to realise he had neither the inclination nor the ability to do that successfully. He would use his power over the budget. There was ample scope for manoeuvre on this front as costs were generally rising and the hotel was a particular offender in this regard. However, it soon became apparent that what had started out as something of a fabricated issue on his part was turning into one that was all too real.

It often happened that when Bethany was chatting with Pashetta in the outer office, she would hear Elliot arguing with Wolf about one thing or another. At other times, she heard him having a go at Bima who was convinced that only the best quality materials were good enough for the hotel and that cost over-runs didn't matter very much. In fact, it soon became apparent that everyone except Catherine and herself was lectured on the importance of keeping expenses down. Catherine, Bethany suspected, was let off simply because she could do no wrong in Elliot's eyes while she herself probably escaped a ticking off because the budget for her work was so small — just enough for a few notebooks and pencils and for the meagre salaries of Santuk and Sarika.

After a while the constant battles about costs began to take their toll on Elliot's spirits and it occurred to him that it had been more than two and a half years since he had taken any of his annual leave. In fact Annie, who rarely complained about anything, had mentioned this in several of her last letters. Perhaps he should arrange to go home for a while and see if they could get their marriage back on track. Not that it was really off track, he reminded himself, just a bit in the doldrums, but then what could you expect after twenty-eight years?

Annie was a great girl, really. She had a way with animals, almost seemed to read their minds. She was constantly grooming them and fussing over them. She fed them too much, though. He was always telling her that. Casper was getting quite fat as a result and Rory was almost as bad.

Of course, Annie had spoilt the children, too, especially Christopher. He hated to think about the vast sums that had been wasted on school fees. The boy was barely literate. The only three words in his vocabulary were fuck, crap and shit and he doubted he could spell them. Nor did he seem able to pass an exam or hold down a job. He was good at eating and sleeping. That was about all but apparently it was enough to convince Annie that he was some kind of undiscovered genius. As for Annabel, she could hold down a job but it seemed to be a different one in a different place every year or two. She was in New York at the moment, working in a television studio and, he suspected, having sex with half the men between Wall Street and the upper reaches of Central Park, the better looking ones, anyway. At least, the canine contingent in the family had turned out alright, he told himself. Rory and Casper were a credit to them - well, mostly to Annie, actually.

Yes, he decided, what he needed was to get away from Kanyalang for a while, read the riot act to Christopher, give Annie a hand with the dogs, that sort of thing. Poor old Rory was getting on a bit. Perhaps they should get a new puppy in preparation for the day, hopefully not imminent, when Rory wouldn't be around anymore. If so, he should be at home to help Annie break the little fellow in.

In the meantime, he assured himself, a few more cases of whisky should see him through.

It wasn't long before Marguarita began to notice that each shipment of supplies from Putussibau included a private order of Elliot's favourite tipple that was immediately carted off to his room. Only rarely was one of the bottles brought out and passed around for general consumption. Bethany saw it too and mentioned it to Marguarita but, search as they might for signs that his drinking was affecting his performance during the day, they didn't find any evidence of it.

When they were together they usually talked about traditional Dayak medicines. Marguarita even started going along to Nanga Palin sometimes although she found Kati's tight-lipped responses to her questions exasperating.

Even so, these visits were not entirely wasted. Some of the cures for minor ailments were general knowledge amongst the grannies and they enjoyed showing off their expertise. The older men also responded to the unexpected interest of a new listener by proudly telling her about the poisons they put on the tips of the arrows for their blowpipes.

'Why do you want to hear about poisons?' Bethany asked her as they were walking back to Kanyalang after one of these visits.

'Because they might be useful.'

'Who are you planning to poison?' Bethany teased, 'Wolf?'

'Not a bad idea,' Marguarita laughed, 'but I'm mostly interested in their potential as medicines.'

Bethany was baffled. 'But —'

'All medicines are poisons, really,' Marguarita continued. 'It's just the dosage and the method of use that makes the difference between healing and harming.

'Still, I'm surprised you're so interested in them,' Bethany said.

'There's no mystery about it. I'm trying to recast myself as an ethno-botanist, that's all.'

'I didn't know there was such a thing.'

'Until recently, there wasn't. But it's the fashion these days, politically correct, if you like, to put 'ethno' in front of practically everything to do with the rainforest.'

'Isn't that a bit silly?'

'It would be if it didn't act as a magnet for pulling in the research grants, funds for conservation, too, by convincing whoever is

165

parcelling out the money that we're frightfully sensitive to the concerns of the local people.'

'A bit of a sham in your case, isn't it?' Bethany observed.

'Perhaps,' Marguarita shrugged indifferently, 'but what does that matter if it gets money for the rainforest?'

Bethany countered with a question of her own. 'Don't you ever think you should care more about the people in the rainforest than about the plant life?'

'No, they don't deserve it,' Marguarita replied without hesitation.

'You seem very certain about that,' Bethany said.

'I am. People often turn out to be quite hateful when you get to know them but that never happens when you're dealing with flora. No orchid ever turned into a Venus fly trap on closer acquaintance.'

Bethany smiled at this comparison but said, 'I think your attitude is rather appalling, actually.'

'Think what you like. It's actions that matter. Do you realise those bloody loggers have probably wiped out thousands of species of orchids already, to say nothing of other types of vegetation? God only knows how many of them have vanished without anyone knowing they ever existed.'

'Who's vanished?' asked a masculine voice from somewhere in the foliage. 'No one I know, I hope.'

A moment later, Wolf appeared. He had been trying to follow a troupe of pig-tailed macaques that had been brachiating through the forest canopy but hadn't been very successful. Human beings, he had concluded reluctantly, just weren't designed for that form of locomotion.

He greeted Bethany with a curt nod but then excluded her from the conversation by talking to Marguarita about the drift of dipterocarp seeds for the rest of the walk back to Kanyalang.

Bethany was not remotely interested in this topic so she disregarded the intended slight and pressed on ahead of them, her mind on the annoying letter she had had from Nigel. He claimed that he had finally found out what love really meant and that this revelation had come in the form of Samantha. It had taken

Bethany a few minutes to remember who this paragon was but then it had dawned on her that the dippy little receptionist at the health club they had gone to was called Sam. Could it be the same one, she wondered, not that it really mattered. It was just that it would have been nice to think Nigel had missed her a little longer.

Actually it was silly to think that way, she told herself. She would put him out of her mind and focus on the long cool bath she would have when she got home. She might even go down to the river and have it there. She hadn't really mastered the technique of soaping herself under a sarong the way the Dayaks did but if she didn't start doing it she would never get the hang of it. She had tried it a couple of times at Nanga Palin but had been so worried about being seconds away from a Lady Godiva moment that she had more or less forgotten about the soap.

She had also been rather put off by the dual function of the river, serving as both village toilet and community bathtub, and hadn't actually felt very clean afterwards. But the river in front of Kanyalang wouldn't be as bad and somehow she felt more adventurous today. The thought of the dreary bathroom at the end of the veranda with all those fish in the bath water – they seemed to be getting bigger every day – suddenly depressed her. She would definitely give the river a try.

As soon as she got back to her room she changed into a sarong, tied it as securely as she could and set out for a spot well upstream, she hoped, from any human contributions the Dayak workers might have left behind.

Taking care to avoid the rocks that littered the riverbed, Bethany slipped down into the deliciously refreshing water and felt cool for the first time that day. Heaven couldn't be better than this, she thought, as she paddled lazily over to the far bank and surveyed the clearing around the longhouse from this new perspective. She was just wondering why she had been such an idiot, not bathing in the river before, when something small and hard hit her just below her left shoulder.

Turning swiftly around to see what it was and where it could have come from, she spied Wolf – or a creature that would have

167

resembled Wolf if it hadn't been totally green – some twenty or thirty feet away. In any case, with its face, arms and upper torso covered with greenish soapsuds, it looked so much like some kind of sea monster that she burst out laughing.

Wolf, thoroughly mystified, stopped soaping himself and gaped at her.

Eventually Bethany collected herself and, remembering the flying missile, gasped, 'What did you do that for?'

'Do what?'

'You know perfectly well what.'

'No, I don't. I swear to you, I didn't do anything except come here, my favourite place, by the way, for a bath.'

'You threw something at me and –'

'Sh,' he said, cutting her off and pointing to a nearby tree. Sitting on one of the extended branches and leaning back against the trunk, very much in the posture of a contented man relaxing in the shade, was a proboscis monkey. It was peeling a papaya and tossing the inedible bits down onto the ground while several females – Wolf counted five of them – alternately kept an eye on him and watched a scattering of juveniles who were frolicking around in the tree.

Bethany scarcely dared breathe for fear of scaring the family group away. Then, ping, something hit her right on her neck. This time it really hurt and before she could stop herself she gave an inadvertent squeal of protest. It wasn't terribly loud but the patriarch of the monkey family heard it. In a flash, he threw down what was left of the papaya, lifted and extended his impressive nose and, with a loud honking sound, broadcast a warning to his wives and offspring that their tree was no longer safe.

Seconds later the entire troupe was gone.

'Here we are,' Wolf said, scooping an illipe nut off the surface of the water and holding it out to Bethany. 'This must have been what hit you, a present from one of those little villains in the tree.'

'I'm so sorry I scared them away,' she said, taking the nut and agreeing that it felt like the size and shape of the thing that hit her.

'Don't be too sorry. That's what made it so interesting. It showed how incredibly smart they are. They just ignored us as long as we

168

were only talking to each other but as soon as you made a sound that Big Daddy didn't like – he must have considered it hostile and assumed it was directed at them – he told the rest of his family to clear out. They didn't waste any time doing it either.'

'How do you know it really was a family and that Big Daddy, as you call him, was the head of it?'

'His size, for one thing, and the fact that only the males have a nose like that, even bigger than mine, enormous in proportion to their size. And they're very highly sexed. The males have got to have a lot of females. If he only had one he'd probably kill her with too much of a good thing. They're very possessive too. A guy won't tolerate other males hanging around, eyeing up his wives.'

'You talk about them as if they were almost human,' Bethany observed.

'They are.'

'Does that describe you too,' she teased, 'almost human, I mean.'

'What have I done to deserve that?'

'You've turned green. It's like being in the river with Kermit the frog.'

'Thanks a lot,' Wolf said, holding out his arm, considering its colour and laughing, 'don't tell me you've only just noticed.'

'Of course I noticed but the monkeys were so interesting, I forgot about you.'

'More compliments, maybe we should take up a collection to send you to charm school or something.'

'There'd be no point trying to send you,' she retorted. 'You'd be expelled.'

He responded by chasing her with a handful of green soapsuds, catching her and smearing her face, back and shoulders with them. She wriggled free and retaliated by splashing water, mixed with some of the soapsuds, back at him. Within minutes she was as green as he was and they were both laughing too hard to notice that they were actually speaking to each other again.

CHAPTER EIGHTEEN

Jim Nathan, whiling away his time in the bars of Balikpapan, was speaking to just about anyone he thought might put him onto the scent of a job. His bank balance was nearing the desperate stage. He just wasn't finding work and he had the feeling that options were running out for him.

'Hey, why so glum?' a familiar voice from the next bar stool demanded. 'Lost your last friend or something?'

Jim turned toward the speaker and saw that it was his old drinking buddy, Matt, looking at the top of his form.

'Those Koreans must be treating you right,' Jim observed.

'Yeah, it turns out they're okay. The top dog speaks English, almost as good as you or me. Says he picked it up in some college in California. And he's no fool, I'll tell you that. What he lacks in cash, he makes up for in smarts.'

'How do you figure that?'

'Well, he's the new kid on the block, right? But he sure learns fast. He's got hold of some great maps, bought them on the sly off some project in a conservation area that hasn't been logged yet. Apparently they were done from satellite photos. That's an expensive proposition, in case you didn't know. A nickel-and-dime operation like these Koreans are running couldn't possibly afford that sort of thing. The detail's so good they show practically every fucking tree.'

Jim frowned but Matt didn't notice.

'And they ain't gonna have any problems about permits or crap like that,' Matt continued, 'because they've managed to pay off one of the big shots, and I mean very big shots, in the Ministry of Forestry. So now they can just target the areas they want to get into, you know, send in a bunch of Madurese guys with chainsaws, and walk away with top quality tropical hardwoods. If that doesn't sound like money in the bank, I don't know what does.'

Jim's reaction lacked the enthusiasm Matt expected. He just gave an indistinct grunt and muttered, 'Fairbanks, the company I used to work for, had some maps like that. These might be the same ones.'

'Don't think so. These are brand spanking new.'

'How do you know?'

'They show areas that I happen to know were only cleared a couple of months ago.'

'Funny,' Jim frowned.

'What's funny about it?'

'The guy who filched the maps I saw and who sold them to Fairbanks is dead.'

'So? Somebody else saw a chance to make a few bucks doing the same thing. What's so weird about that?'

'Nothing, I guess.'

Yet when Jim thought about it later, he decided that it did seem strange. He would have sworn that those people he met at Kanyalang would have auctioned off their grandmothers before they would have sold their precious maps to a logging company. Of course, every barrel had its rotten apple and Marguarita's project had had Tarique Radjeb. But that guy was six feet under now so his little business deals were at an end. And, how could any outsider have gotten access to those maps? He was sure of one thing, though. If someone was raking in a little extra cash at the expense of the rainforest, it wasn't Marguarita. She was the last person to do that sort of thing. But what the fuck, it wasn't any of his business anyway.

As more time passed and his wallet grew even thinner, Jim was increasingly forced to put his newly-minted ideas about the rainforest aside. He found himself latching onto just about anybody who might have news about a job, any kind of job at all.

Every day he wore down the patience of the recruitment people in the mining companies and the oil companies with his constant presence. And every night he got very drunk hoping to be the beneficiary of a hot tip from one of his fellow bar flies.

Luck just wasn't with him though. He was still bemoaning that fact several weeks later when Matt, looking considerably less jovial than when Jim had last seen him, put in another of his intermittent appearances at the Mermaid.

'Hey, where've you been?' Jim demanded. 'I haven't seen you around.'

172

'I'm spending so much time in the jungle I'm turning into a fucking ape-man.'

'Those Koreans work you pretty hard, do they?'

'Hard? They're frigging slave-drivers. They think if they pay you, they own you.'

'Well, at least, they're paying you. That's something.'

'At the moment that's exactly nothing, if you want to know. They owe me three weeks salary and they're giving me the run-around.'

'They sound like real shits.'

'You're telling me,' Matt said, finishing his drink and ordering another.

'Make that two,' Jim told the bartender. And as the skeleton of a plan flashed into his mind, he turned to Matt and added, 'this one's on me.'

'You struck gold or something?'

'No, but I've got a proposition for you.'

Matt eyed him suspiciously.

'How about getting me a photocopy of one of those maps you were talking about. You know, the ones made from the aerial photographs of that conservation area.'

'You gotta be kidding. Those things are kept under lock and key.'

'Yeah, but some smart guy who thought the company wasn't treating him right just might figure out how to pry them loose long enough to make a quick copy.'

'You're nuts,' Matt declared.

'I know a few guys who'd agree with you,' Jim laughed, but he quickly became serious again. 'There'd be something in it for you, of course.'

Matt's interest was instantaneous. 'How much?' he demanded.

'A hundred bucks.'

'Have you gone soft in the head? I'm not going to risk my arse for peanuts like that.'

'You're not risking anything if the bastards aren't paying you.'

'They say they'll have the money on Thursday,' Matt growled.

'Okay, I'll double it,' Jim said. 'Make it two hundred.'

'Forget it.'

But Jim didn't forget it and after downing another beer he said, 'If I were you, I'd get a real kick out of doing the dirty on a bunch of guys that were fucking me over.'

Matt reconsidered the proposition in this light. 'A thousand bucks and you're on,' he said.

'Sorry. That's way out of my league.'

Matt's curiosity, always a little slow to be activated, was finally aroused. 'What the fuck do you want the things for anyway?'

Jim hesitated. There was no way he was going to tell this gorilla about Marguarita. And there was something else, too. It wasn't the main thing but somehow it was bothering him. He didn't much like the idea of a bunch of loggers going into that conservation area with their chainsaws and turning the place into a wasteland and if he alerted the Kanyalang bunch to what was going on they might be able to do something to stop it.

When no explanation was forthcoming Matt became impatient. 'You must have some kind of racket going,' he said. 'What is it?'

'There's no racket. I just want the maps for my collection. I'm an amateur cartographer.'

'Yeah, sure, tell me another one.'

Jim shrugged this off with a laugh while he did some quick mental arithmetic. He grimaced as he wondered how much further he could squeeze his bank balance. 'Five hundred bucks,' he said, 'that's my final offer. Take it or leave it.'

'I'll think about it,' Matt replied, warily.

Jim, convinced by his tone of voice that there was going to be no deal, put the matter out of his mind.

His pessimism proved unwarranted. A few nights later, when the promised Thursday had passed and there had been no sign of a pay cheque, Matt reappeared with a rolled up copy of one of the maps in his hand.

'You got the dough?' he demanded, stuffing the map back into his pocket before Jim could take it from him.

'I'll write you a cheque.'

'Are you out of your fucking mind? Cash only.'

'You can't expect me to have that much on me.'

'Well, when you got it, let me know. Then you'll get your maps.'

'It'll have to be rupiah, then. I can't get you greenbacks.'

'That's okay. I'll be around,' Matt said, and sauntered off, leaving Jim to quell his apprehensions about what this would do to his finances by getting thoroughly pissed.

The next day, fighting a monster hangover, Jim went to the bank. His stomach turned a couple of somersaults when he saw how much, or rather how little, was left in his account. It was noticeably less than he had thought when he had rashly made the deal with Matt.

Was he being the world's greatest chump, or what, he asked himself? But there was definitely something underhand about how those maps were getting into general circulation and if he was the one who sounded the alarm it just might get him the shag of a lifetime. And allowing this thought to overpower his better judgement, he drew out the required sum.

With the money in his wallet, he turned out onto the sun-drenched street. The yellow glare made his head throb and, spotting a Chinese apothecary shop on the opposite side of the street, he decided to give the place a try. After all, the Chinese were clever bastards. Maybe they'd have some secret cure for a monster hangover. He wouldn't care if it were made from fresh lizard blood or ground up rat testicles if it would do the trick.

The shop was not well lit and it was not until his eyes had adjusted to the dimness that he took a good look at the customer ahead of him. To his astonishment he saw one of those freshly scrubbed, healthy-looking, blonde girls who abounded on college campuses in the States but who hadn't crossed his path in years. Either his hangover was giving him hallucinations or one of them was in front of him now, trying to explain to the man behind the counter – a guy who didn't seem too swift with the sign language – that she wanted something for a headache.

The one thing that was clear was that her efforts were being seriously hampered by the language barrier so Jim went over to her and said, 'Can I help? My Indonesian's pretty basic but I'll give it a shot if you want me to.'

'That would be wonderful,' she exclaimed, rewarding him with a bright smile and the information that her name was Judy Whitmore. Then she stood back and waited as he arranged for the purchase of the required remedy and bought a small vial of round silver pellets for his hangover.

'You don't look like someone who's got a headache,' he observed, as they strolled out of the shop together.

'I'm not,' she replied, 'but my mom has one and I promised I'd get her something.'

'What in the world brings you and your mom out to a godforsaken place like this?'

'My parents live here, at least they've been here for the past two years. Daddy works for Calco and I'm taking a term off from college so I can sort of see the world.'

'Your dad must be a pretty big deal in the company if he's got his family here with him,' Jim said, immediately seizing on the possibility that this 'Daddy' guy might be a useful contact.

'Where do you go to college?' he asked, to prolong the conversation.

'University of New Mexico. I'm a junior. At least, I will be when I get back.'

'Is that where you're from?'

'Oh, no, I'm from Southern California.'

'Then why New Mexico?'

'It has a really good geology department.'

'Not many girls go in for that.'

'Some do,' she shrugged. 'I got interested because of my Dad. He's a geologist.'

'So am I.'

'Oh,' she said, her expression indicating that she thought this was a splendid thing to be, 'you should meet Daddy then.'

'That would be great,' he agreed.

The result was that he saw her home and enthusiastically accepted her mother's invitation to stay to dinner.

During the course of the best meal Jim had had in months, it became clear that 'Daddy' had risen well above the ranks of the humble rock-hunters and now presided over the company's entire operation in Indonesian Borneo. It was equally apparent that he was not in a good mood.

'A bunch of vice-presidents from the Houston office are going to descend on us next week,' he fumed, 'and they want a four-day jungle tour laid on for them. Can you imagine what that means?'

'No,' replied Judy, indifferently.

'It means I've got to find a guide to take them up-river,' he explained irritably, 'make sure they've got the right gear — how the hell am I supposed to know what they'll need — and make a thousand and one other arrangements for them. And when is all of this happening? Right after the only secretary in Borneo who is half-way competent manages to get herself pregnant and resigns. That means that I'm going to have to do everything myself. I just wish someone would realise that I don't have thirty-six hours in every goddamn day.'

Jim, motivated by a combination of self-interest and good manners, feigned sympathy as he listened to these complaints.

'And finding a guide is going to be a real bitch,' Mr Whitmore continued. 'If the guy's not reliable, and none of them are, or if he doesn't really know the country and speak passable English, there'll be hell to pay. And who around here's going to have the slightest inkling what a bunch of American VIPs are going to want on a trip like that? Tell me that, will you?'

He glared at the others around the table as if they were responsible for bringing this scourge on him.

'I've spent a lot of time in the jungle,' Jim began, as casually as he could, 'so I think I've got a fair idea what they'll need and where they might like to go. And I don't have much to do right now. If I can help you out, let me know.'

Mr Whitmore did not appear grateful. 'Why aren't you doing anything?' he demanded, suspiciously.

'I'm sort of between jobs at the moment.'

'I'm looking for a tour guide, not a geologist.'

'I understand that, sir.'

'We don't hire geologists here. They're hired out of the head office in Houston.'

'I've been thinking I'd kind of like to branch out a bit, do something different for a while,' Jim said, trying to put a positive slant on his current unemployed state. 'Something like taking tourists up-river, for instance, might be just the thing, as a stop-gap measure, of course, just until things ease up in geology.'

'Why, that's your solution, isn't it, darling?' Judy's mother exclaimed.

Mr Whitmore glowered at his wife. Jim's presence prevented him from pointing out that he could do very well without her advice so he ticked off Judy instead. 'You let that cat of yours get in my study again this afternoon.'

'Oh, Daddy, what does it matter? She won't hurt anything.'

'I'll thank you to remember, young lady, that animal peed on my computer last week.'

Judy did remember and had difficulty suppressing a giggle. Fortunately the maid came in at that moment bringing ice-cold dishes of chocolate mousse that her mother had made that morning and her father's attention was diverted from the misdeeds of the cat.

With an inward sigh, Jim resigned himself to not getting any help on the job front from Mr Whitmore. But as he was leaving, the old tyrant surprised him by saying, 'If you really meant what you said about pitching in with these visitors I've got on my hands, come see me in my office tomorrow.'

Jim could hardly believe his luck.

By the time he set off for the Mermaid Bar, Jim's hangover had vanished and he had decided that 'Daddy' might be almost human. As for Judy and her mother, well, people didn't come any nicer than that. It was just a shame that Judy was such a kid. Although the truth was that even if she was a little older he didn't really go for the squeaky clean super-wholesome type. In any case, why would she want to be stuck with a loser like him? She deserved someone a hell of a lot better.

When Jim arrived at the Mermaid he found Matt well on his way to getting pissed but not too far gone to have let the possible acquisition of five hundred dollars slip his mind, even if it was going to be all in rupiah.

After the money and the maps had changed hands, Jim took his prize back to his room and examined it carefully by the light of the florescent lamp that stretched along the ceiling.

It was with no surprise that he found a stylised line drawing of a rhinoceros hornbill – called a Kanyalang in the local language, he reminded himself – in the lower right hand corner. He recognised it immediately as the logo Bima had designed for their project.

The next day he went to see Mr. Whitmore and was hired to make all the arrangements for the Houston vice-presidents' visit and to take them up river.

The trip went so well that when it was over a couple of other companies signed Jim on to take their people on jungle tours. Then travel agencies began using him, often just for day trips but sometimes for excursions that lasted a week or more. It wasn't really what he would have chosen to do but it paid enough to restore a little life to his bank balance and it certainly beat working in an office. Mr Whitmore even flew him out to Singapore for a couple of days so that he could come back into the country on a new visa under the Calco umbrella. This strategy would, Mr Whitmore hoped, relieve him of the bother of providing recreational travel for any future VIPs or potential clients.

All things considered, Jim found himself enjoying his new job more than he could have imagined. Of course, it did nothing for his career as a geologist but, looking at it just as an interim measure, it fit the bill exactly. He was getting paid for being in the rainforest without having to be part of its destruction.

Talk about a lucky break, little Judy Whitmore had delivered one in spades.

CHAPTER NINETEEN

Bethany's idea of a lucky break would have been one that took her out of the rainforest instead of keeping her in it. The suspicion that she might be happier in a very different sort of job in a very different sort of place had been niggling at her for some time.

Had she come out here with too many illusions about non-Western cultures, she asked herself? Or had Marguarita been right when she had claimed that anthropologists were all trying to escape something? If so, it wasn't working very well in her case.

There were times when a feeling of being terribly alone pressed in on her. The jungle wasn't at all her natural habitat in the way it was Wolf's or Marguarita's or even Mike's. It would help if she could like her colleagues a little better but, except for Catherine, she just couldn't. And the relationships she had with people at Nanga Palin were such one-way affairs – it was always incumbent on her to understand them, not the other way around. Of course, that was her job. She was an anthropologist, wasn't she? The trouble was that things like loneliness and isolation hadn't crossed her mind when she was back in London deciding on a career in anthropology.

Well, she wasn't going to worry about that tonight. Everyone at Nanga Palin was getting ready for an evening of feasting and dancing to propitiate the rice goddess, Ambong, and she wasn't going to miss the fun. She would just let herself be swept up in the prevailing mood of eager anticipation and not think about anything else.

The only problem was that the festivities didn't begin until evening. Staying at Nanga Palin until then meant taking her afternoon bath in the river right in front of the longhouse and she was still a bit worried about having her sarong float away halfway through it all.

'I think I'll bathe a little later,' she told Thumbi, on the theory that any embarrassing moments would be less obvious after dark.

The headman's wife was horrified. 'Bad spirits come out at night,' she cried. 'You do not want to be in the river with bad spirits, do you?'

Bethany quickly assured her that she did not and, to her considerable relief, the bath went off without incident but to her dismay other tortures lay in wait for her.

Sarika and some of her friends dressed her in an intricately woven skirt. It had been designed to reach the knees of its diminutive owner but was a mini on Bethany. She desperately wished that she had had a chance to go on a diet, get a tan on her legs too, before wearing it but that hadn't been possible. Defending herself against insects, leeches and various species of sharp-edged attack-plants had generally precluded wearing anything but jeans. And, as for a diet, the thought hadn't even occurred to her until tonight.

The bad thing — or perhaps it was a good thing — about Kanyalang was that there wasn't a scale anywhere around the place. Nor was there a mirror larger than one designed for shaving so it was relatively easy to forget about painful things like losing weight.

What she didn't realise was that the heat, Kolop's cooking, the daily treks to and from Nanga Palin and the absence of a corner shop selling Mars bars were having a visible effect on her figure. Of course, she had noticed that her clothes were getting a bit loose but she had put that down to the rough treatment they were receiving at Kolop's hands when he did the washing.

Her main concern at the moment was that she was being made to look ridiculous. Sarika and her friends were insisting that she stand still while they bedecked her with a plethora of traditional finery; a beaded cap and jacket, a heavy silver belt, a long silver necklace and a vast number of silver bracelets that would, she was certain, make her look like an over-decorated Christmas tree.

She dreaded the arrival of the guests, especially the testosterone-crazed youth from neighbouring longhouses. Unlike her friends at Nanga Palin, they wouldn't be used to seeing a foreigner in their midst and she knew she would be the object of unrelenting curiosity.

The heat of the day had given way to the coolness of evening by the time the first of this over-sexed brigade, along with older, less hot-blooded relatives, began to arrive and were welcomed with generous portions of tuak.

The serious purpose of the event was addressed with offerings of rice and flowers. These were set out for the goddess Ambong on the veranda and her blessings were sought for the prospective planting. Then when the appropriate rituals had been completed, manioc cakes cooked in pig fat were passed around and Bethany, unusually hungry because of the enticing aromas that had been emanating from the cooking veranda all day, devoured hers quickly.

'Delicious,' she lied, hastily gulping down more tuak to get the taste and the texture of the pig fat out of her mouth.

The next item on the bill of fare, a generous portion of the succulent wild boar meat that had been roasting on a spit all afternoon, was more to her liking. It was piled on individual banana leaf plates and supplemented by various kinds of fish which had either been baked over charcoal or boiled up in a stew.

In the months since she had been coming to Nanga Palin, Bethany's skill in eating soupy things with her fingers had greatly improved. Now, with the aid of the rice balls that generally accompanied such dishes, she was able to scoop them up without disgracing herself.

Tuak and laughter flowed unceasingly during the feast and Bethany was just debating whether or not to have a bit more of the wild boar meat when Sarika brought her a salad that looked especially delicious. Made with a mixture of greens plucked from the jungle and seasoned with garlic, ginger and chilli peppers, it was light and leafy and seemed like the perfect complement to the protein-rich meal that had preceded it.

The first bite thoroughly fulfilled the high expectations Bethany had for it but a moment after swallowing it was all she could do to keep from retching. Nestled amongst the blameless vegetables lurked several pieces of – could it be, she wondered – snake? From its pasty-white appearance and its unpleasant smell she was almost certain that it was.

Her appetite evaporated completely and she fled to a shadowy corner of the veranda and pushed the revolting mixture down between the floorboards.

The recipients of this largess, the hungry dogs and pigs beneath the house, responded with snorts and growls.

Bethany glanced around hastily to see if anyone had noticed what she was doing. Luckily, Mike had arrived just at the crucial moment and everyone's attention had been diverted to him so no one had. But her pleasure at this happy coincidence of events quickly turned to consternation when she realised that Mike was followed by the last person she ever wanted to see at Nanga Palin again – Wolf.

'A couple of my rangers told me about this thing tonight,' Mike explained to Bethany, after the two men had paid their respects to Lunsa, chatted with various members of the longhouse, and quenched their thirst with the ever-present tuak. 'They asked me if I wanted to come along so I thought I'd bring Wolf, too.'

'He decided I needed some fun,' Wolf added, 'and these Dayak bashes can turn into real orgies sometimes.'

'Is that why you came?' Bethany asked coldly, thinking that if he had been nicer to Pashetta, he might be less in need of an orgy but she held her tongue. Instead, she turned to Mike and asked, 'How come you didn't say anything about coming?'

'I didn't hear about it until this afternoon,' he replied. 'You know what these guys are like. Advance notice just isn't their thing.'

'I must say you seem to have gotten into the spirit of things,' Wolf observed, looking her up and down with a mixture of amusement and approval.

'I'm trying,' she replied, curtly.

'Looking pretty sexy, too,' Wolf continued, 'which is right on brief for an orgy.' And nodding in the direction of a group of visitors who were ogling Bethany, he teased, 'I hope your participant observer skills are up and running tonight because I can guess what those guys have got on their minds.'

'Shagging the informants wasn't actually included in my job description,' Bethany retorted.

'A grave oversight,' Wolf asserted, shaking his head in mock distress, 'because I was relying on you to set me straight about something.'

'What?'

'Well, Mike's been saying ... no, never mind he's got to be bullshitting me.'

'I doubt it,' she said. 'He knows a lot about what goes on here.'

'Okay, here it is then - just how far are these Dayak guys willing to go to make their girlfriends happy?'

'Rather far, actually,' Bethany replied, under the mistaken impression that the conversation had shifted onto safer territory, 'and they used to go even farther.'

'Farther?' Wolf repeated, looking surprised.

'Yes,' she declared, 'like giving their girlfriends a freshly killed head when they proposed to them. It's a pity the custom died out, your head would have been just the thing.'

'Jesus, I never knew you were so bloodthirsty,' Wolf exclaimed drawing away in feigned horror, 'but we seem to have got our signals crossed. I was thinking of a different, but equally quaint, custom that Mike claims is still going strong.

'What's that?'

'It's the thing these guys do to their dicks to give their girlfriends an extra tickle.'

'Oh, shut up,' growled Mike, looking suddenly embarrassed.

Wolf ignored him and went on, 'it's more than I'd do for any woman, I'll tell you that.'

A mischievous glint came into Bethany's eyes and she said, 'How very selfish of you.'

'So you know what I'm talking about, do you?' Wolf demanded, feeling quite certain that she didn't.

'If you mean putting sticks through their willies,' she said, as carelessly as if she was talking about straightening their ties, 'of course, I know.'

Wolf gaped. This was not the reaction he had expected. 'Can I ask exactly how you found out?'

'Let's just say I may be a better participant observer than you gave me credit for,' Bethany returned. And silently congratulating herself on having left him thoroughly stunned, she breezed off to

185

watch the musicians taking their place on the other side of the veranda.

Christ, Wolf thought, he had certainly gotten her all wrong. She was nothing like the dippy little innocent he had taken her for and, as he was getting his head around this startling idea, it occurred to him that she just might turn out to be more interesting than he had thought.

Bethany, her spirits high after scoring one-up on Wolf, turned her attention to the cacophony of sounds that were beginning to fill the jungle night.

Drums, gongs, flutes, a three-stringed lute, and a sort of bamboo zither infused the air with a spirit of bacchanalian revelry and she soon realised that, tenuous as her own hold on sobriety had become, most of the people around her were even more sozzled than she was. Voices rose, laughter became more raucous and then, in response to some signal that she had neither seen nor heard, everyone began to gather round in a circle to watch – she didn't know what.

An expectant hush fell over the crowd.

Then she saw what everyone was waiting for. A man dressed in a loincloth and bedecked with feathers sprang into the centre of the circle and began to dance. One by one other performers followed him, all brandishing long curved swords in a terrifying display of ferocity. Suddenly Bethany was conscious of a collective intake of breath as, with a gravity-defying leap, the most brilliant dancer of them all bounded into view. Wielding the feathers of an enormous hornbill, he soared and whirled and virtually flew through the air in a dazzling portrayal of the winged messenger of the gods.

When his performance was over, the level of the entertainment descended to more earthly levels and bawdy comedy became the order of the night. It culminated in the depiction of an old man staggering around the impromptu stage as if he could hardly stand up under the weight of a gigantic erection. The on-lookers were convulsed with laughter.

Eventually the hilarity died down and the prevailing atmosphere changed again. This time it was the women's turn to dance. A line of girls waving hornbill feathers in slow seductive arcs swayed enticingly to the insistent beat of the drums and used their large dark eyes to flirt outrageously with any male who attracted them.

As she watched their dance, Bethany became increasingly aware of the undercurrent of eroticism that charged the humid air, fanned by the plaintive tones of the jungle orchestra, the flickering light of the kerosene lamps and the oceans of tuak that had been consumed.

Then Sarika's beautiful cousin, Giri, glided into the centre of the circle and began performing a solitary dance that sent the senses of any male in the audience reeling. Vibrant sexuality radiated from every movement of her body and, as the musicians urged her on with ever more pulsating rhythms, the fervour of the audience rose to fever pitch.

Giri, in response to their reaction, began running her hands over her body in ways that were at first teasingly suggestive, then frankly erotic and finally unequivocally obscene.

The untamed sexuality of it all, Bethany knew, was to ensure the fertility of the land and indirectly that of the people and animals that lived on it by propitiating the rice goddess.

When the dance was over she glanced at Mike and she could tell from the expression on his face that he had been turned on by it all. What man wouldn't have been? She knew that Wolf was standing next to him but she determinedly avoided looking at him. His reaction didn't bear thinking about.

As a diversion, Bethany quickly sought Sarika's face in the crowd, thinking that because she took her Catholicism so seriously, she must surely disapprove of Giri's performance. But if she did, she was showing no sign of it – quite the contrary. Sarika, along with some of the other girls and many of the younger men, was getting up to dance. Nobody had partners. The girls formed one line, the boys another, and with slow, sensuous movements, they glided past each other in two concentric circles. Questions and answers, sometimes accompanied by invitations, smouldered in their eyes as they appraised potential partners for the night.

Bethany watched this mating ritual with detachment until she saw Giri break away from her companions long enough to draw Wolf toward the line of swaying men.

What does she want with him, Bethany wondered, and then

realised that it was all too obvious what Giri wanted. Well, she'll be in for a disappointment, Bethany told herself, as it was a virtual certainty that Wolf wouldn't have any sticks through his willy. It struck her that Wolf looked revoltingly pleased at being singled out by Giri. Bethany didn't want to watch and yet it was hard not to. He was so much taller than the Dayak men that she couldn't help seeing him whenever she looked in the direction of the dancers.

A moment later Bethany felt the tugging of a small hand on hers and, looking down, she saw that Jarani, Kati's youngest granddaughter, was urging her to come and join the dance.

Shit, Bethany thought, participant observer or not, she'd feel like a combination of giraffe, hippopotamus and elephant in the midst of those lovely tiny girls, and it would be so awful if people actually thought she was on the pull along with them. But when additional friendly hands began pushing her to follow Jarani, she decided it might be better to acquiesce than to make a scene by refusing. Mike, she noticed, was allowing himself to be led toward the swaying circle and this made her feel slightly better about it.

Wolf gave her an approving grin as she passed him but, caught up as he was in the throbbing tempo of the dance, rapidly turned his attention back to Giri.

Bethany pretended not to see him and instead concentrated on trying not to feel huge, as well as ridiculous, in the midst of her petite companions. Fortunately the tuak, gave her the courage to carry on but she soon began to notice that the number of dancers was diminishing. They were drifting off, mostly in pairs, to make love in the darkened inner rooms of the longhouse or in the small huts that were scattered about in the rice fields for use during planting and harvesting.

At last, Bethany began to get tired but she saw that Wolf and Mike were still dancing, only detaching themselves from the circle now and then to fortify themselves with additional servings of tuak.

Giri, she observed, was still dancing, too.

Was she waiting for Wolf, Bethany wondered, reining in a sudden desire to rush over and remind him of Pashetta and tell him to be faithful to her. Then she remembered that something was clearly amiss in that relationship and that, in any case, what Wolf did was no business of hers.

She'd better go to bed before she made a complete fool of herself, Bethany decided, so she slipped away from what remained of the festivities and went in search of the bamboo mat she knew Sarika had laid out for her.

The mat did little to cushion the hardness of the floor and she slept lightly at first, making it easy for male voices not far from her door to penetrate her consciousness. One of them sounded like Mike's.

Waking, Bethany propped herself up on one elbow and listened for Wolf's American accent, as well, but didn't hear it. As far as she could tell, the group was made up of male guests who hadn't managed to, or hadn't chosen to, find a companion for the night amongst the Kanyalang girls.

This was not, she surmised, a group that included Wolf.

I know where he is and what he's doing and who he's doing it with, Bethany told herself, and for the rest of the night Wolf and Giri wove their way in and out of her dreams.

CHAPTER TWENTY

Bethany's conviction that Wolf had had it off with Giri was strengthened the next day when she went into Elliot's outer office and saw that the usually busy and efficient Pashetta was staring gloomily at a blank computer screen.

'What's the matter?' Bethany asked.

'Nothing.'

'There must be something. You're looking miserable.'

'I don't like this place.'

'Why not?'

'The jungle is for animals, not for people,' Pashetta declared.

'But people live in it, too,' Bethany protested.

'Dayak people,' Pashetta said, disdainfully, 'but I am not Dayak. I am Orang Melayu. I am not like these people.' She waved her arm to indicate the surrounding forest. 'I'm from Pontianak. I was brought up in the city.'

'None of us grew up in any place that was remotely like this,' Bethany reminded her, 'but you don't usually look so depressed. Something must be up. Is it anything that I can help with?'

'No,' Pashetta stated firmly, but then relented and confided, 'Wolf and I do not see each other anymore. Maybe you know that already.'

Bethany nodded. 'I sort of guessed,' she replied, not mentioning that it had been rather obvious.

'But I am happy about it,' Pashetta declared, in a voice that would have convinced no one. 'He is monster.'

'I've often thought the same thing,' Bethany agreed.

'I used to think he loved me,' Pashetta continued, 'but now I know he does not.'

'How do you know that?'

'He is bad to me.'

'Bad? What do you mean?'

'He does not want to marry me, take me to America.'

'Lots of men have a problem with commitment,' Bethany observed.

'What is commitment?'

'Saying you want to spend the rest of your life with someone.'

'Just saying or really doing it?' Pashetta asked.

'It's supposed to mean really doing it.'

'Then why not say 'marry'?'

Bethany couldn't help agreeing. 'Yes, why not?' she replied, lamely.

'Wolf does not want to commitment with me,' Pashetta went on. 'In the beginning, he was very strong making love. He just look at me and want to do it, sometimes over and over again. Now he does not want to do it at all. He says we are finished. Ogre. I hate him.'

'Maybe he's just not the right person for you,' Bethany suggested. 'You shouldn't worry, though. You'll find somebody better.'

'Where?'

'I can't exactly draw you a map,' Bethany said. Then, seeing the hurt look on Pashetta's face, she quickly added, 'I don't know. I can't see into the future, can I? But someone with your looks and ability shouldn't have any trouble.'

Pashetta tightened her lips in displeasure, seeming to consider this a rather stupid remark.

It took Bethany only a moment to realise that it probably was. So many of the men in the world were rats that the chances of meeting a non-rat were slim at best, even if you weren't buried in a jungle outpost like Kanyalang, and even if you weren't desperate to escape to the freer society of the West.

Just how clever had Pashetta been to pin all her hopes on Wolf rather than on Mike or Bima? Surely either of them would have been more amenable to a long-term relationship with a possibility of marriage. But then, perhaps Wolf had been the first to let on that he fancied her and after that –

Bethany's speculations were interrupted by a mind-boggling suggestion from Pashetta.

'Maybe you like Wolf. Maybe you want him for yourself.'

'Don't be absurd. You aren't the only one in the world who thinks he's an ogre. Most of us would agree.'

'Catherine wouldn't. And he likes her too much. He likes her more than he likes anybody else.'

'But everyone likes Catherine,' Bethany exclaimed. 'It would be hard not to, wouldn't it?'

Pashetta actually thought it would be quite easy but maintained a sullen silence.

'And everybody likes you, too,' Bethany continued, quickly perceiving that further praise of Catherine would do nothing to lift Pashetta's spirits. 'I can't imagine how Elliot would get on without you, or how any of us would, for that matter.'

Pashetta brightened a bit at the idea of being indispensable so Bethany carried it a step further saying, 'Your family probably cares more about you than you realise, too.'

The sunshine vanished from Pashetta's face. 'You don't understand what a Muslim family is like,' she said.

Bethany had to admit this was true.

'If a girl brings dishonour to her family, they don't care about her anymore. They beat her and turn her out. She is dead to them.'

'Is that what happened to you?'

Pashetta nodded. 'So you see, I can never go back.'

'I didn't think Muslims here in Indonesia were that strict about things. I mean, this isn't the Middle East, is it?'

'Some people very strict, especially if they are Orang Melayu like my family.'

'Do you miss them terribly?'

An expression of nearly unbearable longing flickered momentarily across Pashetta's face before she squared her slim shoulders and said, 'I would like to see my younger brothers and sisters again. I used to take care of them, carry them around, feed them. They loved me very much. I would like to see my mother and grandmother, too.'

Then the tone of her voice changed abruptly and her dark eyes flashed with anger as she lashed out, 'But I never want to see my father or my older brothers again, ever.'

The intensity of feeling in Pashetta's voice shocked Bethany and left her completely at a loss for an adequate response. She was almost glad to see Wolf striding into the office because of the distraction he provided.

'Have either of you seen Rajang around?' he demanded.

'No,' replied Pashetta.

'Shit. Well, find somebody who can kill a snake, will you,' he ordered. 'There's a cobra coiled up on the john. The thing must be four or five feet long and I haven't got time to deal with it. The helicopter's waiting for me.'

'Where're you going?' Pashetta asked.

'Putussibau.'

'Lucky you,' said Bethany, the image of a cobra on the loo making the idea of a few hours escape from Kanyalang particularly inviting.

'Come along, if you want to,' he replied, indifferently.

Bethany was almost tempted to say she would, when the reproachful expression on Pashetta's face made her hesitate. 'I don't think —' she began.

'Suit yourself,' he replied curtly, wondering what had gotten into him to make him suggest such a thing in the first place.

'Be sure and get someone onto the snake thing right away,' he told Pashetta, as he started toward the door, 'before some poor fool sits on it and gets a rude surprise.'

Bethany had trouble pushing this distressing possibility out of her mind but Pashetta's attention was entirely focused on Wolf's disappearing form.

'You see how he does not love me,' she declared ruefully when he had rounded the corner onto the veranda.

'He was in rather a hurry, you know,' Bethany pointed out, lamely.

Pashetta ignored this. Instead she lowered her voice to something close to a whisper and said, 'If you really don't want him for yourself, prove it.'

Bethany stared at her, incredulously. She had a feeling she shouldn't let herself be drawn into this conversation but her curiosity got the better of her. 'However do you expect me to do that?' she asked.

'Very easy. You just buy something for me in Putussibau.'

This time her better judgment triumphed over her curiosity and she refrained from asking, 'What?' Instead, she declared, firmly,

'I'm not going to go to Putussibau.'

'You're not? Why?'

'I don't really feel like it,' Bethany replied, resorting to the easiest explanation, 'and besides, I have work to do.'

Pashetta looked sceptical. 'Maybe you change your mind.'

'How can I? He's leaving in about two minutes.'

Pashetta paid no attention. 'There is a kind of medicine,' she explained, as if Bethany actually had asked what she should buy. 'Chinese medicine, it is called sehat laki laki. There are many kinds and some are no good so you must make sure you get the right one. I will write the name down for you so you do not forget.'

'What is it for?' Bethany asked suspiciously as, in spite of herself, she took the piece of paper and examined it. She knew that sehat meant health in Indonesian and laki laki was the word for men. What was Pashetta up to, anyway?

'It is for man. Make him strong in bed. Like this.' And Pashetta raised her forefinger to a stiff upright position.

'If you think for one minute that I'm going to buy anything of the sort, you're mad,' cried Bethany.

'It's very easy,' Pashetta went on, oblivious of any objections. 'Many Chinese shops have it. You just ask. Then I know if you want Wolf for yourself or not.'

'Come again?' said Bethany, thoroughly baffled.

'If you give me the medicine, I put in Wolf's drink, make him crazy for sex with me, make him commitment with me and take me to America, then I know you don't want him for yourself.'

'Of all the absurd —'

'But if you keep the medicine, you give it to him, you make him want to have sex with you — then I know you lied to me. You really do want him for yourself. Very easy. Very clear. We both know.'

'And suppose Wolf finds out what I've been buying. How embarrassing would that be?'

'If you are clever, he won't find out,' Pashetta declared. And reaching into a drawer of her desk, she took out a small purse and said, 'You don't have to pay. I pay. Here, I give you money.'

'Pay me later, if I buy it,' Bethany said. Then deciding that a hasty departure would be the best way of ending this absurd conversation, she abruptly said that she had to go and hurriedly left the office.

She was so preoccupied with Pashetta's outrageous request — it was all too easy to picture Wolf's leering grin if he caught her buying an aphrodisiac — that when she reached the veranda steps she unthinkingly turned in the direction of the landing pad instead of toward Nanga Palin. It only took her a split second to realise her mistake, ask herself what in the world she was doing and readjust her trajectory but now that the prospect of a day out had entered her mind, it suddenly seemed too tantalising to be turned down.

Sod it, she told herself. I don't care if the devil himself is on that plane. I haven't had a single day away from Kanyalang since I arrived and I'm not going to miss the chance to have one now.

A few breathless moments later Bethany was at the landing pad.

She found Wolf lounging against the side of the plane, waiting for the pilot to signal that everything was ready.

'So you decided to come,' Wolf remarked, wondering if he had been an idiot to suggest it.

The problem was that he hadn't been able to get her out of his mind since her astonishing revelation about having screwed around with some guy who had sticks through his cock. And he still wasn't sure whether it had been with just one guy or with half the longhouse, not that it mattered anyway.

Admittedly he had been severely tempted by Giri the night before but he hadn't quite come to terms with the idea of having sex with her just a few feet from where her mother and grandmother, and God only knew how many other relatives, were sleeping. Alternatively, the prospect of trudging out to one of those empty huts in the rice fields like some of the Dayak couples had seemed too daunting a prospect in his inebriated state.

The result had been that he had slept alone on a pandanus mat, surrounded by a bunch of sex-starved adolescents who had drawn the short straw in the midnight grab-arse. That was the trouble with those festivals at Nanga Palin. When it came to the crunch, they rarely turned into anything more than a hyped-up prick tease, not for him anyway. But last night had been particularly bad because he had kept wondering what Bethany was up to and how she was coping with Granny on the next mat, to say nothing of getting fucked by a human porcupine.

What kind of woman, Western woman, that is, would go for that sort of thing, he wondered? It seemed kind of sick to him and totally out of character for Bethany, of all people. There must be hidden depths to her character that he had been totally unaware of up to now. Maybe having her come along today hadn't been such a bad idea, after all. Getting a handle on what made her tick, especially if he could steer her onto that subject, might do a good deal to liven up an otherwise tedious day.

CHAPTER TWENTY-ONE

The pilot leaned out the window and gave the signal to come aboard.

'Hop in,' Wolf told Bethany. 'You're just in time'.

She regarded the fragile-looking aircraft apprehensively.

'What's the matter?' he demanded. 'You've been in this baby before.'

'I know but somehow I must have been too excited to notice how small it was or how...' She paused, searching for the right word.

'How what?'

'How flimsy.'

'Don't let the pilot hear you say that or he might toss you out,' Wolf teased. 'Come on, be brave. It generally stays up when it's supposed to.'

She didn't think 'generally' sounded very encouraging but she climbed in anyway. It was like being inside some sort of ghastly vibrating machine, Bethany decided as the helicopter lifted into the air but she managed to shout over the throb of the engine, 'Why are you going to Putussibau, anyway?'

'Somebody's got to do Tarique's job and as usual Elliot has shoved all the shitty stuff onto me.'

'What sort of stuff?'

'Going to the bank, getting money for the locals' salaries, settling the accounts with our purchasing agent, a bandit named Chen. He's a cousin, or at least a relative of some sort, of Liu's and he's got a strong preference for being paid in cash. Plus there's the post office and some telephone calls – you know what Elliot's like about using the iridium phone – and a few other boring errands that our great and mighty chief doesn't want to bother with himself. If it sounds deadly, that's because it is. I expect you'll be sorry you came along.'

'Oh, I doubt it,' she assured him, not caring much what they were going to do as long as they would be doing it away from Kanyalang or Nanga Palin. She was painfully aware that it was shameful to be so glad to get away but she couldn't help it. It was rather like being a little girl again and having a day out from school.

The ride seemed appreciably shorter than it had when she had first arrived in Borneo and she was surprised how soon the red tile roofs of Putussibau came into view.

After landing at the tiny airport they hired an antiquated taxi, one seemingly unencumbered by any functioning brakes, for the short ride into town. After some instructions from Wolf, it brought them to a row of open-fronted Chinese shop-houses where a nearly identical array of plastic pails, tin cooking pots, and other household paraphernalia overflowed onto the pavement from each enterprise.

'Why do all these places sell the same thing?' Bethany demanded.

'Who knows? It's the Chinese way, I guess,' Wolf shrugged.

Mr Chen, Kanyalang's primary purchasing agent, as well as the proprietor of one of the shop-houses, gave them a curt welcome and showed them to a small back room. Once there, he ejected two petulant children and an indignant cat from a sofa, neglected to turn off an enormous television and invited them to sit down.

After calling to a servant to bring tea, Mr Chen took out the latest Kanyalang invoices and handed them to Wolf, who perused them with an expression of sharp-eyed suspicion that Bethany thought was extremely rude, even for him. It also, she noticed, made his nose seem even more beaky than usual.

To break the uncomfortable silence that ensued, as well as to satisfy her curiosity about this strange establishment, Bethany made an effort to draw Mr Chen into conversation. This wasn't an easy task, as he apparently considered verbal communication to be a tool that should be reserved for doing business and not wasted on idle chatter.

In such heavily accented English that he almost made it sound like a tonal language, Chen informed her that he lived with his father who had emigrated from China many years ago, his wife who helped out in the shop and his five children, three of whom were in school.

'You're very lucky to have such a nice family,' Bethany observed, politely, in the hope of encouraging further revelations about his life.

Chen frowned slightly, not wanting to tempt fate by colluding in any complement to his family. 'School too much expensive,' he said, curtly.

'But I thought Indonesia had nine years of free education,' she objected.

The idea appeared to astonish him. 'Must go school nine years, yes. Free, no. Must pay.'

'But what happens if you don't have the money?' she asked.

To her surprise, he gave a short laugh. 'Problem,' he said. 'Big problem.'

'That's terrible,' she cried.

He didn't argue.

'How many years did you go to school?'

'Me? Five years. My father say that enough. Read, write, learn numbers enough for business. More school waste of money. Work more better. Make money. My father work very hard. No read, no write, only numbers. He very good with abacus.' Here Mr Chen broke into another laugh, much heartier than the first, and announced proudly, 'Me, I have computer. Big change. World change. My father say time he die.'

'That's a dreadful way to think.'

'He old man. Mostly sleep,' Mr Chen declared, unsentimentally. But his father wasn't sleeping at that particular moment.

Glancing down a dark corridor leading from the room, Bethany saw the old man approaching. He was frail and nearly toothless and was leaning on the shoulder of a middle-aged woman who Bethany took to be his daughter-in-law. Yet when he came nearer, she saw that his ancient eyes looked far more alert and open to the world than those of his son and he soon verified this by setting out to discover as much as he could about the visitors.

The old man spoke no English so the conversation switched into Indonesian. What country did they come from, he wanted to know. How long had they been here? What did they think of Indonesia? How many children did they have?

Bethany quickly disabused him of the idea that she and Wolf had produced any children together at all.

'Very sad,' old Mr Chen said 'but you are still young.' Then he turned his attention to the question of what they were doing in Putussibau. 'Logging business?' he asked eagerly.

Wolf looked up sharply from the invoices and snapped, 'Definitely not.'

The old man appeared disappointed. 'Big money,' he said regretfully.

Wolf couldn't deny this so, after responding with a swift glare, he returned to his reading without saying anything.

Bethany, thinking there was no need to be impolite, tried to make up for Wolf's behaviour by quizzing the old man about his past.

'When I come here, I young man,' old Mr Chen told her, 'strong but poor, very poor. For long time everyone very poor.' He went on to recount some of his youthful struggles in more detail than Wolf would have tolerated but Bethany found it all quite interesting. 'Then logging companies come,' he said, happily waving his blue-veined hand in the direction of the huge television set to indicate the consequent affluence. 'You can see.'

'All too well,' Wolf muttered under his breath in English.

If this comment was heard by either of the Mr Chens, it wasn't understood. But Bethany heard it and, feeling impelled to try to combine honesty with some modicum of tact, said, 'It's dreadful the way they've turned the jungle into something that looks like the surface of the moon.'

This negative attitude astonished old Mr Chen who shook his head and concluded that foreign females had no head for business.

Young Mr Chen was by that time looking pointedly at his watch. 'I very busy man,' he said.

'I bet you are,' Wolf retorted, 'and creative, too, judging by these invoices.'

But the dart missed its intended victim by a linguistic mile so Wolf resorted to unmistakable body language. Slamming the offending papers down on a low table near the sofa, he barked,

'You can't seriously expect me to believe this crap, can you?'

Chen's face went white with anger. 'You no like — your problem.'

'Yeah, it's my problem and you can bet your arse it's going to be your problem too because if the prices on these invoices don't check out, you're going to be up shit creek. And let me tell you —'

The pressure of a hand on his upper leg made him break off. Casting a glance of undisguised astonishment at Bethany, he demanded under his breath, 'Are you trying to grope me or is this just your subtle way of conveying a message?'

'Definitely the latter,' she hissed back, punctuating her response with a sharp pinch perilously close to a point where it would inflict considerable pain.

When Wolf had scraped himself off the ceiling, he found that she was politely thanking the Mr Chens for the tea and saying good-bye.

The moment they were out on the pavement, Wolf demanded, 'What the fuck did you think you were doing, damn near castrating me in there?'

'Just trying to hint that it was time to leave.'

'If that's your idea of a hint, I hate to think what a strong statement would be like.'

'Sorry,' she said, not sounding very sorry, 'but you were being so unreasonable in there that —'

'Bullshit. I'm never unreasonable.'

'You were then. You were going out on a completely unnecessary limb and absolutely inviting him to saw it off after you.'

'How do you figure that?'

'You were insisting those invoices were false before you had actually checked them out. That couldn't have been the best way to go about things, could it? And I don't suppose being rude and horrible to him was going to be any help either.'

Wolf responded with a growl, recalling that Marguarita had had a go at him for much the same thing after those two gold mining bastards had been at Kanyalang.

'So I just thought we should leave before you alienated Mr Chen completely.'

'You know, you may have more smarts than I've been giving you credit for,' he admitted, although he was still annoyed.

'That's a pathetic compliment if ever I heard one,' she complained, hoping he didn't see that she was secretly pleased.

He didn't. His mind was still on Chen. 'But the thought of what that tripe-hound's up to makes me want to spit nails.'

'You don't know for certain that he's up to anything,' Bethany reminded him.

'I haven't got iron-clad proof yet if that's what you mean but I've got a gut feeling that's so strong it's just gotta be right.'

'And how far do you think that will get you?'

'We'll just have to see, won't we?' he snapped. 'Come on, let's get some lunch. Padang food, okay?'

'I'm not quite sure what that is but I'll give it a try.'

'Good because that's about all there is here.'

They walked on in semi-hostile silence until they came to a wide boardwalk some thirty feet above the Sibau River. It was crowded with market stalls selling everything from colourful batiks to fiery chillies, and Bethany would have liked to linger in the midst of its cheerful chaos but Wolf, declaring that getting pissed off always made him hungry, steered her firmly into the only visible restaurant.

'I'd kill for a cold beer right now,' he declared when they were seated in the dismal little eatery, 'but the Melati Hotel's the only place in town that's got a refrigerator and they only put drinks in it if you order them far enough ahead of time for them to cool down.'

Bethany was diverted from this curious style of hotel management by a waiter who began flinging an assortment of small dishes down on their table. Peering into them, she discovered that each one contained a portion of beef, chicken, fish, or eggs swimming in its own spicy sauce. Nobody had ordered these things. They had just arrived. And the waiter, who appeared to be on the receiving end of some sort of telepathic communication, was soon ladling mountains of fluffy white rice onto their plates.

'However did he know what we wanted?' Bethany asked, after the man had hurried off to display similar feats of intuition at other tables.

'He didn't. He just brings whatever's available and if it appeals to you, you eat it and they charge you for it. If you don't want it, you leave it and that's the end of that. You don't pay for it.'

'Well, it looks delicious,' Bethany said, thinking this was an odd way to run a restaurant but helping herself to several of the more inviting items. 'I'm starving.'

Disappointment was soon written across her face.

'You don't look like you're enjoying it very much,' Wolf observed, 'too spicy for you?'

'It's not that,' she declared. 'The sauces are lovely. It's just that somehow the cook seems to have managed to get a mixture of bone, gristle, fat, and some skin in every bite. I don't think I can eat it.'

'Try the egg dish then. That should be okay. And you can dip the sauces out of the other things and just put them over the rice.'

It didn't sound like a great solution but it helped her take the edge off her appetite.

'You know, I've been thinking,' Wolf mused, as he crunched a chicken bone.

Bethany, more interested in Wolf's bone-pulverizing expertise than in his cerebral gymnastics, asked, 'How can you just eat the bones like that?'

'Teeth like a wolf, I guess,' he grinned, helping himself to another chicken wing, 'goes with the name. But don't you want to know what I was thinking?'

'Not very much.'

'Then you don't deserve to know but I'm such a nice guy, I'll tell you anyway.'

'If you like,' she replied, indifferently.

'I was thinking that I owe you one.'

'You do? Whatever for?' she asked, interested now in spite of herself.

'For keeping me from climbing out on a limb back there with Chen.'

'Oh, that,' she said, dismissively. 'That was nothing.'

'I'd say it was something, even if you did choose to express it in a particularly vicious form of sign language.'

'You can't mean that one little pinch,' she exclaimed. 'It was hardly life-threatening.'

'Maybe not to me but it sure as hell threatened the life of any future off-spring I might have,' he said, trying to sound disgruntled but sabotaging his performance by laughing.

'Hey, I've got an idea,' he said, when they had finished the meal and were leaving the restaurant. 'How about taking a short detour by the Melati Hotel and getting them to put a couple of beers on ice for us? After the thoroughly shitty afternoon we've got in store for us, we're going to be desperate for a swig of something cold.'

CHAPTER TWENTY-TWO

It didn't take Bethany long to discover that Wolf hadn't painted an unduly dismal picture of what lay ahead of them. The cauldron-like heat, combined with the pushing and shoving crowds at the post office, left her feeling drained and exhausted. And this ordeal, she soon discovered, was only the beginning. It was followed by a more orderly but seemingly interminable queue at the bank. As the time crawled by she began to wonder whether her inevitable death would actually be caused by thirst or by boredom. She tortured herself by picturing the tall green bottles of beer that had been put in the fridge for them. Were they covered with frost by now, she wondered? Had their contents begun to freeze? These speculations were so tantalising that, when Wolf announced that there were yet more errands to do, she could cheerfully have strangled him.

'Try and bear up,' he said, reading her expression. 'We'll do the wartel next. It shouldn't be too bad.'

'What's a wartel?'

'A place with public telephones. I've got some calls to make but I'll try not to be too long.'

As far as she could see, he didn't try very hard. Perching on a narrow bench in a crowded stifling little room while Wolf shouted over a very bad line to a succession of suppliers in Pontianak and Singapore was definitely not Bethany's idea of a pleasant way to spend an afternoon. She tried to hurry him along by means of a succession of death-stares but they proved ineffective.

To make matters worse, she began to worry about the Chinese medicine. The best solution to the problem would probably be just to forget about it, but she wasn't sure Pashetta would believe that she really hadn't bought it. It would be too embarrassing if she suspected her of just keeping it to use for her own purposes.

It doesn't matter what she thinks, Bethany tried to tell herself. Yet somehow it did matter. The idea of anyone believing that she was chasing after Wolf with aphrodisiacs, or even without them, was too appalling. She couldn't let that happen.

Leaping up, she went over to Wolf and hissed, 'Back in a mo.'

He nodded and returned to his conversation.

It wasn't hard to find a shop that sold Chinese medicines, they had passed several on the way to the wartel. The difficulty was that there were several different packets labelled sehat laki laki so she fished into her handbag for the paper, now a bit crumpled, where Pashetta had written the full name of the one she wanted. Bethany smoothed it out and showed it to the shopkeeper who, after giving her a look of mild curiosity, opened a locked drawer beneath the counter and took out the requested item.

Bethany quickly paid for it, squirreled it away in her handbag and reclaimed her place on the bench in the wartel.

By the time Wolf finished his telephoning, she was hot, thirsty and thoroughly tired of waiting and had neither the inclination nor the ability to hide her irritation. 'Couldn't you have waited and rung those people later from Kanyalang?' she demanded.

'On the iridium phone,' he exclaimed, 'when it costs a fucking fortune just to say 'Hello' on the damn thing? You know what the old man's like about money these days, not that I blame him. He hasn't much choice.'

'But what's the point of having an iridium phone if it's too expensive to use?'

'Emergencies, we've got to have some contact with the outside world besides the old single-side-band radio. Neanderthals had things like that during the Ice Age. But here,' his voice waxed sarcastic, 'in the great metropolis of Putussibau, we've got access to an ordinary telephone and I had a lot of calls to make.'

'So I noticed.'

'Yeah, well, I wanted to do a bunch of quick price checks.'

'Quick? You were ages.'

'Maybe,' he admitted, 'but if I want Elliot to listen to me about the way Chen's been ripping us off, I've got to make sure I've got all the facts. Otherwise, I'm not going to be able to convince him of anything.'

'And did you find what you were looking for?'

'In spades. And let me tell you, that horse's arse, Chen, has been fucking us over in a way that's nothing short of highway robbery.

I wouldn't squawk if it was just ten percent or so, that's Indonesia for you. I'd expect a little padding in the accounts, but this is something else.'

Bethany saw that once again he was knitting his brows together in a way that made his nose seem even bigger.

'And if I've got anything to say about it,' he continued, 'heads are going to roll. But I can't do anything about it now so let's hit the bazaar and then we can crack open that beer.'

'The sooner the better,' Bethany agreed emphatically.

'Poor kid, I guess I've given you a rotten afternoon.'

Bethany made no attempt to deny this but she forgot her misery once they were strolling from stall to stall bargaining for what Wolf called 'jungle luxuries'. She treated herself to several bars of peanuts hardened in palm sugar and to a bag full of individually wrapped sesame sweets but she drew back at the prospect of crocodile tongue shampoo.

'Whoever would want to put something like that on their hair?' she exclaimed, in disgust.

Wolf laughed. 'Don't worry, it's just made from a leaf that looks like a crocodile's tongue.'

'Are you sure?'

He shrugged. 'It's what I heard.'

'From whom?'

'My ex-wife, if you must know. She used to use it.'

'Your ex-wife?' Bethany was stunned. 'I didn't know you had ever been married.'

'I wasn't for long.'

'You've never mentioned her, your wife, I mean.'

He shrugged. 'No reason to.'

A million questions flooded Bethany's mind but she decided this wasn't the place to ask them, no place was, really. After all why should she care if he had had ten wives, or a hundred? She was just being a nosey parker that was all.

She went ahead and bought the crocodile tongue shampoo but she was still so distracted by Wolf's bombshell that she walked away and left it on the table. Then her eye was caught by a pile of sarongs, all different designs and colours, on a near-by stall. She selected two, and was doing her best to bargain for a good price, when she saw a third one she liked even better.

'Damn,' she exclaimed, 'now I don't know which ones to choose.'

'Get all three,' Wolf advised. 'You don't get a chance to go shopping very often.'

'Good idea,' she agreed but revised her opinion when she took out her purse and realised that, after buying the sex pills, she didn't have quite enough money for all of them. 'I suppose I'll just have to choose,' she sighed.

'No, you won't,' he said, 'because I'm going to get you the third one as a present.'

'I'll pay you back as soon as we get back to Kanyalang.'

'Forget it. I told you I owe you one for getting me away from Chen's when you did. And on top of that, I've given you a shitty afternoon so regard the sarong as a gift of conscience.'

'I didn't know you had one,' she teased.

'It comes and goes,' he grinned. 'Now you see it, now you don't. But never mind about that. Help me find a new pair of rubber sandals. Mine are practically in shreds.'

Although this type of footwear was one of the most ubiquitous items in the market, their search proved fruitless. Wolf had American-sized feet and they couldn't find any big enough.

Replenishing his supply of clove cigarettes was an easier task. He bought two cartons, one for himself and one for Kolop, who also liked them.

'I don't think I've ever seen you smoke,' Bethany said, wondering how many new things about Wolf were going to come to light during the course of this afternoon.

'I don't very often. I'm one of those few people who can have one now and then and not get hooked. But I like the smell of these Indonesian ones because of the cloves. They make me think of my grandparent's house at Christmas.'

'What a sentimentalist you are,' she exclaimed, amazed.

He grimaced, as though unsure this was something he wanted to be. 'Come on,' he urged, 'let's go unchain that beer we ordered.'

They retraced their steps to the Melati Hotel but found the

atmosphere there so hot and oppressive that Wolf suggested taking the bottles, now icy-cold, to an open-sided summerhouse perched high on a promontory above the river.

Bethany readily agreed and while Wolf, with the aid of his Swiss Army Knife, set about opening the beer, she amused herself by watching the life on the river. A longboat, so crowded with villagers, vegetables and squalling piglets that it was riding perilously low in the water, made its way downstream while a houseboat was being tied up at the dock. A woman was hanging the family wash out on a line strung across the rear deck, seemingly unfazed by the active child and the dirty puppy that darted back and forth amidst the waving clothes, narrowly avoiding tumbling over the side.

'Here, take this,' Wolf said, handing her one of the icy bottles.

She did, and it was heaven. The best champagne in the world could not have tasted more delicious at that moment. Yet when she glanced over at Wolf, she was surprised to see that he was scowling.

'Whatever's the matter?' she asked.

Wolf waved his beer bottle toward another houseboat, one that was towing a trail of logs downstream while a hapless child was being dangled over the side to pee.

It was the damage to the rainforest, not the possible discomfort of the toddler that was infuriating him. 'I can't look at those damn logs on their way to some sawmill somewhere without thinking about Chen and all the fucking bastards like him who are savaging this place. God, how I'd love to go back there right now and tell him exactly what kind of shit I think he is. Nothing would give me more pleasure than lowering the boom on any future dealings with him but, of course, I can't do that without an okay from the big boss. And Elliot opposes everything I want to do, just on principle.'

'I thought it was the other way around,' Bethany said.

He frowned. 'I don't get it. What do you mean?'

'I thought you were the one who liked to cut him down.'

Wolf shrugged. 'Maybe two can play that game.'

Bethany regarded him doubtfully.

'Listen, I'm not really suffering from any of those delusions of grandeur you accused me of that day at Nanga Palin. The last thing I want to do is strut around as if I'm the leader of the band when I'm not. For one thing, I can't imagine a faster way to get my arse shipped out of here. For another, I'd feel phoney as hell doing anything of the kind.'

This astonishing evidence that he had taken her remarks to heart delighted Bethany but she did her best to conceal any outward show of triumph. Instead, she said, 'You shouldn't have trouble with Elliot this time, should you? I can't imagine that he'll be happy to hear what Chen's been up to.'

'Yeah,' Wolf agreed, 'for once, we might actually see eye-to-eye on something.'

Thinking about it brought to mind some of the recent exchanges he had had with Elliot, particularly that awful one about Bethany.

'You know,' Wolf said, after giving due attention to his beer, 'I was just thinking about the time you made that little trek into Elliot's office to complain about me.'

'Come again?' she said, looking at him blankly.

'The time you told him I was interfering with your work at Nanga Palin.'

'Excuse me but I never did any such thing.'

'You must have. He told me exactly what you said.'

'He couldn't have because I didn't tell him anything.'

'Then there must have been some kind of jungle telegraph at work that day because as soon as I got back he chewed me out, repeating almost verbatim, the same crazy accusations you had flung at me earlier that afternoon.'

'That's impossible,' she cried but an instant later she realised that actually it was possible. 'Perhaps he did hear it from me,' she acknowledged, slowly, 'but I didn't tell him.'

'Run that one by me again, will you. The logic of it kind of escapes me.'

'I told Marguarita about it,' Bethany explained. 'She was on the veranda when I got back from Nanga Palin that afternoon and she could see from my face that something was wrong. She asked me what it was and I told her. I was absolutely livid so I probably spared no detail.'

'So that was it,' he said, a grimace. 'Well, I always suspected she had the makings of a top-notch spy.'

'Don't be silly. She's just observant, that's all.'

'That's putting it mildly. I'd say she's got eyes like a lynx and she could probably be just about as dangerous.'

'Rubbish.'

'You've got to admit she apparently wasted no time in repeating everything you said to Elliot.'

'I don't admit that at all.'

'We're not coming back to the jungle telegraph theory again, are we?'

'Of course not, it's just that we were standing by the thermos outside Pashetta's office at the time so if Elliot's door was ajar he could have overheard everything we said.'

'He always keeps it closed,' Wolf declared.

'Perhaps not always – he might have had it open for some reason. I didn't notice. I was upset and Marguarita was there so I told her what had happened, that's all.'

'Well, that's not quite so bad,' he acknowledged.

'You mean, I'm not the nasty little sneak you took me for?'

'Yeah, that's pretty much what I mean. Tell me, are you still raging mad about all that?'

'Yes, now that you mention it. But somehow, I haven't been thinking about it today.'

'Any chance of extending the truce?'

'I might be willing, if you are,' she replied cautiously.

'Good,' he said, 'that makes two of us then.'

He stretched out his hand to touch her fingers and Bethany responded by reaching out to him. As she did so, she dislodged her handbag from its position on her lap. It tumbled upside down at her feet and its contents fanned out across the pavilion floor.

Wolf immediately caught sight of the box with the words Sehat Laki Laki printed on them. 'Jesus Christ,' he exclaimed, breaking out in raucous laughter, 'who's the lucky bastard you're planning to give that to?'

It was one of those moments when Bethany wished an earthquake or a bolt of lightning or possibly a hungry tiger would come along and put her out of her misery. In desperation she toyed with the idea of telling Wolf about Pashetta's plan but that seemed like such a shabby thing to do. Eventually, for lack of a better alternative, she merely snapped, 'It's none of your business.'

'Okay,' he said, grinning, 'fair enough. But I've got a piece of advice for you.'

'I'm not interested,' she declared, frantically gathering up her scattered possessions and thrusting them helter-skelter into her handbag.

'I'll tell you anyway,' he said, bending down to help her. 'If a guy needs stuff like that to get it up, he's not worth bothering about. Write him off your list. Christ, that longhouse over at Nanga Palin must be chock full of guys who've got testosterone up to the eyebrows. You shouldn't have any trouble finding one who can do the job without any pharmacological help.'

Bethany looked at him in astonishment. Did he think ... surely, he couldn't. She wouldn't, especially not at Nanga Palin where even the tallest man barely came above her shoulder. And even if they did think ...

'But I must say,' he went on, 'I've got to hand it to you for being the most conscientious anthropologist Kanyalang could ever hope to have, as well as for turning into the most surprising woman I've ever met. You know, when you first came to Kanyalang I had you pegged as a real life, walking, talking Alice in Wonderland.'

'I could see that and it was very irritating.'

'Was it? Sorry. Well, if it makes you feel any better, I now know how wrong I was. I mean, you can imagine how startling it's been to find out that Alice had not only grown up but had shagged her way through half of Wonderland, that is, if Nanga Palin can be considered Wonderland. That's really taking the duties of a participant observer to an impressive level. And now to top it off I see that you're even resorting to Chinese aphrodisiacs to keep

Wonderland sex up to your undoubtedly high expectations. If that isn't dedication to science, I don't know what is.'

Bethany didn't know whether to laugh at him or kill him.

'Of course, I'm going along with the highly dubious proposition that anthropology can be considered a science,' he continued, 'but leaving that aside for the moment, let me tell you that a woman who's prepared to go that far for the sake of a job well done is my idea of a seriously intriguing female and if —'

'Where in the world did you get the ridiculous idea that I've shagged my way through Nanga Palin?' she gasped.

'From you, actually.'

'From me?'

'Yes, the night of the festival for the rice goddess. You made no secret of the fact that you were in on the weirder aspects of Dayak sex life, including the barbaric things they do to their dicks, so don't try to tell me you found out about it through some kind of divine revelation.'

'I won't, because as it happens Giri and some of the other girls told me about it. That's how I know.'

'Shit, you don't mean that all my admiration for the world's most dedicated anthropologist has been wasted.'

'I'm afraid it has.'

'God, I haven't been so disappointed since some sadistic creep on the school bus told me there was no Santa Claus.'

'Then perhaps you're the one who's been living in Wonderland,' she observed dryly.

'Ouch,' he exclaimed, 'but I guess I deserved that one.'

'I think you did.'

'Well never mind that, if your little purchase here isn't going to be used for research purposes, who's going to be the happy beneficiary?'

'Why ever would I tell you?'

'Because I'm already in on the scheme — partially anyway.'

'Not good enough.'

'Let me think, then. If it's not anyone at Nanga Palin, it's gotta be someone at Kanyalang, though probably not Elliot, not unless you've got some kind of father fixation. And I doubt if it's Mike.

He's a great guy, the best, but not your type, somehow. The same goes for Bima, in a different sort of way. Of course, there's always my charming self but I've got a feeling we'd have to be stranded on a desert island for ten or twenty years first.'

'Try fifty.'

'Okay, fifty, so that brings us back to life and love among the Dayaks. Are you sure you're not about to embark on any first-hand research along those lines?'

'Actually,' she teased, deciding she was enjoying this, 'that's for me to know and you to guess.'

This response, and the change of mood it indicated, gave Wolf an uneasy feeling that he had missed something vital along the way. He always liked to feel that he was in control of a situation but this one had somehow slipped out of his grasp. He glanced down at his watch and wasn't sorry to see that it was time to go.

When the helicopter put down on the landing pad at Kanyalang, Wolf, faithful to his plan, went straight to Elliot's office to report what he had learnt about Chen, but Bethany, deciding that it was too late to try to do any work, went directly back to the longhouse.

No sooner had she reached the top of the veranda stairs than she came face to face with the person she least wanted to see.

'Did you get it?' Pashetta whispered, without preamble.

Bethany was tempted just to hand over the troublesome medicine and be rid of it but a sudden doubt about how subtle Pashetta would be in giving it to Wolf made her hesitate. If he figured out that she had colluded in an attempt to trap him, as he certainly would now that he knew she had bought the stuff, he would go ballistic. But then, why should she care? Didn't he deserve anything Pashetta could throw at him? And yet somehow she couldn't go along with it.

'I'm afraid, I didn't get it,' she lied.

'But you promised.'

'No, I didn't. I only told you I might get it,' Bethany insisted, even though she couldn't remember exactly what she had said. 'Anyway, Wolf didn't give me a chance. He stuck with me like glue.'

217

This was not something that Pashetta enjoyed hearing. 'I think you did not want to get away from him,' she declared.

'That's not it. Really, I'm sorry but I couldn't, at least, I didn't.'

Pashetta's eyes smouldered with recriminations as she muttered, 'You want him for yourself, I know.'

Bethany, knowing that denials would be useless, seized on the first excuse she could think of to get away. Mumbling something about washing her hair, she hurried down the veranda to her room.

During the rest of the evening Bethany tried to avoid Pashetta's reproachful glances. Luckily at dinner everyone's attention was focused on Wolf's recital of Chen's transgressions and, for once, Elliot and Wolf actually shared the same feelings of outrage and anger.

By the time the inevitable plate of bananas and green tangerines arrived at the end of the meal, Pashetta was thoroughly fed up with the subject. Of course, Chen had been padding the accounts, she thought, and Liu was certainly doing the same thing. How could foreigners be so stupid that they didn't know this? If they sent Chen and Liu away, the next people they hired would do the same thing and take just as much, maybe more. Why not? Foreigners were so rich they probably wouldn't even notice, at least, not right away, and that would give the new people time to help themselves to something worthwhile.

When everyone had left the table, Pashetta wandered listlessly out onto the veranda and surveyed the scene around her. She wasn't quite sure what to do with the rest of the evening. Wolf had brought out his laptop but he was too intent on what he was typing, something that looked like notes and prices, to pay any attention to her. Elliot had disappeared into his room, very likely to enjoy the contents of a bottle of something called Glenlivet. She had seen it on top of his chest of drawers that afternoon when he had sent her in search of a diskette he had left there. She had asked him later if Glenlivet was like whisky and he had just laughed. Still, she was quite certain that it was.

Pashetta had no desire to join the conversation Marguarita was having with that traitor, Bethany. They were going on about leaves and fevers and Dayak cures. Boring. In any case, Bethany was the last person she wanted to talk to at the moment and she always found something just a little scary about Marguarita.

A squeal of delight drew her attention to a small table where, in the course of a chess lesson, Catherine had just taken Bima's bishop. These lessons had become a near-nightly event over the past few weeks and apparently Catherine was proving to be a singularly apt pupil. At least, that's what Bima claimed. But then, Pashetta reminded herself, he was getting almost as bad as Elliot, always thinking that everything Catherine said or did was perfect. How did she manage to convince so many people of this, Pashetta wondered? Could it be that there was some kind of Australian magic behind it all?

Just as Pashetta was considering this possibility, Mike emerged from his room with a small knife in one hand and a block of wood that was beginning to take the shape of an owl in the other. He was relatively new at woodcarving, but watching the old men at Nanga Palin had inspired him to take it up, not that he would ever be able to fashion wonderful gods and elaborately decorated objects the way they did, he knew. The thing was that he had to do something with his evenings. He wasn't much of a reader and in the normal course of life at Kanyalang he had already become as much of a social being as his nature and upbringing permitted. Although if asked, Mike would have denied having any kind of artistic sense or particular feeling for beauty, it would not have been strictly true. His self-knowledge was limited and his modesty was immense with the result that a great deal of his potential went unappreciated, particularly by himself. And while he thought it was okay for guys like Bima to be a little on the arty-farty side, it wasn't a label he would have cared to have pinned on himself.

He had quickly discovered that woodcarving wasn't nearly as easy as the old men at Nanga Palin had made it look but he had persisted and, like Catherine with the chess, was proving to be unexpectedly adept at his new hobby. Of course, his early efforts had been dreadful. Anyone rummaging around amongst his socks and underwear would find a horse with uneven legs that wouldn't stand up, a dog whose tail had been accidentally sliced off, and a crocodile that was in dire need of a set of false teeth. But now, finally, an owl that looked quite promising was beginning to take shape.

Pashetta, for lack of anything better to do, went over and watched the increasingly life-like figure emerge from the wooden block.

At first Mike was rather disconcerted by her presence but after a while he decided that he rather liked having her there and gradually he became so absorbed in his creative efforts that he almost forgot about her. It took a particularly loud and raucous call from a lizard directly beneath the floorboards to restore his awareness of his surroundings. The unfortunate result of this unexpected sound was that he let his knife slip.

'Fuck!' he exclaimed, surveying his damaged bird with dismay. 'Feathers are shit.'

A startled Pashetta leapt off her seat.

'Sorry,' he mumbled, inwardly cursing himself for not being able to talk to a woman without scaring her, boring her or somehow making her angry. How did guys like Wolf do it, he wondered?

'Feathers are not like shit,' she corrected him primly when she had settled back onto her chair. 'Why do you say they are?'

'I meant they're hard to carve, hard for me anyway because I'm no good at it.'

'I think you are very good.'

'If I was any good, I wouldn't have done this, would I?' he said, pointing to the spot that no longer had a feather.

'Never mind. You can fix it, can't you?'

He scanned it doubtfully.

'Just change the other side to match this one,' she suggested, helpfully. 'Then no one will notice.'

'But it won't be right,' he replied, ruefully.

'Who cares about 'right' as long as nobody knows what really happened?'

Mike wasn't quite sure how he felt about this attitude. Still, there might be something in it.

Following her advice, he made a small alteration in the design on each side of the figure. The result was, if anything, an improvement on his original concept. Reassured, he went on carving and by the time he put down his knife for the evening and began clearing up the wood shavings Mike was actually feeling pleased with the owl, pleased with Pashetta and even a little bit pleased with himself.

He had always rather fancied Pashetta and it occurred to him that he could make a move on her now without worrying about horning in on Wolf. The problem was, how to go about it? He wished he was one of those men who understood women but he was sure that would be too much to hope for. Even now, Pashetta had a rather odd expression on her face that made him wonder if she was thinking what an idiot he was.

It would have surprised him to know that she was actually thinking how stupid Bima was being. The chess game had finished and Catherine was going on about the gliding radius and dietary habits of flying foxes and Bima was drinking up every word as if he thought those dreadful creatures, sort of like bats, were the most interesting thing in the world.

The amazing thing was that it wasn't long before Marguarita and Wolf were listening to what Catherine was saying, too. Well, what could you expect, Pashetta thought irritably? Marguarita was interested in everything about the jungle and so was Wolf, especially if it involved Catherine. And now Mike was gazing over in her direction, too, straining to hear what she had to say.

Only Bethany appeared to be indifferent to the prowess of the flying foxes. Pashetta was happy to see that she, at least, was buried in Elliot's discarded copy of the Times, even though it was probably a week or two old. Then a wave of anger swept over her as she remembered the Chinese medicine but she consoled herself with the thought that Mike now seemed to like her and she probably wouldn't need any sex pills with him. If they had some really good sex he might even want to marry her and take her to Australia.

The more she thought about it, the more she liked the idea. Australian men were nicer than Americans and, she decided, remembering her misadventure with the English teacher, very much nicer than British men. They were the worst of all. Maybe all the good English, if there ever were any, left their country a long time ago and went to Australia. Well, that was alright with her because that was where she was going, too.

Eventually the lateness of the hour began to make itself felt. Yawns preceded 'goodnights' and soon everyone except Wolf and Bethany had drifted back to their own rooms.

Wolf sauntered over to the veranda railing, as he liked to do before he went to bed, and gazed out at the silhouettes of the trees, black against the moon-lit sky. It calmed his spirits, cleared his mind, and gave him a feeling of kinship with the jungle creatures around him.

Bethany regarded him thoughtfully for a moment and then put down the Times and joined him at the rail.

'Thanks ever so much,' she said.

'What for?' he asked, in surprise.

'The day, it was great.'

'In spite of the post office and the wartel and all that?'

'Yes, a bit of a change was the thing I needed, even if it wasn't heaven every minute. But there's just one thing –' She broke off, regretting that she had started.

'What?'

'Whatever made you take me along? I mean, face it, we've both been avoiding each other recently, haven't we?'

'Maybe I don't like to lunch alone,' he said.

'Perhaps, but that isn't much of a reason, is it? There must be something else.'

'Not really. I acted on impulse, that's all.'

'A curious impulse under the circumstances.'

'Well, let's just say that you looked particularly attractive at that moment.'

'Nonsense.'

'In fact, you don't look too bad right now.'

'That's something anyway,' she smiled.

He grinned back at her in a way that gave her the idea he might be about to come on to her and for a breathtaking moment she almost wished he would.

Then Marguarita's voice, asking if she had finished with the Times, shattered the mood and brought her back to reality.

It appeared to have the same effect on Wolf because he abruptly gathered up his laptop and his notes, said 'Goodnight all,' and headed off to his room.

'It's on the table by the sofa,' Bethany told her tersely.

'Did I interrupt something?' Marguarita asked with a mixture of curiosity and amusement.

'No, of course not.'

'I'm not sure I believe that.'

'Does it matter?'

'Not really.' There was more wistfulness than envy in Marguarita's tone as she added, 'I'm a little jealous, that's all.'

'Jealous,' exclaimed Bethany, scarcely able to believe her ears.

'Oh, not of Wolf,' she assured her, 'but of the situation. It looked like a rather romantic little scene there and it made me wish…' Her voice trailed off.

'Wish what?'

'Nothing,' Marguarita replied, unwilling to let on that the wish concerned Jim and his unpalatable gold mine.

CHAPTER TWENTY-FOUR

Jim was too busy to think much about gold mining these days. His new business had taken off at a very satisfactory rate and was now consuming most of his non-drinking time. The number of visitors to the area who wanted a guided tour up-river, preferably at Calco's expense, continued to amaze him. And he was profoundly grateful, not only for the effect they had on his bank balance, but for the sheer pleasure of being able to immerse himself in the rainforest without leaving any indelible scars on it.

Good God, he thought, he was actually beginning to think like those guys at Kanyalang. Still he hadn't yet acted on his determination to go back there and alert them to the fact that someone was filching their maps and selling them off to some two-bit loggers. Not only had he been busy but he wanted to have a chance to come to terms with the changes in his feelings and in his attitudes before he saw Marguarita again. They needed time to take root and flourish if he wasn't going to botch things with her a second time. He couldn't rush things because, if he did, not only Marguarita, but that whole bunch would see right through him and sling him out on his arse.

The worst of it was that he couldn't exactly blame them for being suspicious. After all, what kind of guy would be perfectly happy to carpet the jungle with mercury seepage from a gold mine one minute and then swear to all sorts of lofty ideals about the rainforest five minutes later?

A liar, that's what kind of guy. He knew plenty of sons-of-bitches who'd be glad to do exactly that and they'd all be collecting their pay cheques from oil or mining companies. He knew that if he didn't tread very, very carefully, that's what Marguarita and her gang of environmentalists would think he was doing.

He did have one thing going for him, though. He'd be bringing those maps that had the Kanyalang logo right on them and he'd be blowing the whistle on some dirty dealing that wasn't about to do their conservation area any good. Hopefully that would give him the credibility he needed.

Still, he reminded himself, there'd be one person for sure who wouldn't thank him for bringing the situation to light. That was the guy who'd filched the maps in the first place. He'd bet it would turn out to be that American with the animal name. What was it? Jackal? Hyena? No, nobody had a name like that. Wolf, that was it. God, whoever hung that label on him must've been a fucking genius.

Wolf, at this moment, was on his way back to the longhouse for lunch but had stopped to inspect the enclosure that had recently been built for the piglets. He frowned as he gazed at the picturesque roof that extended over part of it. The rains were getting heavier now that it was December and it didn't look very strong. The thatch, doubtless one of Bima's arty-farty ideas, ought to be replaced with some kind of plastic or metal sheeting.

Wolf reached through the wire and tickled the largest animal on the snout. 'Poor old guy,' he murmured, 'I'm afraid you won't be around much longer.'

The idea of becoming a vegetarian flashed into his mind and then out again as quickly as it had appeared. He knew how he would react to the first whiff of Kolop's spicy pork stew.

A darkening sky, along with a distant rumble from the heavens, cut short his chat with his curly-tailed companions and convinced Wolf that he would do well to get back to the longhouse quickly. He made a dash for it but was less than halfway there when the deluge broke and giant sized raindrops began to fall.

By the time he reached the shelter of the veranda he was so wet that the only course of action seemed to be to shake himself dog fashion.

'What are you doing?' cried Bethany, as the second-hand raindrops blurred the ink on the letter she was reading.

'Sorry. I didn't see you. What are you looking so happy about? Is that a love letter or something?'

'No,' she laughed, 'people don't write love letters anymore, do they, not to me, anyway.'

'I've never gotten one either,' Wolf admitted, 'but if that's not a love letter, what the hell is it? Have you won the lottery or something, or did you inherit a million dollars?'

'Neither one, I'm afraid. It's just a letter from an old friend.'

'He must be a damn good friend.'

'He's not a he. He's a she. And she's not actually that good a friend. We were at school together, that's all. I haven't seen her or heard from her in years.'

'Then why the euphoria now?'

'Because she's here in Kalimantan, teaching English in a place called Sanggau. That's not far from here, is it?'

'No, it's about half way down the Kapuas River on the way to Pontianak.'

'Brilliant.'

'Scarcely that. It's just a little market town, a hole, if you want to know.'

'That doesn't matter. The great thing is that she heard I was out here and got my address from another girl in our class. She wants me to come and visit her. Isn't that fantastic?'

'If you've hardly thought of her in the past hundred years or so, what's the great attraction now?'

Bethany considered this for a moment and then said, thoughtfully, 'To be honest, I don't quite know. It is a bit silly, isn't it? But perhaps it's because she belonged, still does, I suppose, to a world that's sane and rational and comprehensible and…'

'And this one isn't?' he suggested.

'Well, I know it's an awful thing to say, but…' She hesitated.

'Go ahead. I'm broadminded.'

'Oh, perhaps it's just all this rain,' she said, trying to make light of her feelings, 'but there's so much of it these days it's beginning to get on my nerves.'

'Yours and mine, both, everyone's, in fact.'

She looked at him in mild surprise. Of course, people complained about the rain all the time but she hadn't realised that anyone minded in the same way she did. 'Sometimes when it comes streaming down in sheets like this, I feel like a great wall is closing in on me.'

'Well, in a way, it is.'

'And somehow everything's become… well, just so frightfully dull and routine.'

227

'Was it ever anything else?'

'Yes, in the beginning. I mean, just the idea that I was actually here in Borneo made everything, even terribly ordinary things like speaking Indonesian or Dayak, seem challenging and exciting.'

'And they don't anymore?'

'No, now it's all just a nasty slog in languages I can't express myself in very well. Not that that really matters because I don't think the people at Nanga Palin would understand me in any language.'

'Isn't it your job to understand them?' he asked. 'After all, you're the anthropologist.'

'Oh, don't remind me,' she said, gloomily. 'That's another thing that's depressing me. I never thought I'd hear myself say this, but I'm getting to hate always trying to understand other people without ever being understood in return. Do you know what I mean?'

'I can make a guess.'

'I never should have become an anthropologist in the first place,' she said, vehemently.

'Bullshit. You're just caught in a mid tour trough, that's all.'

'What's that?'

'Just what it sounds like. It's when the initial enthusiasm has worn off and 'exotica' isn't so fucking exotic anymore. But it's before you've been here long enough to see any satisfying results from your efforts.'

'Centuries will pass before that happens,' she groaned, 'if it ever does.'

'It sounds to me like you need a change of scenery, even if it's just to a dump like Sanggau. You better go and see this girl, what's her name?'

'Amanda.'

'Spend a few days with Amanda and I dare say you'll feel better when you get back.'

Remembering what just one day in Putussibau had done for her outlook on life, she was inclined to believe him. Her face brightened for a moment and then darkened again. 'But she says she's going to Yogyakarta for Christmas. She wants me to come in January.'

'What's the matter with that?'

'It's weeks away,' she said, as if it had been years.

'Look here,' he grinned, amused at her impatience, 'weren't you just complaining about the rain?'

She nodded.

'Believe me, this is nothing. In January it can last all day sometimes, not just for a few hours like it does now. That means you'll either get stuck at Nanga Palin for a lot longer than you want to be there, or else you won't be able to get there at all. So you might as well be in Sanggau.'

'I suppose so but it does seem such ages.'

'What's going to be ages?' asked Catherine, arriving at the top of the stairs in time to hear this lament.

'Probably lunch,' declared Bima. 'It's always late when I'm starving.'

Wolf and Bethany turned toward him in surprise. Neither of them had noticed that he was sitting at the dining table, absorbed in a set of elevations he had spread out in front of him.

It occurred to Bethany that he hadn't shown any inclination to join in their conversation until Catherine appeared on the scene.

'It's been ages since I came here and it's going to be ages before I have a chance to get away and go anywhere,' replied Bethany in answer to her question.

'It doesn't have to be,' objected Catherine. 'Christmas and the New Year are coming up and Elliot said just a skeleton staff here will be alright.'

'Who gets to be the skeleton?' demanded Wolf.

'Probably you,' she laughed. Then, turning to Bethany, she suggested, 'Let's go to Singapore.'

Bethany looked doubtful. 'Why Singapore?'

'Mostly because it's not Kanyalang but it's near-by and it's as different as any place could possibly be, all well-ordered and clean and modern. Let's go. It'll be fun.'

Bima looked like he'd say 'yes' in a minute if the invitation came his way but it didn't. Marguarita made certain that she wouldn't be one of the 'skeletons' by arranging to visit an orchid-collector friend in Irian Jaya. And Wolf tried to make up his mind whether to go to Bali or to the more-distant Phuket. Which one, he wondered, would offer the best chance of coming across a flock of sex-starved females sunning themselves on the beach, just waiting for him to come along and give them the vacation of their dreams?

All this left Elliot, with the assistance of Mike and Pashetta, to hold the fort during the holidays.

The Singapore plan proved to be an excellent one. The luxury and comfort of a modern hotel was sheer heaven after Kanyalang. Bethany quickly decided that there was much to be said for having pavement, rather than leaves and leeches, under her feet. And, although she wasn't usually much of a shopper, it was exciting to try on clothes for the slim new figure she now realised she had. Added to that was the glorious relief of being able to speak English to everyone she met, even though the reply often came in that baffling linguistic hybrid known as Singlish.

'But I think the very best thing was the restaurants,' she confessed to Mike and Wolf after she got back to Kanyalang. 'I know Kolop tries his best but I swear I had forgotten what really delicious food tastes like. And I didn't see snake or monkey or lizard on any of the menus.'

'You just didn't go to the right places,' claimed Wolf. 'You can find all of those things in Singapore if you try.'

'I can't say I wanted to,' she declared, 'and in any case, I had better things to do.'

'Lucky you,' said Mike. 'I wish I did.'

'You need a vacation,' declared Wolf. 'It should be your turn next. Come to think of it,' he grinned, 'why don't we make Bethany stay here and you go visit that friend of hers in Sanggau.'

'Great idea,' Mike said, laughing. 'Is she pretty?'

'Is she?' demanded Wolf, turning to Bethany.

'I really don't know,' she replied, finding it difficult to picture her former classmate as an adult. 'We all looked so awful in those days, you know, school uniform and spots and all that.'

'You must be able to give us some kind of hint,' urged Wolf.

'Well, she had sort of mousy-blond hair and,' Bethany frowned, as she struggled to remember, 'she was good at hockey, played centre forward, I think.'

'Sounds promising. I like athletic girls, especially blondes,' Mike said, hoping he sounded cool.

'Blondes with spots?' laughed Wolf.

'Yeah, I don't mind spots,' Mike said, generously.

'I also remember that she was very intelligent,' Bethany declared, regretting that she had colluded in the speculation about Amanda's appearance. Couldn't men ever think about anything except sex? Or was the claustrophobic effect of the monsoon making them even worse than usual about that sort of thing? It was certainly reducing the amount of time they could spend taming their libidos by tramping through the jungle.

Yet if Bethany had actually been able to read Wolf's mind she would have realised that, at least at the moment, his thoughts were not being propelled by his libido. The mention of Sanggau had brought a very different subject to his attention and it was one that troubled him.

Disquieting rumours had come his way and, unsure just how much credence to give them, he turned to Mike and asked, 'Have you heard anything about this squabble between the Dayaks and the Madurese?'

'Not much,' Mike replied, 'just that there've been a few scuffles around Pontianak. Apparently one of them was set off by a Madurese guy going off with a Dayak girl, or maybe it was the other way around, I can't remember.'

'Hardly the real issue,' observed Wolf.

'Right, but the thing got way out of hand and a couple of people were killed,' Mike said. Then turning to Bethany, he asked, 'Did they say anything about it at Nanga Palin today?'

'No, but then I spent most of my time talking to the women and their horizons are a bit limited.'

The second these words were out of her mouth, she could have cut out her tongue, and Wolf immediately made it all worse by doubling over with laughter.

'Jesus Christ,' he exclaimed, when he could control himself enough to speak, 'that's the most gloriously politically incorrect remark I've heard in years.'

Bethany turned magenta. 'I don't mean intellectually limited,' she retorted. 'I'm talking about their experiences. Some of the grannies haven't even been as far as Putussibau in their entire lives. How can things that happen way off in Pontianak possibly be important to them? They must seem light years away.'

'Dayaks and Madurese never like each other,' declared Pashetta, arriving back from the office looking very wet. 'It's raining dog and cat out there,' she added, flashing a quick smile at Mike who had taught her this curious expression.

'I don't think anyone at Nanga Palin likes them,' Bethany acknowledged. 'Laban and some of the others were shocked when I told them a Madurese doctor comes to Kanyalang sometimes. They say he might poison us and claim no Madurese can ever be trusted.'

'Yeah, my rangers say the same thing,' Mike agreed.

'I quite liked that Madurese doctor,' said Bima, who had just come up the veranda steps and was busy shaking water off a large banana leaf. 'God, I'm soaked to the skin. This damn leaf was the only thing I could find for an umbrella.'

'The Dayaks seem to think it does the trick,' Wolf pointed out.

Bima was about to point out rather sharply that he wasn't a Dayak when he was interrupted by Kolop announcing that lunch was ready. Everyone except Bima gravitated toward the table.

'Need a map?' asked Wolf, seeing him turn in the opposite direction.

'Just letting Catherine know about lunch,' Bima replied, testily.

'Don't worry, she'll figure it out if she's hungry,' Wolf said.

'That's the trouble,' Bima argued. 'She's never hungry these days. Haven't you noticed she hardly eats anything?'

'Probably just watching her figure,' suggested Wolf.

Bima didn't look convinced. 'No, I think it's more than that. She's the kind of woman who needs a man to take care of her, that's all.'

He wondered why Marguarita, passing them on her way to the table, burst out laughing when she heard this.

CHAPTER TWENTY-FIVE

When lunch was over Bima, ostensibly because of the rotten weather, lingered on the veranda, secretly hoping Catherine wouldn't be any too eager to go dashing out in the rain either. In any case nothing could be done on the hotel on a day like this. The builders hadn't even shown up for work this morning and he couldn't say he blamed them. He had a distinct aversion to getting wet himself.

Today, however, the showery weather was proving lucky for him. Catherine was amenable to an after-lunch chat even though she didn't share his feelings about the rain. She actually claimed to like it and seemed disappointed when the sky began to clear.

'Let's go for a walk,' she urged. 'I adore the time right after a rain, you know when the air is still damp and the leaves are all glistening.'

Bima had never paid much attention to this sort of thing but he liked doing just about anything with Catherine so he was more than willing to fall in with her suggestion of a walk. And he had to admit that there really was something quite lovely about the rainforest that afternoon even though he was fairly certain that it didn't have much to do with glistening leaves or clinging rain drops.

Nevertheless their walk proved to be short-lived. They hadn't gone very far beyond the outer perimeter of Kanyalang when it started to rain again in earnest.

'Come on,' Bima urged, 'run. If we go fast enough we might not get too wet.'

He knew this was a forlorn hope but couldn't think of anything better to do.

A few breathless minutes later, Catherine surprised him by proposing a very different strategy. Instead of racing along as he wanted her to, she slowed her steps to a leisurely stroll.

'Don't you think we'll get awfully wet this way?' he protested.

'Of course,' she laughed.

'Don't you mind?'

'Not a bit. Do you?'

'Not really,' he said, unconvincingly.

He had never been a good liar.

'Just regard it as a delicious outdoor bath,' she urged.

This wasn't easy for a lifelong rain-avoider to do but he gave it his best try and it wasn't long before he was actually enjoying the deluge, too.

Barely able to see through the sheets of rain, they splashed along for a while without paying much attention to where they were going. Then, either by accident, or because the hotel acted like something of a magnet for Bima, they found themselves in front of the formidable ancestor figure now standing tall and occupying pride of place at the entrance to the hotel.

'He doesn't look like he's about to invite us in,' Catherine remarked, looking up into the ferocious wooden face.

Bima felt a little deflated at this observation. It seemed to reflect badly on the image of the hotel so he felt obliged to put the record straight. 'It's supposed to look fierce,' he explained.

'Why?'

'To keep evil spirits away.'

'And does it?' she laughed.

'Let's go in and see,' he suggested, suddenly eager to show her everything that had been accomplished so far.

She agreed and, as they made their way through the various rooms, he found that he wanted to do more than just display what had already been done. He wanted her to see it all, not as it was but as it was going to be, finished, decorated, and ready to receive its first guests.

'Like at Nanga Palin, like our place, too,' he began, as they mounted the steps, 'all the communal sorts of things, eating, drinking, sitting around talking, will happen on the front veranda. There'll be lounges on this side,' he continued, waving his hand to the left, 'furnished with chairs and tables made from local materials and decorated with cloths and beading, silver working, too, done with traditional Dayak motifs and patterns and styles. The blending of indoor and outdoor space will be the key here, with the furnishings and decorations giving it an interior feel but the absence of a fourth wall drawing in an exterior element. Everything will be made of local materials, bamboo, rattan, hand-woven cloth and the lighting will be entirely from oil lamps and candles.'

'It sounds beautiful,' she said, looking around her as if she could almost see it, lamp-lit and lovely, in the tropical night.

'The bar will be here in the middle, directly behind the ancestor figure,' he continued, encouraged by her obvious appreciation and going to the spot in question, 'and it will be carved from one enormous log and look like something right out of a Somerset Maugham story. I practically had to beat Elliot over the head to get him to authorise it. He didn't like spending the money for it even though we were getting it for practically nothing. All we had to pay was the cost of getting it here because the loggers had gone off and left it behind.'

'Why would they do that?' she asked.

'It's got some occlusions in it that weaken it for building purposes and mess up basic furniture designs so they think it's not worth the cost of transport. That's what they said, anyway. But there's a brilliant woodcarver in a longhouse five or six hours' walk from here. He can design it around any imperfections and get a bunch of his mates to help him do the carving. The thing is more than fifteen metres long so it'll be a big job but it's going to be absolutely gorgeous.'

'Well, people will probably need a drink after encountering that fierce ancestor figure,' Catherine suggested.

Bima looked hurt and Catherine immediately felt repentant.

'But it will do great things for the atmosphere,' she said, encouragingly.

He brightened and took her to the dining area at the far end of the veranda where, later, she could almost swear that she had seen the candles glowing on the tables and the oil lamps flickering around the edge of the room.

'It's the interplay between form and function that's the key,' Bima went on to explain, 'as well as the linkages between traditional and futuristic ways of thinking. That's why we were all so desperate to have an anthropologist on the scene and why the architect has to be on site all through the building process. That's unusual, you know.'

Catherine smiled. 'Lucky for me, though,' she said in a tone that gave Bima the idea that perhaps he was going to get lucky, too.

'Anyway, I've got a bit off the subject,' Bima said, not want to risk having her suspect what he was thinking. 'The cooking will be done in a separate hut, built to look like a rice storage barn, and there'll be a wooden walkway connecting it to the dining room.'

'Why not just have a cooking veranda?' Catherine asked, remembering the one at Nanga Palin.

'No, too many intruders.'

Catherine looked surprised.

'Monkeys, frogs, lizards, birds, ants by the millions – you know the cast of characters around here better than I do,' he said, with a laugh. 'Anyway the plan is to partition the back veranda into individual areas, one for each room, so that the guests can relax in their own space and look out over the river. We'll have a pool, of course, to amuse them when they're not tramping through the rainforest but it won't be visible from the longhouse. It will be a little way away, surrounded by jungly trees and plants and things, designed to look like natural watering hole.'

'That sounds great,' she said, approvingly. 'I just wish we had it already.'

Bima was so delighted with her enthusiasm that he suggested climbing up to the rafters. That way she could not only see where the pool would be but she could have a view of the entire complex of Kanyalang, research centre, longhouse, landing pad and everything. 'And this is the perfect time to do it,' he told her, 'because the scaffolding is still up.'

'It's fantastic,' she exclaimed when, feeling she was taking her life in her hands, she stepped out onto the rickety bamboo platform that had been put up for the installation of a carved finial. 'I feel like I could reach up and touch the clouds – well, not quite,' she laughed, after stretching her arms skyward.

Then she made the mistake of looking down to the clearing below and her mood abruptly changed. The ancestor figure looked so different from this new perspective. Instead of appearing

236

formidable, almost scary, as it had when she had been on the ground looking up at it, it now seemed almost friendly, as if it were inviting her, luring her, pulling her down to it.

'No,' she screamed, turning to Bima and gripping him in a near strangle hold, 'don't let me fall.'

'You're alright,' he assured her, freeing himself from her clasp so he could steady her, 'I'm here. I won't let you fall. Just don't look down, that's the thing to remember,' and pressing her face into his shoulder so that she couldn't see anything but the blue of his shirt, he added, 'you're just having a touch of vertigo, that's all. It can happen to anyone, especially if you look straight down.'

His words had a calming effect but she was still reluctant to let him go.

'Come on,' he said, gently disentangling himself, 'let's go down to some place a little more sensible.'

Holding onto him as tightly as she could, she allowed him to lead her down to one of the guest rooms where a scattering of straw mats, a couple of thin blankets, a tin thermos and a chipped enamel cup gave evidence of recent habitation by the night watchman and possibly some of the workmen.

Bima picked up the thermos and shook it. 'There seems to be a little something left in it,' he said.

'What is it?'

'Tea, I expect,' he said, pouring some into the cup, taking a sip himself and handing it to her. 'I can't say it's hot but it might be better than nothing.'

She took a sip and pulled a face.

'Pretty awful?'

'Frightful.'

'You'd better get out of those wet things then,' he said, 'and wrap up in one of those blankets.'

She nodded in agreement but made no effort to do it so he lifted up her top and began to undo her jeans, convinced that at any moment she would stop him.

She didn't. She merely stood there like a doll while he relieved her of the rest of her clothes and tucked a blanket around her.

'What about you,' she said, 'you're wet, too.'

237

'It's okay. I don't mind.'

A mischievous twinkle came into her eyes. 'Are you shy,' she asked, 'or do you not catch cold very easily?'

He shifted awkwardly. The truth was that if he took off his clothes she would see that he was in the throes of a major erection – he didn't trust the blanket to conceal the evidence – and he wasn't sure just how she would react. He didn't want to risk being rejected.

He needn't have worried.

With a knowing smile, she murmured, 'It wouldn't do for you to start sneezing now, would it?' and began unzipping his jeans.

He didn't stand there like a doll. He did everything he could to further the proceedings but when he drew her down on to one of the mats and positioned himself on top of her, things didn't turn out as well in reality as they had in his dreams – at least, he was sure, not for her. The embarrassing problem was that he had wanted her for so long, wanted her so badly, that it was all over in something close to the speed of light. He rolled off her knowing there wasn't any point in even asking how it was for her.

Catherine was really nice about it though. She claimed she didn't mind so they just lay in each other's arms and talked about things. And before the rain had begun to let up, he was ready for action again.

This time the action was slow, sensuous and unhurried. As far as Bima was concerned they had all the time in the world and before the afternoon was out, he was convinced that they had had all the pleasure in the world as well.

Catherine, somewhat to her surprise, thought much the same thing. Sex with Bima, she reflected, was so different from sex with Tarique that she could scarcely believe the same word could be used to describe the two experiences. With Tarique they had been like two wild animals, tearing at each other, biting and clawing in a frenzy of passion. The climax had been totally fantastic, of course, but when she thought about it she wasn't certain it had really been better than the one she and Bima had shared. They hadn't tried to tear each other apart, quite the opposite. They had done everything possible to give each other pleasure and the amazing thing was that they had succeeded beyond anything she could have imagined. Just thinking about it made her reach out and stroke his face, unconsciously inviting him to have another go.

By the time they drew apart for the third time the rain had stopped.

The usual pre-dinner drinks were in progress when they got back to the longhouse.

'Hey, where the hell've you guys been, the local swimming hole?' Wolf exclaimed when he saw their still-wet clothes.

'I've been showing Catherine around the hotel,' Bima said.

'But it stopped raining over an hour ago,' Wolf pointed out. 'Didn't it occur to you two idiots to get out of those clothes before embarking on any sightseeing jaunts?'

Bethany thought she saw Catherine's lips frame the words, 'We did,' but she wondered if she had just imagined it.

Out loud, Catherine cried, 'Being wet is lovely. I haven't felt so deliciously cool in ages. And the rain made it the perfect time to get a little exercise.'

Sexercise, more likely, thought Marguarita, accurately summing up the situation.

Bethany rather expected her friend to confide in her but Catherine did not, and in any case Bethany soon became too preoccupied with her own life to pay much attention to anyone else's.

The main thing on her mind was her upcoming trip to Sanggau but on the morning when she was supposed to leave, she stepped out onto the veranda only to find her plans frustrated by another day of heavy rain. The helicopter was clearly not going to fly in this weather.

'Hey, things can't be that tragic,' Wolf said, when he saw the devastated expression on her face.

'But I can't go in all this,' she lamented.

'It might clear later,' he said, with a cheerfulness that showed her he didn't begin to understand her feelings.

'Even if it does,' she told him, 'I will have missed the flight on to Pontianak from Putussibau.'

'That's hardly the end of the world. There's another one on Monday. I know because I've got a reservation on it, myself.'

'You do?' said Bethany, less than pleased at this prospect. She had been looking forward to her visit to Amanda as a total escape from Kanyalang and every minute counted. The Singapore trip had been great but Catherine's presence had been a constant reminder that a return to Borneo was looming on the horizon. 'What do you have to do in Pontianak?'

'Talk to some of those pricks in the governor's office. They like to keep tabs on what we're up to.'

'The governor?' she said, surprised.

'Oh, not the Big Cheese in person. If it was a question of seeing him, Elliot would do it himself but since it's just routine stuff with a lot of dolts who really couldn't care less, he shoves it off on me. So you see I should be the one who's standing around here with the long face, not you. After all, you'll be seeing a friend and Sanggau will still be there on Tuesday or Wednesday.'

'I doubt it,' she cried. 'It's probably going to rain like this for weeks and weeks and Sanggau will be washed away by the time I get a chance to go.'

'Idiot,' he said, laughing. 'Since when are you a meteorologist, anyway?'

'Since about five minutes ago.'

'Come on, let's get some coffee. That'll make you feel better.' And, taking her arm, he propelled her toward the breakfast table.

Mike, Elliot and Catherine were already there.

'Looks like your trip's pretty much on hold,' Mike observed, digging into his fried eggs.

'Just postponed until Monday,' Wolf pointed out, giving Bethany an encouraging grin. 'It's a good thing, though. Now we can go as far as Pontianak together and entertain each other on the way. And on top of that, it saves a helicopter call out.'

'You really should have planned it that way in the first place,' Elliot told Bethany, reproachfully. 'You're only going on holiday. You can leave anytime. And the helicopter doesn't come here for nothing, you know.'

Catherine leapt to Bethany's defence. 'But she's in a hurry to see her friend. I would be, too, if I had one in Sanggau.'

'Quite,' Elliot replied, stiffly. Then in the fatherly tone he often used to conceal his very unfatherly feelings for Catherine, he added, 'You should have something for breakfast besides tea. You're too thin.'

'I can't eat much breakfast in this heat,' Catherine said.

'It's not hot. It's raining,' Elliot pointed out.

'That doesn't lower the temperature by more than two degrees,' declared Catherine. 'It just turns everything to steam. But don't worry about me. I'll eat a big lunch.'

Pashetta heard Elliot mumble something about low-flying pigs and looked around her apprehensively. She didn't care for pigs, low-flying or otherwise.

Bethany caught her glance but misinterpreted it. Perhaps Pashetta minds as much about the rain as I do, she thought. No one else seems to, though. But then nobody else had any place they wanted to go.

Bethany remained on edge all weekend as more rain streamed down but her pessimism about Monday's weather proved unwarranted. Early morning sunshine drove the last drops of moisture away and shortly after breakfast she was in the helicopter, watching Kanyalang get progressively smaller as they lifted off into the sky.

Of course, the downside to the way things had turned out was that Wolf was there too but she comforted herself with the thought that as soon as they got to Pontianak she would be on her own.

'Hey, I've got an idea,' she heard him shout over the noise of the engine.

'What about?'

'What would you think of spending a couple of days in Pontianak and coming along on some of these ghastly visits to government officials with me?'

'Whatever for?'

'To talk about the Dayaks, what else?'

'I thought the government people weren't very interested in the Dayaks.'

'Generally, they're not,' he agreed. 'But this flare up between the Dayaks and the Madurese might be enough to make them sit up and take notice now. Of course, it's all still small potatoes but it could get out of hand fast. It has before. And if it does again, it could be the kiss of death for the governor and his inner circle.'

'What makes you say that?'

'The powers-that-be in Jakarta want this province in the hands of someone who's strong enough to keep order.'

'I can see that but —'

'The simple fact is that blood and chaos are bad for profits. There's big money to be made around here, not only in timber but in oil palm, gold, and god knows what else, illipe nuts, maybe. And, believe me, plenty of Suharto's relatives and cronies know it. They've got major, and by that I mean mega-gigantic, fucking enormous, investments all through the area. But if the Madurese and Dayaks start killing each other again, they'll kill off a good chunk of the returns from those investments. The super rich in Jakarta might even have to start cancelling their orders for their fifteenth Mercedes, for God's sake. And if that happens, I promise you heads will roll in the provincial governor's office here in West Kalimantan. And they know it, too.'

'Maybe I'm being thick,' Bethany said, 'but I fail to see what I can do about it.'

'Then you certainly are being thick.'

'Thank you very much,' she retorted, indignantly, 'but you can't tell me that Dayak genealogies and longhouse social systems, the sort of thing I've been working on, have any effect on profits in the logging business.'

'Right, but what you apparently haven't figured out is that it's harder than hell to get on the inside track with the Dayaks and that you're one of the few people around who's succeeded in doing it.'

'Perhaps, but —'

'No 'buts' allowed. Just listen, will you. There're only two ways the government can forestall more, and probably worse, outbreaks of violence. One is to shoot any possible perpetrators but that'll look bad if the papers get wind of it. The other is to quietly bribe the relevant parties into co-operating.'

'Doesn't that take more money than the government is apt to have?' she asked.

'Right, you can be quick to catch on when you want to be,' he said, approvingly.

'And since there's no budget for little sweeteners in the form of ready cash,' Wolf continued, 'the government has to resort to other methods, like throwing each group a few fish in the form of political favours, to put a lid on things. But for that to work, they've got to have reliable information about what particular fish would do the job. That's where you come in, on the Dayak side, that is, so I've got a gut feeling that under the circumstances they'll be very interested in what you have to say.'

Bethany looked unconvinced so he went on.

'Look, you're the one person who can put these guys in the picture about what the Dayaks problems are, more specifically, what might persuade them to tolerate the continued presence of the Madurese. After all, it's a virtual certainty that those paper-pushers in Pontianak have never set foot in a longhouse so they won't have a clue where to start in terms of a deal.'

Bethany looked doubtful. 'I wouldn't want to do anything that betrayed the people at Nanga Palin,' she said.

'Nobody's asking you to, quite the opposite, in fact. What's wanted from you are suggestions about ways the government can improve the Dayaks' situation.'

'I'd have to give it some thought.'

'No law against that. We wouldn't be seeing anyone until this afternoon, anyway. That'll give you some thinking time and give us a chance to conjure up a joint act. I'll make the case for the economic benefits the rainforest can bring to the area, if no one's allowed to reduce it to ashes and sell it for plywood, that is, and you do the Dayak stuff. And we'll even make the package more digestible by not lighting directly into anything that smacks of corruption. That's another place where you come in.'

'Me?'

'Yeah, for damage control in case things go west. You're good at that sort of thing.'

'Whatever gives you that idea?'

'Don't you remember when we were at Chen's place in Putussibau? You were right on the ball that day. Tact, you may have noticed, is not exactly my strong point. Part of your job will be to throw a muzzle on me if I start to shoot off at the mouth and antagonise people.'

'Well —' she hesitated, still reluctant.

'And there's another thing,' he continued. 'When there's any kind of unrest anywhere, the first thing the officials are likely to do is boot the foreigners out. We don't want that to happen to our bunch, do we?'

'God, no,' she exclaimed, genuinely shocked.

'But if you can shed a little light on what might be done to soothe the Dayaks, it could bolster the impression that Kanyalang's a project worth keeping. So how about it, will you help?'

'I'd like to but, you see, I promised Amanda —'

'Screw Amanda. You haven't even thought about her for years, so what difference can a few days make?'

It wasn't easy to counter this argument.

'Well, perhaps —' she began.

This was all Wolf needed to hear. 'Good girl,' he said, 'I knew you'd come through. And a minor benefit is that you can charge your travel time and expenses to work instead of vacation.'

'I'm not sure Elliot would agree to that,' she pointed out.

'To hell with Elliot. I'm in charge of this little jaunt now and I authorise it.'

'Are you sure you can do that?'

'Why not? I generally figure out some way to get the old fart to do what I want.'

Bethany knew this was true but his confidence annoyed her. A touch of petulance crept into her voice as she replied, 'I really hate to have my plans messed up. And there are Amanda's plans to consider, too. I can't just —'

'Yes, you can. Come on, here's your chance to make a real difference, to do something important for Kanyalang and for Nanga Palin, too. You can't say no.'

She knew she was being bullied but it was so exhilarating to feel that she was a valued member of the team, someone whose help

Wolf was actually seeking, that she found herself giving in to his heavy-handed tactics without further struggle.

After all, Amanda could wait.

CHAPTER TWENTY-SIX

'You'll like the hotel in Pontianak, you know,' Wolf said encouragingly as they were strapping themselves into their seats on the Das Airways plane. 'It's a bit run down but it's got a great restaurant overlooking the river, views of the ships all lighted up at night, fantastic prawns, a top notch chef, now tell me what's so bad about that?'

'Nothing, I suppose,' she replied, although her enthusiasm for ships was limited and she had never been terribly keen on prawns.

Nor, she later realised, could she endorse his description of the hotel. In her opinion it was not only dingy and shabby but an interior decorator's nightmare. The only good thing about it, she decided, was the balcony outside her room. She had to admit that deserved the rave notices Wolf had given the place.

The Kapuas River lay directly beneath her, the cool breeze from the water blew through her hair, and the mesmerising panorama of river life, from ocean-going freighters to rafts and row boats, animated the scene in front of her. She almost felt as though she was on the deck of one of the ships, going to ... anywhere. It didn't matter where. It felt almost as if she were sailing into a thrilling and liberating unknown, beyond the jungle, beyond the heat and humidity of Borneo, beyond the oppressive world of Kanyalang.

A sharp knock on the door roused her from her thoughts and she reluctantly turned away from the river scene.

'Ready?' Wolf asked, coming into the room. Then seeing that she wasn't, he exclaimed, 'Hey, you were supposed to be changing. You can't go to government offices wearing jeans, for God's sake.'

'I thought we didn't have appointments until this afternoon.'

'We don't. But it wouldn't be a bad idea to make some courtesy calls on a few lower forms of life before that. You know, massage their egos a bit, make them think we think they're important. And, in a way, they are. Of course, they can't really help us much but they can sure as hell hurt us if they want to, so it's best to keep on the right side of them.'

'I didn't realise you were so calculating.'

'Might as well call it by its real name,' he said, with a harsh laugh, 'arse-kissing. I hate it and I'm notoriously bad at it.'

'You could call it diplomacy,' she suggested.

'I'm not very good at that either.'

She didn't contradict him but wondered, as she took a blue skirt and a white top out of her rucksack, if perhaps he wasn't a bit better at it than he claimed.

'Back in a mo,' she said, as she tossed the two rather crumpled garments over her arm, picked up her sponge bag and disappeared into the loo.

She was as good as her word and soon re-emerged, clean, dressed, and ready to go.

'What a transformation,' he said, with more appreciation in his eyes than in his words, 'you look almost human.'

'Is that so unusual?' she laughed.

'I'm not going to commit myself on that one,' he teased. 'Come on, let's get out of here.'

A brief taxi ride brought them to a large but unprepossessing building where they made the requisite rounds of official visits. Whenever Wolf brought the conversation around to the Dayaks, as he did repeatedly, everyone listened politely to what she had to say and when it was all finally over she had high hopes of being complimented by Wolf.

Much to her annoyance, that didn't happen. Instead, she was obliged to listen while he congratulated himself on the success of his strategy for the day's meetings. 'Kanyalang's coming out of this looking really good,' he claimed. 'We're showing those guys that we've got our finger right on the pulse of what's going on. Now the thing to do is convince them that our monitoring of the situation is indispensable. Then no paper-pushing jackarse can give us the shove.'

Bethany had difficulty concealing her irritation and was not in any mood to hear that he had invited three friends of his to have dinner with them that evening. She felt that she had met quite enough people for one day. After all, talking about sensitive issues like the government's treatment of the Dayaks without alienating the very people who might be able to do something to improve the quality of their lives hadn't been easy. She felt that she had earned a relaxing evening, just calling for a cold beer on the balcony, followed by room service, but decided against saying anything.

When the friends arrived she had a pleasant surprise. They were relaxed, fluent in English and far easier to be with than the government officials had been.

This was especially true of Jun Yon Wong, the most articulate of the three. He was the son of a wealthy Chinese import-exporter, had been educated in America and was now being groomed by his father to take over the family business.

Bethany could see that he was chaffing under the restraints this return to a more traditional society imposed on him. Laughter and intelligence sparkled in his dark eyes and she suspected that this brief interlude in the company of foreigners was just what his spirits craved. However he could be serious when the occasion called for it and he clarified a number of things for her.

'We're all a little nervous these days,' he told her, 'because of this trouble between the Dayaks and the Madurese. But then, you must know a lot more about it than I do.'

'Actually, I don't,' she replied. 'Kanyalang is a bit isolated you see and there're not many Madurese in our area.'

'Even so, you must know about all the problems the Madurese are causing here in Kalimantan,' exclaimed Eta, a lecturer in political science at Pontianak University who didn't trouble to hide her impatience with people who were ill-informed on public affairs.

Her appearance, as tall as a European woman but with a slim and delicate build that a strictly English ancestry effectively precluded, didn't help Bethany to like her any better.

Good heavens, am I jealous, Bethany asked herself, horrified at the thought. Certainly Wolf was making a perfect idiot of himself over her, looking at her like she was a combination of Cleopatra and the Oracle of Delphi rolled into one, but then she supposed any man with his hormones up and running would probably do the same.

Well, she wasn't going to let herself be intimidated by Eta no matter how brilliant and beautiful she was, Bethany decided, so she went back to the subject of the Madurese. 'I've heard a little about them,' she said, 'although I don't actually know what brought them here in the first place.'

'Madura is too small an island to support so many people,' Eta said, making it clear that she was explaining the obvious.

Adnan, a reporter for one of Indonesia's major news magazines, added, 'They thought they could make a better life for themselves here but —' He spread his hands in a gesture that indicated these hopes had not been realised.

'Some of them have succeeded, haven't they?' replied Bethany, thinking of the Madurese doctor.

'Perhaps,' Eta admitted, 'but they take land away from the Dayaks and that causes trouble for everyone.'

'The problem,' said Jun, turning to Bethany, 'as you probably know, is that the Madurese don't understand the Dayaks' practice of shifting agriculture. They see land that looks like it's been abandoned and think they can help themselves to it. They can't get their heads around the idea of allowing large tracts of it to lie fallow for ten or fifteen years and then going back and planting them again.'

Adnan nodded, gloomily. 'And now tension is building up again,' he added.

'At least the government people we talked to today seemed quite interested in the Dayaks' situation,' Bethany replied, exchanging glances with Wolf. 'I was rather surprised actually.'

'I'm not,' Jun said. 'The government doesn't want to admit it but they're secretly afraid of more bloodshed. Still you guys shouldn't have to worry up where you are. It's the area between here and Sanggau, and on up toward the Sarawak border, that's a tinderbox.'

'But I'm going to Sanggau the day after tomorrow to visit a friend of mine,' Bethany said.

'I don't think that's a very good idea,' Jun warned.

Eta disagreed. 'Oh, you don't need to worry,' she said, turning to Bethany, 'you'll be fine. This little squabble is strictly between the Dayaks and the Madurese. No one will bother you.'

Bethany began to warm to Eta.

'You won't be a target,' Jun agreed, 'but that doesn't mean you couldn't be caught in the middle of a nasty scene. It would be better if your friend went to Kanyalang to visit you.' Then looking over at Adnan, he asked, 'What do you think?'

'I think you are being very pessimistic,' Adnan replied. 'It is really just more of the same, you know. The Madurese will always claim the government gave them the right to the land and the Dayaks will always say the Madurese cheated them.'

'After all, the Dayaks are just forest people,' Eta said, as if that explained everything, 'so, of course, everybody cheats them.'

'But that's dreadful,' Bethany cried.

'Well, people are like that, aren't they?' Eta said, coolly. 'Everyone is the same.'

'Not quite the same,' Jun corrected her. 'The Chinese cheat them honestly.' Then in response to Bethany's look of astonishment, he added, 'I hope you don't think I'm just saying that because my family originally came from China.'

'No,' she replied, smiling, 'I think it's because you like to tease and that's very wicked of you. But you couldn't really have expected me to believe that you could cheat someone honestly, could you?'

To her amazement, Jun took the question seriously and set about answering it. 'The way it works,' he said, 'is that the Chinese buy forest products, you know, rubber, illipe nuts, rattan, that sort of thing, from the Dayaks. They cheat them on the weight and on the water content, everyone knows that. But once they've made an agreement, they don't go back on it. Their scales are crap but their word is good and the Dayaks respect that.'

'That's a rather odd way of looking at things, isn't it?' Bethany said, convinced that she must have missed some vital element in his argument.

'Not really,' Jun replied, 'especially when you put it together with the fact that the Chinese are businessmen so they want to live in the market towns, not on the Dayak's land. And, as I'm sure you know, the Dayaks don't have much interest in living in the towns. They just want to buy the things the Chinese sell and take them back into the jungle or the rice fields or wherever. So when you put it all together, you have a relationship that works.'

'Yes, but it's still cheating, isn't it?' Bethany persisted. 'And you can't persuade me that there's really an honest and a dishonest way to cheat someone.'

'The Dayaks seem to think there is,' Jun contended.

'What there is,' said Eta, 'is a standard method of cheating that's generally accepted as part of the cost of doing business. But other ways of cheating are not seen in the same light.'

Everyone except Bethany nodded in agreement. 'Then what are the unacceptable ways the Madurese use?' she asked.

'When they make a deal to buy Dayak land,' Adnan replied, 'they take it over and then don't pay. That makes the Dayaks hopping mad and they never, ever forget it.'

'But what can they do about it with just a few knives and blowpipes, poor things,' Eta said.

'Don't underestimate those blowpipes,' warned Wolf. 'I've seen them in action and, let me tell you, I wouldn't care to be on the receiving end of an arrow shot from one of them. The poison on the tips can have you barking out a death rattle before you know what's hit you.'

'The machetes the Dayaks use aren't any joke either,' added Jun. 'You could slice someone up very nicely with one of them.'

'Don't forget, some of them have got guns too,' Adnan pointed out.

'A few maybe, but not very many,' said Jun.

'And they're not much use without bullets, are they?' put in Eta.

Adnan shrugged and the question went unanswered as a magnificent red snapper topped with shredded ginger and smothered in a sweet and sour sauce was brought to the table and set down in front of them.

A waiter skilfully set about the task of filleting and serving it and, while the attention of the other diners was focused on his stellar performance, Jun took the opportunity to study Bethany.

A nice girl, he thought, the sensitive type, intelligent, too, but a bit naïve, especially about the Dayaks. He had a feeling she hadn't taken his earlier warning seriously enough so he decided to repeat it. 'You know,' he said, 'I really think this isn't a good time for anyone to go to Sanggau.'

'It's too late to change my plans now,' she told him, although she knew it really wasn't.

After all, why should she give up her trip, she thought stubbornly, when Jun was the only one who seemed to think there might be a problem. Eta and Adnan clearly didn't agree with him. And none of the government officials they had seen that day had said anything that would discourage her from going. Adnan must have been right about Jun, she told herself. He was an alarmist, that was all.

As soon as the three guests left, Wolf not only made it clear that he didn't consider Jun's alarm bells out of order but, to her surprise, he went on at considerable length about Eta's poor judgement on the matter of Sanggau.

'She may be smart as a whip about some things,' he said, as they made their way up the stairs to their respective rooms, 'but in spite of having spent three or four years here in Pontianak —'

'I thought she was from here,' interrupted Bethany.

'God, no, she's Javanese, from Jakarta. Couldn't you tell?'

Bethany shook her head. She wasn't sure how she was supposed to know this but she let the matter slide.

'I guess she's not as clued in to what's going on around here as I thought,' Wolf continued. 'Now Jun, he's lived here all his life, except when he was in the States, and he knows what he's talking about. I really think you should follow his advice. Wait and go to Sanggau some other time.'

Bethany shook her head. 'I can't imagine that anything dreadful is going to happen,' she said, firmly. 'People here in Pontianak, even your friends, are obviously prejudiced against the Dayaks.'

'Possibly,' Wolf admitted, 'but don't forget, Jun's a pretty sharp guy.'

'That doesn't mean he knows everything, does it?'

'Of course not but —'

He broke off, thinking that maybe Bethany did have a point. Just because Jun was smart, didn't mean he was a fucking fortune teller. He could be wrong.

'Well, sleep on it,' Wolf suggested, 'and see how you feel in the morning. If you're still determined to go then keep your eyes open and don't hang around if the locals seem nervous. Get the hell out of there on the double.'

Bethany nodded. That was something she could agree to easily.

'Well, good night, then,' he said, making no motion to leave.

'Good night,' she replied, lingering in the half-open doorway.

There was an awkward silence as neither of them moved.

Deciding that the situation was fast becoming ludicrous, Wolf resorted to a playful threat. 'If you're not in that dining room by eight o'clock tomorrow morning, I'll break into your room and pour cold water all over you.' And on this note of mock-ferocity, he turned and left her.

'I'll be there,' she called after his retreating form.

Bethany kept her word and shortly before eight she found him having coffee at a table near the window, reading the English version of the news magazine Adnan worked on.

'Sleep well?' he asked, looking up to greet her.

Erotic images from a dream she had had during the night flashed through her mind . 'Yes,' she replied, the colour mounting in her face. She was terrified that Wolf would somehow be able to read her mind.

Bethany sat down and ordered coffee hoping that as she sipped it the memory of the dream would go away, but it didn't. It had been such a turn-on that when she thought about it she could almost feel him pressing against her, beside her, on top of her, inside her, touching and kissing her in places that didn't bear thinking about, at least not when the star performer was sitting across the table from her in a hotel dining room.

She made a valiant effort to focus her attention on her breakfast but had barely made any inroads on it when Wolf jolted her out of her reverie.

'You're not coming down with some kind of jungle fever, are you?' he asked, regarding her flushed countenance with concern.

'Whatever makes you think that?' she replied, as she speared a piece of papaya and popped it into her mouth.

'You've gone all red.'

This observation made her swallow the fruit so quickly that she barely avoided choking. 'It was hot in my room,' she improvised, hastily. 'I suppose I haven't quite cooled off yet.'

He looked at her quizzically. It was true that the flush was beginning to fade but he had a distinct feeling that she wasn't telling him the truth. He didn't pursue the matter though and, to Bethany's relief, he began instead to outline his plans for the day's official visits. She regarded them with more interest than she had the previous day because of the opportunity they offered to sound people out on the subject of Sanggau.

To her relief, everyone assured her that there was nothing to worry about. Even the deputy governor confirmed this, declaring firmly that there wouldn't be any trouble and politely hoping that Bethany would enjoy her visit with her friend.

That settles it, she decided, as they left his office. He must know.

She was in high spirits when they got back to the hotel. She treated herself to a lovely cool shower with proper running water and no danger of having a fish slither down her back and had just changed into jeans and a sleeveless blue top when Wolf knocked on her door and called out, 'How about a gin and tonic on my balcony? Believe it or not, there's actually something of a breeze.'

Warning bells resulting from her dream sounded off in her head but she told herself not to be silly. It wasn't as if anything real had happened or was going to happen.

'Well, what's your verdict?' Wolf asked, when he had poured the drinks. 'Are you sorry you decided to stop over here?'

'No, not at all although —'

'Although what?'

'I can't help wondering whether the people we talked to today were telling us the truth or just saying what they thought we wanted to hear — about the possibility of trouble in Sanggau, I mean.'

'Most likely what we wanted to hear, it's their idea of the polite way of doing things, you know.'

She nodded. 'Still, it sort of pisses me off.'

'Well, you can hardly expect them to tell us the truth, can you?'

'Why ever not?'

'Because they know we're trying to protect the jungle from all the things that bring them a quick buck. And if, by some miracle, we ever succeed, it will hit them right where it hurts, in their wallets. And believe me, anything that looks like a threat to their envelopes –'

'You mean their bribes?'

'Right. Anything like that would be arsenic in the soup to them.'

'But don't at least some of them care about the rainforest?'

'Who knows,' he replied, with a shrug, 'but if they do, you can be damn sure they won't speak out.'

'What's preventing them?'

'Everything, if anyone squealed, his arse would be in a sling before he knew what hit him. Don't forget, these guys have their jobs to think about. After all, their families are a hell of a lot more important to them than some fucking monkey in a tree or a weird plant somewhere.'

'I know but –'

'There aren't any 'buts' about it. Their salaries are so low they can't make it from one paycheque to another without a steady stream of supplements. And, just in case you're in any doubt about what those 'supplements' consist of –'

'I'm not.'

'Good, because they're bribes, pure and simple and without them these guys just can't make it, at least not in the way they want to. Their kids' education would go up in smoke and so would all the other goodies they're currently enjoying. So you can be damn sure that no one is going to be fool enough to blow the whistle on that gravy train.'

'But that doesn't mean it's right for us to go along with a thoroughly rotten system like that, does it?' objected Bethany.

'Not up to your exalted moral standards, is it?' he jeered.

'I suppose you could put it that way if you want to.'

'As it happens, I don't want to put it any way at all. But just

256

suppose for a minute that we don't go along with this 'rotten system', as you put it. Suppose we storm into their offices and tell them exactly what we think of their little games. What would happen then? Where do you think we'd be?'

'At least, we'd be standing for something.'

'Bullshit, we wouldn't be standing at all. We'd be sitting on the next flight out of here. And what would that do for the rainforest – exactly nothing.'

'In the long run, it might be better than putting on blindfolds and pretending all this corruption's not happening.'

'In the long run there won't be any trees left to protect. No, our best bet is to stay put and do what we can to save this particular corner of jungle. That means speaking up when it will do some good, even if that's not very often, and shutting up when it won't. That's the best –'

The horn from an ocean-going ship drowned out the end of Wolf's sentence and he strolled over to the balcony rail to watch it go by. Dusk had fallen and a number of the bigger ships were ablaze with lights while many of the barges and small water taxis were illuminated only by the modest glow of a paraffin lamp.

'There's something about a ship lighted up at night, even if it's just a rusty old tub, that always makes me want to get on it and go wherever it takes me,' Wolf mused. 'Do you ever feel like that?'

'I didn't until now,' she replied, joining him by the rail. 'But I can see what you mean. There's something compelling about it and if you have a natural wanderlust –'

'I guess we've both got that,' he said, 'or you'd be back in England and I'd still be in the States.' And feeling that it was nice to be on the same wave length with someone – unusual, too, when that 'someone' was a woman – he put a companionable arm around her and leaned toward her, intending to plant a friendly kiss on her forehead.

The problem was that something didn't go according to plan and somehow he found that both his arms were around her and the kiss that he was pressing on her lips was far more than friendly. It was long and deep and dangerously like the prelude to something more.

257

Jesus, he told himself as he went on kissing her, this was a seriously bad idea. The last thing he needed was another entanglement with a woman at Kanyalang. But of course they were in Pontianak now, so maybe tonight didn't count. She didn't seem to be protesting anyway. She didn't even pull away when his hands went up under her blue top so maybe she was thinking more or less along the same lines that he was – a night away from real life, a one-off in a setting that even he had to admit was kind of romantic.

This reading of her thoughts was given added credence by the sensuous way she rubbed against him when he slid the tips of his fingers down inside her jeans. The trouble was they were too tight-fitting for his hand to progress very far without unfastening them but he noted that fortunately the balcony was protected from prying eyes on three sides. And after glancing toward the river to see that no small boats were loitering nearby, he began to undo the zipper.

'But this isn't fair, you know,' she protested.

'Fair?' he repeated, unsure what equality and justice had to do with their present situation.

'Exactly,' she said and to his surprise, and even to her own, she opened the zipper on his trousers, pulled out his dick and, using it as a handle, drew him into the room.

This was not a scenario that Wolf had any trouble going along with and it was close to midnight before it occurred to either of them that they had completely forgotten about dinner.

Wolf roused a sleepy room-boy and persuaded him to go out and get them chicken satays with peanut sauce and fried rice while he mixed them more gin and tonics on the balcony.

'You're not going to go ahead with this Sanggau jaunt tomorrow, are you?' Wolf asked.

'I don't know,' she said, happily downing the remains of her drink and holding out her glass for a refill, 'I can't think about that now.'

'Okay, I'll think about it for you,' he replied but he had already decided that now there were two reasons to call off that little excursion. The first was, of course, that it might be dangerous but the second was that he was beginning to rethink the idea of a one-off. A few re-runs might not be such a bad idea after all.

'Cancel Sanggau or at least postpone it,' he urged, 'and come back to Kanyalang with me.'

Bethany didn't argue – she didn't see any reason to spoil a thoroughly enjoyable midnight feast – but she'd let him know in the morning that she was still going. No matter how spectacular their romp in bed had been, it didn't mean she was going to let him do her thinking for her.

CHAPTER TWENTY-SEVEN

The first thing Bethany was aware of as she woke the next morning was a deep, rhythmic sound coming from the direction of the river. Boats, she thought, there must be a thick fog. The problem was that it seemed closer than that, almost as if it were right in the room. And opening her eyes to see just what it was, she was for a moment surprised to discover Wolf snoring on the side of the bed nearest the river.

Why, she wondered, briefly, was she only ever attracted to men who snored?

The question remained unanswered as the events of the previous night went tumbling through her mind. My God, she thought, how could she have done that? With Wolf of all people! She must have been thoroughly pissed or else completely out of her mind. But the details of what happened, from the time she took his dick in her hand, to the moment she had it in her mouth, to the time he was doing gloriously comparable things to her, came back to her so clearly that she must not have been too pissed.

But if she hadn't been drunk or crazy, how in the world could she explain it all? She hated Wolf — well, perhaps that was a bit of an exaggeration but she seriously disliked him. How could he possibly have seemed so attractive last night, she wondered, attractive enough for a blow job, something she generally avoided? But the undeniable fact was that he had.

Now looking over at him in the cool light of morning — actually it was a soft pastel light that was flickering in through the thin curtains, she noticed — she was assailed by a frisson of something akin to fear. The feelings he had aroused in her were too powerful, too intense. Her overwhelming instinct was to distance herself from them by getting away from him.

She got up, wrapped a sarong around her and went out on the balcony.

The morning was beautiful, she discovered, not foggy at all, and the water was alive with small boats taking people to work. A few larger ocean-going vessels were visible in the distance and she wished she could get on one, anyone, going anywhere that would offer her an escape from the swirling array of conflicting emotions that were besieging her.

Getting away would an easy proposition, she reminded herself, since the plans for Sanggau were already in place. All she had to do was carry on with her existing itinerary and use the time away from Kanyalang to reassert control over her jumbled mix of feelings. But there was something else, too, she realised. Sex had never been quite like it had been last night. Was it because of Wolf, or the romantic setting by the river, or the freedom of being away from Kanyalang? Why did it make her head ache so much to think about it? Perhaps that was just because she was hung over. Yes, that must be it, she decided.

Wolf did his best to dissuade her from going to Sanggau but he was much too far from understanding her state of mind to be able to influence her decision. His arguments were based on political insecurity and personal discomfort and, as such, didn't reach her at all.

By mid-morning she had hired a rattle-trap car and set off for Sanggau.

During the drive Bethany, desperate to turn her mind from thoughts of Wolf, tried to remember Amanda as she had been at school, tall for her age, sort of gangly and uncoordinated, shy, studious, smart, always a bit left out, good at games, though, but when she tried to picture her as an adult she failed completely. Well, she'd find out soon enough.

Amanda greeted her with a joyous warmth that touched Bethany's heart, although at the same time it set off a pang of guilt at the recollection of how little she had liked her in the old days. But now as Bethany surveyed her hostess, she could detect no trace of the schoolgirl shyness or the prefectorial authority that had marked her adolescence.

Another surprise, completely inexplicable in Bethany's view, came during the course of one of their first conversations together. It was that Amanda could claim to be so happy in a life that seemed little short of achingly austere and deadly dull.

'You see, I'm really living like a daughter in an Indonesian family,'

Amanda explained, as they lounged on a bed in her cell-like room. 'And I'm seeing so much that I would never have dreamt of before I came out here.'

'That's great,' Bethany said, trying to sound like she really thought it was. But if she looked unimpressed, Amanda didn't appear to notice.

Carrying on with undiminished enthusiasm, she said, 'Bapak, that's what we call the father of the family, is the District Officer for Sanggau. He is a Coastal Melay, all the family is, so of course they're good Muslims and everything has to be very strict and traditional. Ibu, that's what I call my Indonesian mother, and Tini and Wati, my sisters in the family, all wear headscarfs whenever they go out. Of course, there's not much to go out for, except school and a bit of very basic shopping.' An expression of concern flitted across her face as she added, 'I do hope you won't be too bored while you're here.'

'Oh, don't worry,' Bethany said, attempting to repress the suspicion that Wolf had known what he was talking about when he had described Sanggau as a 'hole'. 'I just wanted to see you again after all this time. I mean, it's been ages, hasn't it? And besides, I was dying to get away from the project and the people I work with for a while.'

Amanda looked reassured and hastened to describe the various attractions of the town. 'There's a cinema,' she said, 'and a place that has lovely ice-creams. Plus there're lots of Chinese shops, although they don't really sell much that you'd want to buy.' She didn't mention that on her volunteers' salary she was barred from buying much beyond the bare necessities anyway. 'The school where I teach is about a twenty-minute walk away. You must come with me tomorrow. The students would love to meet you. It would be a great chance for them to practice their English.'

Amanda, who never ran out of stories about her surroundings, then treated Bethany to a spirited description of the lives, the foibles and the struggles of her students. Sanggau with its varied groups of people, its strange customs, so very different from those at home, its many conflicts, some trivial, others deadly serious, was a never ending subject of fascination for her. And because she was so interested in everything herself, she endowed it all with a magical quality that made it interesting to her listener.

Bethany was constantly amazed at the way Amanda could, without telling an outright lie, make a place with as little to offer as Sanggau sound intriguing and exotic.

'You're the one who should have been an anthropologist, not me,' Bethany told her with a rueful laugh, 'or even better, a travel writer, the kind who sends articles to airline magazines and makes absolute hell-holes look like some kind of paradise.'

'I couldn't do that, wouldn't do it,' Amanda exclaimed, offended. 'I've been telling you bad things, too, haven't I?'

'Yes, sometimes, but it's just that the total effect of what you say is…' Bethany groped for the right word. 'You make it all sound so colourful and alive the way you describe it that even the bad things, not that there're very many, sound more like exciting challenges than anything else.'

Amanda tried to demur but Bethany went on, 'You see, I couldn't talk about Nanga Palin that way. The awful truth is that I'm feeling rather fed up with the place at the moment.'

'Everyone feels like that sometimes,' Amanda said, soothingly. 'I can tell from the things you've said that you really care about it. And you know so much about what the people there think and feel.'

Amanda had arrived at this conclusion after besieging Bethany with questions, surprisingly well-informed ones, Bethany thought, about the Dayaks. And without realising what she was doing, Bethany gradually began to look at Nanga Palin through a lens that was nearly as rose-tinted as the one through which Amanda viewed Sanggau.

Yet the surroundings of their current lives were not the only object of Amanda's interest. She laughed with Bethany over shared memories of their school days and they brought each other up to date on the more recent events in their lives.

'Whatever made you want to come here?' Bethany asked.

'I'd never been anywhere,' Amanda explained, 'except Spain and Greece on package holidays. Of course, they were full of people from the UK but even so they gave me a glimpse of life in other sorts of places. That inspired me to take a three month course in teaching English as a second language and when it was over I found out that the school here was looking for someone.'

'But what made you come out as a volunteer? I mean, with a certificate in teaching English, you could have found a real job with a real salary, couldn't you?'

'Perhaps,' she acknowledged, 'but you see the package holidays showed me how useless it is to come abroad and find yourself surrounded by hordes of people from your own country. You might as well stay at home, don't you think?'

Bethany hadn't quite looked at it that way but she nodded.

'What I wanted,' Amanda continued, 'was a chance to be involved in a completely different culture and find out what other people are really like. And being a volunteer with VSO seemed the best way to do it.'

'Well, you certainly succeeded.'

Amanda looked pleased.

'But don't you sometimes miss being around other people you can talk to?' Bethany persisted.

'Not really,' Amanda replied, and then added, hastily. 'Of course, I'm frightfully glad to see you but basically, I like being the only foreigner in Sanggau. It makes it so much easier to fit in and be accepted. Unfortunately, though, four or five Germans are coming here soon, working on an irrigation project, I think, and I've heard they're bringing their families with them.'

'Well, you might not have to see much of them.'

Amanda brightened at this thought and reverted to the subject of her students.

Bethany met some of them when she went to school with Amanda the next day. She sat in on her classes and chatted with some of the braver students who dared to try out their newly-acquired English. Most of them however were too shy to do this so Bethany talked to them in Indonesian and was rewarded with lots of polite compliments, ones she wished she deserved, on her linguistic ability.

Although she found the first day at the school genuinely interesting, she began to be a bit bored by the second, and on the third morning it took a major effort to stifle her yawns and keep her mind from drifting back to Kanyalang and Nanga Palin wondering what was going on there.

In spite of the concerted effort Bethany had made to avoid thinking about Wolf and reliving the night they had spent together, she hadn't been very successful. She was constantly forced to drive away visions of what their future relationship might be like, if they were to have any relationship when they got back to Kanyalang. And all too frequently, she caught herself wrestling with the problem of how it all could be kept under her control rather than his.

Left to entertain herself in the school courtyard while Amanda went to a meeting with the other teachers during the lunch break, Bethany had been quietly dwelling on this problem when the sound of crying roused her from her thoughts. Looking around her, she saw a girl with a tear-stained face clutching a crumpled letter in her hand while sympathetic friends clustered around her. Bethany's first thought was that some rat of a boyfriend had let her down. Then she remembered that Indonesian schoolgirls weren't supposed to have boyfriends.

Well, that didn't mean anything, Bethany told herself. Human nature was the same everywhere, wasn't it? And perhaps this girl who looked like she was about seventeen or so was one of the rebellious ones, a bit like a younger version of Pashetta. But on closer inspection, Bethany could detect nothing of Pashetta's precocious manner in this demurely dressed girl in school uniform. She had straight black hair that fell just below her ears, high flat cheekbones that were at the moment damp with childish tears and large expressive eyes that gave her a serious and sensitive air.

In an effort to keep a rein on her imagination, Bethany found herself straining to overhear what the girl was actually saying but the friends around her all seemed to be talking at once and this, combined with the girl's continued crying, made her difficult to understand.

Oh, well, I shouldn't be such a nosey-parker, Bethany told herself.

A few minutes later her attempts at eavesdropping were put to an end by the resumption of lessons but the unhappy girl made no effort to join the horde of students pressing back into the building.

Within a few minutes she was left alone in the schoolyard so Bethany, driven by a mixture of curiosity and compassion, and half-expecting a rebuff, went over and asked her in Indonesian, 'What's the matter? Can I help in any way?'

The girl regarded her warily for a moment and then silently handed her the letter.

Bethany looked at it but frowned as she realised that she couldn't make it out.

'I forgot,' the girl apologised, taking it back. 'It is in my language, Madurese.' Then she added, 'It is from my mother.'

With the boyfriend theory out the window, Bethany's thoughts turned to a death in the family and she frantically groped for something appropriate to say.

The girl saved her the trouble. Switching into English, she explained, 'My father stop to send money. I must leave school. Go home.'

Knowing this was not a boarding school, Bethany asked, 'Don't you live at home now?'

'No, I live with aunt. My mother sends money every month. She works for oil company near Balikpapan. She washes and irons all day. Very hard work. She looks very old. I do not want to wash and iron all my life. I want to be teacher like Miss Amanda. My mother want me to be teacher, too, but now —'

'Surely, you still can,' Bethany interrupted. 'There must be a school near where your mother lives.'

'If no money, how I can go to school? I have younger brothers and sister. They must eat. I must go home now and help my mother. I want to help her but I do not want my life be finished.'

'But surely it needn't be,' Bethany protested. 'You can get a job, can't you? Not washing and ironing but something better than that.'

The girl looked unconvinced and remained silent, so, in an effort to keep the conversation going, Bethany said, 'Will you tell me your name?'

'Kartini.'

'Mine's Bethany.' Then a thought stuck her and she continued, 'You must already have more education than your mother, don't you?'

Kartini nodded. 'Yes, but job very difficult to find. If I cannot be teacher I like to be secretary but I cannot if I not finish SMA. I will just have very low work all my life.'

After struggling for a moment, Bethany recalled that SMA was secondary school in Indonesia. 'How much longer do you have to go?'

'This year and one year more.'

Thinking how dreadful it would be to have to drop out without a qualification at that point, Bethany decided to talk to Amanda about it and see if there was anything that could be done.

She raised the subject as they were walking home.

'Yes, I heard,' Amanda said, ruefully. 'Her cousin brought the letter just before break. And it's such a pity. She's one of the best students in the school. Didn't you think her English was absolutely brilliant, for a schoolgirl who's never been out of Kalimantan, I mean.'

'She must be smart,' Bethany agreed, 'and it's so sad that she seems to think the rest of her life is totally ruined.'

'The awful thing is, she's not far wrong. She had her heart set on going to teacher training college and she was almost certain to get an oil company grant to go to the one in Banjarmasim.'

'Isn't there some way she could carry on here? Doesn't the school have some kind of help it could give her?'

'You must be joking,' Amanda exclaimed, with a bleak laugh that contrasted dramatically with her usual positive attitude.

They walked on in silence for a while until Bethany said, 'How much money do you suppose her mother sends her every month?'

Amanda made an educated guess.

'I could help her get through the rest of this year,' Bethany calculated, 'and then maybe –'

'Careful,' Amanda warned, 'if you start giving money to every needy person you meet, you're going to be totally inundated before you know what's happened. I'm lucky in a funny kind of way because I barely have enough to scrape by so I just can't give any more than a few rupiahs here and there. But you do have money so —'

Bethany started to protest but Amanda cut her off.

'By Indonesian standards, you do,' she insisted, 'and you live way up there in the rainforest so you don't know what it's like to be surrounded by people in desperate need of money.'

'Some of the people at Nanga Palin could use a little help,' Bethany replied, truculently.

'What do you do about it?'

'I had to make a rule in the beginning that I didn't lend money.'

'Well, there you are then,' Amanda exclaimed.

Bethany acknowledged that her friend had a point but as the day wore on she found she couldn't get Kartini out of her mind.

Bethany looked for Kartini at school the next morning and was told by one of her classmates that she wasn't coming anymore.

'Not even to finish the term?' Bethany asked.

Her informant shook her head so Bethany asked where Kartini's aunt lived and was given directions to a narrow alleyway not far from the town centre. An early morning rain had left it slippery with mud but, after careful navigation, Bethany found herself standing in front of a small house that was sadly in need of paint. She had to knock on the door a number of times before it was partially opened by a gnarled old crone whom Bethany later learned was some sort of indigent relation.

'Yes, Kartini lives here,' the old woman said, eyeing the foreign visitor suspiciously.

'May I come in and see her?'

The response was a sharp, 'No.'

Bethany was taken aback. 'Just for a minute,' she pleaded.

'Kartini isn't home. She went away.'

Bethany had barely digested this unwelcome news and was turning away when she glimpsed the figure of a girl in an upstairs window — a girl who looked very much like Kartini.

But why should she want to hide from me, Bethany wondered?

Perhaps the old witch was right and Kartini wasn't there. It might have been someone else in the window, some other girl with black hair and dusky skin. After all she had only seen her for a second.

Thoroughly put out by her lack of success and plagued by the suspicion that she had been lied to, Bethany trudged back to the main street.

Although the day was overcast, the morning was already getting hot and the humidity felt like it was high enough to support marine life. Deciding she needed something to soothe her spirits, she directed her steps toward the one café in town that served cold drinks, went in and ordered a coke.

A few minutes later, three women, two rather large and blonde, and one small and dark with an Asian cast to her features, came in and sat down not far away.

Surprised at seeing other foreigners there, Bethany wondered what language they were speaking. She listened and decided it must be German. Perhaps they had something to do with that irrigation project Amanda had mentioned.

God, I'm becoming a frightful eavesdropper, she thought. I'm even trying to listen in on conversations in languages I don't understand. How despicable is that?

As a defence against this reprehensible tendency she picked up a copy of a magazine that had been left on a near-by chair and began to read it. It had a lot of words she didn't know and she was concentrating on it rather hard when a Teutonic voice interrupted her.

'Excuse me.' The words were heavily accented but clear. 'Are you Karen?'

Bethany said she was not.

The owner of the voice looked disappointed but then, seeming to think that her intrusion required some explanation, she gestured toward her companions and went on, 'We only arrived here yesterday. Our husbands are going to be working on an Asian Development Bank project here. And there is another man on the team, a Dane. He is coming with his wife, Karen, but we haven't met her yet.' She paused a moment and then added, reproachfully,

'We expected you to be Karen.'

'Oh,' Bethany replied, feeling that she really shouldn't have to apologise for not being Karen.

'My name is Gretchen,' the woman continued. 'Are you a tourist here?'

Bethany repressed a smile. What in the world would bring a tourist to Sanggau, she wondered? 'No, I'm visiting a friend,' she said.

The woman waited as if she expected her to elaborate, so Bethany added, 'I work on an eco-tourism project farther up the river, past Putussibau.'

'What do you do up there?'

'I'm an anthropologist.'

'How interesting. And you speak Indonesian, I see,' she said, glancing down at the magazine.

'More or less,' Bethany acknowledged.

By this time the other two women had stopped talking and were regarding Bethany with interest. The blonde one leaned over and asked, 'Will you care to join us?'

Bethany didn't really care to but she didn't want to be rude so she closed the magazine and took her coke over to their table.

She was immediately deluged with a long list of their woes. Sanggau was an unspeakable place to live, they told her. Indonesian was an impossible language and they couldn't find anyone to translate for them or to help them. Their husbands were hopeless – they were at work all day and had callously left them to manage on their own. Men were so selfish, they declared, all they cared about was themselves. They had people at the office to help them cope with everything so they didn't give a thought to the fact that their wives were being left to struggle by themselves.

'We were told,' continued a woman who had been introduced as Helga, 'that English was the second language in this country but nobody speaks it.'

'Some people do,' Bethany said, 'you just haven't met them yet.'

'We certainly haven't,' Gretchen agreed, 'and I would very much like to know where they are hiding.'

'Don't they learn English in school?' asked the dark-haired woman whose name was Deng. She was Thai, married to a German, and her voice was softer than that of her companions.

'Yes, they do, actually,' Bethany replied.

'Then where are they?' Gretchen demanded. 'Tell me that.'

It suddenly occurred to Bethany that she could tell her. At least, she could tell her where one was.

'I know a student, a girl about seventeen, who speaks English,' she told them as a plan began taking shape in her mind. 'Her name's Kartini. She might be able to take you shopping in the afternoons after school and translate for you. And maybe she could give you Indonesian lessons, too. That would make your life here much easier, wouldn't it?'

Everyone agreed that it would.

'Of course,' Bethany continued. 'Kartini would expect to be paid.'

'Naturlich,' agreed Helga.

Gretchen's eyes narrowed as she asked, 'How much?'

Bethany equivocated. 'I don't know exactly,' she said.

A conversation in rapid German ensued.

Bethany had difficulty concealing her stunned disbelief at the munificence of the hourly sum mentioned. It would be a fortune in Sanggau. Kartini would make as much in two hours as Amanda did in a week.

'I'll speak to her about it,' Bethany said, and after making arrangements to bring Kartini to meet them, hurried away.

She lost no time in retracing her steps to the house where she was now convinced that the girl she had seen in the window really had been Kartini.

This time when she knocked on the door it was opened by a middle-aged woman whom Bethany later learned was Kartini's aunt. She appeared unruffled by the presence of a foreigner at her door but, like the old servant, she assumed that Bethany must be an English teacher, come to extract more school fees from the family.

'Kartini isn't here anymore,' she said, before her visitor had a chance to ask.

This time, Bethany stood her ground. 'It's very important that I see her,' she insisted. 'Can I come in and wait?' And regardless of the fact that no invitation was issued, she determinedly made her way inside and launched directly into an explanation of why she had come.

Kartini must have been listening from the hallway because the moment she heard about the job, she burst into the room, glowing with happiness.

The necessary introductions were made the following day and the presence of Deng made the two German women seem less intimidating to Kartini. She was able to bring out her very best English and do justice to Amanda's high opinion of her.

I can hardly believe it, Bethany thought, as she half-walked, half-flew back to Amanda's house. It all seems too good to be true.

CHAPTER TWENTY-EIGHT

Two days later Bethany and Amanda were strolling down Sanggau's main shopping street after school when they noticed that the Chinese merchants were drawing protective metal grating across their usually open storefronts and their would-be customers weren't complaining. Instead they were hurrying homeward with worried expressions on their faces.

'What's going on?' Bethany asked her friend. 'Why is everything closing up so early?'

'I've no idea,' replied Amanda, trying to catch what two old man were saying but failing because they were speaking Chinese.

Bethany questioned several passers-by but no one appeared to have the time or the inclination to enlighten her.

'Let's forget it,' Amanda said. 'We'd be better off going straight home. The family will be able tell us what's going on.'

They had almost reached the now familiar neighbourhood when Bethany's attention was caught by three house-maids speaking Dayak. She paused and listened for a moment and then, puzzled by what they seemed to be saying, went up and spoke to them.

At first they showed the same curious reluctance to explain anything that the people on the main street had shown but their astonishment at hearing a foreigner speaking their language soon overcame their reserve. The result was a jumbled account of their version of events that left Bethany thoroughly confused.

This time it was Amanda's turn to ask for a translation.

Bethany frowned. 'Their accent's a bit different from the one I'm used to and —' She broke off, asked the girls a few more questions and then, turning back to Amanda, shook her head hopelessly. 'I must have got it terribly wrong,' she said, ashamed that she couldn't do any better.

'Why? What do you think they said?'

'A load of absolute rubbish — something about a king sitting on a leaf and calling out an army. I mean, how absurd is that? Then there were some things I missed and some nonsense about a cup

275

of blood that somehow had something to do with the Madurese.' With a self-deprecating laugh, she added, 'I'm really mortified that I can't do any better than that.'

'Never mind,' Amanda said, soothingly, 'I'm sure those girls don't know nearly as much as Bapak does. We're almost home and we'll find out everything from him.'

Bapak was already home when they got there.

'There is very bad news coming out of Pontianak,' he told them in his softly spoken but authoritative Indonesian. 'The Dayaks and the Madurese are killing each other again and –'

'Are you quite certain?' exclaimed Bethany, not wanting to believe it.

Bapak was shocked. This girl had absolutely no manners, he thought, interrupting her elders like that. He congratulated himself that up to now he had managed to have very few dealings with foreigners even though he had let his wife convince him to host this temporary 'daughter'. He had resisted the idea at first, he remembered, but she had insisted that it would be good for the children's English so had given in.

He looked approvingly over at Amanda. She hadn't known their ways when she had first arrived but she had a natural sense of politeness and had learned quickly. She was almost like an Indonesian girl now, so he didn't mind having her around but this friend of hers was a different matter.

'The Dayaks and the Madurese have had many wars,' Bapak told her, sternly, 'maybe five or six, many people killed. Now they start again.'

'But why?' Bethany asked, wondering if he could cast any additional light on what she had already learned from Jun.

Bapak concealed his irritation with difficulty. What was the matter with this girl, he wondered? One of the first things a well brought up child was taught was not to ask questions. 'The Dayaks are very simple people and the Madurese are very clever,' he told her, reflecting a commonly held view. 'They steal and cheat. This makes the Dayaks very angry.'

Bethany jumped rapidly to their defence. 'I'd be angry too if people did that to me,' she replied, 'wouldn't you?'

Bapak silently agreed but didn't choose to reward the girl's impertinence by saying so. In any case, the situation was more complicated than it appeared on the surface and a foreigner couldn't be expected to understand.

'The Dayaks are very fierce,' he explained, patiently. 'They like to kill.'

'That's not true,' Bethany cried.

Bapak could scarcely believe he had heard her correctly. Being flatly contradicted was so unthinkable in the hierarchical world of his home and his office that it took him a moment to know how to deal with it.

He regarded his visitor with a mixture of anger and contempt. 'You don't know anything about it,' he said, with a deliberate rudeness that was quite out of character. This girl must be incredibly stupid, he decided. Didn't she live up there with the Dayaks? How could she be so ignorant about them? Then he recalled her saying something about working with a little group of Dayaks up beyond Putussibau. He supposed it was the Maloh. He had heard that they were relatively peaceful, not like the Iban and some of the other Dayaks. She clearly didn't know anything about them. Well, it just showed what happened when foreigners tried to meddle in Indonesian affairs.

'You stay in the house,' he ordered the two young women, afraid that Bethany's foolish ideas might lead them into some kind of trouble. If that happened, and if it was seized on by the press, it could make him, as District Officer, look bad. And, after a moment's consideration of how quickly the situation could become dangerous, he also forbade his wife and daughters from venturing out the next day.

'What should I do about my classes?' asked Amanda, who had learnt how to put things tactfully.

'Forget them,' he said, firmly. 'Everyone else will. You stay home until it is safe to go out.' He gave a nod in Bethany's direction to emphasise that she was included in this command. Then he dismissed his listeners by picking up his newspaper and beginning to read.

277

'How annoying,' Bethany exclaimed, when they were back in Amanda's room. 'I can't bear the thought of sitting around the house when all sorts of interesting things are going on outside.'

'I know it doesn't sound like much fun,' Amanda said, apologetically, 'but if Bapak thinks it's the best thing to do, it probably is. He's very clued in to everything that's going on. Nothing much escapes him.'

'I'm not so sure about that,' Bethany fumed. 'How much does he really know about the Dayaks? He seems to have the idea that they're still head-hunters, for God's sake. I mean, is that about a hundred years behind the times, or what?'

'You're probably right but while we're here we sort of have to do what he says.'

Fuck, Bethany muttered under her breath. The prospect of submitting to obtuse and arbitrary patriarchal authority did not appeal to her at all. How could Amanda be such a wimp? After all, there was such a thing as carrying this idea of being a daughter in an Indonesian family too far.

The obvious rebellion on Bethany's face alarmed Amanda. 'You know, it would be terribly awkward for me,' she said, 'if you didn't go along with what Bapak wants.'

'Oh, alright,' Bethany agreed, reluctantly. 'I don't want to cause you problems.' Still, she couldn't resist adding, 'But there can't be many Dayaks here in Sanggau because they don't like to live in towns so I don't know what Bapak's all bothered about.'

'There are some Dayak maids like the ones you talked to,' Amanda pointed out. 'They generally come here to work for a couple of years and then go back to their villages.'

'Yeah, and they looked pretty scary, didn't they?' Bethany said, sarcastically.

Amanda shifted uncomfortably and changed the subject. 'It's almost time for dinner,' she said, looking at her watch. 'Shall we see if it's on the table yet?'

It wasn't so they peered into the kitchen and were surprised to see Ibu ladling rice out of a rice cooker and Wati standing over a gas burner frying a mixture of sliced soybean cakes, red chilli peppers, and thin strips of potato in a large pan.

'Where are the maids?' Amanda asked, surprised to see Ibu doing the actual work herself rather than merely giving instructions.

'They've gone,' Wati said.

'Gone where?'

Wati shrugged. 'I don't know,' she replied.

'They were frightened and ran away,' Ibu explained. 'It was very foolish of them. They would be safer here.'

'What were they afraid of?' Amanda wanted to know.

'They think maybe Dayaks come tonight and kill them,' Wati told her.

'What rubbish,' Bethany whispered in English to Amanda, confident that even if Ibu heard her, she wouldn't understand.

Bethany was right about Ibu's English, virtually non-existent, but she underestimated her ability to figure things out.

'Our maids are Madurese,' Ibu told Bethany, reproachfully, 'so they are right to be careful.'

'Where did they go?' Amanda asked.

'They have an older brother who works as a night watchman. Probably they went to him. How should I know? They didn't tell me. I looked for them and they weren't here, that's all.'

'May I help, then?' Amanda asked, taking the ladle from Ibu's hand and filling a colander with fluffy white rice. Bethany watched awkwardly, wanting to help but not knowing quite what to do.

Wati solved the problem for her by handing her a large pineapple and assigning her the daunting task of peeling it, removing the eyes and slicing it. Bethany did her best but the result was ragged and she noticed that Ibu did not look too pleased.

The atmosphere at dinner was unusually subdued. Bapak scarcely spoke and Bethany wasn't sure whether the look of displeasure on his face was for her or for the general situation.

'Don't you wish we could go out and see what's happening?' she said to Amanda after they had helped with the washing up.

'Not really. Maids sometimes know things. They have a sort of grapevine that works better than the newspapers. In fact, they hear things the papers wouldn't even be allowed to print.'

'Like what?'

'Oh, I don't know – things the government wouldn't like.'

'What would happen if they did? Print it, I mean.'

'They'd be closed down and the editor would probably be arrested.'

Bethany gave a grimace of distaste.

'But on the servant's grapevine,' Amanda continued, 'news just seems to float through the air. And the great thing is, it's uncensored.'

'But how often does it turn out to be right?' Bethany returned, with a touch of scorn.

'Most of the time, I think.'

For Amanda's sake, Bethany made an effort to restrain her frustration at being confined to the house but she found the imprisonment particularly grating when Bapak decreed that all the women in the family should stay home for still another day, even though he himself continued to go to work as usual.

Fortunately Ibu always kept a large store of rice in the larder so no one actually had to leave the table hungry but the supply of fresh vegetables and other food diminished rapidly and each meal became plainer and skimpier than the last.

When Bapak came home on the third evening his countenance was grim. 'The Dayaks are coming from everywhere,' he reported, 'even from as far as Sarawak, killing, killing, killing, and taking heads.'

Bethany stared at him in stunned disbelief.

'In a village on the Sarawak road they put the fresh heads, still dripping blood, up on poles along the road,' he continued. 'The passengers on a bus going through there reported seeing it.'

'I don't believe it,' Bethany protested. 'There must be some mistake.'

'There were many witnesses,' he said tersely.

'But —' she hesitated, frantically searching her mind for a way to show that it couldn't be true. It simply had to be unsubstantiated rumour, or possibly the work of a gang of hardened criminals.

Yes, that was it, she decided, blame the Dayaks. Lots of people would be ready, even eager, to do that. But when she propounded this theory to Bapak, he refused to dignify it with a reply.

'Anyway, Dayaks couldn't possibly have come from all over Borneo,' she argued, determined to convince him that she was right. 'How could they have got in touch with each other? The rainforest isn't exactly littered with telephone boxes or internet cafes, is it? There is no way they could have got word to so many other Dayaks so far away.'

'They used magic,' Bapak told her, with every evidence of seriousness, 'and the cup of blood.'

Bethany could scarcely keep from laughing as she asked, 'What on earth do you mean?'

'It's a Dayak tradition, used in time of war,' Bapak told her. 'A young man fills a cup with the enemy's blood, Madurese blood in this case, and the fastest runner takes it to the next village. All the young men there drink from it and then another runner takes it on to the next place. Just the smallest sip gives anyone who tastes it a raging blood-lust and he is immediately filled with the spirit of war and the desire to kill.'

Bethany was surprised to see Ibu nodding in confirmation of this outlandish tale, Wati and Tini looking frightened, and Amanda apparently struggling with the question of whether to go along with it all or not.

'For one thing,' Bethany exclaimed, with mounting exasperation, 'running through the rainforest from village to village just isn't something that can be done in a matter of hours, or even a few days. It would take ages. And how can one cup hold enough blood for all those men all over Borneo to have a drink? You'd have to have a whole lorry full of blood and how would that get through the jungle where there aren't even any roads? And how —'

She stopped. It was clear from the faces around her that no one, with the possible exception of Amanda, was listening. Perhaps tearing down irrational ideas with rational arguments just wasn't possible, she decided, and yet there must be some way to get through to these people.

Overwhelmed with frustration, she suddenly remembered that the Dayak maids they had passed on the street had been saying something about a cup of blood. Had everyone in this place gone stark raving mad?

All at once, Bethany was terribly sorry she had come to Sanggau. All her hopes that a visit to Amanda would restore her perspective on the world and on her life were being thoroughly demolished by the incomprehensible attitudes of the people here. It was worse than being at Nanga Palin because Bapak and his family were educated people so she couldn't help expecting more of them. Plus Amanda - how could she possibly even flirt with these outlandish ideas? Just thinking about it made her want to scream.

Later that evening when she gave vent to her indignation Amanda's reply was far from satisfactory.

'Some of these ideas may not be rubbish, you know. People here are convinced that the Dayaks in the forest have special powers and,' Amanda hesitated for a moment before adding, 'they may be right. After all they've spent their whole lives here. They must know, don't you think?'

'Amanda, you must have been out in the sun without a hat. Otherwise, you couldn't be saying these things.'

'I'm not saying I definitely believe them —' she began.

'Well, you've just given me a colossal fright because you certainly sounded like you did.'

'I just meant they might have some truth to them.'

Bethany didn't find this reply very comforting. She didn't want to think that Amanda was going round the bend.

CHAPTER TWENTY-NINE

As she was drifting off to sleep that night, or trying to, anyway, Bethany asked herself how everyone at Kanyalang, one person in particular, would react to this nonsense about the Dayaks' magical powers. And she smiled in the darkness as she thought of the raucous laughter the very idea of it would produce.

'Jesus, what a lot of crap,' she could almost hear Wolf say. The others would agree and unflattering comments about Amanda's gullibility would flow thick and fast.

The thought made her feel better but the beneficial effect was short-lived. It was quickly superseded by the troublesome realisation that her attempt to re-establish contact with a familiar and rational world had only led her farther than ever away from it.

Fuck, I wish I had actually listened to Wolf and not come here at all, she admitted to herself. I wonder if he's thinking about me. God, I hope so.

Her thoughts went back to their night together and she hoped that it had left him wanting her as much as she wanted him. It didn't seem very likely though. There had been too many women in his life for it to have meant much to him. After all, she might even get back to Kanyalang and find that he had sorted things out with Pashetta and they were together again.

In an effort to put this horrible scenario out of her mind she turned her attention back to the current trouble in Sanggau. It was frustrating to think that all sorts of interesting things, some undoubtedly involving Dayaks, were going on out on the streets and the only things she'd ever know about them were the meagre bits of news Bapak chooses to pass on to her.

My God, if Dayaks were really coming from as far away as Sarawak, they might be coming from Nanga Palin too, she reasoned. Could that mean the men she saw there every day were drinking from that cup of blood — if the thing really existed, which of course it couldn't possibly. All that simply had to be a load of rubbish. And as for thinking of anyone she knew being filled with an uncontrollable blood lust — it was preposterous. No one who'd spent any time at Nanga Palin would believe that anyone from there was rushing around cutting off Madurese heads.

Then an awful thought struck her. Bapak was the highest government official in the district and if he persisted in believing the Dayaks were doing things like that who knew what completely unwarranted measures he might take against them, or against foreigners working in the area? Would he revoke their visas, for instance, and make them leave the country to keep them from reporting any trouble?

Somehow she would have to convince him that he was wrong. But how was she going do that when she was caged up in the house with no independent access to information?

She simply had to go out and see for herself what was going on. Perhaps the press would listen to her even if Bapak did not. She could get in touch with Adnan and perhaps with the foreign press too. At least, they'd see her as being neutral in the whole thing — but was she actually neutral?

Oh, well, she told herself, she couldn't worry about that now. She had to figure out how to escape from this prison without waking Amanda and the entire family. She knew that Ibu had ears like a lynx and her obsession with the evil effects of night air would probably make them extra sharp when it came to detecting anyone climbing in or out of an open window.

But Bethany knew she had to risk it. Pushing the bedroom window open a little farther, climbing out and jumping down to the garden would present no problem.

She could just slip out for a little while, she decided, and unless she discovered something really drastic, no one ever needed to know.

Fortunately Amanda was a sound sleeper so Bethany was able to get up, dress and get away without waking her. After hurrying across the garden she hesitated when she reached the street. How still everything was, she thought. Where was the music that usually blared from the radio next door, or the sputtering noises emitted by the three-wheeled taxis as they rattled by, or the calls of the food vendors as they pushed their lamp-lit carts through the neighbourhood? Even the dogs and cats seemed to have received the message that tonight their howls and yowls would not be appreciated.

Was she doing the right thing, Bethany wondered nervously as she made her way along the curiously silent streets? Somehow the absence of the usual night time sounds was unsettling and she was almost at the point of turning back when a collective cry of terror pierced the stillness and banished any thought of retreat.

An instant later the air was filled with a cacophony of desperate shrieks followed by screams of agony.

Determined to find out what was going on, and hoping she could help the victims of whatever terrible accident had occurred, she ran through a maze of narrow lanes that took her ever closer to the source of the cries.

Then her feet froze to the ground in front of a scene of unmitigated horror.

Bodies covered in blood lay everywhere. Panic-stricken people, driven mad with the fear of being stabbed to death by the razor-sharp blade of a Dayak's knife or of being decapitated by a Dayak's long sword, darted everywhere. Some were desperately clutching children who were too terrified to cry, while others were forced to abandon companions who were too badly wounded to follow. Everyone ruthlessly trampled over the bodies of those who were already dead while blowpipe-wielding men ringed the periphery of the massacre and hastened the butchery by reining poisoned arrows down on the hapless victims.

A throng of young boys crazed with fright ran into Bethany and knocked her to the ground in their frenzied attempt to escape their attackers. She felt her head crack against something hard and then everything went blank.

When she regained consciousness, the first thing she noticed was that an ominous quiet had replaced the shrieks of terror. Wondering if she was in the throes of some kind of nightmare, she cautiously opened her eyes to the sickening spectacle of heads being severed from the remaining corpses.

Too horror stricken to move, she could only lie there paralysed with fear, watching and waiting for the end to come.

But the end didn't come. The unbelievable happened instead. The assailants, convinced that their task had been fully accomplished, were disappearing into the night. She had been passed over.

Her head throbbed and she could feel stabs of pain in one of her legs and in her chest but the all-important thing was that she could feel. Thinking was more problematic. Her head hurt so much she felt as if she would never be able to think again and she was sore and aching all over. Had people kicked her or stepped on her or what? It didn't matter. She didn't care. She was alive.

As the first, faint rudiments of rational thought gradually began to return, she started to wonder how these ghastly atrocities could possibly have been carried out by Dayaks? She pictured Lunsa and Thumbi and Sarika and all the kind people who lived so simply at Nanga Palin but who had received her into their midst with such hospitality. She'd have to be out of her mind to believe that the Dayaks were still the fearsome head-hunters of history and legend. The Dayaks of today would never ever have done the unspeakable things she had just seen.

Yet, as Bethany looked around her, the carnage told a very different story. Decapitated bodies, some with their heads still near severed torsos, others with no head in sight, were jumbled over the ground around her. The neck-to-toes form of a baby lay nestled in the arms of his headless mother. The mutilated remains of other children, red with the blood that must have spurted from their necks or drained from the stubs of their hacked off arms or legs, were scattered near their motionless parents.

Bethany stared in disbelief at the evidence of such savagery. Then she shut her eyes in the hope that when she opened them again, she would find that it had all been merely some ghastly hallucination. But something jolted against her forehead and forced her to confront reality once more. Opening her eyes, she discovered that a severed head had rolled against her own and its blank, unseeing eyes were only inches away from her. Then a trickle of blood from a cut across her scalp mercifully blurred her vision and gave her a temporary reprieve from this nearest of horrors.

By the time she managed to regain her sight, the head that was refusing to be stilled was no longer there – somehow it had rolled away. She tried to sit up but a wave of dizziness swept over her. She leaned over and threw up, her stomach heaving until she had no strength left to do anything but lie there amongst the mutilated corpses, close her eyes and hope that everything around her was a dreadful nightmare that would vanish with the dawn.

How long she lay there amidst the slaughter, a few minutes or a few hours, she never knew. Nor did she have any recollection of getting shakily to her feet and stumbling through the empty streets in search of Amanda and the haven of Bapak's house.

Suddenly Ibu's capable hands were cleaning the blood from her face as she tried to learn exactly what had happened.

Bethany related the horrific events of the night as best she could but her answers were confused and disjointed. Only someone as well versed in the background of the situation as Ibu would have been able to make any sense of her story.

'But why?' Bethany asked, as Ibu pressed a cool compress on her swollen temple. 'Why didn't they kill me, too?' Her voice grew hysterical as she went on, 'I mean, they were cutting off heads everywhere. It didn't matter if the people were already dead. They took the heads, anyway so why didn't they cut off mine? Why am I the only one out of all those people who's left alive?'

'Because they could see you were not Madurese,' Ibu said, simply.

'But the children, the babies,' Bethany wailed. 'Why did they want to kill them?'

'Because they were Madurese children,' Ibu explained, slightly impatient at having to explain the obvious.

Bethany had neither the strength nor the inclination to pursue the matter further. She was too exhausted to do anything but acquiesce as she was half-led, half-carried to her room, undressed and put to bed.

If they reproached her for her nocturnal excursion, her recollection of it was obliterated by their subsequent kindness.

The first thing Bethany was aware of when she woke up the next morning was a headache of such mammoth proportions that it was a few minutes before the gruesome events of the night burst in on her consciousness.

'No,' she cried, almost aloud. It couldn't have happened. It didn't happen. But another voice within her throbbing head told her that it really had. And at the thought that it surely couldn't have been Dayaks who did those unbelievably grisly, brutal things, she was faced with the question of who else would have taken heads like that?

If only she had some air, she thought, but in the light of her recent misadventure, Ibu had made certain that no window was left unlocked at night. Now, in the late morning, the sun was already turning the room into a furnace.

Trying to move her head as little as possible, Bethany made her way over to the window and, in spite of the pain the motion caused her, managed to get it open. She took a deep breath and was trying to come to terms with things she didn't want to admit had happened, when Tikus, the family dog, tore over to the garden gate and began barking wildly. She ignored him at first but when the sounds turned into menacing growls and then to something more like high-pitched wolf-howls, she peered through the metal grillwork to see who or what was antagonising the normally friendly little fellow.

She saw four men sauntering by and heard them speaking in such loud clear Dayak that she had no trouble understanding. Three of them had human heads swinging from their belts and it was the scent of dried blood emanating from the severed necks that had set off the dog. Then to her horror Bethany recognised one of the heads.

It was Kartini's.

CHAPTER THIRTY

It took Bethany less than a minute to come to a decision. Whether or not anyone from Nanga Palin had been involved in the horror of the previous night, she could never, ever, work with Dayaks anywhere again. And as far as Nanga Palin went, even if the people there hadn't taken part in the massacre themselves, she couldn't bear to watch them glorying in a great Dayak victory. And they would certainly do exactly that. She could just hear them. No, it was too awful. It would have been their relatives, neighbours, friends, even lovers, who had done it so there was no question about whose side the inhabitants of Nanga Palin would be on. What would the screams of the dying children, the blood spurting from their necks, matter if those children had been Madurese? And who would care about trampling over the headless corpses if the mutilated remains were those of a hated enemy.

No, she couldn't face it. She wanted to go home, back to a place where there were civilized standards of behaviour, where nobody took heads or sliced people to death with long knives, and where machetes weren't considered an essential part of everyday attire. She simply couldn't work with people who kept up a tradition of such appalling brutality. And if that meant an end to her career as an anthropologist – well, so be it.

'But you must go back, at least to collect your things,' Amanda protested, when Bethany announced she was never going to set foot at Kanyalang or Nanga Palin again. 'And who knows, once you're there you might change your mind about staying.'

'Not a chance. And after last night, I couldn't care less about getting my things,' Bethany declared. 'What do I have there, anyway, except a few old clothes?'

'Somebody named Wolf?' Amanda suggested with a smile.

Bethany's mouth went down at the corners. 'I had him, as you put it, for one night, that's all. I don't think it meant much of anything to him and I'm not going to let it mean anything to me either. I mean, in the face of all that's happened, how could I? I'd just lie in bed and close my eyes and see all the blood and hear the screams and relive the terrible fear. Admittedly, sex with him was fantastic, better than I ever thought it could be, but I won't go back there just for that. I'm never going to be the kind of woman who's going to let herself be enslaved by a man. I've seen it happen to other people. I've told you a bit about Catherine and that awful Tarique – and in way it was a little like that for Pashetta with Wolf, though not nearly as bad – but it's never going to be like that with me.'

'I'm not saying you should be some kind of sex slave,' returned Amanda, with a laugh, 'but none of what happened was Wolf's fault. And breaking off with him isn't going to do anything to bring those people back.'

'Yes but if I'm back at Kanyalang it will be impossible for me to put it all behind me.'

Amanda could see her point so she took a different approach. 'There're your notes,' she reminded her, 'and your books, plus all the work you've done so far. You can't just leave all that.'

'Why not? I won't want any of it because I'm leaving Borneo the minute I can get a flight out of here.'

'But you might come back sometime and –'

'Never, there's no way I'm coming back, ever.'

'Doesn't it matter about your contract? I mean, it's not as if the men who did those dreadful things last night were actually from Nanga Palin.'

'Some of them might have been,' Bethany argued. 'They might have come there for one of the festivals or even just dropped in for a shag.'

'But you don't know that for certain,' Amanda pointed out. 'Shouldn't you at least find out before you do anything drastic like throwing over a career you've spent years preparing for?'

'No, because it doesn't make any difference whether anyone from Nanga Palin was actually in that mob of murderers last night or not.'

'But you've been saying –' Amanda protested.

'You see,' Bethany explained, 'if it's a question of Dayaks versus Madurese, there's no doubt about where they'll all stand. And I just can't go there and chat and be friendly with people who think it's alright, possibly even a good thing, to cut off the heads of little children, or of anybody else for that matter. There's a point at which being a participant observer just won't do anymore.'

'Well, when you put it that way,' Amanda agreed, 'I see what you mean. But you'd better give yourself a few days to recover before you think about going anywhere.'

'I'm alright.'

Amanda looked unconvinced but didn't argue. 'In any case,' she declared, 'you can't possibly leave until the road to Pontianak is safe.'

'How soon will that be?'

'Who knows? Not until everything settles down, I suppose.'

Ibu added her voice to Amanda's in insisting that Bethany stay until it was safe to travel and Bapak converted the invitation into a command, declaring that she mustn't go anywhere while the situation was still so precarious.

Eager as she was to put all the distance she could between herself and Sanggau, she was touched by the family's generous hospitality and decided that perhaps it wouldn't be such a bad thing to stay on for a few days. It would give her a chance to pull herself together so that she could, hopefully, face the future with some measure of equanimity.

On the day following the massacre, the house seemed particularly crowded as no one, not even Bapak, went out. The news of the night's bloodshed had spread through the town like wildfire, whispered over fences and through the iron grill-work on locked garden gates.

'But why isn't there anything about it on the news?' Bethany asked Bapak, after joining the family in front of the television set.

'It is not always wise to announce these things,' he told her, 'at least, not until they are a little clearer. It might make the whole province of West Kalimantan look bad.'

'But people should know what's happening,' she said, indignantly.

Bapak felt a flash of pity for all the men in England. How did they manage to live with such disobedient and argumentative women, he wondered? Why didn't they train them better?

He sighed as he reminded himself of his responsibilities as a host. He would not be sorry when it was safe for Bethany to leave.

Virtually everything in the town, including the food market, had closed down, leaving the resources of Ibu's larder severely strained. A breakfast of fried rice with chillies was followed by a lunch of fried noodles with onions and chillies. Bethany cheered up at the thought of the evening meal until she saw that the rice, although plentiful, was supplemented only by a dish of three hard-cooked eggs smothered in a sauce of onions, garlic, ginger, and, yes, she knew it, chillies. But it didn't seem like very much for six people and she felt a stab of guilt at the thought that she was eating some of the family's food.

A picture of the abundant provisions on the table at Kanyalang flashed through her mind and, for a fleeting instance, she almost wished she could somehow spirit herself back there.

As it happened, Bethany had been quite wrong in thinking that Pashetta was still suffering from Wolf's defection.

As soon as Mike had realised that Pashetta and Wolf were no longer an item, he had felt free to try to move in on her. As a result, he had found himself spending more and more time talking to her – not, he realised, that talking was exactly his specialty. Any meagre talents he might have had along those lines had been effectively stifled during his childhood.

His father and brothers had only talked to each other when they had a specific piece of information to convey. Of course that made a lot of sense, he decided, but it didn't get you very far with women. Females expected you to rattle on whether you had anything to say or not. They seemed to do this quite effortlessly themselves and appeared to take great pleasure in it. The funny thing was that he was beginning to feel that there was something rather nice about sitting around and having a beer with someone and saying anything that came into your head, even if nothing much did. People got to know what was on each other's minds that way and it made you feel kind of close to them.

Pashetta liked to talk and it was easy to have a conversation with her because she relieved him of the necessity of saying very much, himself. Unless she asked him a direct question, which didn't happen all that often, he only had to listen.

Mike didn't realise how much the warmth and sympathy she detected in his eyes encouraged her to make further revelations about herself. He only knew that she had told him a lot about her family and her life and that some of it sounded pretty awful.

Of course, he had always thought she was the sexiest woman at Kanyalang – even when all he had really known about her was that her face and figure didn't exactly hurt the eyes. Now she seemed more attractive than ever but the trouble with all that conversation business was that it left him really hesitant about coming on to her in the way he was burning to do. He had never felt any similar reservations about having sex with a woman before but maybe that was because he had never really talked to one, at least not in the way he talked to Pashetta. That made things different, somehow. What if he made a move on her and she turned him down? He'd feel like he'd lost his closest friend.

Wolf at that moment was feeling the loss, temporary, he assumed, of Bethany. Conversations over lunch and dinner were a crashing bore because he couldn't watch Bethany's face or see her reactions. He didn't go for a glass of cold water from the thermos outside Pashetta's office nearly as often as usual because there was no chance of running into her there. And he drank more in the evenings, accepting Elliot's offers of a whisky so often that he felt obliged to order him a new case on the next flight from Putussibau.

This newfound camaraderie improved the relationship between the two men but it did nothing, in Wolf's view, to make up for the fact that Bethany wasn't there.

He was, he admitted to himself, behaving like a teenager. And the worst thing about it was that he was making an idiot of himself over a woman he had spent just one night with, a woman who romanticised the rainforest in a way that drove him to distraction.

It was all too easy to look into the future and see what she would do after her little Borneo adventure was over. She'd go back to some dreary university job in the UK and spend the rest of her life lecturing spotty adolescents about the Dayaks.

Then after class she'd get into some rattletrap car and go home to some hearth-and-slippers husband and a couple of squalling brats.

Ugh, he thought with a shudder, what a life!

Having sorted this out, Wolf glanced at his watch and decided it was time for a nightcap, one that would have more punch to it than a beer. He could do with a shot or two of whisky. As he went in search of it he passed the door of Tarique's room and on impulse, pushed it open and went in.

It still bugged Wolf that he hadn't been able to find a single clue about what the arsehole had been up to. It didn't make sense that he had kept no personal financial records, left no paper trail about anything at all. There just had to be something on his computer or somewhere. Maybe if he tried again – he flicked Tarique's laptop on but a further perusal of the files revealed nothing that hadn't surfaced in previous searches.

He was about to give up and call it a night when he was startled by a feminine voice from behind his chair.

'What are you doing?' Marguarita asked, leaning over him and looking at the screen.

'Isn't it obvious?' Wolf replied, testily.

'Transparent as glass,' she said, laughing, 'you're snooping around Tarique's files, still hoping to dredge up something on him.'

'Got it in one.'

'You're wasting your time, you know.'

Thoroughly exasperated at having spent almost an hour doing exactly that, he retorted. 'You wouldn't like to just fuck off, would you?'

'You're very rude tonight, even for you,' she observed, choosing to be amused rather than offended. 'You should be glad to see me.'

'Tell me why.'

'Because you'll never make a detective on your own, you know.'

'If you've got something helpful to say, spill it,' he snapped. 'I've been through every goddamn file on this computer, and the one

294

in his office, but I can't find a damn thing to suggest the guy was anything but squeaky clean.'

'It's remotely possible that he actually was squeaky clean.'

'Don't be an idiot.'

She shrugged. 'Perhaps the way to find out is by asking.'

'Yeah, ask a dead man — great idea. If you've got anything else to suggest, stick around. Otherwise —'

'Actually, I'm talking about asking someone who's alive.'

'Who, you?'

'Sometimes you can be astonishingly dense,' she observed. 'Who knew Tarique the best?'

'Catherine but —'

'Do I detect a glimmer of human intelligence, after all?'

'She won't be any use,' Wolf said. 'She didn't know a damn thing about his financial dealings — at least, not about any underhand stuff. I asked her.'

Marguarita raised her eyebrows. 'You can ask her again, can't you? Of course, she probably won't tell you the truth but if you know what you're looking for you might be able to read between the lines. She's not a good liar, you know.'

'Unlike you.'

'Unlike me,' Marguarita agreed, coolly.

Wolf regarded her suspiciously. 'Look here,' he said, 'have you got it in for her or something?'

'Whatever gives you that idea?'

'I don't know. Maybe you're jealous or something.'

'Jealous of Catherine,' Marguarita scoffed, 'Why?'

'Because of Tarique, maybe.'

'You must be mad.'

'Well, something doesn't add up.'

'It adds up perfectly. You just don't see it. Catherine was the one who had the closest relationship with him, wasn't she?'

'Right.'

'And isn't it just possible that she's not the angel you take her for?'

'Bullshit, I don't take her for an angel,' Wolf retorted, thinking there were times when he'd truly like to throttle Marguarita. 'And I know her every bit as well as you do.'

'I doubt that,' she replied, 'but you could still have a little chat with her couldn't you, sort of skate around the subject of Tarique's financial dealings.'

'Sorry, I don't skate,' he said, sharply. 'If you want to sharpen your claws on Catherine, you'll have to do it yourself without any help from me.' And with that he closed up the computer and stalked off to his room.

CHAPTER THIRTY-ONE

As the days passed Wolf began to wonder what could be keeping Bethany in Sanggau so long. Surely she must have had enough of that dump by now and of darling Amanda, too. Or could she be staying away because of him, regretting the night they spent together and figuring that once she got back to Kanyalang she'd be faced with the prospect of running into him every five minutes? That was probably it, he thought, dismally, but it certainly wasn't a great testimonial to his talents in the sack.

The bill of fare at dinner did nothing to raise his spirits.

'Not fish again,' he exclaimed, as they sat down at the table. 'I swear, I'm beginning to grow gills.' And lifting one of his arms, he pointed to a likely spot on his rib cage and added, 'I can feel them starting just here.'

'We could hide Kolop's fishing line,' suggested Mike, 'except it wouldn't do any good because he catches the damn things with his hands.'

'River fish have too many bones,' complained Pashetta. 'I like ocean fish.'

'I've told Kolop that Catherine doesn't like it,' Bima added.

'Where is she, anyway?' asked Elliot, noting that her place was empty.

'In her room lying down,' said Bima. 'She wasn't feeling very well.'

'She was looking frightfully pale this morning,' Marguarita added.

'Doesn't she always?' Elliot frowned.

'It's not surprising,' Bima said. 'She hardly eats anything.'

It was true that in recent weeks Catherine had fallen prey to a sort of mid-day lassitude that she was finding harder and harder to overcome. She tried to hide it from the others, especially Bima, but today it had taken several cups of Kolop's strong coffee after lunch and another one, heavily laced with sugar, about four in the afternoon to get her through the day. Worst of all, her butterflies and beetles just weren't as compelling as they had been only a short time ago and the same thing could be said about the human fauna. Even Wolf, while terribly sweet, didn't seem particularly attractive anymore.

The only person who had lost none of his lustre was Bima. She was constantly amazed at what an extraordinary person he was, kind and gentle and loyal, qualities she would have considered boring before she had known Bima. How odd it was, she thought, that they had now become the ones that attracted her the most.

When the meal was over and Catherine had still not appeared, Marguarita filled a plate and knocked on her door.

'May I come in?' she called.

'No, I'm sleeping.'

Marguarita ignored the rebuff, went in, and turned on the light. 'Look, I brought you some dinner,' she said, holding out a tempting selection of pork strips cooked in a sweet soy sauce, potato slivers fried with red chillies, slices of a green squash that Kolok called labu siang, a generous helping of white rice, and a green tangerine. 'When Bima found out that the rest of us were having fish he persuaded Kolop to do pork for you.'

Catherine took one look at it and pushed it away. 'I don't want it,' she said, petulantly.

'You can try a bite or two, can't you?'

'No.'

'I'll leave it here then, shall I?' Marguarita said, setting it down on the dresser. 'You might want it later.'

'I doubt it.'

Marguarita frowned, annoyed that her efforts at being a ministering angel, a role it took some effort for her to assume, were meeting with such little appreciation. 'No wonder you don't feel like eating,' she said, 'it's like a furnace in here. Why haven't you put the air conditioner on?'

She was about to remedy this apparent oversight when frantic squeals from Catherine stopped her.

'No, don't. It's not hot, really it isn't.'

'Well, you need some air in here anyway,' Marguarita declared, giving in on the air conditioner but opening the window and locking the wire screening into place instead.

The warm dampness of the jungle night crept into the room, bringing with it the sound of croaking frogs, calling gekkos, and buzzing insects. Catherine shivered and Marguarita stared with concern at her chalk-white face. There was a nearly translucent quality about it that gave a wraith-like cast to her features but Marguarita's scientific mind was not predisposed to linger on the supernatural. It gravitated to the subject of blood chemistry instead and she felt that something must be seriously amiss with Catherine's and guessed that her red blood count must be extremely low.

Snatches of a conversation she had interrupted between Wolf and Catherine a number of months ago came back to her and, after fitting various pieces of the puzzle together, she hazarded, 'That wasn't actually a mega-hangover you had, was it — you know, when you and Bethany spent a couple of days at Nanga Palin?'

'Yes, it —' Catherine began and then broke off. Why bother arguing about it now?

Marguarita answered for her. 'That was an abortion, wasn't it?' she said, in a voice that invited no denial.

Catherine didn't reply.

'You idiot, you might have died, you know.'

'Well, I didn't, did I?' Catherine retorted, with more vigour than Marguarita had expected.

'Do you know what it was they gave you for it?'

Catherine shook her head.

'Didn't you ask?'

'That old woman — witchdoctor or whatever she was — said it was 'obat'.'

'That just means medicine,' Marguarita said, impatiently.

'I know that,' Catherine sighed, not wanting to talk about it, 'but I didn't much care what it was.'

'I'd have thought you might have been curious.'

'Why? What difference would it have made? The old bat would only have told me some Dayak name that wouldn't have meant anything to me.'

'It might have helped us find the English name, if there is one, or the Latin name.'

'What's the point of bothering about all that now?' Catherine said, crossly. She just wished Marguarita would go away and leave her alone. 'It's all ancient history, for God's sake.'

'Not necessarily. You're looking rather awful and –'

'Thanks.'

'Well, it's the truth. You have huge dark circles under your eyes.'

'They might go away if you would let me get some sleep.'

'Perhaps,' Marguarita replied and, making a mental note of the bluish tinge to Catherine's lips, wished her good night and went in search of Elliot.

She found him pouring himself a whisky on the veranda. 'I think we should ring for the doctor tomorrow morning,' she told him. 'It's my guess that something's definitely wrong with Catherine.'

For once, Elliot was unconcerned about the cost of the iridium phone or the helicopter and he followed Marguarita's advice as soon as he reached the office. But he encountered an unexpected difficulty when he actually spoke to the doctor.

'Fucking hell,' he exclaimed into the expensive instrument, 'you've simply got to come.'

Pashetta, who had never heard Elliot use that sort of language, widened her eyes in astonishment and Mike, who was lounging beside her desk, muttered, 'Whatever's got into the old boy today?'

'I think maybe the doctor does not want to come,' she suggested.

She was right. He didn't.

'But it's perfectly peaceful here,' they heard Elliot say. 'I can assure you, there's absolutely no danger.'

Mike frowned. The doctor's unwillingness to come didn't really surprise him. Nearly half of his rangers hadn't turned up for work that morning, or the day before, for that matter, and there seemed to be a vague feeling of tension in the air. It gave him the distinct impression that something ominous was afoot.

'What did the guy say?' Mike asked as soon as Elliot put down the phone.

'That the Dayaks are running amuck,' Elliot explained, 'killing any Madurese they can find. I told him there was no problem here but he's being stubborn and refuses to come.'

'The doctor is Madurese,' Pashetta reminded him.

'Bugger,' muttered Elliot and since it had been Marguarita's idea to bring in the doctor he decided to talk to her about what to do next.

He found her at her desk pouring over a large book and looking rather tired.

After telling her about the unsatisfactory telephone conversation, he asked, 'Do you think a doctor's really necessary?'

'Absolutely essential.'

Surprised that she seemed so adamant, he ventured, 'You don't think a little rest —'

'No, I don't. You see, it wasn't a monster hangover that kept Catherine at Nanga Palin a few months ago. It was an abortion.' She paused and then added, 'Dayak style.'

Elliot was stunned. 'Good God, why didn't she go to —'

'I don't know. She tried to make me believe some nonsense about being away from work but that couldn't have been the real reason.'

'What was it then?'

'My guess, but it's only that, is that Tarique had somehow managed to get his hands on her money and she couldn't afford to go anywhere else.'

Elliot turned purple with rage at this idea and for a moment Marguarita feared that Kanyalang might have two cases for the reluctant doctor. But he mastered his emotions and even managed to evince some concern for Marguarita. 'You're not looking very well, yourself,' he said.

'I've been up a good part of the night,' she explained, 'reading up on some of the plants in the area to see what they might have given her at Nanga Palin.'

'Did you find anything?'

She nodded. 'Yes, several possibilities so far, but I think the most likely one is something called croton tiglium. The Dayaks call it

Chengkian. When the roots are boiled the liquid makes a fairly effective abortificant, sometimes too effective.'

Elliot frowned. 'What do you mean by that?'

'I mean that a bit too much of it can kill the woman at the same time that it destroys the embryo.'

'Good God,' he exclaimed in horror, 'Catherine might have died.'

'Quite,' agreed Marguarita, 'but it's the same thing with most of these local medicines, you know. It's the dosage that's the dodgy thing, too little and it doesn't work, too much and that's the end of the patient. And if the ingredients aren't measured accurately, or if they haven't been properly adjusted to suit the size and weight of the person who's going to take them – well, that's when you have a problem. Fortunately Catherine's taller than the Dayak women so if she was accidentally given a dose that was a bit on the strong side she could have tolerated it, more or less. I wouldn't be surprised if that's what happened.'

'What makes you say that?'

'Of course, I'm a botanist who dabbles in traditional medicines, not a doctor,' she reminded him, 'but I gather that a substantial overdose of croton tiglium can kill off a dangerous, and potentially fatal, number of red blood cells. Now we've all noticed that Catherine's been dragging around lately, always tired and eating almost nothing. And of course anyone can see that she's white as a ghost. All that sounds like a dearth of red blood cells to me.'

'But she's always been pale,' Elliot protested, in the hope of easing his growing alarm.

'I know. She might just be a bit anaemic,' Marguarita said, doubtfully. 'Perhaps she has been all along. But if so, that might have made the effect of the croton tiglium worse.'

Elliot felt himself succumbing to a mounting panic. Sorting out the after-effects of an abortion just wasn't within his designated scope of work. But if Catherine's health, possibly even her life, was in jeopardy he had to make sure he did the best he could for her. Jesus, he thought, what a time for that damn fool doctor to get cold feet about coming to Kanyalang.

'What do you suggest we do about it?' he asked, suddenly feeling rather helpless.

'Get her to a doctor as quickly as possible. Since he won't come here, one of us will have to take her to Putussibau. I'll do it, if you like.'

Elliot gave her a look of infinite gratitude. 'If only I had had any idea…' he began.

'If any of us had known,' Marguarita interrupted, 'anyone except Bethany, that is – I assume she was the one who arranged it.'

Elliot had difficulty keeping himself from trembling with rage. 'If so, she's off the project the minute she gets back from her holiday.'

'No need to be hasty,' Marguarita pointed out. 'You can't think she would do anything that stupid a second time.'

'I'm not sure I share your optimism,' Elliot snapped.

'She is quite good at her work, you know,' Marguarita pointed out. 'You wouldn't be able to replace her easily.'

'Well, never mind about that now,' he replied, testily. 'I'm going to order the helicopter. How soon do you want it?'

'Just give me a couple of hours.'

'Good,' he said and feeling that it was a relief to be able to do something, he went back to his office and picked up the iridium phone.

Elliot was still trying to digest everything Marguarita had said when Wolf appeared at his door, so he told him about it.

'Hell, that abortion was months ago,' Wolf exclaimed. 'Catherine's probably just getting her period or something.'

'But Marguarita said –' protested Elliot.

'What the fuck does she know? She's not a doctor. She's got a bee in her bonnet about some of these Dayak cures and for some crazy reason she wants to ring the alarm bell, that's all.'

'I don't agree with you,' Elliot said, firmly. 'In fact, I've already called for the helicopter so Marguarita can take her to the doctor in Putussibau.'

'Well have it your own way,' Wolf said.

'I intend to,' Elliot returned icily.

Marguarita and Catherine left on the helicopter shortly before lunch. Without them, it was a significantly diminished group that sat down to the mid-day meal.

Mike, prompted by the doctor's refusal to come, had spent much of the morning finding out as much as possible about what was becoming known as the seventh, and possibly the worst, of the Madurese-Dayak wars. 'Rumour has it there've been thousands of deaths,' he said at lunch.

'Madurese or Dayaks?' Wolf demanded.

'Mostly Madurese. Apparently swarms of Dayaks, armed with machetes, swords, blowpipes, you name it, have been pouring out of the jungle, some from as far away as Sarawak.'

'You're kidding,' Wolf exclaimed, hoping that he was.

'No, I'm serious. A couple of my rangers told me they're taking heads in the villages along the road to Kuching and as far up-river as Sanggau.'

'Sanggau?' interrupted Bima. 'Isn't that where —'

Wolf cut him off. 'Jesus Christ, that's where Bethany is. We've got to get that helicopter back here right away.'

Elliot looked at him in amazement. 'Whatever for?' he asked.

'For me,' Wolf declared. 'I'm going to Sanggau and get Bethany out of there.'

'Aren't you being a little overly dramatic?' Elliot suggested. 'If there's trouble on the streets she'll be far better off staying where she is and keeping away from crowds. Having the conquering hero arrive in the midst of it all will just stir things up and make them worse.'

'Anyway, they're only out to get the Madurese,' put in Mike, in an attempt to calm Wolf down, 'so she'll probably be alright.'

'Probably isn't good enough,' Wolf retorted. 'If the Dayaks run amuck, she could be caught in the middle of it and anything could happen.'

'Most unlikely,' Elliot declared, 'so I advise you to cool down and remember that the helicopter's an expensive proposition. It's already been here once today and I'm not going to call it back just for some madcap scheme of yours.'

'Is that what you call concern for somebody's safety — a madcap scheme?' Wolf asked in an outraged voice. 'Well, I'd call it something different, like a sense of responsibility, and if you won't order the goddamn helicopter, I'll do it myself.'

'If you do, it will be on your own account and it will be charged against your salary,' Elliot warned.

'I don't give a flying fuck who or what it's charged to.'

'Very well, then,' Elliot said, coolly, 'you can ring from my office.'

'Thanks for nothing,' Wolf shouted back from the veranda stairs as he hurried off to the iridium phone.

'Temper, temper,' Elliot muttered under his breath but nobody paid any attention.

Wolf needn't have rushed. When he landed in Putussibau he was told that hiring a taxi to take him on to Sanggau was out of the question. More than twenty kilometres of road had been built over peat bog and now, with the rains, it had become impassable. Why did he want to go there anyway, he was asked? Didn't he know there was trouble in the area?

Eventually Wolf had to resign himself to the prospect of cooling his heals in Putussibau until the next morning when he could catch the regularly scheduled flight to Pontianak and then try to get to Sanggau from that direction.

With nothing particular to do for the rest of the afternoon, he decided to see what was up with Catherine. He had told Bima he would try to check on her if he had time. The poor guy was feeling guilty about not having been the one to take her to the hospital but he was squeamish about health issues and the thought of dealing with the after-effects of a hatchet-job abortion had completely freaked him out.

Wolf could understand how he felt but, since it wasn't incumbent on him to do anything more than pop round and ask how things were going, he set off on his mission without any qualms.

After a little preliminary research he found Catherine asleep in the town's stark, ill-equipped hospital. Marguarita, buried in a book, was ensconced in a chair not far away.

'Florence Nightingale, I presume,' Wolf remarked, dragging a chair over next to her. 'I must say, this is an unsuspected aspect of your character.'

'Isn't there anything at Kanyalang you could be doing?' she retorted.

'About a hundred things, but never mind about that, what does the doctor say about Catherine?'

'He thinks she has something called haemolytic anaemia and that it could have been triggered by a heavy dose of croton tiglium.'

'Does he agree that that's what they gave her for the abortion?'

'He says that it's likely, although he doesn't pretend to know much about Dayak medicines. But he's put her on something called prednisone and we'll see how it goes.'

'How long is he going to keep her in this place?' he asked, brushing a persistent fly away from his face and looking around at the mildew-streaked walls.

'Just a few days, assuming she responds well to the treatment.'

'You'll stay with her, won't you?' Wolf asked.

'Until Bima comes – that should be tomorrow.'

'That's not so bad then,' Wolf said, with relief. 'For a while there, I was afraid it might be something serious.'

'It can be fatal if it goes untreated long enough,' she informed him tartly. 'Is that serious enough for you?'

'Holy shit,' exclaimed Wolf, turning pale beneath his tan. And not wanting to dwell on such a dire eventuality, he launched into an account of his frustrations in trying to get to Sanggau.

'But what's the point?' Marguarita asked.

'I'm just worried that something might happen to Bethany, that's all.'

'Bollocks, you're just dying to play the hero.'

'That's not true. I just want to make sure she's okay.'

Bethany's name had penetrated Catherine's consciousness and she asked, sleepily, 'Is Bethany in some kind of trouble?'

'Not really,' they both assured her.

'The Great Wolf, the leader of the pack, is charging forth single-handedly to defend her against a horde of raging head-hunters,' Marguarita added, mockingly.

'Don't be an idiot,' he snapped.

'I'm not sure I'm the one who's being an idiot,' she relied.

'Elliot agrees that I'm wasting my time,' Wolf confessed.

'I don't,' Catherine said, weakly. 'It's really scary to think of Bethany being in the middle of ... you did say head-hunters, didn't you? I'm glad you're going.'

'It's really nothing to worry about,' Wolf said, seeing that Catherine looked distressed.

'But if she's caught somewhere and needs help, or even if it turns out that she doesn't,' Catherine continued, 'I think it's lovely that somebody cares enough about her to go and find out.'

Wolf scowled. For the life of him, he couldn't remember ever having had anything he had done described as 'lovely' and it didn't quite suit the persona he liked to think he projected.

'I just wish it wasn't taking so damn long to get there,' he grumbled. And shortly after that, he conjured up an appointment and made his escape.

Wolf had many more occasions during the course of the next twenty-four hours to wish it was easier and quicker to get to Sanggau.

When he arrived in Pontianak he found that even though the road to Sanggau was passable, it was hard to find a taxi driver who was willing to go there. It was too dangerous, they claimed. There had been trouble along that road. But eventually money worked its magic and Wolf found one who was tempted by his offer of a highly inflated fare and agreed to make the trip.

After four hours of death-defying driving they arrived in Sanggau, and Wolf surveyed the town's deserted streets and closed-up shops with misgiving. Fortunately Bethany had mentioned that her friend lived with the District Administrator's family, but there were so few people on the streets that it wasn't easy to find anyone who could give him directions. Eventually he succeeded however, and the taxi drew up in front of the designated house.

Bethany glanced out the window at the sound of a car screeching to a halt at the garden gate. Then seeing that the unexpected visitor was Wolf, she rushed to the door, flung it open and threw her arms around him.

307

'My God, is it really you?' she cried. 'I don't believe it. You can't imagine how glad I am to see you. But whatever are you doing here?'

'I'm damned if I know,' he replied, grinning at the enthusiasm of the welcome he was receiving.

'Who cares why you're here,' she declared, pulling him into the dim interior of the house. 'Just come in and don't dare think of going away.'

Then, in a display of emotion that left Wolf thoroughly confused, her squeals of delight gave way to gut-wrenching sobs.

'Hey, there,' he said, disentangling himself from her grasp and wondering why, with only two sexes in the world, one of them had been made completely irrational, 'if my being here is making you go on like this, I'd better get the hell out.'

This threat only seemed to bring on a fresh flood of tears.

'Hey, are you okay?' Wolf asked hopefully but since she clearly wasn't, he said, 'Come on, you can tell me. What's the problem?'

She tried to tell him but her words poured forth in such a jumble that he could make absolutely no sense of them so, after a few futile attempts to figure it all out, he gave up. They'd have plenty of time to talk going back in the car.

'Come on, enough of that,' he said, gently brushing her tears from her cheeks. 'Get your kit and caboodle together. I've got a taxi waiting to drive us to Pontianak and we can sort all this out on the way. We might even go AWOL for a couple of days, catch a flight to Bali or somewhere, before we go back to Kanyalang.'

Bethany pulled away from him in alarm. 'I'm never going back there,' she cried, 'never, ever.'

Stunned, Wolf demanded, 'Why not?'

'Because of everything I just told you,' she said, dismayed that he could ask that after everything she had said.

'I'm afraid I didn't quite get it straight,' he confessed. 'You'll have to take it a little slower.'

She tried starting again but the result was no clearer than before.

'Listen, you're overwrought,' he said, cutting her short. 'Don't try to decide anything now. Things will look different tomorrow.'

'No, they won't,' she declared, vehemently, 'and if you can't understand that – well, that's just too bad. But I can't go back there now, not after everything that's happened.'

Amanda, who had been drawn into the hallway by the commotion, decided to step in. 'Perhaps I should explain,' she said.

'I could use a translation, that's for sure,' Wolf agreed, with relief. 'You must be Amanda.'

She nodded and then described, as best she could, what had happened to Bethany during the events of the preceding days.

'Good God,' Wolf exclaimed, when he had heard it all. Then turning back to Bethany, he said, 'Okay, I think I get it now but you can't spend the rest of your life here in Sanggau, you know.'

'No, of course not,' she agreed, trying to regain control of herself.

'Right, and you can't go anywhere from here without going through Pontianak,' he reminded her, 'so you might as well come with me now. Once we get there you can think about what you want to do.'

She didn't reply.

'Come on,' he urged, taking her silence as a good thing – at least, she wasn't refusing. 'The bandit who's driving my taxi is already charging me a fucking fortune and the more I keep him sitting here, the higher the price is going to go.'

He could tell from the sudden eagerness in Bethany's eyes that she found his suggestion seriously tempting. The problem was that she appeared incapable of forward motion.

'Okay, goodbye then. I'm going without you,' he threatened, although he had no intention of doing any such thing.

The stratagem worked. Bethany flew into action and crammed a few things into her rucksack. Within minutes she was thanking Bapak and Ibu for everything.

Then she threw her arms around Amanda, saying, 'I can't tell you how wonderful you've been. I'll never forget it as long as I live. Nobody in the world ever had a better friend than you. Keep me up to date with what's happening in your life and I'll see you the minute you get back to London. Just tell me what flight you're on and I'll meet you at Heathrow.'

309

Wolf was mystified at this outpouring of affection for a friend she hadn't bothered with in years, but he merely shrugged, picked up Bethany's rucksack and led her to the taxi.

He had an uneasy feeling as they drove through the too-quiet town. He knew it shouldn't have been like this and it made him nervous. There must be rumours afloat that today wasn't going to be an ordinary day. The sooner he got Bethany out of there, the better.

He frowned as he thought of her farewell to Amanda. All that business about meeting her at Heathrow sounded like Bethany was really determined to go back to the UK and he couldn't let that happen.

Quite aside from his personal feelings, he told himself, it would be a disaster for Kanyalang if she left. It could take several months to find a replacement for her and then, unless the new guy was as quick at picking up the language as Bethany had been, it would be at least a year before he'd be able to jabber away in Dayak and be of any real use. That could mean a loss of as much as a year and a half's work, and the project simply couldn't afford that.

But was that really what was bothering him, he wondered, or was he just kidding himself? Maybe the real problem was that he knew that if Bethany went back to England, he would lose her. Was that what was worrying him? But it shouldn't because he wasn't going to let it happen. He was going to do something that would make her change her mind and stay. The question was – what?

CHAPTER THIRTY-TWO

As soon as the car shifted, with much noise and difficulty, into high gear and they left Sanggau behind them, Wolf returned to the subject of what had happened there and got Bethany to flesh out Amanda's account of the massacre.

'So you see,' she concluded, 'I know I'll never be able to think of Dayaks again without seeing Kartini's head dangling from that man's belt. And working with them, being with them every day, is so completely out of the question, I can't begin to tell you.'

'But they wouldn't be the same Dayaks,' Wolf pointed out, his thoughts running along much the same lines as Amanda's had done. 'You're dealing with a completely different set of guys at Nanga Palin.'

'Not necessarily. The mob that night came from all over Borneo so God only knows who was in it.'

'Did you recognise anyone?'

'No.'

'Well, there you are then. If anyone you knew had been there, you would've spotted them right away.'

She regarded him doubtfully. 'Perhaps not – it was dark and everything was so chaotic. I can't really be sure.'

'Okay then just for the sake of argument let's say that there were a couple of guys from Nanga Palin there. If so, you'll hear about it fast enough when you get back there, won't you?'

'But I'm not going back.'

'Why rush into any decisions now?'

'Because I know how I feel and that's not going to change.'

'Listen, it can't do any harm to check the situation out before you do something rash like chucking the job and getting in an aeroplane, can it?'

'I don't see any point in wasting time when I've already made up my mind.'

'Okay, fair enough. But what's your hurry anyway?'

'It isn't really a question of time,' she said, backtracking a little.

'It's more that I can't even bear the thought of looking at Dayak faces, much less working with them every day.'

'Even if you found out that nobody from Nanga Palin had had anything to do with the massacre?' he demanded.

'Even so,' she said, firmly, 'because there would still be all the weddings and festivals and things like that when I'd have to see people from other longhouses.'

'And would that be such a problem?'

'Yes, because I'd look at each of the visitors, the men that is, and wonder, were you one of the ones? I couldn't stand that.'

'Couldn't you just give those occasions a miss?'

She gave a derisive laugh. 'I'd be a fine anthropologist if I did that, wouldn't I?' Then she frowned and went on, 'But that's not everything. There're all those times when men from other villages come over to see the Nanga Palin girls and the same thing would happen. I would wonder. And I don't think I could bring myself to speak to a girl if there was a chance she'd been sleeping with one of those murderers from Sanggau. I wouldn't even be able to be civil to her family.'

'Isn't that going a bit far?'

'I don't think so because her relatives would have been right in there, sleeping in the same room with them.' Then, with an unexpected giggle, she added, 'Although how they manage to do that when their daughters or granddaughters or their sisters are bonking away on the next mat, I can't imagine.'

'Pretty sound sleepers, I guess,' Wolf grinned, relieved that the conversation had taken a lighter turn.

To his disappointment, it didn't last.

'Almost everyone at Nanga Palin has relatives from other longhouses who come to visit,' Bethany continued, 'and if some of those people had been in Sanggau I wouldn't have recognised them.'

'Couldn't you just consign it all to the past and put it out of your mind?' Wolf asked, without much hope.

'Hello,' she said, looking at him aghast, 'haven't you heard anything I've been saying?'

Shit, he thought, his arguments were getting him exactly

nowhere. But he'd have to come up with some strategy for keeping her from leaving the project and, more important, to keep her from leaving him.

'Don't you see,' Bethany continued, feeling increasingly exasperated at not being understood, 'that the men in Sanggau, and other places, too – wherever they slaughtered Madurese – will be heroes to them. They'll think of them as warriors in the best Dayak tradition and after what happened I just can't live with that.'

Wolf turned away from her and looked out the window, racking his brain for a way to make her see things differently. After a while, he came up with a possible avenue. 'Listen, the Nanga Palin people are Maloh Dayaks, aren't they?'

She nodded.

'And in the old days, the serious head-hunting days –'

'Sanggau was serious, for God's sake,' she cried, outraged at hearing the killings there trivialised.

'Okay, okay, bad choice of words, let's just say that back in the days before anybody tried to put a stop to head-hunting, the Maloh were relatively peaceful, weren't they?'

'Yes.'

'And wasn't it the Iban Dayaks who were the really bloody-minded ones?'

'Apparently.'

'Okay then, let's take that as given. Now, if you want to talk about glorious warrior traditions –'

'I don't. I can't think of anything I want to talk about less.'

'Okay, we don't need to,' Wolf said, recognising that a touch of hysteria had crept into her voice. 'Let's just talk about the fact that head-hunting was more of an Iban thing than a Maloh one.'

'Alright.'

'So doesn't it follow that you may not find as much enthusiasm for blood sports, human blood that is, at Nanga Palin as you might think?'

Wolf studied her face as she appeared to consider this. At least, she wasn't denying it outright.

Encouraged by this, he went on. 'There's another thing, too. The Maloh are a small group, aren't they?'

'What are you getting at?'

'Just this, the Maloh are concentrated in the area above Putussibau but the Iban are all over the place. And the Dayaks involved in this recent violence have come from just about everywhere. So doesn't it look like it must be mostly Iban who are running amuck and doing those God-awful things?'

'Not necessarily, and if you're suggesting that the people at Nanga Palin won't support what happened if turns out that it was Iban who did it, then I think you couldn't be more wrong. The Maloh and the Iban are a bit different but not all that much.'

'Well, you know best,' he conceded, deciding that strategic retreat might be the best policy at this point. 'But will you just think about it for a little while before you make any definite decision?'

'I'll think about it over night,' she agreed, reluctantly, 'but tomorrow morning I'm going to the airline office and booking my flight back to the UK.'

'But that's no time at all,' he protested.

'It's enough. What's the point of sitting around Pontianak thinking about a decision I've already made? If there's a plane leaving for Singapore —'

'There isn't. There're only three flights a week and tomorrow isn't one of the days.'

'Alright, to Jakarta, then, or any place where I can get on a plane back to London.'

Crap, Wolf muttered to himself and, realising that he wasn't getting through to her at all, he turned away and gazed out the window. Bethany, reacting in similar fashion, stared out the window on her side and pretended a fascination with the passing landscape that she was very far from feeling.

A hostile silence hung like a wall between them until Bethany began to feel a pang of conscience. Considering how much trouble Wolf had gone to on her behalf, she decided that perhaps she was being a bit churlish. In an effort to make amends, she changed the subject and asked, 'How are things going at Kanyalang?'

Glad for the opportunity to try and take Bethany's mind off of Sanggau, Wolf launched into an account of recent happenings on the project. But when he told her about Catherine, he stopped short of mentioning any possible connection between her current illness and the abortion medicine. He didn't want to say anything that might make her feel bad about her role in that episode or add fuel to her desire to put Kanyalang, and everything associated with it, behind her. He related the doings of everyone else in considerable detail though and, thanks to the terrifying speed set by the driver, they drew up in front of the hotel in a remarkably short time.

Bethany felt a pang of sadness as she looked up at the slightly dilapidated building. This was the place where she and Wolf had spent that unforgettable night together and now there would never be another one like it — certainly not tonight when the horrors of Sanggau would still be raging through her dreams. She wondered if they should even find another hotel and get separate rooms to make sure they did everything possible to put their one night together behind them.

She was about to suggest this when it occurred to her that she hadn't spent a night alone since the massacre. Amanda, so understanding and so kind about being woken up, had always been there on the other side of the room, ready to drive her nightmares away. But what if she woke up and no one was there? How would she dispel the horrible images of her dreams without the warmth of human contact? And if that warmth came from Wolf, and if sex came along with it, well, why not? After all, another night with him wouldn't have to be like the first one, would it?

It wasn't.

It was gentler and less intense but more beautiful in its way. And when she finally drifted into sleep she had the first peaceful dreams she had known since the massacre.

The next morning she watched drowsily as Wolf got up, tied a sarong around his waist and went out into the corridor in search of the room boy.

'I ordered coffee for us,' he said when he came back and got into bed again, 'but it's sure to take a while so in the meantime —'

'We can go out on the balcony and watch the river boats,' she teased, knowing full well that that wasn't what he was about to suggest.

'Not yet,' he replied firmly and proceeded with his original plan.

When they lay quietly back against the pillows again, Bethany said, 'You do understand why we can't go on like this, don't you? Why I have to leave?'

'I'm damned if I do. Everything could be so great if you'd just put that ghastly business in Sanggau behind you and carry on as before.'

'But don't you see —' she began and then realised that he didn't see and probably never would.

The room boy arrived just then with the coffee and Wolf told him to take it out on the balcony.

'Good idea,' Bethany said, glad to enjoy the early morning sunshine, the fresh breeze and the passing parade of river traffic.

Wolf watched too but he didn't say much until he had drained his cup. He was surprised how gutted he felt about going back to Kanyalang without her. 'Are you sure you won't change your mind about leaving?' he asked.

'Positive.'

'Okay, then,' he said curtly in an effort to keep her from suspecting how he felt, 'we'd better get a move on. The airline office opens at nine o'clock and we should be there early if you want to get on one of today's flights.'

She was a bit taken aback and not entirely pleased at the brusqueness in his tone. 'What's the matter? Are you pissed off about something?' she asked.

'Well, you can't expect me to be glad that you're running out on the project, and running out on me, too.'

'Oh, don't think of it that way,' she pleaded. 'I'll never forget our time together, with you coming to get me and all that. It's been wonderful. It's just that I can't stay now, I really can't.'

Fuck, he thought. It's supposed to be the man who gets up in the morning and says, 'It's been great but I've gotta go.' How had she managed to turn the tables on him?

'You see', she continued, 'if I did stay, feeling the way I do about my work, it would only be because of you. And that wouldn't be any good, would it?'

316

'It might be alright,' he said.

She laughed but added, firmly, 'Not for me, it wouldn't. I won't orient my life around any man, ever.'

'That makes us even then,' he declared, 'because I feel the same, only reversed, of course.'

'At least we agree on something. That's not a bad note to say goodbye on, is it?'

'I guess not,' he agreed, forcing a jaunty demeanour to show that he was fully on board with their going their separate ways.

They set out for the airline office a few minutes later, only to be told when they arrived that all the flights that day were fully booked.

'But you must have something,' Bethany insisted, 'just one seat.'

The ticket agent, who had assumed they were travelling together, scanned the computer screen again. 'I do have one seat on the two o'clock flight to Surabaya and you can get the shuttle to Jakarta from there.'

'Brilliant, I'll take it,' Bethany said.

'When you get to Jakarta, you better go over to the RRF office,' Wolf advised, as they left the building. 'They should be able to get your ticket back to the UK for you and, hopefully, pay for it.'

'Good idea,' she said, but her manner was suddenly cool. Wolf was actually being a little too helpful, she thought, and it gave her a niggling feeling that he wasn't quite as sorry as she would like to see her leave.

He continued to be annoyingly useful when they were out on the street, flagging down a taxi and giving the driver the name of their hotel.

'We've got to get you back to the room so you can pack up,' he explained. Then, as the vehicle lurched erratically through the traffic, forcing an arthritic old man to leap out of the way like an acrobat to save his life, Wolf went on, 'You know, everybody's going to hit the ceiling when I break the news to them.'

'The news?' she repeated, enquiringly.

'That you're not coming back, you idiot.'

A thrill of pride and pleasure rippled through her at the idea that she would be seriously missed. Elliot had made his opinion of her work all too clear and she was very much afraid that some of the others, Wolf included, shared his view. It was heaven to think she might have been wrong.

'With Catherine sick, Tarique dead, and you hot footing it back to the Land of Beans on Toast,' Wolf continued, 'we won't be much above half-mast in terms of our expat staff. Of course Elliot and I can more or less pick up the pieces for Tarique. I never realised how little he really did until he wasn't around anymore. But that still leaves Catherine's spot vacant and I can't think she's going to be back on the job any time soon. Now with you going too, we'll really be up shit creek. No one can step in and do your work, or Catherine's either, without years of training, topped off by a few brain cells to go with it. So until you're actually on that plane, I'm going to keep hounding you to change your mind.'

Bethany, feeling she'd rather die than let him know how pleased she was to hear this, quickly turned away before he could see her face. And just to make sure that he didn't suspect, she declared, firmly and truthfully, 'You'll be wasting your breath.'

In any case, she couldn't quite convince herself that her departure would cause a problem for long. The RRF would send out another anthropologist to replace her. Wolf would find another girlfriend. And when it came down to it, the only person who might seriously miss her was Catherine, especially now that she was ill.

'Just how bad is she?' Bethany asked, changing the subject. 'Catherine, I mean.'

He shrugged. 'Like I said, she's in the hospital in Putussibau. That's all I know. Marguarita's the only one who seems to have much of an idea what's wrong with her.'

'You didn't tell me she was in hospital,' Bethany exclaimed.

'Yes, I did, when we were driving down from Sanggau, remember?'

With a pang of guilt, Bethany did remember. 'How awful of me,' she cried, feeling really terrible. 'I must have been so wrapped up in my own problems that I just didn't pay attention to anyone else's.'

'It's not too late to start. I happen to know she's very worried about you, being caught up in all this Dayak-Madurese trouble and all that. Seeing you might go a long way toward reviving her spirits.' Then fearing that it would be counter-productive to push too hard, he added, 'But, of course, you've already done your bit for Catherine.'

'I have, how?'

'You saw her through that abortion, didn't you? You really don't owe her anything more,' he declared, giving negative persuasion a try since he hadn't got anywhere with a positive approach. 'Remember, she's got Marguarita with her for now and hopefully Bima will turn up before Marguarita's limited supply of saintliness runs out. That should be enough. Catherine doesn't need a whole troupe of hand-holders.'

'I'm not sure I'd like to be ill out here with only Marguarita to rely on.'

'She's got Bima,' he reminded her, 'and of course the rest of us, too. We all love Catherine.'

Bethany looked at him sharply. Who exactly was 'we' and what kind of love was he talking about? But they had reached the hotel before she had a chance to pursue the subject and when they got to their room she changed her mind about asking.

Instead she set about gathering up her scattered bits and pieces.

'You're going to freeze your arse off in London,' he observed, as she tucked her thin tropical clothes into her rucksack. 'It's January, you know.'

'I don't have anything else.'

'You better call someone in England and get them to meet you at Heathrow with a coat,' he suggested, being annoyingly helpful again. 'You can do that when you get to Jakarta, you know.'

'Not a bad idea,' she agreed, but without any noticeable appreciation in her voice.

'Well, that's it then, isn't it?' he said, as she fastened the rucksack. 'Anything else you need to do before your plane takes off?'

'Nothing special,' she replied, trying to push an unwelcome thought from her mind.

'Something's the matter,' he asked, picking up on her darkened expression. 'I can see it.'

'Does whatever's wrong with Catherine have anything to do with the abortion?' she demanded.

Confronted with a direct question, Wolf decided not to keep anything back. It obviously wasn't going to make any difference now.

'Marguarita thinks it might have,' he said.

'How – did she pick up some kind of infection then?'

'No, Marguarita thinks the medicine they gave her at Nanga Palin might have brought it on.'

'Does she know what it was? It was practically impossible to get anything out of Kati, so we were never sure.'

'Her guess is that it was something called trigli… oh, hell, I can't remember exactly. But according to her, it can attack the red blood cells and possibly, if you get too much, induce some funny kind of anaemia.'

'Is it serious?'

'According to her it can be, if it's not treated.'

Bethany looked stricken. 'Did the doctor in Putussibau agree with her?'

'I think so but I didn't get a chance to talk to him. Of course, Catherine's so pale that it doesn't take four years of medical school to suspect that she's a little short on red blood cells.'

Again Bethany's conscience gave an uncomfortable lurch. She was supposed to be Catherine's good friend. Why hadn't she noticed something was wrong?

Wolf, seeing guilt, anxiety and indecision flicker across her face, decided to press his advantage. 'Don't worry, though,' he said, almost cheerfully, 'the hospital in Putussibau isn't too bad. At least, it's okay as long as someone's around to make sure the nurses use disposable needles whenever they give her an injection.'

Bethany was deeply shocked. 'But is there someone around who'll keep doing that?'

'Like I said, there's Marguarita at the moment.'

'But how long is she prepared to stay?'

He shook his head, gravely. 'A couple of days, I think, or until Bima shows up. So try not to worry.'

'That's easy enough to say,' Bethany replied, as she absent-mindedly took a hairbrush and a tee-shirt out of her rucksack and then put them back in again.

'What are you doing?' he demanded.

'Thinking of changing my flight.'

'It's a bit late for that, isn't it?' he replied, hiding his glee behind a reproachful tone.

'Not really, I can always book another one when I have a better idea of how Catherine is. But if she's ill because of the abortion, well, then I'm largely responsible. I can't just go away and leave her in a mess that I got her into, can I? I'm not that much of a worm.'

'You've never looked very worm-like to me,' agreed Wolf, reaching over and drawing her towards him. Then glancing down at his watch he added, 'Maybe we'd better get busy and cancel your reservation on the Surabaya flight. Then we can hot foot it over to the Das Airways office and see about getting back to Putussibau.'

Bethany nodded, picked up her handbag and would have started for the door if Wolf hadn't suddenly gripped her by the back of the neck and held her.

'On the other hand,' he said, 'fuck Das Airways. It will still be open an hour from now.'

'Alright,' she said, laughingly pulling him down on the bed, 'fuck me, instead.'

That's exactly what he did.

CHAPTER THIRTY-THREE

Wolf and Bethany were not the only ones who were trying to get to Putussibau just then. The heavy January rains had brought Jim's burgeoning guiding business to a temporary halt and revived his determination to see Marguarita again, this time not only for the hoped for shag but also to let her know that the precious maps coming out of her project were ending up in the hands of at least one logging company and possibly more.

The problem, he soon realised, was that getting from Balikpapan to Kanyalang wasn't easy in any weather but particularly not in January. If they hadn't been in the full throes of the rainy season, he would have enjoyed trekking across the Muller path and, from there, making his way alternately by boat and by foot over to the Kapuas river basin and up to Kanyalang. But a trip like that was out of the question at this time of year so he decided to check with the local office of the Missionary Air Fellowship and see what they were up to. Their single-engine Cessna planes went around from time to time dropping off supplies of bibles and bibelots and he had heard that they were occasionally willing, for a suitable monetary contribution to their efforts, to take on an extra passenger, even a reprehensible one such as himself.

He was in luck. In a couple of days one of their planes would be leaving for a missionary outpost not far from Putussibau so they could make an extra stop and drop him off at the airport there. Then he'd be able to hitch a ride on the helicopter that took mail and supplies to Kanyalang a couple of times a month and, if the fates were still on his side, he wouldn't have to wait too many days for it.

He waited a week.

Jim barely managed to conceal his disappointment when he arrived at Kanyalang and found that Marguarita had taken an ill colleague to the hospital in Putussibau but, on hearing that she would probably be back soon, he decided to settle in and wait.

No one appeared very pleased to see him but they were all sufficiently tired of each other's company that they weren't prepared to turn away a diversion. Jim's connection with Calco wasn't viewed with enthusiasm but at least his job as an environmentally-friendly tour guide was relatively harmless and they certainly couldn't fault him for bringing small groups of tourists, properly leashed, de-clawed, and supervised, into the jungle. Wasn't that what their own project was about?

It didn't take long for Jim to decide that with Wolf away somewhere, Kanyalang was an unexpectedly pleasant place to spend a little time. Mike, on closer acquaintance, proved to be a regular guy which didn't surprise him, really. He generally hit it off with Australians. There was a no-nonsense quality about them that he appreciated and he spent a couple of enjoyable days going along on forest patrols with him.

It was after the second of these that the two men came back to the longhouse to find to their surprise that Marguarita was relaxing on the veranda reading one of Elliot's outdated copies of the Times.

'Hey, how's Catherine?' Mike demanded, immediately.

'Sleepy but the doctor said I could bring her back, although she's still on rather heavy medication.' After going into some detail about the red blood cells — or shortage of them — but skipping over any mention of the possible cause, she concluded by saying, 'Anyway I think she's on her way to recovery.'

'Great,' said Mike, 'I'll just pop in and say hello, if that's okay.'

Marguarita nodded approval. 'Don't knock though. Just have a look and make sure she's not asleep before you charge in.'

'Right.'

It was only after Mike had hurried toward Catherine's room that Marguarita gave any sign she had noticed Jim's arrival at all.

'You again,' she observed, indifferently, 'that's a bit of a surprise.'

'It shouldn't be. I told you I'd be back.'

'You didn't expect me to believe that, did you?' she said, laughing.

'I always expect to be believed.'

'You must suffer a lot of disappointments.'

He was taken aback at her coldness. He hadn't remembered her as such an ice-goddess, quite the opposite, in fact.

'Well, I kinda wandered back, like I said I would,' he muttered, awkwardly.

'So I see. How's the gold mine?'

'Dead in the water.'

'That's good.'

He gave a non-committal shrug. 'Anyway, I'm out of that racket now.'

To his chagrin, she didn't appear particularly interested. An awkward silence that he found hellishly uncomfortable fell between them, but Marguarita seemed quite unperturbed by it.

Then in a moment of inspiration, Jim ventured, 'In fact, I've been getting into something kinda along the lines of what you guys are doing.'

'Oh?'

'Yeah, eco-tourism – I'm taking groups of people up river from Balikpapan so they can get a feel for the rainforest.'

'St Augustine of the Jungle,' she observed, scornfully.

'I don't get it,' he said, thoroughly confused.

'I'm raising you to the status of our revered saint, you must know the one who led a swinging and thoroughly wicked life until he was too old to enjoy that sort of thing anymore. Then he reformed and set about reforming everybody else.'

Jim was baffled. 'Hey, I'm only twenty eight.'

His confusion drew a mocking laugh from Marguarita. Then deciding it would be fun to tease him, she added, 'I notice you're not denying the wicked part.'

He squirmed, feeling that somehow he was being censured and ridiculed at the same time and not enjoying either one. 'Well, I guess it all depends on how you look at it,' he replied, lamely.

'Doesn't everything?'

'Yeah, sure but I still don't get this St Augustine thing.'

'Well, you were in the gold mining business, weren't you? Killing off everything in sight with that poisonous sludge you mining people like to spread around.'

'Hey, wait a minute –' he protested.

'But then when the company you worked for collapsed and you were out of a job, you decided to take the high road – very noble.'

Now he was angry. 'Look, I don't have to stay here and listen to this.'

'Quite right, you don't.'

'I'm getting out of here first thing in the morning.'

'Have a good trip,' Marguarita smiled and returned to the Times.

Jim stalked off in the direction of the kitchen hoping to find a drink that was cold and alcoholic enough to assuage his fury and humiliation.

He settled for a beer, took it into Tarique's old room, which had now been converted to guest quarters, and sat down on the edge of the bed.

Christ, he thought, I never realised she was such a bitch.

As the amber liquid in the bottle diminished, his anger at Marguarita mounted until, in a sudden reversal of direction, his rage turned inward and he began cursing himself for being a fool.

After all, he admitted to himself, she was right. He would never have gone green if Fairbanks hadn't folded. And if he could've gotten work as a geologist for some other gold mining bunch he'd have jumped at it. He'd probably do that now if he had the chance – or would he? He wasn't quite sure.

The trouble with hanging around these Kanyalang types was that they made him think of stuff that had never bothered him before. Maybe he should stop letting them mess around with his head so much. They were turning his world upside down.

And the hell of it was that Marguarita was still as attractive as he remembered. He guessed he just hadn't ever thought about what kind of person she was. Then it occurred to him that he hadn't really cared if she was the all-time bitch from hell. He wasn't looking for a wife, for God's sake, just for a really great lay. And that was still what he wanted, in spite of everything, including all that stupid St Augustine crap.

After finishing off the remaining contents of the bottle, he felt an urgent need to pee and set off in the direction of the loo at the far end of the veranda. When he came out he found Elliot, Mike, Bima, and Pashetta, all talking more-or-less at once, hurling questions at Marguarita about somebody named Catherine. Although he couldn't work up much interest in this chick, he had had quite enough of sitting alone in his room with only an empty beer bottle for company. It would be better to hang around with the others and hope they'd get onto a more interesting subject.

They didn't but it wasn't long until Marguarita surprised him once again.

Listening to her, it occurred to him that sitting around that hospital for days couldn't have been any picnic so maybe she wasn't quite the bitch he had taken her for, not if she was willing to put up with all that for her friend.

Then why had she been so horrible to him, he wondered? He didn't think it could be because he had put the make on her. After all, an attractive woman like that must be on the receiving end of that kind of thing all the time. And she hadn't exactly given him the push that night either, at least, not until the very last minute.

Maybe he had gotten it all wrong the first time, he decided, maybe she just didn't go in for one-night stands. She had known he would be leaving the next day and she obviously hadn't believed him when he'd said he'd be back.

Maybe after the way he had come on to her that night and then hadn't made any effort to contact her for months, she had every right to be mad at him. That would explain why she'd gone into that sting-like-an-adder mode just now. If so, he couldn't really blame her. He'd just have to hope she'd calm down and give him another chance.

Without intending to, she did.

It happened later that evening and it wasn't entirely fortuitous. Jim had seen her stop by Catherine's room after the beer-drinking group had broken up for the night and he had lingered near-by, hoping for just such an opportunity.

The plan worked.

'How's the patient?' he asked, hoping he sounded like he really cared.

'Alright, I think she'll sleep through the night.'

'You sure are a good friend.'

Unfortunately for Jim, this was exactly the sort of maudlin sentimentality that Marguarita couldn't bear. 'The project needs a zoologist, doesn't it?' she snapped. And when he looked at her blankly, she added, 'Catherine's our zoologist, although she's having to be more of an entomologist here.'

'They do bugs and things, don't they?' Jim said.

Marguarita nodded. 'I'm afraid we're a little short on the cuddlier forms of life around here, both human and non-human.'

'I dunno about that,' he returned with a grin. Then, reverting to the subject of their earlier conversation, he asked, 'Did you really think I wasn't coming back?'

'To tell you the truth, I didn't think about it at all.'

'You really do know how to hurt a guy.'

'Sorry,' she said, indifferently.

After a moment's hesitation, he confessed, 'I thought about it a lot.'

She gazed at him in astonishment. 'Why? This kind of project surely isn't your sort of thing.'

'It wasn't the project I was thinking about, at least, not entirely. It was you.'

She laughed, thinking that it really was rather sweet of him to have taken her so seriously and that maybe he had a few redeeming features, after all.

A tempting thought darted into her mind. An attractive, albeit slightly wooden-headed, geologist didn't turn up on the veranda every night. And, after playing nurse to Catherine, an occupation for which, she realised, she was not temperamentally suited, she could use a good shag.

It would have been unthinkable if he had still been in that gold mining company but now – why ever not?

'Well, you did come back, that's the important thing,' she said, with a smile that sent a wave of optimism surging through him.

'Right,' he agreed, cheerfully. 'What do you say we celebrate with a drink? I brought some whisky with me from Balikpapan.'

'Strategic planning must be your forté.'

He looked at her suspiciously. Was she poking fun at him again? He hoped not but he wasn't quite sure so he hid his discomfort by saying, 'Hold on a minute. I'll get it.'

Ordinarily, Marguarita wasn't fond of whisky but tonight she felt she could use something really strong. Not only had sitting around the hospital been something of an ordeal, but Catherine's fading-away heroine routine was getting on her nerves. A few shots of whisky, followed by sex with a good-looking stranger, might be just the tonic she needed.

The question that bothered her though was – what he was doing here? She didn't believe for a minute that he had come back because of her. Perhaps, after a few drinks, she would be able to find out what he was really after.

It took only the smallest expression of interest on her part for him to launch into an account of his recent doings, waxing particularly loquacious when it came to explaining his change in attitude toward the rain forest.

Marguarita listened to it all with ill-concealed scepticism.

'So you see,' he went on, oblivious of her reaction, 'as soon as I heard about the maps those Korean loggers had – well, right away I had a hunch they might be from here.'

Marguarita was instantly alert. 'What maps?'

'You know, the ones Elliot does from satellite photographs. That guy, Tarique, the one who died, sold some of them to Fairbanks Mining and Exploration. That's how I first knew about them. And now the Koreans have gotten hold of them, except they've got an updated version.'

'How do you know?'

'I heard about them from a guy in Balikpapan so I figured you people here would want to know about them.'

'And there were others?' An unsettling array of possibilities swirled around in her mind.

'Yeah, I'm kinda ashamed to admit it but those maps were the real reason Don and I came to see Tarique that time, you know, before we knew he was dead. We wanted to do a deal for an up-date then but do it directly with this guy, Tarique, and cut Chen out.'

'Chen?' Marguarita was momentarily baffled.

'Yeah, that agent you people have in Putussibau.'

'What does he have to do with all this?' she demanded.

'He was the one who fixed up the first deal. He bought the maps from Tarique and then sold them to us. But we didn't see any reason to shoot any of the spoils his way the second time around.

At least that was Don's way of thinking. Don, as you may have guessed, was quite an operator and not exactly the Sunday school type. So when he had done a little snooping and found that the contact man here was Tarique, he even managed to sell him some stock in the company. Chen, of course, was too smart to bite.'

'So that was why you were here. I always wondered,' she mused, turning this new information over in her mind. 'I knew Tarique was up to something, several of us did, but we never succeeded in finding out exactly what it was. God, selling Elliot's maps, Kanyalang's maps, to a gold mining company, and to you!'

'He didn't exactly sell them to me,' Jim interrupted. 'It was to Fairbanks.'

'But you worked for them, didn't you?' she said, angrily.

'I know,' he agreed, ruefully. 'I regret it now.'

'Do you? I doubt it.'

'Jesus, don't you ever believe anything?' he exclaimed.

'It's generally safer not to.'

'Well, you've got to believe me tonight.'

'I don't see why.'

'Because the other reason I've come back, besides seeing you I mean, is to clue you in on the fact that the theft's still going on.'

'That's impossible. Tarique's dead.'

'I know.'

'Dead men don't steal maps.'

'Yeah, but live ones do, some of them, anyway.'

Seizing on the implication of his words, she demanded, 'Are you saying someone here at Kanyalang now is stealing and selling them?'

He hesitated, feeling suddenly awkward. 'Yes and no.'

'What does that mean?'

'It means that someone, somewhere, is stealing and selling them and this is the most likely place to start looking.'

'Don't you think the same maps Tarique sold are just being passed around and resold?'

'No, because the ones these Korean guys have got show areas that have only been burned off in the last few months.'

'Are you certain about that?'

'I've got a photocopy of one of them.'

'With you here, now?'

'You got it.'

'Show me.'

'It's in my room. You'd better come with me. It's too dark out here to see it very well.'

'But a logging company would surely do its own mapping, wouldn't it?' she protested, as they went along the veranda and turned into his room.

'Yeah, as long as it was a big, well-heeled outfit,' he agreed, beginning to rummage through his rucksack. 'But there're a lot of two-bit operators out there who'd jump at the chance to piggyback onto what someone else had already done. Just think of the money they'd save,' he pointed out, as his fingers closed around the map. Then smoothing it out and handing it to her, he added, 'For a small company that's short of working capital, it could be a God-send.'

Marguarita scarcely heard what he was saying. Her attention was riveted on the line drawing of the hornbill in the lower right hand corner.

'Can I keep this?' she asked, after studying it for several minutes.

'Why do you want to do that?' he demanded, an unthinkable suspicion springing into his mind.

'There's someone I want to show it to before the others see it.'

'Elliot?'

'No, not Elliot, someone else.'

He wondered whether his horrible suspicion was out of the question after all. Could Marguarita be the culprit? The idea was preposterous and yet –'

'I think I'd kinda like to keep hold of it myself,' he told her, hoping she wouldn't be able to read his thoughts.

This hope was quickly dashed.

'What's the problem? Don't you trust me?' she demanded, a flicker of amusement playing about her lips.

'Now don't get mad –' he began.

But she merely laughed, bade him a brusque good night and left him alone with the map.

The odd thing was that he didn't really mind about the shag that wasn't going to happen. Sometime during the last few minutes his desire to screw Marguarita had taken second place to a new and highly inconvenient determination to protect the rainforest, even if it meant saving it from her.

CHAPTER THIRTY-FOUR

The thing that Marguarita minded just then was that Wolf still wasn't back from his absurd little jaunt to get Bethany away from Sanggau. She wanted to discuss this map business and all it entailed with him. He was the only person around, except Pashetta, who hadn't endowed Catherine with a sort of angelic aura and who therefore might be able to view her actions with some degree of objectivity.

What was he doing anyway, she wondered? It had been five days since she had seen him at the hospital in Putussibau. Could he actually have run into some kind of real problem? She didn't think so. He was probably just being his usual annoying self and causing trouble somewhere.

That wasn't exactly the case. Despite the fact that the interior of Borneo was not a favoured destination at the moment, he and Bethany were having unexpected difficulties getting on a flight. There were only four a week from Pontianak to Putussibau, one of which had failed to take off because of poor visibility while a second had been cancelled due to that mysterious phenomenon known to the travelling public as 'technical difficulties'. By the time the weather cleared and the necessary repairs had been carried out the backlog of passengers was considerably greater than the nine-seat plane could accommodate. Wolf and Bethany were forced to wait so long for a flight that when they finally arrived in Putussibau they were informed by the hospital staff that Catherine had been discharged the previous day.

They had no inclination to linger in the drab little market town so they found the helicopter company and arranged for a chopper to take them back to Kanyalang. As soon as it settled down on the landing pad and the rotor blades had come to a halt, Bethany leapt out. Kartini had been beyond her help but there might be something she could do for Catherine, something that would go a little way toward making up for the harm the abortion had done her.

'What's the big rush?' Wolf called after her.

'Catherine, of course, I want to see how she is,' Bethany called back as she hurried on ahead of him up the path.

Deciding that Catherine shouldn't have to cope with an entire herd of visitors at once, Wolf didn't try to follow her. Instead, he stopped by the office to see what was going on there.

He had just reached the veranda steps when Marguarita emerged from the lab with a stack of plant presses in her hand.

When she saw him she didn't waste time on preliminaries. 'I've got something to tell you,' she said, not considering his trip worth enquiring about. Wolf noticed this but, recalling how much of the last few days he had spent in bed with Bethany, he decided her lack of interest was a good thing.

'We can talk in my office,' she said, pushing the door open with her foot and, once they were inside, kicking it closed behind them.

'I gather that's not just to keep the air conditioning in,' he observed.

'No, it's not,' she agreed, putting the presses down on her desk and turning to him.

'Okay, I'm listening,' he said. 'What's up?'

'Well, surprise number one is that we have a visitor.'

'Anyone I know?'

'Yes, as a matter of fact, Jim Nathan.'

Wolf looked blank.

'You surely remember him. You took such a virulent dislike to him when he was here before.'

'Christ, I hope you don't mean one of those arseholes from the gold mining company.'

'I'm afraid I do.'

'Shit.'

'He may not be as bad as you think.'

'The hell, he isn't.'

'Actually it's been rather interesting talking to him.'

'I hope talking is all you did.'

'Does it matter?' she said, laughing.

'Damn right, it does.' Then noticing the quizzical expression mingled with the look of amusement in her eyes, he hastened to make himself clear. 'It makes me sick to think of a guy like that, someone who's been lining his pockets at the expense of the jungle, getting first class treatment around here.'

'Alright, I see where you're going,' she replied, not laughing anymore, 'but you can climb down off your hobbyhorse. Jim didn't get what you think, not from me, anyway. But don't you want to hear what else I have to tell you?'

'Okay, shoot. It can't be any worse than the news that the guy is here.'

'Actually, it can.'

Wolf groaned. 'Spill it anyway.'

She did.

Marguarita told him everything she had learned from Jim and concluded, saying, 'So you see, they're undoubtedly our maps. The question is, how did they get into the hands of that logging company?'

'Well, that's pretty obvious, isn't it?' Wolf asked, amazed that Marguarita was being so obtuse. 'But at least the bastard's dead now so it can't happen again.'

'Apparently, I didn't make myself clear. The map shows recently deforested areas,' she replied, taking great care to emphasise the word 'recently'.

'You can't mean since Tarique died?'

'That's exactly what I mean.'

Wolf gaped at her. 'Then who –'

'I'm afraid the finger points to our lovable little friend and colleague …' She paused, waiting for him to twig but he merely looked at her blankly.

'Catherine, of course,' she said, impatiently.

'Bullshit.'

'Don't be too sure of that. I think we might find she was Tarique's little helper all along and that after he died she carried on as best she could alone, pocketing the profits for herself, of course.'

'You must be out of your fucking mind,' he said, aghast.

'I don't think so,' she returned, calmly.

'Well, I do. You've had it in for Catherine for a long time and you know it. But this time you've gone too far.'

'Would the fact that she and Tarique had a joint bank account in Singapore convince you that I actually haven't gone too far?'

'It might, if I believed it.'

'But you don't?'

'Of course, I don't.'

'You will,' she said with conviction, 'when I show you the cheque book for it, along with Tarique's chequebooks for his own accounts, one in France and one in the Channel Islands.'

'You can't mean —'

'Yes, I can and stock certificates, too,' she continued, with a note of triumph in her voice, 'and a CD-ROM with recent financial records on it.'

Wolf gasped.

'And do you know where I found them?'

'I'm not psychic, for God's sake,' he barked. 'Anyway, Elliot and I looked all over the place, absolutely everywhere, for Tarique's financial stuff and it didn't turn up.'

'Did you look in our dear Catherine's underwear drawer?'

'Of course not.'

'That's where I came across them, underneath a pile of knickers.'

'You've gotta be kidding.'

'I'm totally serious.'

'What the fuck were they doing there?'

'You better ask Catherine.'

'Don't worry, I will. But what in the world were you doing pawing through her panties, tell me that?'

'Getting some things together for her to take to hospital.'

'How come you didn't tell me about all this when I saw you in Putussibau?'

'Because at that point I hadn't really looked at them. I just assumed Catherine had slightly weird ideas about where to keep her bank books but it wasn't any of my business. It was only after I heard Jim's story about the maps that I decided to take a closer look so this morning while she was having a bath I went in and, well, you could say 'borrowed' them.'

'Filched them, you mean.'

'I suppose you could put it that way. Anyway that was when I seriously began putting two and two together.'

'Are you sure you're doing your sums right,' he demanded, 'not making two and two add up to something like five or seven?'

'Quite sure,' she said, firmly. 'If you think about it, it's all too clear that Catherine had something to hide.'

'Not to me, it isn't. At least, it wasn't —'

'As a starter, think about this. It takes brains to get a doctorate in zoology, doesn't it?'

'Some minimal amount, maybe.'

'But Catherine acts like a ditzy blonde.'

'Well, she's free of your intellectual pretensions, if that's what you mean.'

'Not exactly, but never mind. There's something else, too. Can anyone really be as sweet as Catherine seems to be?'

'Certainly not you.'

'Undoubtedly not me,' Marguarita returned, smiling, 'but don't you think there's something there that doesn't add up?'

'Not necessarily, it depends on what you found out from your little discovery.'

'Well, for one thing the French account looked pretty normal.'

'Normal?'

'Yes, it had deposits for his salary and withdrawals for his family's living expenses, for his own expenses, too, you know, the sort of thing you'd expect, but the other one was rather different. It was the US dollar account in the Channel Islands and the activity in that one is harder to explain unless you bring something else, probably Catherine's contributions, into the picture.'

'You've lost me there.'

'During the year before Tarique died,' she explained, 'there were deposits into the joint account in Singapore, also a US dollar account, every month, all for the same amount. It would have been something close to three quarters of my salary, so probably roughly the same percentage of Catherine's. Then with about a week's time lag that amount was invariably transferred into his solo account in the Channel Islands. And there was a much larger deposit into it about six months before he died.'

'That must have left him pretty flush.'

'It didn't actually because every couple of months he brought the balance down close to zero by writing checks to your favourite gold mining company, Fairbanks Mining and Exploration.'

'Jesus Christ,' he gasped. 'Why the —'

'And there were stock certificates in Tarique's name for shares in Fairbanks.'

This revelation drew a guffaw from Wolf. 'They must be worth exactly nothing,' he jeered. 'The company's gone belly-up.'

'That's hardly the point, is it?'

'No, I guess it isn't,' he said, grimly, as the full import of her revelation crashed in on him. 'Christ, to think the bastard was doing that right under our noses! And all the time we were working out butts off to save this fucking jungle.'

Marguarita nodded in bleak agreement.

'But Tarique was always grousing about being broke,' Wolf exclaimed, 'complaining that it cost a fucking fortune to keep his family in France. Said his kids ran through money like water and his wife was worse. Of course he just brought out that story to try to soften people up before touching them for a loan. But it didn't work with me.'

'Nor with me,' Marguarita said emphatically. 'I didn't listen to that rubbish either. And I can't believe he got anything out of Elliot – Bima, perhaps, although I doubt it – but how about Catherine?'

'Oh, God,' groaned Wolf, 'I bet you anything that's where her money went.'

Marguarita nodded. 'I think she would have given it to him, lent it to him, whatever. And that would certainly explain her choice of a place to have an abortion.'

'Christ, I'd like to find the snake that killed that mother-fucking shit and pin a medal on him,' Wolf said.

Marguarita smiled to herself but didn't indulge in any speculation about whether or not she deserved to share the medal with snake.

'At least, all this pretty much lets Catherine off the hook,' Wolf continued, 'except for the charge of being idiotic enough to lend the arsehole all her money.'

'Does it?' exclaimed Marguarita, indignantly. 'You must be joking. When you look at the joint account in Singapore it does no such thing. Why do you think she latched onto all the evidence of Tarique's financial dealings the way she did if she hadn't played a part in them? And how do you explain the fact that she didn't say a word about them when she knew, we all knew, that you and Elliot were turning the place upside down looking for exactly that sort of thing?'

He grimaced but didn't reply.

'There's only one explanation, isn't there?'

Again he was silent.

'She was in on the map theft with him and she didn't want that awkward little fact to come to light.'

Wolf was about to condemn this theory as utter crap when a sudden recollection sealed his lips. Catherine had completely flipped out when she had come across him going through Tarique's desk the day after the funeral.

Shit, he muttered to himself as he began to wonder if perhaps Marguarita could be right after all.

Sensing victory, she pressed on. 'And how do you suppose Tarique got his hands on those maps?' she demanded.

'How the hell should I know? Went into the Big Chief's office and took them out of the map cabinet, I guess.'

'Elliot always keeps his office locked when he's not around,' Marguarita pointed out, 'and I don't think he would have given the key to Tarique. There were too many suspicions floating around about him even then, remember?'

'Yeah, but the old man was never really convinced there was anything to them. At least, he made a major effort not to see what he didn't want to see.'

Marguarita nodded. 'Quite, but I'm sure he would have given Catherine the key in a flash if she had fabricated some plausible reason to ask for it. You know how besotted he is with her. Or she might have just allowed herself to be invited into his lair for a few drinks and, after a bit of a snog, persuaded him to give her anything she wanted.'

Wolf viewed this theory with scepticism. 'I think your lurid fantasies are running away with you,' he warned. 'You're overestimating Catherine's sex appeal and underestimating Elliot's good sense.'

'Possibly, but doesn't the bottom of an underwear drawer strike you as an odd place to keep chequebooks and financial records, particularly someone else's?'

He gave a reluctant nod of assent. He hated it when Marguarita was right.

'And explain to me, if you can,' she persisted, 'why she didn't mention the existence of that stuff unless she was afraid it would somehow incriminate her?'

'There're two possibilities,' he argued.

'I can't imagine what they are.'

'Well, she might have had some personal stuff of her own mixed in with –'

'She didn't.'

'She might have at the time she first put them there.'

'Sorry, I'm not impressed with that possibility. What's the other one?'

'She might have been protecting him, or thought she was. She was always trying to do that.'

Marguarita raised an eyebrow. 'It was a bit late for that, wasn't it? He was already dead, for God's sake. It's far more likely that she was protecting herself. And even if she wasn't directly involved, even if she wasn't the one who actually pinched the maps, she must have known what was going on or she wouldn't have seen any need to shield him.'

'You've got me there,' Wolf admitted. 'Have you tried asking her about any of this?'

'No, I thought I'd wait until she was a little better.'

'That's surprisingly generous of you.'

'Not really. I just want to be sure she won't be able to use any of her near-death rituals to avoid answering questions.'

'I don't think she'd do that.'

'Wouldn't she?' Marguarita laughed. 'Just watch her.'

'Okay, I will. I'll talk to her right now and see what I can find out.'

CHAPTER THIRTY-FIVE

Instead of going directly to Catherine's room, Wolf stopped by Elliot's office for a brief chat first. Then having obtained the information he wanted, he continued on his way.

When he reached Catherine's door Wolf knocked on it sharply, waited a moment, knocked again and then pushed it open.

He had forgotten how pale she had looked in the hospital bed and now her appearance startled him into a gentler manner than he had intended to use.

'How're you feeling?' he asked.

'Not too bad.'

'Glad to be out of that hospital?'

'Very.'

'Look, I've got something serious to talk to you about,' he said, sitting down at the foot of her bed. 'Are you up to it?'

'Perhaps, I'm not sure,' she replied, weakly.

'Marguarita tells me she found some of Tarique's paraphernalia, chequebooks, stock certificates, a floppy disk, that sort of thing, squirreled away in one of your drawers.'

He thought he detected a fleeting look of apprehension cross her face before it was replaced by a flush of anger.

'What was Marguarita doing going through my things?'

'Getting clothes for you to take to the hospital.'

Catherine digested this explanation in silence.

'How come you never let on that you had all that crap when you knew Elliot and I were busting our arses going through Tarique's papers and computer files, trying to get some idea of what he'd been up to?'

'I don't know,' she whimpered, 'I suppose I just forgot about it.'

'That's quite a trick when the people around you are talking about it non-stop,' he pointed out.

'I suppose it was incredibly dozy of me,' she admitted, 'but I was distraught. It was such a terrible time, with Tarique suddenly dead like that, and being pregnant and having no money and —'

'Yes, yes,' he interrupted, impatiently. And then to her

astonishment, he demanded, 'Don't you ever wear any underwear?'

'What kind of question is that?'

'Marguarita says she found a whole lot of financial stuff tucked away underneath your knickers. How come you didn't notice it when you were getting out a fresh pair? I'd have thought the sight of it would've jogged your memory a little.'

'Marguarita should stay out of my dresser drawers,' Catherine exclaimed, angrily.

Ignoring her indignation, Wolf pressed on. 'You didn't want any of us to see that little treasure trove of information, did you? You wanted to keep it to yourself.'

'I don't know what you're talking about.'

'I think you do. Marguarita's right, you're a terrible liar.'

Catherine clamped her hands over her ears. 'Marguarita again, Marguarita thinks, Marguarita says,' she cried. 'Fuck Marguarita. Why don't you believe me for a change?'

'I'd like to but I'm finding it difficult.'

'I don't see why,' she said, her voice trailing off into a whine.

'Because you didn't level with us — you had exactly the sort of stuff we were looking for and you didn't say a word about it. That's gotta mean you had something to hide. Either you were protecting Tarique or protecting yourself. Which was it?'

Her face remained expressionless as cresting waves of exhaustion swept over her.

'And don't try to give me that bullshit about forgetting you had it,' he continued, 'because I won't believe it and I can promise you no one else will either.'

He waited, fixing her with an accusing gaze until she murmured, 'I was protecting Tarique.'

He was quick to pounce on her words.

'Then how do you explain that little conversation we had a few months ago when you promised me you wouldn't do that anymore? Were you lying then or are you lying now?'

'I don't know. I changed my mind, that's all. Leave me alone.'

'No,' he said, taking her hand and holding it with a disarming gentleness, 'I won't leave you alone, not until you've told me everything.'

'I can't talk about it now,' Catherine moaned, turning her head away. 'I'm too tired.'

'Okay then. Don't say anything. Just lie still and listen. I'll do the talking.'

Seeing no way of avoiding this, she acquiesced.

'You gave Tarique money to put in that gold mine even though you knew it was inside the conservation area,' he said.

The very mention of this injustice hit on a nerve that was still frayed and raw. 'But he cheated me,' she blurted out. 'He was supposed to be buying those stocks for both of us, in both of our names, but he didn't do it. He just took my money and bought the stocks for himself.'

'Was that what that joint account the two of you had in Singapore was for?'

'It was for our future together in Canada,' she said, tears coming to her eyes at the thought of the future that had eluded her. 'That's where we were going to go after everything was finished here. At least, that's what I thought, so when I looked in his desk and saw –'

'And saw what?'

'The stock certificates – they were only in his name. My name wasn't even on them at all. I had put practically my whole salary in it for months and months and he said he was putting his into it too, except of, course, for what he had to send back to France for his children. It was supposed to be an investment in our life together, our future.'

She broke down in sobs but Wolf ruthlessly cut her off.

'When did you look through his desk?' he demanded.

'I don't know.'

'You must know.'

'I think it was a few hours after the funeral.'

'Were you looking for anything in particular?'

'No,' she faltered, 'not really.'

'Personal stuff, I suppose,' he suggested, offering her an excuse.

She seized it, eagerly. 'Yes,' she said, 'and –'

'And financial stuff.'

'No, yes, that's when I found out he'd taken everything, all the stocks that were supposed to be in both our names. He had

343

told me the broker in Anchorage was holding them so you can imagine how I felt when I found they had been here all the time. He just hadn't wanted me to see that my name wasn't on them even though I had contributed more than half of the money to buy them. That's why I couldn't afford to go anywhere better for an abortion.'

'Look, you don't have to convince me the guy was a total shit. I've known that for ages. What I didn't know until today was that he had somehow gotten his paws on Elliot's maps and sold them to those guys from Fairbanks Mining, or maybe exchanged them for some worthless stock, whatever the deal was. Anyway one of the guys is back here again and he told Marguarita all about it.'

'You'd believe anything, no matter what kind of rubbish it was, if you heard it from Marguarita,' Catherine cried.

'I wish I could believe this was rubbish,' Wolf replied, his voice bitter with disappointment. He had come into the room hoping, even though it was a very small hope, that Catherine would say something that would completely pulverise Marguarita's theory.

'What's more,' he said, recovering himself and continuing, 'you were the one who got hold of Elliot's office keys and made photocopies of those maps for Tarique, weren't you?'

Her disclaimer was swift and emphatic. 'Don't be absurd.'

'Am I being absurd? I just had a little chat with Elliot and he recalls an evening, back when Tarique was still alive, when you asked for the keys to his office. You said you wanted to get some lab notes you had left there so you could work on them that evening.'

'Perhaps I did,' she shrugged. 'I might have. I really can't remember.'

'And it seems that that wasn't the only time you were careless about leaving your belongings strewn around his office.'

'You know how disorganised I am. I'm always leaving things about. That doesn't mean anything.'

'It doesn't prove anything, that's true, but when you put everything together, it's highly suggestive.'

'It suggests that someone's spreading a lot of venomous lies about me. That's what it suggests,' she retorted.

344

'Does it? Tell me, how much did you get out of that little deal?'

'What deal?'

'You know damn well what deal I'm talking about, the sale of those maps.'

'I didn't get a thing.'

'So there was a deal.'

'I didn't say that.'

'You didn't deny it either, at least not in any convincing way.'

'You're just twisting everything I say to make me look bad.'

'I want to know what part you played in what went on.'

'I didn't play any part.'

'Why the hell did you do Tarique's dirty work for him? Didn't you see what you were letting yourself in for?'

'There was nothing to see because I didn't do anything.'

'Are you trying to tell me that you didn't have a clever little scheme going, one that would give you the chance to enjoy the money together with Tarique if everything went smoothly but would let him swing for it alone if it all went west? I bet you did. You just didn't foresee the arrival of that snake and lover-boy's quick exit from the land of the living, that's all.'

'Marguarita's put you up to all this,' she cried. 'I know the way her mind works.'

He couldn't completely deny this and Catherine, quick to perceive her advantage, lost no time in exploiting it. 'As for having the keys to Elliot's office, I only had them a couple of times. And that was just for a few minutes. Pashetta keeps them most of the time. If anyone had access to those maps and copied them for Tarique, she was the one. I'm sure she could use the money. And I don't think she even likes the rainforest, much less cares about saving it.'

For a moment Wolf was genuinely taken aback. He had to agree with her about Pashetta's attitude. Nevertheless he quickly recovered his equanimity and pointed out, 'Yes but Pashetta hasn't tried to hide anything. You have.'

'Bollocks, you're just making a silly fuss about my being a little absent-minded.'

'Am I? I don't think so.'

'But you are,' she insisted. 'And what makes you so obsessed with that stupid disc anyway? Have you actually seen it, or do you just know what Marguarita chose to tell you about it?'

Again he had to credit her with having scored a point. 'She knows I'm going to look at it,' he replied, gravely 'so it wouldn't make much sense for her to lie about it, would it?'

'And have you actually seen those maps that supposedly came from here?'

'Not yet.'

'Well, other people can make maps, can't they?'

'Yes, but they're not apt to put the Kanyalang logo on them.'

'How do you know these maps have it?'

He hesitated, reluctant to credit Marguarita as his source.

'I know,' she cried triumphantly, 'Marguarita told you. It sounds like something she'd think of.'

He had to admit that she was right.

'It's nothing but a stream of her vicious lies,' Catherine scoffed. 'You just wait, you'll be sorry you listened to her and sorry you've been so hateful, accusing me of all these dreadful things when I didn't do any of them.'

'There's one more thing, though —' he began.

'Don't even tell me about it,' she cried. 'I've never felt so betrayed in my life. And I'm too tired and too miserable to listen to anymore.'

Tears filled her eyes and splashed down her pale cheeks and for just a moment Wolf felt like a first class bastard. Then he reminded himself that he wasn't in the running for 'Mr Nice Guy' and pressed on. 'One of the times Elliot gave you his office keys was after Tarique died, wasn't it?' he said.

'What does that matter?' she sniffed.

'It matters because there's a Korean logging company that's got a recent version of the maps. Someone's been carrying on with Tarique's little games now that he's six-feet under and can't do it for himself anymore. And I think that someone is you.' He paused and waited, watching her stricken face for a tell-tale reaction. Then he said gravely, 'Tell me, am I right?'

'No, you're not right,' she declared vehemently. 'You're more than wrong. You're totally ridiculous. How could I even find the name and address of a logging company, for God's sake, much less go around selling them maps?'

'That's what I'd like you to tell me.'

'Oh, stop bullying me and go away,' she cried. 'Go bully Bethany or Pashetta or someone.'

'Just now I'd rather stay here and bully you,' he said, furrowing his brows as various possible scenarios ran through his mind. 'Now, if you won't tell me how you contacted the logging company, I'll just have to make a few guesses.'

'Go ahead, I could use a giggle,' she declared but he thought he detected a nervous tremor in her voice.

'It would only take a stroll across the compound for you to have a chat with our faithful contractor, Mr Liu, wouldn't it?' he began.

'I suppose so.'

'And any information you let drop in that quarter could be passed along pretty quickly to his cousin, Chen, in Putussibau, couldn't it?'

She shrugged. 'I wouldn't know.'

'I think you would.'

She ignored this.

'Well, something I happen to know is that Chen does deals with gold mining operations, Fairbanks, to name one, and doesn't care too much about the niceties of the situation. So if Liu tipped him off that you had some interesting maps to sell, what's to stop him, Chen, I mean, from contacting some cheap-shit logging company, one that would rather buy stolen maps than fork out the money to do their own reconnaissance? Liu and Chen both take a cut and everybody's happy — at least, everyone who doesn't care a damn about the rainforest.'

'Stop it,' she cried, putting her hands over her ears, 'stop it. I won't listen to another word of this rubbish. I've told you the truth. It's not my fault if you refuse to believe me.'

'You're making it damn difficult,' he returned, forcibly removing her hands from her ears, 'but never mind. I've got a proposition for you.'

She looked up in surprise.

'If you level with me now,' he continued, 'and really tell me the truth, I'll help get you a medical evacuation back to Australia. That way nobody outside of Kanyalang ever needs to know about all this. But I warn you, if you don't come clean within the next five minutes, I won't lift a finger to help you.'

'I don't need your help, thank you,' she said, recovering her composure, 'and I don't want to go back to Australia.'

'It might be a good idea to rethink that one,' Wolf said, finding it difficult to restrain the impulse to slap her. But he had never actually hit a woman and wasn't going to let Catherine drive him to start now. 'Not only will it be better for the project if we can keep this whole thing quiet, but it will be one hell of a lot better for you.'

'I fail to see that it will make any difference to me at all, one way or the other.'

'Then you must not be the smart cookie I took you for.'

'I'm smart enough to see what Marguarita's done to you.'

'Done to me?'

'Yes, she's turned you into some kind of giant sponge, absorbing every malicious rumour she concocts about me. But you can't prove a single one.'

'Possibly not, but I'm not talking about a conviction in a court of law. I'm talking about your future career. Who the hell do you think is ever going to hire you for another job if word gets around about what you've done on this one? And word will get around, you know, unless we all make a concerted effort to see that it doesn't.'

'Only because you and Marguarita will do everything possible to see that it does,' she retorted, anger bringing a flush of colour to her cheeks.

'Neither of us is going to do that,' he said, firmly, 'although we probably should. God only knows what harm you could do on another rainforest venture.'

'Don't worry, there's never going to be another one, not for me, anyway. I've had enough of the jungle, and enough of this place, if you want to know, to last me the rest of my life.'

'Can I take it that you agree to the medivac option then?'

'I suppose so,' she replied, hoping this half-truth would be sufficient to get rid of him without really committing her to anything she couldn't get out of later.

'Good. That's settled.'

'But,' she objected, not at all ready for it to be settled, 'how about Elliot? He won't agree to it, will he?'

'Just watch him. I've just been having a little chat with him and he's worried about how bad this Borneo climate is for your health. He'll jump at the excuse to get you back to Australia.'

'Oh,' she said, trying to keep the dismay out of her voice. Would he really let her go just like that — surely not, she told herself. He wouldn't believe all those dreadful things about her.

'I've done a little preliminary work on him already,' Wolf told her. 'You know how he adores you. He's not going to let one mistake, no matter how serious, ruin your career. And don't forget how important Kanyalang's reputation is to him.'

'How about the others — will they go along with it?'

'Nobody's going to want to see you suffer. But I don't think they'll exactly want to sit back and watch you sell any more of our maps to gold miners or loggers either.'

'Will they really believe I've been doing that?' she asked, in a quavering voice.

'I don't see how they can do anything else,' he replied. And ignoring the tears that were once again welling up in her pale eyes, he went on, 'so I suggest you pack up anything you can't live without and be ready to get out of here pretty much a.s.a.p. In the meantime, I'll try to convince everyone to keep a lid on this whole shitty business.'

'You're not angry, then?' she asked, in a trembling voice.

'Are you kidding?' Wolf barked. 'I'm so fucking mad, I can't see straight. And if you think I've cooked up this medivac plan just to save your skin, you couldn't be more wrong. I'm doing it because I don't want any lingering stink from your dirty little schemes to hang around this place and muck up everything we're doing here.'

'Thank you very much,' she retorted, 'but you're not head of this project, you know. Elliot is. And he's not going to believe your lies, or Marguarita's either. And he won't send me away on some horrible medical thing. I know he won't.'

Wolf managed to keep his temper in check just long enough to stride out of the room before slamming the door with an earth-shaking crash behind him.

CHAPTER THIRTY-SIX

Catherine was right that Elliot's first reaction to Wolf's account of her treachery would be to spring to her defence. He simply couldn't believe, wouldn't believe, that his lovely Catherine had done such a thing. It was all a despicable lie, formulated no doubt by Marguarita out of jealousy. He had always suspected her of having a ruthless streak — cold, efficient, intelligent women like that so often did.

Yet he hadn't been able to console himself with this thought for long. He was still in the throes of telling Wolf off for spreading wild rumours when a sudden recollection made him break off in mid-sentence. It was the expression he had seen in Catherine's grey eyes one day when she had watched him take the key to the map cupboard out of his desk. The intensity of interest shining in them had momentarily unnerved him. And he realised that it was only shortly after that he had, for no definable reason, stopped leaving that particular key in the top drawer of his desk. Instead, he had added it to his key ring and carried it, along with the office key, in his trouser pocket. He was quite certain that since then he had only given it to only two people, and Catherine was one of them.

Pashetta, of course, was the other. She was in and out of the map cupboard all the time but it was always during the day when other people were around and it would have been almost impossible to do a bit of secret photocopying.

On the other hand, his key ring had only been in Catherine's possession on two occasions that he could remember. Both times had been when she had accidentally left something in his office that she wanted to work on in the evening. She would have had ample opportunity to take the maps out of the drawers and photocopy them without anyone being the wiser. And that, he concluded, after bitter reflection, was probably what happened.

After a long conversation with Marguarita, followed by a look at the Kanyalang logo on Jim's map and a few faltering efforts to deny the likelihood of Catherine's guilt, Elliot agreed that a medical evacuation would be the best solution all around.

In any case, he told himself, it was clear that Catherine's health wasn't improving the way it should so he needn't feel any pangs of conscience about banishing her with slightly less than rock-solid proof of her role in the affair. He would be sending her to a place with better medical care and that had to be a good thing even if by some chance they were all misjudging her.

Another benefit of the plan was that only the expat staff, and of course Pashetta, would ever need to know the real cause of Catherine's departure. He fervently hoped that no one beyond the bounds of Kanyalang, not even the RRF people in Geneva, would hear of it. Liu and Chen would be sacked and with any luck the project would continue with a minimum of disruption and no stain whatsoever on its reputation.

Mike and Bethany were completely stunned at the news of Catherine's perfidy and Bima staunchly refused to accept the possibility that there was any truth in it at all. Only Pashetta, who had been convinced all along that Catherine didn't deserve the affection so liberally bestowed on her, could have said that she wasn't surprised.

Bima's first inclination was to go to Catherine and assure her that there was no way he would believe these preposterous lies about her, that he couldn't imagine what Marguarita and the others could be thinking of, that they must have gone mad. But he was thwarted in his attempt to do this by the reception he received when he knocked on her door.

'Don't come in,' Catherine called.

'But it's me, Bima. I just want to –'

'Go away.'

'Please, just for –'

'No. Can't you understand? No.'

Shocked, hurt, and feeling thoroughly rejected, he gave up and turned away.

A similar conversation took place through the same closed door a few hours later but with a different outcome. Bethany disregarded Catherine's objections and pushed open the door and charged in.

'Do you have any idea how late it is?' Catherine cried indignantly, after Bethany had flicked on the light and sat down on the bed. 'It's almost midnight, for Christ's sake.'

'I don't care what time it is. I want to know why you did it, that's all. Then I'll go.'

'Did what?'

'You know exactly what I'm talking about.'

'No, I don't, honestly.'

'Alright, if you insist on being dense, I'll spell it out for you, m-a-p-s. You took them and you know it. We all know it now. But what I want to find out is how you could have done such an awful thing. I mean, why?'

'Why do you just believe everything Wolf tells you?' Catherine flung back at her.

'I don't. It's just that in this particular case it's painfully obvious that what he's saying is right.'

'I can't believe you're turning on me like this,' sobbed Catherine. 'I thought you were my friend.'

'I'm not turning on you – not necessarily – I'm trying to understand you. And it's because our friendship has been really important to me that I'm doing my best to figure out why you did what you did. I mean, you must have had some reason although – well, to be honest, it's awfully hard to think of anything that would justify it.'

'Then you're not my friend,' Catherine said, resentfully.

'I was until tonight.'

'Then you're not anymore?'

'How can I be?' demanded Bethany.

Catherine considered this for a moment and then with a note of pathos in her voice asked, 'Have Wolf and Marguarita turned the others against me, too?'

'We're all absolutely furious, if that's what you mean. We feel betrayed.'

'Even Bima?'

'I'm not certain. You'll have to ask him.'

Catherine's pale lips trembled and her eyes filled with tears, but Bethany gave no sign of being moved by her distress. Instead she pressed on with her questioning.

'Pashetta says you did it for the money. Did you?'

'Pashetta,' Catherine almost spat out the name, 'she's always hated me. She's jealous, that's all.'

'Nobody hates you,' Bethany replied testily, 'at least, they didn't until now. Tell me, if it wasn't for the money, what was it?'

Catherine turned her face to the wall and let the tears trickle down her face.

'Come on, there's no point in playing innocent,' persisted Bethany. 'I won't believe it. Neither will anybody else so you might as well tell me why you did it. Then I can at least try to understand.'

Catherine, who chronically felt herself misunderstood, turned over and looked balefully at her visitor.

'It was for the money then, wasn't it?' Bethany persisted.

'Not exactly.'

'What does that mean?'

'Well, I suppose the money was part of it.'

'What was the other part?'

'Tarique.'

'Tarique?'

'Yes, you know what he was like.'

'Only what I've heard.'

'I forgot, you weren't here when he was still alive, were you? If you had been, you would have seen that he had a kind of hypnotic power over people. At least, he did over me. And he was so goddamn attractive and I wanted him so badly that I couldn't see straight.'

She paused, searching Bethany's eyes for a touch of sympathy. 'I just couldn't help agreeing to do whatever he wanted,' she continued, 'and borrowing the maps, only long enough to make copies, you understand, seemed like such a small thing. I couldn't believe they were going to be of much use to anyone.'

'Shouldn't you have known better?'

'Perhaps, but tell the truth, would you have realised there would be anyone who would give a damn about them?'

Bethany hesitated. 'Possibly not,' she admitted, 'but it might have occurred to me that there was something a little sinister about lying to Elliot and slipping into his office at night to make secret photocopies of his stuff.'

'But it was just the maps. Elliot was never going to miss them. And if you had any idea how important that money was going to be for Tarique and me – it was going to be the start of our new life together in Canada – you'd understand.'

'And you actually believed all that was really going to happen?' asked Bethany incredulously.

'Don't rub it in,' Catherine replied in an anguished voice. 'I loved him. You don't know what that's like because you've never loved anyone but that stepbrother of yours and that never amounted to anything but a school girl crush. If you'd ever really loved someone you'd know how important it was to believe him and trust him. But maybe you'll find that out some day and then you'll understand how much I wanted to believe Tarique.'

Catherine paused, hoping her darts had struck home, but Bethany showed no sign of allowing herself to be diverted from the subject at hand so she went on, 'And I had all sorts of reasons to trust him.'

'Like what?'

'Like a bank statement from our joint account in Singapore that had both our names on it just like it was supposed to. How much evidence did I need, for God's sake? Wouldn't you have been convinced by that, especially if you didn't have any reason to doubt him? And I didn't at the time.'

'How did you find out what was really going on then?' Bethany asked.

'I went through the papers in his desk the night after he died. That's when I discovered that he had drawn our joint account almost down to zero and moved all the money into another account that was only in his name. He must have been doing that every month, almost from the beginning.'

'But how could he –'

'It was disgustingly easy. You see, I had arranged with the RRF to have my salary checks deposited directly to the Singapore account instead of to my Melbourne one. And after Tarique had shown me one or two bank statements, well, just the one, actually, I didn't ask to see anymore. I mean, you wouldn't, would you, not if you loved someone? You'd trust him. So, of course, I had no idea that he was transferring all the money into his own account and that when he was buying the shares in the mining company he was putting them just in his own name instead of in both our names, not when it was supposed to be our investment for the future.'

'Christ,' Bethany exclaimed, fighting off a touch of sympathy, mixed with impatience, for her former friend, 'when it comes to having crap taste in men, you really take the biscuit.'

'I know that now,' Catherine said, bitterly. 'I can't believe what an imbecile I was, letting myself be blinded by my feelings that way. I suppose in a way I deserved to be left with absolutely nothing except the threat of having a baby. But anyway, you can see now why I couldn't ask anyone to lend me money to go away somewhere for an abortion, why I had to risk having it locally.'

'Well, no, I can't see —' Bethany began.

'Don't be an idiot. I couldn't have people delving into my finances, asking questions about where my money had gone —'

'They wouldn't.'

'Of course they would, like a shot.'

'Who knows,' Bethany said, dismissing the argument as pointless. 'But the thing I really don't see is why you carried on photocopying and selling the maps after Tarique died.'

'Revenge,' Catherine declared with unexpected ferocity.

'A bit late for that, wasn't it?' Bethany observed. 'How can you take revenge on someone who's dead?'

'I suppose you can't really,' Catherine acknowledged, 'but the one thing I could do was get back the money he had stolen from me.'

'Even though you weren't getting it back from him?'

'I admit it wasn't quite as satisfying that way but it was better than nothing. At least, I didn't have to feel that I'd been quite so totally fucked over. You can understand that, can't you?'

For a moment Bethany almost felt that she could but then her perspective returned and her sympathy evaporated. 'But how could you possibly forget about the rainforest just like that,' she cried, 'and Kanyalang and everything we're all trying to do here? Don't you care about it at all?'

'Of course I do.'

The expression on Bethany's face hardened. 'If you're going to lie to me, at least try to make it a vaguely believable lie,' she said, angrily.

'I'm not the one who's lying. You are.'

The look of stunned outrage on Bethany's face made Catherine want to laugh but she pressed on, 'You're lying to yourself if you think that what we're doing here is going to make any difference at all. It's not, you know. The rainforest is doomed no matter whether Bima builds his precious hotel or a few benighted tourists come to stay in it or not.'

'But the research centre —' Bethany began.

'The research centre is going to be about as helpful as a raindrop in the Sahara. And as far as what happens to a few silly maps, nothing could matter less. The rainforest has had it. It's finished. What the loggers don't cut down, the plantation owners will — that is, unless the gold miners get there first. You know that every bit as well as I do.'

'I'm not sure I do, actually,' Bethany replied icily.

'If you were half-way honest with yourself, you would, so would Wolf and Elliot and all the others. The whole idea of an eco-tourism project in a place like this is just one big exercise in make believe. Ask Mike. He'll tell you the same thing.'

Bethany longed to deny this but remembered Mike saying something along those lines the day she arrived.

'The tourists aren't going to come,' Catherine continued, 'and even if they did, the money they'd bring in would be a pittance compared with what's needed to save even a square inch of this jungle. So why shouldn't I take back the money that was stolen from me?'

'If you need to have the answer to that question spelt out for you,' Bethany began, getting up and going toward the door, 'then I don't think there's much point in going on with this conversation.'

'I could have told you that from the beginning,' Catherine replied, petulantly.

'I still feel that I'm missing something,' Bethany said, pausing with her hand on the door. 'Once Tarique was dead and the abortion was over, why was the money still so important to you —

357

important enough for you to jeopardise the work of the project, to say nothing of your own career, to get it back?'

Catherine appeared to direct her answer more to herself than to Bethany, 'Because I'd be able to see my face in the mirror again without feeling that a fool was looking back at me.'

'You weren't bothered by the idea of a thief looking back at you?'

'If you nicked a paper clip off Elliot's desk, would you consider yourself a thief?'

'It's hardly the same thing.'

'In your view, perhaps, but I don't see much difference.'

This level of blindness was beyond Bethany's ability to cope with so she went on to the other point that was still troubling her. 'How could you have carried on working here if you were convinced it was all so pointless?'

'It's still an interesting eco-system, isn't it,' Catherine replied, 'even more so actually because it's about to disappear. But never mind about that. It may have been work that brought me here in the first place but it hasn't been work that's kept me here. For a long time it was Tarique, although at this point I wish I had never laid eyes on him. Now it's Bima, sort of, and anyway there's really no place else I particularly want to go.'

'Not even back to Australia?' Bethany suggested.

'Definitely not that.'

'Why ever not? It's supposed to be a great place. Lots of people would love to have a chance to go there.'

Catherine turned her head away. Bethany wasn't proving to be the loyal friend she had thought she was.

'Anyway it's the logical place for you to go on a medical evacuation,' Bethany continued, 'and you surely can't expect to stay here after what's happened.'

'Singapore's closer,' Catherine said, a wave of self-pity sweeping over her, 'not that I really care. There isn't any place I particularly want to be.'

'You'll change your mind about that when you're feeling better,' Bethany assured her as some of her anger began to recede. Catherine had done an awful thing, that was undeniable, but she had suffered too and Bethany couldn't help feeling just a little of the old affection returning.

'Wolf told me you promised never to work in the rainforest again,' Bethany continued. 'That's going to be hard, isn't it?'

'Nothing could be easier. I never want to be trapped in another hell-hole like this as long as I live.'

Bethany, attributing Catherine's heated response to a wave of remorse, decided to leave her to wrestle alone with what she assumed was a belatedly awakened conscience.

But Catherine's conscience, if she possessed one, remained in a state of untroubled sleep.

After the door clicked shut, Catherine turned off the light, fell back against the pillows and tried to relax, but she soon found that even with her hands over her ears she couldn't keep out the hated sounds of the jungle night, the hooting, the yowling, the croaking and the hissing, that were tormenting her. They called up terrifying pictures of crawling snakes, climbing civet cats, and creeping centipedes, all struggling to get into the room through any available opening. And behind them, driving them toward her, was Tarique.

With his mocking laughter ringing in her ears, she decided she wouldn't argue against being sent away. She would be glad to go, the sooner the better.

CHAPTER THIRTY-SEVEN

'God, I feel completely drained after that conversation,' Bethany told Wolf when she found him on the veranda.

Everyone else had gone to bed but he had waited for her. 'Here, this will do you good,' he said, pouring a generous dollop of gin into a glass and handing it to her. 'What did she say? Did you get anything reasonable out of her?'

Bethany did her best to sum up Catherine's reaction.

'It sounds like getting her out of here on a medivac to Australia is definitely the best solution,' he said.

Bethany agreed, set down her glass and announced that she was going to bed.

'And where are you planning to sleep tonight?' he asked, catching hold of her wrist to keep her from turning away.

'In my room, I suppose,' Bethany said, pretending the real meaning of his question had escaped her although of course it hadn't.

'Not with me?'

'We're not in Pontianak anymore,' she reminded him although she made no effort to free her wrist from his grasp.

'Does that matter?' he asked.

'It might – in fact, it almost certainly will.'

'Only if we let it,' he said, although he wasn't sure how true this would be in the cheek-by-jowl proximity of life at Kanyalang. 'In any case, too much has happened today. Things will be clearer in the morning.'

'And in the meantime –' she smiled, knowing the answer.

'In the meantime my room's just down the veranda.'

'So is mine,' she said, suddenly feeling that being in her own place would give her more control over the situation.

In no mood to argue over details, he let her take him by the hand, not by the appendage she had used as a handle in Pontianak, and lead him toward her door even though he had a few fleeting doubts about whether this late night escapade was a very good or . a very bad idea.

If he'd known that Bethany's thoughts were running along similar lines, he would not have been flattered.

Elliot wasted no time arranging for Catherine's departure on the grounds of medical necessity and, almost before she knew it, she was acknowledging the glacial farewells of her colleagues. Only Bima and Bethany went with her to the landing pad to see her off but Marguarita was already there saying, what seemed to Bethany, like a surprisingly affectionate good-bye to Jim.

'Don't worry, honey,' she heard him say, 'I'll be back.'

'I won't forget this time,' Marguarita promised, as he climbed into the aircraft to take advantage of the free ride to Putussibau. Then she joined Bima and Bethany as they stood back to watch the helicopter rise up into the air.

Jim waved madly from the window but Catherine offered no sign of affection for the people whose lives had, for a while, been so closely entwined with hers.

The precipitous ejection of the most-loved member of their little group appeared to have a far more profound effect on the people left behind than it did on Catherine herself. It seemed like a light had gone out at Kanyalang and everyone except Pashetta got thoroughly pissed on the veranda that evening.

Bima and Elliot suffered the most, as they were the ones for whom the disillusionment had been the most profound. A tacit understanding grew up between them as each one took comfort from the knowledge that he was not the only one who had been played for a fool.

In the days that followed, Elliot was more tight-lipped and withdrawn than ever, and by late evening he frequently showed deleterious signs of how much whisky he had consumed. Sometimes he brought a bottle out onto the veranda after dinner and shared it with whoever happened to be around but more often his drinking bouts were solitary affairs, dominated by thoughts of Catherine. He recalled with shame how pleased he had been by the keen interest she had taken in his maps and how he had delighted in showing them to her. He had taken such pride in explaining it all to her. And he had to admit that it hadn't been only his intellect that had been stimulated. God, he thought, what a fatheaded old fart he had been. He wished he could get as turned on when he told Annie about his maps but after twenty-six years of marriage, two children and half a dozen dogs, what could he expect?

Well, perhaps he and Annie could get their marriage back on track one day, make it a real marriage again. The prospect wasn't frightfully exciting but that might be just as well – better to leave excitement to the young. They could better withstand the shocks it so often brought with it.

Bima, like Elliot, wasn't withstanding the shock very well and Catherine's duplicity had left him behaving more like a snapping turtle than like his usually kind and genial self.

Marguarita, by contrast, had become unexpectedly easy to get on with but Bethany suspected that had more to do with the recent presence of Jim than with the absence of Catherine.

Pashetta, too, looked happier but the reasons for this change were more complicated than Bethany guessed. Although she was still vaguely envious of the affection Catherine had seemed to attract so effortlessly, such feelings were rapidly being overpowered by her delight in the latest happenings.

Her first cause for satisfaction was that foreigners were finally getting what was coming to them and in her opinion it wasn't a moment too soon. It drove her mad the way they were always so quick to point their fingers at every sign of corruption they found in Indonesia.

Were those tall, rich, self-assured people from overseas so perfect themselves, she had often asked herself? Was corruption unknown in those magical places they came from? Of course not, any fool knew that. But the tone of moral superiority they assumed when they talked about Indonesians who took bribes or who cut down the forests made her so angry she wanted to scream. Where were the forests in their own countries, she wanted to know? Gone. And why was that? Because the grandfathers of those same, smug, self-satisfied expats had cut them down and had made themselves rich by doing it – that was why.

'Oh, but that wasn't our fault,' someone had once explained to her. 'It happened a long time ago. We can't be held responsible for that.'

Yet when Indonesians did the same thing now, she fumed, that was a different story. They were considered criminals.

Now, thanks to Catherine's little games, she thought with a smile, things would be different. Expats, the ones at Kanyalang, at least, would be forced to face the hypocrisy of their neo-colonial attitudes. And the more she was able to belittle them in her mind, the taller and more confident she felt herself become.

Gradually, she began to give voice to her opinions without first glancing at Wolf or Mike to see what they thought. Occasionally she even found that it was more exciting to argue than to echo. And as her former reticence receded, the intelligent and rebellious being that had been so fiercely repressed by her past experiences began to emerge.

The change, when it was perceived by her companions, did not meet with universal acclaim.

Mike had been having enough trouble trying to bridge the chasm between a friendly relationship with her and a romantic one before this change became apparent. Now he was finding it more difficult than ever.

The trouble, he decided, was that talking to Pashetta, confiding in her and sharing his thoughts with her, was a two-edged sword. Although it brought them so much closer to each other in some ways, it was a colossal stumbling block when it came to having sex. This was because of the possibility that if he tried to come on to her she might turn him down. If that happened he'd lose his soulmate, his playmate and his favourite companion, all at once. His job would have to go, too, because there would be no way he could stay on at Kanyalang and face Pashetta every day after something like that.

As a result, he began to suffer from a problem he had never thought he would have – getting the old boy up. It behaved in its normal way when he was lying in bed at night thinking about her but it went into some kind of coma when he was actually with her and this was beginning to worry him.

Mike wasn't the only one who was worried.

Pashetta couldn't understand why he wasn't making any effort to get her into bed and she spent a lot of time peering anxiously into the mirror wondering if some kind of jungle rot was blighting her appearance. Yet as far as she could see, which wasn't very far because the mirror was small, she hadn't changed. But something had to be different and it was important to figure out what it was. Their long talks on the veranda were great but conversation wasn't likely to get her to Australia while sex just might do it. It was such a shame that Bethany hadn't kept her promise about that medicine.

Pashetta mentioned this as they were strolling back to the longhouse one afternoon.

'Remember the Chinese medicine you were going to get for me in Putussibau,' she said.

Bethany certainly did. She groaned inwardly at the mortifying recollection of Wolf laughing his head off when he discovered it.

'Is there any of it left?' Pashetta asked.

'All of it,' Bethany replied.

Pashetta was astonished. 'Didn't you use it on Wolf?'

'No.'

'Then why didn't you let me have it, like you promised?'

'I didn't promise. I just told you I might get it for you,' Bethany argued, trying to remember exactly what she had agreed to.

'What you really mean is that you used it yourself to make Wolf crazy mad for you,' Pashetta accused.

'That's not true.'

'Then how did you make him want to have so much sex with you?'

'It isn't all that much,' Bethany replied, laughing.

Pashetta looked unconvinced. 'I think you give him lots and lots of Chinese medicine, maybe all of it.'

They were approaching the veranda steps by this time so Bethany suggested, 'If you come to my room I'll show you the box and you can see that it hasn't been opened yet.'

'Okay,' Pashetta agreed, although that didn't quell her suspicions.

A few minutes later Bethany, after considerable pawing around in the disorder of her top drawer, triumphantly held out the box. 'See,' she exclaimed, 'it's all here. I didn't give any of it to Wolf.'

'Why did you buy it if you didn't want to give it to me, or to Wolf either?'

'I suppose I hadn't quite made up my mind what I wanted to do about it,' Bethany confessed, 'and I got tired of sitting around waiting while Wolf made a thousand phone calls. Shopping for an aphrodisiac seemed like a cool thing to do.'

'What is going to happen to it now?'

Bethany shrugged. 'I don't know. I almost forgot I had it.'

'Can I have it then?' Pashetta asked.

'Not for Mike, surely?'

Pashetta nodded.

'You can't possibly want it for him,' Bethany exclaimed. And playfully borrowing her friend's words, she added, 'He's already crazy mad for you.'

'In some ways he likes me but not in that way,' Pashetta corrected her.

Bethany made no effort to conceal her surprise. 'That doesn't sound like Mike,' she said, 'not that I would really know, of course.'

'How much did you pay for the medicine?' Pashetta persisted. 'I will give you the money.'

'No need to do that,' Bethany replied, uncomfortably aware of how differently she felt about letting Pashetta have it now that she knew it was for Mike rather than for Wolf. 'Just take it,' she said, handing it to her. 'Here.'

Pashetta accepted it eagerly and, thanking Bethany, fairly flew off to the seclusion of her own room to think.

She had to figure out some way to get him to take it without realising what it was or that anything out of the ordinary was going on. That wouldn't be easy, she knew but if she tried hard enough she should be able to come up with something.

The place to start would be the kitchen, Pashetta decided. She would have a chat with Kolop and find out when they were going to have something very strong-tasting and very spicy for dinner.

She wasted no time in setting this plan in motion and, as she approached the kitchen, the aromas emanating from a caldron-like pot that was bubbling away over the charcoal fire were encouraging. They suggested that chicken, enhanced by tiny green peppers so fiery they could blister the throat of the uninitiated diner, would soon be on the table so she asked Kolop if she could just try a bit.

'Perfect,' she said, when she had tasted it. And before he could object, she quickly put several spoonfuls of the sauce into a cup and started for the door.

'Hey,' cried Kolop, 'where're you going with that?'

'I'm going to give it to Mike. This kind of chicken is one of his favourite things,' she said and, over his protests, hurried back to her room.

Once she had closed the door firmly behind her, she opened the medicine and cautiously tipped a portion of its contents into the curry. She wasn't certain how much to use and she didn't want to put in so much that he could taste it. Plus she knew that too much might be dangerous and she didn't want to kill him or anything. The trouble was that if she didn't give him enough it might not have any effect. She'd just have to make the best guess she could and hope it would be alright.

She found Mike a few minutes later working on a report at the dining room table. 'I hope you are hungry,' she said, sitting down opposite him. 'Kolop is doing a really delicious chicken for tonight.'

'Good.'

'I thought you might like to try some,' she said, holding the cup out to him.

'I'll wait for dinner,' he replied, indifferently. 'Go ahead, have it yourself.'

It took no theatrical ability for her to look crushed. 'But Kolop made me promise to give it to you because he knows how much you like it cooked this way.'

Her obvious disappointment made him feel bad. 'Okay, thanks,' he said, taking it, 'I'll give it a try.'

He took one spoonful, ate it, choked and tried to hand the cup back to her.

'No, no,' she cried, 'you must finish it. Kolop said he wanted the cup back and if it isn't empty he'll think you didn't like it.'

'No, he won't,' argued Mike. Luckily a thermos of cold water had been left on the table after lunch and he reached for it. 'Only an Indian fire-eater could scoff up this stuff on its own. Tell him to send some rice with it next time.'

'Don't worry, he always has some around,' Pashetta said and disappeared into the kitchen before he could stop her.

A few minutes later she was back with a plate of rice and, after all the trouble she had gone to, Mike felt obliged to pour the spicy curry over it and act like he appreciated it.

Pashetta gave a sigh of relief when he finally took the last bite. How long would it be before it took effect, she wondered? It would be awful if it worked too quickly and turned him into some kind sex maniac in the middle of dinner.

It didn't.

Mike just seemed like his normal self at the table and didn't even show any sign of being particularly interested in that sort of thing when they lingered over a bowl of prawn crisps on the veranda after dinner.

I must not have given him enough, she told herself later when she was in bed, even though she still half-expected to hear a low rap on her door. She'd just have to try again with a stronger dose.

She was worrying over what to put it in – there was still the problem of keeping him from tasting it – when she heard a loud thump, not on her door but on the roof. It sounded like it was just above her room. She would swear she heard feet scampering here and there, darting across the thick layer of thatch. Musang, she thought. Mike called them civet cats. They often came on the prowl at night, stealing any food that wasn't firmly under lock and key.

They're after the prawn crisps, she thought, remembering that there had been a lot of them and that Mike had muttered something about turning in and had gone off well before the bowl was empty. And in her disappointment with the results of the sehat laki laki she had left the rest of them on the veranda.

Thinking about them now – they were her favourite snack and she had been too preoccupied to eat much during dinner –

Pashetta leapt out of bed to go and rescue them only to find that the thief had got there first. She just arrived in time to see a tawny tail disappearing over the veranda rail leaving a trail of prawn-coloured crumbs behind it.

'Bastard,' she cried, for the benefit of any English-speaking civet cats that might be within hearing, but none appeared to notice.

It clearly wasn't her night. The sex medicine hadn't worked and now the prawn crisps were gone. She wondered what she could do to change her luck.

A possible answer occurred to her as she was passing Mike's door on the way back to her room. Acting on impulse, she quietly turned the handle and let herself in.

Groping her way through the darkness, she could barely discern the outline of Mike's inert form as he lay spread-eagled across the bed. He was taking up so much of the available space that she wasn't quite sure how she was going to slip in beside him. Perhaps it would be better to wake him up first and get him to move over, she thought. She was on the point of doing this when she was put off by the long, low rumble of a snore – one that sounded like she had strayed into a lion's den and was inadvertently treading on its tail.

As the fearsome noise was repeated, her eyes grew used to the darkness and a closer look reassured her that the form on the bed was actually human, and indeed was Mike, so she bent down and kissed him on the lips.

Instead of waking up as she expected him to do, he merely reached up in his sleep and pulled her down on top of him. This solved the problem of where she was going to find room in the bed but it put her seduction plans on hold – temporarily, at least.

What she didn't know was that her arrival in his room had triggered her appearance in his dream and that only gradually as he began to return to consciousness did he realise that she was actually lying there in his arms.

This astonishing fact was such a turn-on that his dick, not one that any woman who had seen it ready for action had ever described as small, grew to gigantic proportions.

The Chinese medicine, Pashetta thought, in panic when she felt it pressing against her abdomen. I must have given him too much,

much too much. And with a cry of fright, she rolled off him and by pushing as hard as she could against his chest managed to hold him away from her.

'What's the matter?' he asked, not letting her get very far away. Instead he climbed on top of her, supporting himself on his knees and elbows and using his enormous cock to caress the soft places between her legs.

'You are,' she protested, 'it is so —'

With a rueful laugh, he stretched out beside her and propped himself up on his left elbow. The situation was not new to him. 'It'll be alright, I promise you,' he said soothingly. 'You should know I wouldn't hurt you.'

She didn't know it. With a dick that size she didn't see how sex could possibly be anything but terribly painful. But no sex would mean no Australia, she told herself disconsolately, so she closed her eyes and mustered up the courage to enclose the scary projectile in her hand.

'Do Australian men always have one this big?' she whispered, wondering how the women in that alarming country coped.

It was not a question Mike wanted to answer. In his world sex was something you did, not something you talked about.

'You're not still worried about me hurting you, are you?' he chided gently. 'I promised you I wouldn't, remember? Don't you believe me?'

She wanted to say that she wasn't stupid, that of course she didn't believe him, but she held her tongue and allowed him to stroke her gently as he tried to persuade her that everything would be alright.

'I won't go inside you,' he murmured, running his hands along her hips and pressing her thighs together. 'For now we'll just do it like this.' And sending a silent thank you to the whore in Sydney who had taught him this ploy, he plunged his cock down again and again into the tight dampness around — but not inside — the opening between her legs.

Not quite as good as the real thing, he reflected when he finally rolled off her, but the next best thing.

Pashetta, stretching happily in the aftermath of successive waves of pleasure, lavished silent praise on the Chinese medicine. She

370

even wondered if perhaps this new way of doing things, rubbing up and down against her in that exciting secret place, wasn't actually better than the real thing.

In any case, her fear of his giant cock had been largely overcome. During the nights that followed she eagerly gave herself up to the thrill of his touch, encouraging his fingers as they played about the secret openings into her body and welcoming his tongue as it teased her in the place it mattered most. And little by little, as the possibility of pain was overwhelmed by the certainty of pleasure, he began to press his cock inside her, at first just a little and then deeper and deeper, until she felt that the only important man in the world was Mike.

Gradually, as the nights grew into weeks, Mike began to have a vague feeling that something extraordinary was happening to him. And the more he mulled it over, the more it seemed that it all revolved around Pashetta – not just having sex with her but lying in bed with her afterwards and talking about things. Talking and talking, he hadn't known it was possible to feel so close to anyone. And even if he had known, he wasn't at all sure he would have taken to the idea – more likely, it would have scared the shit out of him – but with Pashetta it was great.

Of course, talking wasn't something that had to be done in bed. He could talk to her pretty much anytime, anywhere, about anything at all and she always understood – almost always.

There was one subject on which they totally, even heatedly, disagreed. That was the Dayaks. No matter how much he told her about them, she just didn't seem to take on board the fact that they were really terrific people, smart, loyal, brave, resourceful, hospitable and friendly. What more could you ask for?

Pashetta felt she could have given him a long list of things but she tried to hold her tongue. Neither of them enjoyed it when they had an argument so she tried to save her comments about the Dayaks for Bethany.

This arrangement worked well. Bethany missed Catherine more than she would have imagined and she increasingly looked to

Pashetta to fill the void. This was especially true as none of the others, eager as they had been to hear every detail of her misadventure in Sanggau, were inclined to want it repeated over and over again. And great as the nights with Wolf were, there remained the fact that he still couldn't, or wouldn't, understand how hard it was for her to continue working at Nanga Palin after everything that had happened.

Pashetta, on the other hand, revelled in the sensation of having been right about the Dayaks all along and never tired of having her opinion vindicated. She listened with undiminished horror whenever Bethany talked about the massacre and completely understood her reluctance to go back to Nanga Palin. The result was that gradually, in spite of everything, she found herself beginning to like Bethany.

Pashetta and Bethany were not the only ones who spent a lot of time talking about the Dayaks. Conversations on the veranda and around the dinner table often focused on the ever-increasing ferocity of the conflict with the Madurese. Mike heard the Dayak version of what was happening from his men while Bima, who was spending a lot of time with Fang, the new contractor who had replaced Liu, got a very different picture. Like most of the electricians working on the hotel, Fang was a Chinese from Putussibau. He had no particular affection for either the Dayaks or the Madurese.

'The Dayaks are taking more and more heads,' Fang had told Bima that morning, 'and lots of Madurese villages are being burned to the ground.'

Bima related all this and more to the group assembled around the lunch table and it was rather unfortunate that he chose that particular time to add, 'Fang says that the Dayaks are cutting out the fresh livers of the people they kill and eating them.'

'Raw,' gasped Pashetta, 'ugh.'

'Do you think they should be cooked?' enquired Marguarita dryly.

'A few onions might help,' suggested Wolf, 'and bit of garlic.'

'Stop it,' cried Bethany, clasping her hands over her ears, 'I can't stand it. How can you be so horrible?'

'I can't stop being horrible,' Wolf said. 'I'd have to stop being me.'

'Not a bad idea,' observed Marguarita and everyone chorused their agreement.

The only really bad idea, Bethany decided later that afternoon, had been staying on at Kanyalang after everything that had happened. She had only come back from Sanggau because of Catherine so there was really nothing to keep her here any longer, nothing except Wolf. And now with the fighting and all the ghastly things the Dayaks were doing, there was every reason to go.

Even though her closest friends and informants at Nanga Palin, apart from Sarika, were the grannies — and they certainly weren't out there taking Madurese heads, eating human livers, and murdering innocent children — their connection with the men who were doing it was too close. Thumbi and the other old dears she had become so fond of were the repositories of the culture that had engendered all this savagery and they were the ones who had transmitted it to the men carrying out the carnage.

She tried to talk about all this with Wolf while they were sharing a fresh coconut by the thermos outside Pashetta's office but he wasn't very sympathetic.

'How many old grannies in London would like to be held responsible for all the things their delinquent grandsons did?' he demanded.

'Not too many I suppose but it's not quite —' she broke off as a venturesome monkey leapt onto the veranda rail and looked like he was about to snatch the fruit from her hand.

'Get off, you bastard,' said Wolf, grinning at the intruder — a show of teeth was a sign of hostility in the monkey world — and waving his arms menacingly in the animal's direction.

It scampered off into a nearby papaya tree.

'So it does work,' she said, handing him the rest of the coconut, 'that business about never smiling at a monkey.'

'Yeah,' he said and added approvingly, 'you're getting to be something of a jungle creature yourself.'

'Thanks,' she said, realising he had intended it as a complement but knowing it wasn't true — quite the opposite actually.

In the immediate aftermath of Sanggau, Bethany had tried hard to convince herself that what had happened there had been a one-off, more-or-less, and that she shouldn't allow it to affect her attitude toward the people at Nanga Palin. Certainly, she had heard nothing about massacres, head-hunting, or cannibalism when she was there. And when she had cautiously brought up such subjects, in a detached and circuitous way of course, anything of the sort had been thoroughly denounced. Sometimes bad people started vile rumours, the old ladies had told her, but she mustn't believe them.

In truth, Bethany often didn't know what to believe. The Dayak-Madurese War remained a nearly secret war, embarrassing to the government and, for that reason, barely mentioned in the press. News, often in widely contradictory accounts, was spread by 'jungle telegraph'. The latest item wafting through the rainforest by this method was that half-Madurese children were being killed in an effort to rid their longhouses or their villages of the hated enemy bloodline.

The image of this last horror, the murder of the children in their own homes, probably by their own Dayak relatives, haunted Bethany's dreams and, one night when she couldn't sleep, she raised the subject again with Wolf.

'Is anything like that going on at Nanga Palin?' he asked her, although he knew the answer perfectly well.

'No,' she admitted, 'but then, there aren't any half-Madurese children there.'

'Well, that's okay then, isn't it?'

'No, it bloody well isn't okay,' she cried. 'These people are the ones I have to work with every day and I think they actually approve of what their relatives and friends are doing.'

'How do you know that?' he demanded. 'Have you asked them?'

'Yes.'

'And what do they say?'

'Thumbi said it was a bad thing to do,' she confessed.

'So that's probably what the others think too, isn't it?'

'Possibly.'

'Well, what's your problem, then?' he asked, impatiently.

'I'm not at all sure Thumbi was telling me the truth about what she really felt.'

'Bullshit, you're just determined not to believe her, that's all,' Wolf declared.

'Perhaps,' she conceded, doubtfully.

'Anyway, I didn't think anthropologists were supposed to take a moral attitude toward the people they studied,' Wolf reminded her. 'I mean, aren't you people supposed to stand back and record what you see, good or bad, and not impose your own values on other cultures?'

'That's what they tell us at university but it's not all that easy when awful things are actually happening all around me.'

'Well, don't you think you should to give it a try though?' he suggested, hopefully.

'I have been giving it a try. I'm still here, aren't I, or haven't you noticed?'

'You're making it fucking impossible for me not to notice,' he said with a grin as he ran his hands along the pleasant curvature of her backside. 'I know it's been tough with all this ghastly stuff going on but isn't the purpose of anthropology to explore the whole range of human behaviour?'

'That's what they tell us,' she repeated, well aware of where he was trying to lead her, and reluctant to agree.

'And it's not just supposed to be some kind of rose-coloured love fest with the noble savage, is it?'

'Don't be an idiot.'

'Okay, then, look at it this way. If you and your fellow scribblers only write about the good things the Dayaks do – the Dayaks or whatever group is the flavour of the month – then you aren't going to come up with a very accurate picture of the diversity of the world's cultures, are you?'

'I suppose not,' she confessed.

'So wouldn't it be better,' he urged, 'to stick it out here and go for an accurate representation of what the Dayaks are really like, warts and all?'

He waited for her to argue with this suggestion and when she didn't, he let his caresses become more urgent, made love to her and fell asleep.

Yet as the days crept by, Bethany's steps became slower and slower as she approached the notched log leading up to the communal veranda at Nanga Palin. The heat was really getting to her these days. She was fed up with the difficulties of communicating with people who were, culturally speaking, millions of light years away from her. She was bored with observing, or worse, doing, the same repetitive tasks over and over. She was tired of going to the loo in a flimsy little hut perched out over the river and she had absolutely had enough of forcing herself to eat food that revolted her.

It was around this time that she began to notice that some of the younger men at Nanga Palin were disappearing and staying away for days at a time. Thumbi made excuses for them, insisting that they were off visiting girlfriends in other longhouses and, as much as Bethany wanted to believe this, she had trouble doing it.

Fuck Nanga Palin, fuck Borneo and fuck Wolf, Bethany thought, I have got to get away from here.

She just wished she had stuck to this decision when she was still in Sanggau. It would have been so easy then. She could have just left without a backward glance, but it was going to be so much harder now that she was back at Kanyalang. Explanations would have to be made. The helicopter would have to be booked. Farewells would have to be gone through. Promises to return – promises she knew would be lies – would have to be made to the many kind people who had befriended her at Nanga Palin. Worst of all, Wolf would have to be dealt with and that, she realised, as she fell asleep in his arms, would be so hard she couldn't bear to think about it.

So as day followed day, she found reasons to postpone the farewells at Nanga Palin, arrange for the helicopter and book the tickets back to the UK. And little by little, during this interlude of procrastination and uncertainty, things began to change.

The fighting between the Dayaks and the Madurese tapered off. Nobody won. Nothing was really settled but, with an end to the killing and a return to a state of quiescent hostility between the two groups, Bethany couldn't help wondering if the reasons for staying didn't outweigh the ones for going.

The Dayaks had done terrible things. That was undeniable. Even so, she thought, if you looked at the historical record, did the Europeans really come out any better — or the Americans? Perhaps cannibalism wasn't quite their thing and they didn't have a particular penchant for beheading their victims but they had certainly been responsible for their share of atrocities. And were the Africans or the other Asians, people that so often engaged the attention of anthropologists, really any better? She didn't think so.

Bethany voiced these thoughts to Wolf as they lingered on the veranda after the others had turned in for the night.

'You're right,' he agreed, 'human beings are a nasty lot when you come down to it.'

'Animals are much nicer,' she said.

'Especially wolves,' he said, pulling her to him, kissing her and then leading her back to his room.

Within a few moments the complexities of the human condition lay discarded, along with their clothes, on the floor beside the bed.

Gradually Bethany moved her departure plans back from 'as soon as possible' to 'sometime soon' to 'after Giri's wedding' to a vaguely suitable but unspecified date in the distant future. And during that time she was happier than she could ever remember. She scarcely noticed that the expected rains of July and August did little more than dampen the top of the forest canopy.

September was worse. Not only did the expected rains fail to arrive, allowing the temperature to rise to desperately uncomfortable heights, but a more sinister development threatened the well-being of the little group at Kanyalang.

Instead of rain, the air began to fill with smoke.

Initially this was not alarming. Bethany knew that a certain amount of smoke was inevitable as the Dayaks set their annual fires to clear the land for the next planting. It had been done at this time every year for longer than even Thumbi could remember. The problem was that in recent years bigger and bigger fires had been set by plantation owners who wanted to make way for new oil palm production and by logging companies intent on opening up access to valuable tropical hardwoods. And with virtually no rain this year to stop them, these all-embracing infernos were burning out of control, laying waste to everything in their path.

By late September much of the arboreal growth of hundreds of years had been reduced to ashes. Animals, the ones that weren't burnt alive, starved to death as their habitats were incinerated and by the end of the month the morning song of the siamang gibbons no longer wafted through the longhouse at Kanyalang.

The smoke from the fires soon invaded Borneo's towns and cities where it mixed with noxious fumes from badly maintained vehicles and with toxic emissions from factories. Most of the inhabitants merely coughed and choked and wiped their streaming eyes while they tried to go about some semblance of their normal lives. But others, less fortunate than their neighbours, were forced to watch as their young children and elderly parents died from the respiratory infections brought by the poisonous air – an enveloping blanket of death that became euphemistically known as 'the haze'.

Everyone at Kanyalang, from Elliot to Kolop, was enraged by the official greed and deliberate blindness that made all the waste and suffering possible.

'If those arseholes would just put a stop to the illegal incursions into the rainforest,' Wolf fumed virtually every day, 'the fires could be kept to manageable levels.'

Everyone agreed but they all knew that private gain at public expense was too well-entrenched in the system to be likely to disappear any time soon. Too much money had changed hands. So as the deadly haze spread northward to Singapore, Malaysia and even the southern Philippines, there were cries of outrage from Indonesia's neighbours but only muted criticism of the government and of the president's cronies in the local press. Editors were too aware of the dangers of attacking the rich and powerful to give the story the attention it deserved. Nevertheless, mutterings of discontent echoed through the streets of the towns as the noxious haze grew ever thicker and deadlier. Schools were closed. Children were kept indoors. Tourism revenues evaporated. Airline operations were seriously disrupted and foreign businessmen stayed away.

On some days the haze was much worse than on others. There were times when the visibility at airports in the region sank to little more than a few metres. But on relatively good days planes managed to get through and on one of these days a letter from Catherine came for Bethany.

She opened it and read,

Dear Bethany,

I keep starting letters to Bima and then tossing them in the bin when I remember how horrid he was to me about those silly maps so I'm writing to you instead. I'm not going to bother trying to make him understand anymore.

Of course, you weren't much better but at least you stood by me during that dreadful abortion time and that was more important. I won't ever forget that.

Anyway, it all seems so very far away now. But I hope everyone at Kanyalang realises how stupid and mean they were to make such a fuss about what I did. Any help I may have given the loggers doesn't make any difference now, does it? The fires are destroying it all anyway.

I also hope you're not letting that tyrant, Elliot, keep you there in the path of the flames and that horrible haze. Staying there and burning up or choking to death won't do anything for the rainforest, will it?

You'll be glad to know that in spite of what Elliot and Wolf did to me, sending me away like that, everything has turned out really well here. The pittance I got for the maps has been enough to keep me going, barely, for a little while. Then I'm going to start teaching at uni again when the new term begins.

So everything has really worked out for the best, hasn't it?

Love, Catherine

The letter made Bethany feel so sick that she tore it in two when she finished it. Catherine's complacency, her utter self-absorption and her lack of remorse made her want to scream. Then five minutes later she went in search of some tape so she could put it back together again and show it to Wolf.

She found him on the veranda. 'Here, read this,' she said, thrusting it toward him.

Wolf ran his eyes over it quickly and then in disgust read it aloud to Marguarita and Elliot who had already come in search of a beer.

Marguarita was the first to find her voice. 'That letter makes me want to throw up,' she said.

'Who would have thought everything we were doing here could mean so little to her?' Elliot murmured more to himself than to anybody else.

'I sure as hell never guessed,' Mike said, shaking his head in amazement.

'I don't suppose any of us did,' said Elliot, searching his mind for something that would explain away, or at least mitigate, the appalling selfishness expressed in the letter. 'Perhaps it's her illness that's making her say those things. We shouldn't necessarily assume it's the real Catherine speaking.'

'The real Catherine,' exclaimed Marguarita scornfully. 'None of us have ever seen the real Catherine. She was always acting. She was far too sweet and angelic to be genuine – and too dippy, as well.'

'You're not talking about Catherine, are you?' said Bima joining the group and picking up the letter. 'Goddamn Tarique,' he said, 'if it hadn't been for his influence –'

'She would have been just as scheming and self-centred and greedy,' Marguarita pointed out, finishing his sentence for him.

A lively discussion broke out as, with the illumination of hindsight, everyone except Bima began relating incidents when Catherine's behaviour hadn't rung true. And for the first time in days, conversation on the veranda centred on something besides the inexorable progress of the haze.

CHAPTER THIRTY-EIGHT

News of the spreading fires became worse every day. And as the weeks passed and the devastation came ever nearer to Kanyalang, an opaque cocktail of smoke, dust and ash settled over the open veranda of the longhouse, oozed through the half-finished structure of the hotel and coated everyone's throat and lungs with a layer of viscous poison.

'Don't you think it's about time you declared a holiday?' Marguarita suggested to Elliot one afternoon as they converged on the thermos of cool water outside Pashetta's office.

'She's right, you know,' said Mike, coughing loudly as he strode toward the veranda steps.

'Holiday,' Elliot repeated, looking at them as if they had each sprouted a second head, 'what on earth are you talking about?'

'All this,' Mike said, waving his arm in the direction of the open air, 'and there's no guarantee it won't get worse,' he added, ominously.

'Don't you think we should leave while the helicopter can still get here to take us out?' Marguarita urged.

'Close up shop when we're not in any danger?' exclaimed Elliot in the patronising tone he usually reserved for Bethany. 'That wouldn't do at all now, would it?'

'Most of the fires are well to the east and south of us,' put in Wolf, emerging from his office and adding to the general realignment of forces by taking Elliot's part. 'We should be okay at least for the time being.'

'In other words we should wait until we're trapped before we do anything?' snapped Marguarita. 'Brilliant.'

'I don't think that's likely to happen,' Elliot assured her, 'and I can't very well order an evacuation and shut down this entire project without compelling reasons.'

'Forget about reasons. Find an excuse,' warned Mike, 'or by the time you want to sort something out, it could be too late.'

'The airport in Pontianak has been closed for two days now,' Marguarita pointed out, 'and who knows how long it will stay that way. That sounds rather compelling to me.'

'Not to me,' countered Wolf. 'Most of the traffic in Pontianak airport is fixed wing aircraft. We're talking about choppers here and they can fly in almost anything. They'll be able to get through and take us out of here if we need them.'

Elliot nodded, for once welcoming Wolf's contribution. 'Yes, but I don't think it's going to come to that,' he said. 'The wind will pick up before long and that will clear the air.'

'Before long might be too long,' Marguarita retorted sharply.

Yet much to her chagrin she had to admit that the next day proved him right. A gentle breeze dissipated the worst of the haze and the planes began flying again. The air at Kanyalang was breathable once more and excuses to stay within the confines of air-conditioned offices were jettisoned. Life returned to normal – almost.

Some small changes the haze had made in their daily routines weren't dropped immediately. One of these was the attention paid to the nightly weather report, previously considered boring by everyone except Elliot. Now they all gathered eagerly around the shortwave radio hoping to hear that a rain, one heavy enough to tame the fires, was approaching. A fierce tropical downpour would have the added benefit of lowering the pollution level. Although it wasn't as bad at Kanyalang as it was in the towns and cities, it was enough to leave them with reddened eyes and rasping throats.

The strength and direction of the wind was also a matter of intense interest although, unlike the longed-for rain, the wind was a double-edged sword. Not only could it disperse the haze but it could also fan the fires and so was regarded with a mixture of apprehension and hope.

Another change, one that happened so gradually that no one really noticed, was Mike's role in the evening gatherings on the veranda. Instead of being primarily a listener, merely putting in a word or two now and then, he found that he was frequently the one who did the most talking.

It was his sightings of rarely-seen animals from Borneo's improbable menagerie that brought about this miracle. Desperate to escape the smoke and flames that were turning their traditional habitats to ashes, the creatures were venturing farther and farther from their preferred surroundings, enabling Mike to regale his colleagues with stories of his encounters with them.

One day, to Pashetta's distress, he even reported having caught a glimpse of a reclusive sun bear, arguably the most dangerous animal in Borneo. It had been lurking in a thick tangle of leaves and vines when he came across it, he told them, and he had taken great care not to make any noise and to stay down-wind of it. He was well aware that, far from deriving its name from a sunny disposition, this smallest member of the bear family was a fractious creature that needed little or no provocation to go on the attack with the full force of its scalpel-sharp teeth and intestine-ripping claws.

A couple of days later Mike had everyone in stitches when he told them about coming across a bearcat.

'A what?' Bethany exclaimed.

'Make up your mind,' Bima laughed, 'which was it?'

'Neither,' Mike said and went on to describe the animal's very odd appearance, the thing that had led to its name.

'It sounds like a fluffy whiskery offspring of an inter-species romance,' Bethany said. 'Did it try to attack you or anything?'

'No, it was looking very relaxed.'

'How can you tell when a bearcat is relaxed?' Marguarita wanted to know.

'Well, for one thing, it was just sort of hanging there, dangling by its tail —'

'That doesn't sound very comfortable,' Bethany put in.

'If you've got a prehensile tail, a really strong one, and like to swing from branches it might be just the thing,' suggested Wolf and they all laughed.

Of course, many of Mike's sightings were of life forms that were distinctly lacking in the cuddly factor such as unusual varieties of snakes, leeches, bugs, and insects, most of which were highly likely to sting or bite. Nevertheless he soon found that he enjoyed drawing squeals of 'ugh' or 'how awful' or 'yuck' from Pashetta and Bethany. It made him feel like a kid again, the kind of strong brave hunk that all the girls were dying to have sex with, not the useless adolescent he had actually been.

Generally though, he accepted the fact that he was not Crocodile Dundee and he enjoyed relating his pleasanter encounters, such as the one he had with a little tarsier one day. It had been extraordinary, he told them all, because the wide-eyed little primates were definitely nocturnal. This one must have been driven from its habitat by the fires and was so disoriented that it had stayed awake during the day.

'In any case, there it was, staring down at me from the branch of a tree,' Mike said, 'looking very wise and kind of startled, a bit sad and scared too.'

'At Nanga Palin they say that animals know when something bad is going to happen – know it before people do,' Bethany said.

'Animals can sense it somehow,' Pashetta added, 'nobody knows quite how.'

Everyone looked at her in surprise. She was usually so contemptuous of anything that touched on Dayak folklore.

This time it was Elliot's turn to rubbish it. 'How can they possibly have any idea what animals know?' he demanded, not expecting an answer.

Bethany surprised him. 'By their behaviour,' she said, 'they do strange things they wouldn't ordinarily do.'

'That's true, actually,' Pashetta agreed, 'they do. In Yogyakarta they can tell when Mount Merapi is going to erupt because the animals come farther down the mountain. They're always right, you know.'

'I don't know any such thing,' Wolf declared but he turned to Mike and added, 'I'd kind of like to come along with you sometime, maybe this afternoon, if that's okay, and get a look at some of these beasties. You know the ones that don't usually poke their noses out where we can see them.'

'Sure, but I can't absolutely guarantee you any noses.'

'That's okay, I'll take my chances,' Wolf replied, not suspecting what it was that chance had in store for him.

No one else suspected it either and it was only when the two men hadn't come back by the time everyone was ready for drinks on the veranda that Bethany remarked, 'Heavens, they must have gone a long way.'

'Or done something idiotic like getting lost,' laughed Marguarita.

'They wouldn't do that,' retorted Bethany.

'Maybe they were attacked by a dangerous animal,' Pashetta suggested, looking distinctly worried.

Elliot scoffed at this notion but when dinner was over and the two men still weren't back, he got a little irritated.

'They ought to know better than to go wandering around the jungle after dark,' he fumed and as the hours passed without any sign of them, his irritation changed to concern and he had trouble getting to sleep.

Neither Bethany nor Pashetta even tried to sleep very much that night. Instead, they passed the long hours drinking endless cups of tea on the veranda and leaping up at every unexpected sound.

'Do you think they've gone to Nanga Palin?' Pashetta suggested, around midnight.

'Why ever would they want to do that?' Bethany replied and then felt like a fool because she knew exactly what Pashetta had in mind.

'Play with bad girls.'

Bethany smiled at this Victorian description of longhouse sex and said, 'I doubt it, somehow.'

'Wolf used to do it when he was with me. And maybe Mike does it too. All men are very bad, you know,' she added, thinking that Bethany needed a little instruction in the realities of life.

Sleep eluded Elliot as well, and the amount of whisky in the bottle on his desk diminished as the hours passed. He annoyed Bethany and Pashetta by popping out of his room every couple of hours to remind them to let him know the instant the two men came back.

Bima managed to sleep but enormous monitor lizards rampaged through his dreams, savaging his hotel while Saskia stood by watching and crying and saying she wouldn't spend another moment in this horrible place.

Even Marguarita found it difficult to sleep. Each time she slipped into a light doze, sounds that wouldn't have troubled her on an ordinary night – frogs and lizards, rats and civet cats, wild dogs

385

and jungle pigs – conspired to keep her nerves taut and her mind active. Then towards morning, as the buzz of insects swarming outside her window and the crows of the roosters heralding the coming day added their commotion to the night time hullabaloo, she felt a curious sensation of impending evil. Opening her eyes in the semi-darkness she made out the form of a man hovering just above the bed – Tarique.

The sight was so alarming that it woke her up and the idea of a ghostly visitation was quickly laid to rest. It had been nothing but a bad dream generated, no doubt, by her worries about Wolf and Mike. And the curried catfish Kolop had served up for dinner might have had something to do with it too, she decided.

She was just drifting back to sleep when a startling, and not altogether welcome, possibility occurred to her. If Tarique's 'appearance' had been a manifestation of her fears for Wolf and Mike, it must mean she was seriously worried about them. And if this was true, if she cared that much about what might be happening to them, was she really the bitch some people took her for – not that she gave a damn? Or could it be that in some significant way her nature was changing? Was she going soft, sentimental and dippy like the people she had always despised? She wasn't at all sure she liked the idea of the jungle making her into quite a different person from the one she had been when she came to Kanyalang.

She reviewed the recent past in her mind to see if she could find a moment when such a transformation might have begun and lighted on the recollection of the banded krait uncoiling itself to strike at Tarique. She hadn't been troubled by any bothersome milk of human kindness then. She had watched the fatal moment unfold with the same detachment she would have brought to the viewing of a second rate film.

If she had known about Tarique's involvement with the gold mines at the time, or with the maps, that would have been one thing. But she hadn't known. She had merely had a feeling that he was up to something and that, whatever it was, it wasn't doing the jungle any good. She had acted on intuition rather than on evidence and how unscientific was that, she asked herself? Before she came out here she would never have done anything like that. It would have been completely against her nature.

Wondering if the jungle could be having an equally important effect on anyone else, Marguarita paraded them one by one through her mind. Surely there must have been a few changes, she thought, although it wasn't easy to recognise them in people she saw every day.

Elliot, she decided after careful consideration, was getting more and more reclusive, making it much too easy for Wolf to expand his power and grow more assertive and arrogant than ever. And Mike — he had changed more than anyone. He was certainly less introverted then he used to be. He actually talked these days and occasionally showed signs of nearly human intelligence.

Bethany was different too, Marguarita reflected. She's lost that Alice in Wonderland quality she had when she first came here. Of course, being around Wolf as much as she was these days would be enough to turn the Easter Bunny into a cynic. Anyway, she's certainly more jungle-wise and confident now than she used to be.

Actually Pashetta is probably the one who's changed the most, Marguarita concluded, although the jungle might not have much to do with it. She looks so happy these days. It just shows what being in love will do. She lights up like a firefly whenever Mike's around, which is more than she ever did with Wolf. Of course when she was alone with his passport, Marguarita thought uncharitably, it might have been a different story. Not that Wolf deserved any better. He got what he wanted out of that relationship and she was quite certain that he never had any intention of giving Pashetta what she wanted.

Bima was a bit of a mystery though, she mused. Could he be the one person who hadn't been changed very much by his time at Kanyalang, or had he been affected by it in some deep interior way known only to himself?

It was a question she couldn't answer. Outwardly he still seemed much the same and she wondered if his obsession with his work, with the hotel and with 'fusion architecture' as he called it might have been enough to insulate him, to a certain extent at least, from the disillusionment that the revelations about Catherine must surely have brought about.

It would have disconcerted Bima to know how close Marguarita's sharp eyes came to seeing into the deepest parts of his psyche and comprehending the pain that lay hidden there.

What she had no way of knowing, because he didn't talk about it, was the extent to which memories of Saskia, self-possessed and detached yet graceful and alluring as ever, served as a balm to the wounds Catherine's defection had inflicted on his ego. Images of her kept coming into his mind and he became determined that she had to see the hotel standing tall and beautiful when it was finished – if not before. If she didn't, there would always be a part of him that she wouldn't understand. But what did that matter, he asked himself? They had split up, hadn't they? And since then, he had been in love with someone else, disappointing as that love had proved to be.

Of course, he warned himself, there must be someone else in Saskia's life by now, although there was always a chance that her recent love affairs hadn't fared any better than his. He couldn't help hoping that was true because, for the first time in months, he was overwhelmed with a desire to see her again. And perhaps it was just possible that they could take up where they had left off.

On the other hand, why go back to a relationship that hadn't worked, Bima asked himself? Was it that, after having made such a colossal mistake with Catherine, he didn't see how he could ever trust his judgement again? He knew Saskia. He knew what it was like to talk to her, to have sex with her, to wake up with her in the morning. Sometimes he even knew what she was thinking. And the most important thing he knew about her was that she would never betray his trust the way Catherine had.

The trouble was, he thought frowning, that he just didn't know if it would be possible to have any kind of real relationship with someone he didn't actually share a life with. He knew there would be no chance of getting Saskia to live out here in Indonesia, though, of course, it shouldn't be too difficult to persuade her to come out for holidays. Still it wouldn't really be much of a shared life. If they were ever to live together on a daily basis, he'd have to go back to Holland, or at least, to some country in Europe. Would that be so bad, he wondered? Not really, he liked Holland and a part of him, an important part, was Dutch.

The problem was that the Dutch part of him was only one part. There was the Indonesian part too and that would be stifled if he worked in Europe. The climate there simply wasn't suited to the fusion of Western and Indonesian architectural styles that had become the springboard for his creativity. Not even the British were convinced that freezing all winter was a necessary part of life anymore.

Of course he could give up on the fusion stuff, he told himself, and concentrate on conventional domestic architecture but he knew he wasn't about to do that. Two diverse strains of influences had made him the man he was and if he didn't give some measure of expression to each, he wouldn't ever be able to produce anything original or worthwhile.

If Saskia could just see the hotel, Bima thought, perhaps she would understand a bit more about him. Then, if she wasn't involved with someone else by now, perhaps they could work something out. It would inevitably have to be a long distance affair but there could actually be advantages in that. It would mean less intimacy, of course, but it would offer more freedom. And it might even give a romantic charm to the times when they actually saw each other, make them appreciate each other's company in a way that people who were together all the time seldom did.

CHAPTER THIRTY-NINE

No one else at Kanyalang would have been capable of appreciating much of anything the next day, suffering as they were from a combination of sleep deprivation and worry about their missing colleagues.

One of the effects of this was to put a damper on all but the most cursory verbal exchanges at breakfast so, toward the end of the meal, when Wolf and Mike, dirty, exhausted, scratched and bedraggled, climbed the veranda stairs, their first thought was to wonder why everything was so curiously quiet.

Pashetta, who heard their footsteps before anyone else did, squeaked, 'There they are,' and rushed from the table to throw her arms around Mike.

'Where the hell have you been?' barked Elliot, rather like an irate father telling off two wayward teenagers.

'You look awful,' observed Marguarita.

'Thanks,' returned Wolf, with a wry smile, 'I wish I could say the same for you but the truth is you've never looked so good, not to me, anyway.'

'Nor to me,' agreed Mike.

'Whatever happened to you?' cried Bethany.

'Nothing I ever want to happen again,' replied Wolf, 'but I've got to have a bath and a cup of coffee before I tell you about it.'

Mike echoed this view on the urgency of a bath, declared he'd kill for a cup of tea and added that they both were starving.

It was Wolf, partially restored to his old self after the bath and the coffee, who embarked on the tale but his usual facility with speech seemed to have deserted him.

'It all started when I caught a glimpse of the most incredible feathers,' he began, 'bright orange head gear like you've never seen, so of course I knew right away that it couldn't be anything but a rhinoceros hornbill.'

There was a gasp of envy from Marguarita.

'But that's only the beginning,' he went on. 'The thing that made it a once-in-a-lifetime experience was that the bird, a male obviously, was right in the middle of sealing its mate up in the hollow of a tree for the duration.'

'The duration of what?' asked Pashetta.

'Her pregnancy.'

'How horrible,' she exclaimed.

Wolf shrugged. 'If you're a male hornbill, that's what you do,' he said. 'It's an established ritual of the species. But for a guy like me to get a chance to stand there and watch it – I could scarcely believe my luck. I don't think I even let myself breathe, I was that mesmerised.'

'Yeah, that was the trouble,' put in Mike.

Wolf didn't disagree. Instead, trying to put the best possible face on a what had turned into thoroughly embarrassing episode, he went on, 'That's why I didn't notice that there was this scaly bastard circling around in the river giving me the evil eye. It wasn't all that close but crocs can travel fast when they want to and this one was a monster, at least fifteen feet long. And for some reason, I didn't exactly dig the idea of being chewed up like a piece of prime steak.'

'More of a wolfburger in your case,' put in Marguarita.

'Where the hell were you during all this?' demanded Elliot, turning to Mike. 'Why weren't you and your rangers giving Wolf the back-up he needed?'

'We weren't there,' Mike said.

Surprised looks flew around the table.

'Not there,' thundered Elliot, 'why the hell not?'

'Hold on,' Wolf interjected hastily, 'you can't blame Mike, or the rangers either. I ditched them, not the other way around.'

'You can't mean you were just wandering around on your own,' Elliot protested.

'I'm afraid that's exactly what I do mean,' Wolf acknowledged.

'You idiot, not even a boy scout would have done anything that stupid,' fumed Elliot.

'What's stupid for a boy scout isn't necessarily the same thing for me,' declared Wolf.

'A boy scout might have figured out that going off half-cocked on his own wasn't –' began Marguarita.

'Never mind about that,' growled Elliot. 'What I want to know is what the hell made you do it.'

'I know it's going to sound crazy,' Wolf said, 'but you've got to put it in the context of an absolutely mind-blowing day – one that began, believe it or not, with a sighting of a sun bear. Now how lucky was that? It must have been driven out of its usual stamping ground by the fires. I mean you could probably spend the rest of your life prowling around the rainforest and never actually come face to face with one.'

'Face to face,' repeated Elliot, horrified.

'Well, not exactly,' Wolf admitted, 'it was really more like face to arse end, the latter belonging to the bear, so she didn't see me and I took care to stay down wind of her.'

'Don't tell me you followed her,' exclaimed Elliot.

'Of course I followed her,' Wolf said. 'You don't think I'd let a chance to trail a sun bear get away from me, do you?'

'A sun bear with two cubs,' put in Mike, wanting to stress the risk of being anywhere near this fur-bearing concentration of teeth, claws and muscles. 'I wasn't going to put my rangers' lives at risk, or the bear's life either – remember, if it had attacked we would have had to shoot it – just to give Wolf an interesting day out. So that's how he ended up going off on his own and why none of the rest of us were around when he saw the hornbill or when the crocodile, no doubt with a big smile on its face, spotted him.'

'How did you find each other again?' asked Bethany.

There was a moment's silence before Wolf admitted, 'Mike found me.'

'Not till morning, though,' Mike added.

'What took you so long?' asked Elliot who no longer had any sympathy for either of them.

'I wasn't looking in the trees,' Mike grinned.

'The trees?' repeated Marguarita. 'Why would you be looking there?' But the words were barely out of her mouth when she hooted with laughter. 'You don't mean –'

'Yes, I do,' returned Mike, his eyes twinkling with malicious amusement, 'that's where I found him.'

'In a tree,' chorused all three women, laughing their heads off.

The only thing Wolf could do was squirm. It was the most thoroughly mortifying moment of his life.

'What were you doing in a tree?' asked Bima wonderingly.

'Avoiding the fucking crocodile – what do you think?'

'How long did you have to stay there?' Bethany asked.

'All night.'

'You can't mean it was circling around beneath you all that time,' exclaimed Bima incredulously.

'It might have been,' replied Wolf, defensively, 'how was I to know? Once it got dark I couldn't see whether the fucking thing was there or not. And I wasn't about to take a chance.'

'You must have been frightfully cold,' said Bethany, feeling she should show a little sympathy between giggles.

'And hungry,' added Pashetta.

'And exhausted,' put in Bima.

'And feeling like the world's number one fathead,' suggested Marguarita.

'Right on all counts,' Wolf admitted.

'Where were you during all this?' demanded Elliot, fixing Mike with an icy stare.

'Pretty much staying put at first so this idiot', he motioned in Wolf's direction, 'would be able to come back and find us. But of course he didn't so eventually we – the Dayak guys, actually – tracked him to his tree.'

'It was a pretty rough night all around,' added Wolf.

'At least, I had my feet on the ground and had some guys with me,' Mike said, feeling that Wolf had taken enough flak by this time. 'I wasn't alone like he was so I didn't have it so bad.'

'Spending a night up a tree with a crocodile snapping at your toes can't be anybody's idea of fun,' observed Bima.

Wolf, far from appreciating any sympathy at this point, just wanted to die of shame at the memory of the predicament he had got himself into. For years he had prided himself on being jungle-wise, being the one who knew everything worth knowing about the tropical rainforest, the one who was capable of coping with any situation the steamy wilderness could throw at him. In short, he had seen himself as the king of the jungle – until last night.

Now he had to face the fact that he wasn't so great after all and he was so taken aback by this ego-shattering revelation that he didn't even notice that later in the day there was a shift in the direction of the wind.

Kolop was the first one to detect the change.

Although Elliot had ordered one of those foreign fishing lines for him, he preferred to catch his prey with his hands the way he had always done so he had waded out into the centre of the river in search of a tasty specimen for the evening meal. As a result, he was well-positioned to notice when the breeze blowing across his bare chest veered around and started coming from the east instead of the west. He stopped what he was doing, scanned the horizon, didn't like what he saw and glumly clambered out of the water without any fish.

This change in the direction of the wind was greeted with similar dismay at Nanga Palin. Bethany, who had stayed on later than usual to help with the preparations for Giri's wedding, due to take place in a few days, gradually began to notice that the happiness warranted by the occasion seemed to be on the wane. People were gathering in small groups on the veranda, apprehension written clearly on their faces, and talking in low tones about the wind, the fires and the possible anger of the gods.

Bethany, straining to hear what was being said, caught words like 'rice fields' and 'huts' and 'tomorrow morning' and was trying to put them together in her mind when Thumbi, in much sharper tones than she ordinarily used, told her to go back to Kanyalang.

'But why?' protested Bethany, surveying the cloudless sky and seeing no sign of anything that necessitated an immediate return.

Thumbi was not given to answering 'why' questions and her manner was unexpectedly imperious as she reiterated her instruction and added, 'We will go to rice fields far away. You must go with Kanyalang people. They will be worried about the wind too and make plans.'

This seemed rather unlikely to Bethany but, deciding that no good would come from arguing with Thumbi, she obeyed.

When she got back to Kanyalang she saw that she had been right.

The shift in the wind had not aroused the same interest there that it had at Nanga Palin. Kolop, Rajang, and the few other Dayaks who were still about the place late that afternoon were the only ones who had noticed and they slipped silently away. Kolop, who was the last to go, thoughtfully left a large plate of sandwiches and a dish of cut up fruit on the kitchen table.

Everyone else at Kanyalang, the expats, Pashetta, and the skilled labourers working on the hotel, were essentially transplanted city-dwellers and were not in the habit of paying much attention to the wind unless, as it was doing today, it brought some relief from the sweltering heat.

'What a heavenly breeze,' Marguarita exclaimed, as she took a cold beer from the ice chest on the veranda and eagerly began to drink it.

'Not bad,' agreed Bima who, along with Mike, was enjoying his usual evening tipple on the veranda.

Wolf was there too but, still feeling much diminished by his recent folly, was sitting a bit apart from the others and being uncharacteristically silent.

Mike didn't share Marguarita's enthusiasm for the gusts of air now wafting their way. 'I'm not sure it's so heavenly,' he replied, 'more like the breeze from hell, I'd say.'

'You're grumpy today,' she chided him. 'What's the matter with a breath of cool air?'

'The direction it's coming from,' he replied, waving his glass toward the eastern periphery of the project clearing, 'that way.'

'Is that so bad?' asked Bima.

'Damn right it is,' Mike returned. 'The fires are over there.'

'They're not likely to get to us here, are they?' Marguarita asked casually.

'Who knows?' Mike said. 'The wind might change again, but then it might not. In any case I think it's time to read the riot act to Elliot — you know, lay it on the line about getting out of here and getting out fast.'

Elliot who had come out of his room in time to hear his name asked, 'What's all this about?'

Marguarita didn't need time to sharpen her claws. She was more than ready to go on the attack. It wouldn't be the first time she had tackled Elliot about suspending operations until the dangers from the fires and the haze were past.

'Just how long are you intending to keep us here, right in the path of the flames?' she demanded.

Elliot, taken aback at the unexpected ferocity of the onslaught, exclaimed, 'Haven't we discussed —'

'Yes we have,' she agreed, 'but the winds have changed and they're bringing the fires right this way, right towards us. You may want to stay here and let yourself be turned into a human torch but I promise you I don't.'

'Come now, don't you think we should look at this a little more calmly?' Elliot replied.

'I think we can very calmly say,' Mike put in before Marguarita had a chance, 'that you've finally got the 'compelling reasons' for an evacuation you were waiting for. The fires are now a serious danger for Kanyalang.'

'Are you sure you're not jumping to conclusions?' Elliot asked.

'You don't have to jump very high to see that there's a rim of red on the horizon,' Mike pointed out. 'Have a look.'

Elliot went over to the veranda rail and surveyed the sky determined to belittle their fears but he changed his mind when he saw a flicker of pink in the eastern sky. 'I see what you mean,' he admitted, 'but it won't do to rush into anything, you know. The wind may shift again tomorrow and send the fires off in the opposite direction.'

'Sure,' Mike acknowledged, 'that could happen but there's no guarantee.'

'Well, we'll just have to wait and see, won't we?' Elliot said.

'No,' declared Mike firmly, 'that's not an option we've got anymore. It's too risky.'

The temptation to plunge into the fray, seize control and sort everything out was too much for Wolf. 'All this wait-and-see business has gone on too damn long already,' he declared.

'You've changed your tune,' Elliot pointed out, sharply. 'The last time we talked about this —'

'I know,' Wolf replied, impatiently. 'I was wrong.'

'Did I hear you correctly?' exclaimed Marguarita in astonishment. 'Did you actually admit you were wrong about something?'

'No need rub it in,' retorted Wolf.

'I'm not rubbing it in,' she smiled, 'I'm just savouring it to the fullest. After all it's a moment that may never come again.'

'Do any of you have any idea what an evacuation would involve?' demanded Elliot, 'in terms of time and organisation and expense?'

'Do you have any idea that people's lives, our lives, are on the line here?' Wolf flung back at him. 'Everything depends on what that fucking wind is going to do and, since nobody knows for sure, we've no choice but to take the worst-case possibility and run with it. Time and expense don't come into it, nor does the fact that it'll be a pain in the arse to organise. It's just something we've got to do.'

'I'm glad you feel that way,' Elliot said smoothly, 'because now I won't have any qualms about putting you in charge of organising it.'

'You got it,' said Wolf and both men felt they had won a victory of sorts.

'Don't forget the guys working on the hotel,' Bima put in, 'There're a lot of them you know.'

'Yeah, cast of thousands,' agreed Wolf.

'That's going to mean quite a number of helicopter trips,' warned Elliot.

'Don't worry, we'll manage,' Wolf said, with an assurance Elliot found extremely irritating.

'God only knows what it'll cost,' he growled.

'A fucking fortune, I expect,' returned Wolf cheerfully.

'The RRF will just have to come up with money, won't it,' declared Marguarita. 'After all they can't exactly throw us on a funeral pyre just because it's the cheapest way of dealing with us.'

'How about the Nanga Palin people?' Mike said. 'A lot of them work for us too. We can't just leave them and their families to be burned alive.'

'I don't think we have to worry about them,' said Bethany, joining the group in time to hear this. And before Mike could register his indignation at the thought of abandoning them, she explained, 'They seem to have their own solution.'

Everyone looked at her in surprise.

'What sort of solution can they have?' Elliot asked.

They found out the next morning.

CHAPTER FORTY

Elliot was the first one up and hence the one to discover that no preparations had been made for breakfast. There wasn't even any hot water to make a cup of tea and he didn't know how he could possibly start the day without one.

He would just have to fan the damn charcoals and heat up some water himself, he decided.

He struggled with the coals for more than half an hour before he managed to bring a little water to a tentative boil and by that time he was so hot and so cross that he barely wanted the tea. He took a sip anyway and after tasting it he wanted it even less. Perhaps the water hadn't been quite hot enough, he reflected, but, since he clearly wasn't going to get anything better anytime soon, he took the cup out onto the veranda and turned his attention to the question of the prevailing wind.

There was little doubt that the haze was distinctly worse in the east. After peering at it for a few minutes in the hope that it might begin to clear, or simply drift away, he thought he noticed a difference, although not the sort of difference he wanted to see, in the rim of red on the horizon. It was probably just his imagination, he told himself. But if that rim of red in the distance really was getting bigger, if the fires really were coming toward Kanyalang, well, there was only so much he could delegate to Wolf. The ultimate responsibility for getting everyone on the project out to safety would lie with him.

The enormity of the undertaking horrified him. For the first time he found that he was actually glad that Wolf was around. Irritating as the fellow was, his help would be worth having at a time like this. He'd take a reasonable level-headed approach to it all, whereas the others — he just wasn't sure how much he trusted their judgement.

Footsteps along the veranda roused him from his thoughts and he turned to see Pashetta and Mike coming out in search of breakfast. Too bad for them, Elliot told himself, they won't get a decent cup of tea either. But he had to revise this view when

Pashetta, with an expertise acquired in childhood, began fanning the charcoals.

'My granny always cooked over coals,' she explained.

Mike watched her for a few minutes and then, seeing that it was hot work, pushed her aside and took over the task himself. Bethany was the next to come looking for breakfast, followed shortly by a sleepy-eyed Wolf, and soon they were each taking a turn fanning the coals. By the time Bima appeared and wondered what was going on, steaming cups of tea and coffee, supplemented by bread and pineapple jam were spread out on the table on the veranda.

'You know, I never properly appreciated Kolop before,' Bethany confessed. 'Do you realise it's taken four of us to do his job?'

'And we haven't even done half of it,' Mike pointed out. 'Where're the eggs, for a start?'

Wolf raised his cup of black coffee. 'To Kolop,' he said and they all joined in, 'a well deserved salute from all of us.'

Marguarita was the last to wake up and by the time she got to the veranda everyone was looking out over rail. There was no argument about the rim of red on the horizon. Everyone saw it and agreed that it was wider and nearer than it had been the night before.

'I always said we shouldn't have to rely on a rented helicopter,' Marguarita reminded Elliot. 'Now everyone's going to be trying to call one in and it's going to be a nightmare.'

'Quite,' he said, coldly. He hadn't been blind to the usefulness of Kanyalang having its own helicopter and had, in fact, drawn the attention of the RRF to this very subject on several occasions. But they had replied that it was far more cost effective simply to hire one when it was needed.

Well, he'd just have to do his best to see that they got hold of one now, Elliot realised. That was one task he didn't want to leave to Wolf so he'd better not waste any time getting to that iridium phone.

Bima, mesmerised by the ominous rim of red along the eastern horizon, wasn't paying any attention to the talk of helicopters. He was thinking only of his beloved hotel and whether or not it was going to be incinerated by the approaching flames. Were they coming nearer – the question kept pounding through his mind. Was his beautiful creation, the one he had worked on so hard, poured his heart into, going to be reduced to a pile of ashes? If that happened, something in him would die with it, he was certain of that.

'Hey, wake up, mate,' said Mike, coming up behind him and slapping him on the back. 'This is no time for day dreaming, not if we want to be ready to get out of here at a moment's notice.'

There was no arguing with that so, hard as it was for him to do it, Bima pulled himself together and joined the general frenzy of activity.

Marguarita was soon in the throes of preparation, selecting out the most important slides and samples to take with her. It was a daunting task and she was far from finished when the sound of coughing alerted her to the fact that someone was coming up the steps of the office veranda, someone who had not spent the morning in air conditioning.

It turned out to be Bethany, back from Nanga Palin.

'What's it like there?' Marguarita asked, coming out of the lab. 'Are they in as much of a panic as we are?'

'They must have been. The place is absolutely empty. There's not even a pig or a chicken left under the longhouse.'

'Where do you think they went?'

Bethany told her what she had heard about the distant rice fields and the huts.

'But are they far enough out of the path of the fires?'

'I'm not really certain but I trust Lunsa to know what he's doing,' Bethany replied.

Elliot heard their voices and, followed by Pashetta, came out to see what was going on.

'You're back quickly,' he remarked, ready to be critical as ever when his eyes fell on Bethany.

She told them the news.

'So you were right,' he acknowledged with reluctant respect both for Bethany and for the people at Nanga Palin. He found it vaguely irritating that they had managed to decamp with such efficiency while he had made no progress at all getting in touch with the helicopter company. 'Does Mike know?' he asked.

'I shouldn't think so,' Bethany said, 'or he would have told me before I went all the way over there.'

A moment later a distraught Bima bounded up the veranda steps calling out, 'Nobody's working. Everything's come to a complete standstill on the hotel. They're terrified of the fires and all they're doing is standing around talking about getting out of here, back to Putussibau.'

'Calm down,' Elliot told him, sternly, 'just go back and tell them I'm doing everything I can to get a helicopter here and –'

He was interrupted by the arrival of Mike, announcing, 'The wind's picking up. We're going to need those choppers fast.'

'Damn right,' exclaimed Wolf, arriving almost simultaneously, his clothes and face streaked with mud.

'What the hell have you been doing?' demanded Elliot.

'Letting the pigs out of their cages. There isn't going to be any room for them in the chopper.'

'God, no,' exclaimed Elliot, horrified.

'But they should at least have a chance to get away from the fires.'

'I hope they can run like hell,' Mike said, 'just look at the sky now.'

Everyone's eyes turned upward and eastward and a wave of fear, so strong it was almost palpable, swept over them. There was no denying that the band of red on the horizon was considerably wider than it had been at breakfast time.

Elliot, with Pashetta at his side to translate if necessary, hurried back to the iridium phone. Marguarita returned to the task of gathering up the slides and samples she wanted to take with her. Bima hugged the plans for his beloved hotel to his chest while he searched for a protective case to put them in, just in case the unthinkable happened. Then, unable to stay away from his beloved project for long, he hurried back to reassure the workmen that help was on the way. Not, he tried to convince himself, that such help would actually be needed. Surely the wind would shift again before the fires got to Kanyalang – it just had to, it must.

At times the wind picked up, at other times its trajectory shifted slightly, there were even times when it abated for a while or changed direction altogether. It blew, it circled round, it diminished, it teased, only to come on stronger again a little later.

The only thing everyone could be sure of was that the haze was growing ever more opaque as smoke became an increasingly large component of it. Breathing became more and more difficult and any kind of strenuous activity had to be abandoned.

At lunch time, at dinner time, and again for breakfast and lunch the following day they ate ever-diminishing quantities of fruit and bread. Fortunately for everyone, Mike was able to supplement this meagre fare by catching a few fish with the line that Kolop had disdained and Pashetta was covered with praise for roasting them quite expertly on the charcoal burner.

Mike not only put himself in charge of fishing but of bartending as well. 'No point in leaving all this beer to be boiled away by the fires is there?' he claimed.

No one contested this line of reasoning and Elliot even went so far as to bring out all but one of the bottles of whisky in his stash, just in case a last minute shift in the wind made it possible to call off the evacuation.

As time passed, hopes diminished. The fires continued to draw nearer and the need for the helicopter grew more and more desperate. Elliot and Pashetta spent virtually every waking hour glued to the iridium phone trying to get through to the charter service but there were lots of small logging operations in the area and they were equally frantic. When Elliot's call was finally answered, he found that Kanyalang's request could only be placed at the end of a very long queue and the price had shot up to the stratosphere.

'Well, the bastards in Geneva will just have to pay,' Elliot told Pashetta, after he had angrily replaced the receiver. 'We're not going to sit here and choke to death.'

'Or burn up,' she added helpfully.

'Quite,' he agreed, 'just to save a few bloody pounds. Come on, we'd better let everybody know the helicopter will be coming eventually.'

The rapid tropical dusk was falling over the compound as they hurried back to the longhouse and the others were already digging into the bar supplies by the time they arrived.

'What's the news?' asked Mike.

'Are we ever going to get a helicopter?' Bethany asked.

'Of course we are,' Elliot replied sharply.

'When?' demanded Mike. 'We can't wait forever, you know.'

Elliot, all too well aware of this, furrowed his brows as he confessed, 'We finally got through to the company but it might be a while before a helicopter gets here. They say they're besieged with requests and a lot of companies put in their orders ahead of us.'

'Can't we bribe our way to the front of the line?' demanded Wolf. 'A little money, or in this case, maybe a shit load of money, can be pretty persuasive.'

'I've already offered about eight times the normal rate,' Elliot said, 'and they turned it down.'

'Let me talk to them then,' Wolf said. 'I'll read the riot act to them.'

'You'll do no such thing,' replied Elliot sharply.

'Why the fuck not?'

'Because, you adolescent idiot,' Marguarita explained, 'if you antagonise them enough they could just leave us here to be roasted alive.'

'I won't antagonise them,' Wolf objected.

'My dear boy,' said Elliot, for once without rancour, 'you antagonise everyone.'

'Bullshit,' declared Wolf and was astonished when no one seemed to see things his way, not even Bethany. He could scarcely believe it.

'Fucking hell,' he muttered.

The very real amazement in his voice amused Marguarita. 'Hoping for the popularity prize, were you?' she taunted.

Pashetta was more sympathetic. 'Don't worry, you do have some good qualities,' she said.

'Thanks a whole lot.'

'We all know you're smart and work hard and really care about

404

the rainforest,' Bethany said, hoping to soothe his injured feelings, 'that's something, isn't it?'

Wolf continued to look dejected but no one was eager to build up his already overblown ego.

Marguarita compromised by adding, 'It's just that you can be a colossal pain in the arse sometimes.'

'She's right, you know,' agreed Elliot.

Mike was beginning to feel sorry for Wolf. 'Nobody's perfect, for God's sake,' he said.

'And you're not altogether bad,' confirmed Bethany.

'And presumably not bad in the altogether,' conjectured Marguarita generously, 'not that I really know, of course.'

Everyone, including Wolf, laughed and some of the tension in the air evaporated. An alcohol-induced wave of optimism, born partly of denial of the impending danger and partly of relief that help was on its way, soon spread through the group and after copious amounts of Elliot's whisky had been consumed, something like a holiday spirit seized them all. The helicopter would come in time to get them all to safety. Of course it would. It had to. And in the meantime the wind might die down or change course as it had done so many teasing times during the last few days.

No one suspected that before another forty-eight hours had passed the helicopter pad would be red with blood and one of them would lie, crushed beyond recognition, between the body of the over-worked pilot and the remnants of the under-serviced rotor blades.

CHAPTER FORTY-ONE
Two Years Later

A gentle breeze was blowing off the water, ruffling the cocktail napkins on the terrace of the Sea Turtle Hotel in Bali, when Bethany heard an American voice say, 'I don't know if you remember me but —'

She looked up, was puzzled for a moment, and then the speaker's rust red hair sparked a flash of recognition. 'Oh my God, of course I do. You're Jim … I can't quite remember your last name.'

'Nathan.'

'Jim Nathan, of course,' she repeated. 'I'm Bethany Parker and you remember Wolf, don't you?'

'Sure,' Jim said, proffering his hand to the latter without enthusiasm.

'Good to see you again,' Wolf lied.

'Sit down, have a drink with us,' Bethany urged, with extra cordiality to compensate for Wolf's surliness.

If Bethany had been on her own, Jim wouldn't have hesitated but he wasn't sure about putting up with Wolf, even for a quick drink. Then he thought, what the hell and sat down.

'I was really sorry to hear about what happened to Kanyalang,' he began.

'It doesn't bear thinking about, does it,' agreed Bethany, 'especially about Marguarita. That was so awful.'

Jim tightened his lips and an expression of intense sadness clouded his swarthy face as he recalled all he had heard about the accident. He still hadn't found another woman like her and didn't think he ever would. He was pretty damn sure there weren't any.

'At least everyone else got out,' Wolf said.

'Thanks to Elliot's gargantuan efforts,' Bethany hastened to add, 'he was unstoppable. God only knows how he managed to bludgeon the helicopter company into letting one of their precious helicopters take off in that visibility — it was practically non-existent. Elliot really hung in there and wouldn't take no for an answer but the poor pilot had to make three trips and —'

'Three?' Jim repeated, wondering vaguely how that mattered. Marguarita was all that mattered to him.

'Well, we couldn't exactly take off and leave the guys working on the hotel to be roasted alive,' interjected Wolf.

'But that last trip was too much for the pilot, or maybe for the chopper, I don't know,' resumed Bethany. 'Anyway, it crashed just as it was lifting off and that's when Marguarita was killed.'

'A fucking waste of a brilliant mind,' said Wolf bitterly, 'and as for Kanyalang, apparently there's not much left of it now.'

'Nor of Nanga Palin,' added Bethany, 'but the headman there was really smart and persuaded everybody to leave in time to get to safety. Their longhouse is just ashes and cinders now though and so is darling Bima's beautiful hotel. We've seen the aerial photographs and it's enough to break your heart. You remember Bima, don't you? He cared so much about it. We all did, you know, about everything. You can imagine how we felt when so much we had worked for literally went up in smoke.'

Jim couldn't imagine anything except that Marguarita, beautiful, vibrant, sexy-as-all-hell Marguarita, was actually dead.

He had never talked to anyone about her, never shared his memories of the night they had spent together, never let anyone know how he had kept her alive in his imagination and his dreams. Talking about her now with two people who had actually known her and had been there with her during those last fatal moments made her death suddenly seem very new and agonisingly real.

He would have been relieved to know that only a small fraction of these emotions were reflected in his face. They were however enough to convince Bethany that he was taking the fate of Kanyalang surprisingly hard for someone who had spent such a short time there. This reaction touched her and prompted her to try and cheer him up. With this in mind, she launched into what she hoped would be a more up-beat subject. 'What brings you to Bali, anyway,' she asked, 'a holiday?'

'Sort of,' he said, 'and doing a little scouting for this tour guiding business I've got going out of Balikpapan. What about you?'

'We're here to celebrate the soft opening — that's what they call it — of Bima's gorgeous new hotel up in Ubud. It's absolute heaven.

It's already been written up in a whole mess of travel magazines as the perfect blend of traditional form and modern function, Asian elegance and European comfort, all that sort of thing. Of course Bima's over the moon about it. We all are.'

'All?' Jim asked.

'The two of us,' Bethany said, glancing at Wolf, 'and Saskia, Bima's girlfriend. She came all the way out from Holland for the opening but I don't think she appreciates how really brilliant his work is. I'm convinced some men just have a talent for getting involved with the wrong women, what do you think?'

'Absolutely,' he agreed, so emphatically that Bethany gave a little jump.

'Of course, it isn't always like that,' she insisted, wanting to set the record straight. 'You remember Mike and Pashetta, don't you?'

He nodded.

'They're in East Africa now, together, and I think they're absolutely right for each other. They have an adorable little boy, almost three months old now. Pashetta claims he looks exactly like Mike, if you can imagine that.'

'You seem to be very good at keeping in touch with everybody,' Jim observed.

'Bethany's the Information Centre for the whole ex-Kanyalang crew,' Wolf said. 'Without her, we would all have just gone our separate ways and nobody would have known what anyone else was up to.'

'He exaggerates,' protested Bethany. 'I just get the occasional e-mail now and then, except from Mike and Pashetta, of course. They send us pictures of their baby every five minutes. Bima's really the only one who keeps in touch with Elliot. He retired after the accident and is back in Sussex with his wife now but I'm not sure how well that's going. I have a feeling he's not frightfully fond of her.'

'He's crazy about his dogs though,' put in Wolf with a laugh, 'at least that's something.'

Bethany ignored this and added, 'The bad thing is there doesn't seem to be much chance he'll ever walk very well again. His leg was broken in several places when he was thrown from the plane and Bima thinks he'll always have to use a stick.'

'Too bad,' murmured Jim absently, unable to turn his mind from the image of Marguarita lying dead underneath the helicopter blades.

Wolf was getting fed up with Jim's sympathetic noises about what had happened to Kanyalang. The guy had only been there for a few days and nights. The place couldn't have really meant that much to him. Deciding he had heard enough, he gulped down the remains of his drink, said something about checking his e-mails and stalked off.

A gravel path led from the bar to the bungalow where he and Bethany were staying and as he went along he began to wonder if Jim – that big show of interest in people he hardly knew had to be a sham – was trying to put the make on Bethany. If so, tough luck, the bastard was too late. Bethany was with him now and he was pretty sure he could trust her not to go off shagging some orang-utan look-alike, or anyone else for that matter. And if this kind of trust had to be a two-way street, well, he was okay with that. After all, what was the point of chasing other woman when they didn't come any better than Bethany?

The haze and the fires and Marguarita's death had affected her in ways he would never have expected, he reflected. Instead of putting her off the life out here and sending her flying back to London, it seemed to have touched some previously untapped core of adventure and determination within her. Saving the jungle and understanding the way of life of the people who lived in it had taken on a prime importance for her. It was almost as if Marguarita, with her death, had transferred her passion for the rainforest to Bethany.

Hey there, hold on, he told himself, hastily pushing this absurd idea out of his mind. It was alright for Bethany to show a bit of a mystical streak now and then, okay for types like Bima too, but he was damned if he was going to let any of that stuff rub off on him.

In the meantime Jim, relieved that Wolf was gone, cast about for something else to talk about. Bethany was the first real link he had had with Marguarita in two years and she would probably be the last so he wanted to draw out their conversation as long as possible.

'Whatever happened to that woman, Catherine, I think her name was, the one who had that abortion in a Dayak longhouse?' he asked, feigning as much interest as he could.

A grimace of distaste passed across Bethany's face. 'She's alright I think, now anyway.'

'Now?' echoed Jim.

'We don't actually keep in touch,' Bethany explained, 'but somebody said she had a hard time when she first got back to Australia.'

'In what way?'

'Shaking that nasty bout of anaemia she had and then somehow ending up with a kind of nervous breakdown — I always thought she was a bit mental, so did Wolf. Anyway she was in hospital for a while but she must have pulled herself together because the last I heard she was floating around the Galapagos Islands with her new boyfriend, an Italian herpetologist, researching the evolution of some kind of lizard so it looks like she's put Kanyalang and everything that happened there behind her.'

'She's done a better job of it than I have then.'

Bethany looked at him quizzically.

'I know I just spent a few days with you guys,' he said, 'but Marguarita is a hard person to forget.'

'You got that one right,' agreed Wolf, coming back to the table in time to hear this last comment. But he quickly turned his attention to Bethany, waved an e-mail in front of her and said, 'Look at this, will you, it's from Geneva.'

'From the RRF?' she cried hopefully.

'Who else?'

After a quick perusal of it, she explained to Jim, 'They're starting up a new eco-tourism project.'

'In Borneo again?' he asked.

'No, this one's in Irian Jaya.'

'In the Baliem Valley,' added Wolf, 'where fashion designers go broke because all you need for formal wear is a penis sheath.'

'And the brilliant thing,' Bethany continued, ignoring the

sartorial aspects of the situation, 'is that they want both an environmentalist and an anthropologist on it.'

'And that means you and me, Baby,' declared Wolf, catching her up in his arms, swinging her around and barely avoiding knocking the glasses off several near-by tables.

Any doubts Bethany may have had about what lay ahead were lost in the euphoria of the moment. The sex would be great, absolutely fantastic, and Wolf was getting easier to work with all the time. He didn't treat her like a newcomer to the rainforest anymore - well, she wasn't one, was she? And he was reasonable enough to see that.

The night he had spent in a tree with the crocodile circling around just beneath his toes seemed to have had a profound effect on him. He was noticeably less brash, less arrogant, less interfering and bullying than he used to be. In fact, he almost seemed to realise, some of the time, at least, that he might not be the biggest, most important beast in the Borneo bestiary. Of course his basic nature hadn't changed. He was still the aggressive, overconfident, pig-headed bastard he had always been, just not quite as bad. But then with a crocodile for a personality coach, she reflected, it wouldn't be reasonable to expect miracles.

Was she in love with Wolf, she asked herself? The answer came rushing back in less than a nano-second – yes, wildly, madly, passionately. Did she like him? This time her response came more slowly but no less certainly – not very much. And that was the unsettling thing. How long could she go on loving someone she didn't really like?

Perhaps she would find out in the Baliem Valley.